D0950538

#1 *New York Times* Bestselling Author

NORA ROBERTS

AN IRISH WISH

Includes *Irish Rose* & *Irish Rebel*

Silhouette Books

 SILHOUETTE™

An Irish Wish

ISBN-13: 978-1-335-14754-7

Recycling programs for this product may not exist in your area.

Copyright © 2021 by Harlequin Books S.A.

Irish Rose
First published in 1988. This edition published in 2021.
Copyright © 1988 by Nora Roberts

Irish Rebel
First published in 2000. This edition published in 2021.
Copyright © 2000 by Nora Roberts

This edition published by arrangement with Harlequin Books S.A.

For questions and comments about the quality of this book, please contact us at CustomerService@Harlequin.com.

Silhouette
22 Adelaide St. West, 40th Floor
Toronto, Ontario M5H 4E3, Canada
www.Harlequin.com

Printed in Lithuania

MIX
Paper from responsible sources
FSC® C021394

CONTENTS

IRISH ROSE

Chapter 1

Her name was Erin, like her country. And like her country, she was a maze of contradictions—rebellion and poetry, passion and moodiness. She was strong enough to fight for her beliefs, stubborn enough to fight on after a cause was lost, and generous enough to give whatever she had. She was a woman with soft skin and a tough mind. She had sweet dreams and towering ambitions.

Her name was Erin, Erin McKinnon, and she was nervous as a cat.

It was true that this was only the third time in her life she'd been in the airport at Cork. Or any airport, for that matter. Still, it wasn't the crowds or the noise that made her jumpy. The fact was, she liked hearing the announcements of planes coming and going. She liked thinking about all the people going places.

London, New York, Paris. Through the thick glass she could watch the big sleek planes rise up, nose first, and imagine their destinations. Perhaps one day she'd board one herself and experience that stomach-fluttering anticipation as the plane climbed up and up.

She shook her head. It wasn't a plane going up that had her nervous now, but one coming in. And it was due any minute. Erin caught herself before she dragged a hand through her hair. It wouldn't do a bit of good to be poking and pulling at herself. After thirty seconds more, she shifted her bag from hand to hand, then tugged at her jacket. She didn't want to look disheveled or tense…or poor, she added as she ran a hand down her skirt to smooth it.

Thank God her mother was so clever with a needle. The deep blue of the skirt and matching jacket was flattering to her pale complexion. The cut and style were perhaps a bit conservative for Erin's taste, but the color did match her eyes. She wanted to look competent, capable, and had even managed to tame her unruly hair into a tidy coil of dark red. The style made her look older, she thought. She hoped it made her look sophisticated, too.

She'd toned down the dusting of freckles and had deepened the color of her lips. Eye makeup had been applied with a careful hand, and she wore Nanny's old and lovely gold crescents at her ears.

The last thing she wanted was to look plain and dowdy. The poor relation. Even the echo of the phrase in her head caused her teeth to clench. Pity, even sympathy, were emotions she wanted none of. She was a McKinnon, and perhaps fortune hadn't smiled on her as it had her cousin, but she was determined to make her own way.

Here they were, she thought, and had to swallow a ball of nerves in her throat. Erin watched the plane that had brought them from Curragh taxi toward the gate—the small, sleek plane people of wealth and power could afford to charter. She could imagine what it would be like to sit inside, to drink champagne or nibble on something exotic. Imagination had always been hers in quantity. All she'd lacked was the means to make what she could imagine come true.

An elderly woman stepped off the plane first, leading a small girl by the hand. The woman had cloud-white hair and a solid, sturdy build. Beside her, the little girl looked like a pixie, carrot-topped and compact. The moment they'd stepped to the ground, a boy of five or six leaped off after them.

Even through the thick glass, Erin could all but hear the woman's scolding. She snatched his hand with her free one, and he flashed her a wicked grin. Erin felt immediate kinship. If she'd gauged the age right, that would be Brendon, Adelia's oldest. The girl who held the woman's hand and clutched a battered doll in the other would be Keeley, younger by a year or so.

The man came next, the man Erin recognized as Travis Grant. Her cousin's husband of seven years, owner of Thoroughbreds and master of Royal Meadows. He was tall and broad-shouldered and was laughing down at his son, who waited impatiently on the tarmac. The smile was nice, she thought, the kind that made a woman look twice without being sure whether to relax or brace herself. Erin had met him once, briefly, when he'd brought his wife back to Ireland four years before. Quietly domineering, she'd thought then. The kind of man a woman could depend on, as long as she could stand toe-to-toe with him.

On his hip he carried another child, a boy with hair as dark and thick as his father's. He was grinning, too, but not down at his brother and sister. His face was tilted up toward the sky from which he'd just come. Travis handed him down, then turned and held out a hand.

As Adelia stepped through the opening, the sun struck her hair with arrows of light. The rich chestnut shone around her face and shoulders. She, too, was laughing. Even with the distance, Erin could see the glow. She was a small woman. When Travis caught her by the waist and lifted her to the ground, she didn't reach his shoulder. He kept his arm around her, Erin noticed, not so much possessive as protective of her and perhaps of the child that was growing inside her.

While Erin watched, Adelia tilted her face, touched a hand to her husband's cheek and kissed him. Not like a long-time wife, Erin thought, but like a lover.

A little ripple of envy moved through her. Erin didn't try to avoid it. She never attempted to avoid any of her feelings, but let them come, let them race to the limit, whatever the consequences.

And why shouldn't she envy Dee? Erin asked herself. Adelia Cunnane, the little orphan from Skibbereen, had not only pulled herself up by the bootstraps but had tugged hard enough to land on top of the pile. More power to her, Erin thought. She intended to do the same herself.

Erin squared her shoulders and started to step forward as another figure emerged from the plane. Another servant, she thought, then took a long, thorough look. No, this man would serve no one.

He leaped lightly to the ground with a slim, unlit cigar clamped between his teeth. Slowly, even warily, he looked around. As a cat might, she thought, a cat that had just leaped from cliff to cliff. She couldn't see his eyes, for he wore tinted glasses, but she had the quick impression that they would be sharp, intense and not entirely comfortable to look into.

He was as tall as Travis but leaner, sparer. Tough. The adjective came to her as she pursed her lips and continued to stare. He bent down to speak to one of the children, and the move was lazy but not careless. His dark hair was straight and long enough to hang over the collar of his denim shirt. He wore boots and faded jeans, but she rejected the idea that he was a farmer. He didn't look like a man who tilled the soil but like one who owned it.

What was a man like this doing traveling with her cousin's family? Another relative? she wondered, and shifted uncomfortably. It didn't matter who he was. Erin checked the pins in her hair, found two loose, and shoved them into place. If he was some relation of Travis Grant's, then that was fine.

But he didn't look like kin of her cousin's husband. The coloring might be similar, but any resemblance ended there. The stranger had a raw-boned, sharp-edged look to him. She remembered the picture books in catechism class, and the drawings of Satan.

"Better to rule in hell than to serve in heaven."

Yes... For the first time, a smile moved on her lips. He looked like a man who'd have similar sentiments. Taking a deep breath, Erin moved forward to greet her family.

The boy Brendon came first, barreling through the doorway with one shoe untied and eyes alight with curiosity. The white-haired woman came in behind him, moving with surprising speed.

"Stand still, you scamp. I'm not going to lose track of you again."

"I just want to see, Hannah." There was a laugh in his

voice and no contrition at all when she caught his hand in hers.

"You'll see soon enough. No need to worry your mother to death. Keeley, you stay close now."

"I will." The little girl looked around as avidly as her brother, but seemed more content to stay in the same place. Then she spotted Erin. "There she is. That's our cousin Erin. Just like the picture." Without a hint of reserve, the girl crossed over and smiled. "You're our cousin Erin, aren't you? I'm Keeley. Momma said you'd be waiting for us."

"Aye, I'm Erin." Charmed, Erin bent down to catch the little girl's chin in her hand. Nerves vanished into genuine pleasure. "And the last time I saw you, you were just a wee thing, all bundled in a blanket against the rain and bawling fit to wake the dead."

Keeley's eyes widened. "She talks just like Momma," she announced. "Hannah, come see. She talks just like Momma."

"Miss McKinnon." Hannah kept one hand firmly on Brendon's shoulder and offered the other. "It's nice to meet you. I'm Hannah Blakely, your cousin's housekeeper."

Housekeeper, Erin thought as she put her hand in Hannah's weathered one. The Cunnanes she'd known might have been housekeepers, but they'd never had one. "Welcome to Ireland. And you'd be Brendon."

"I've been to Ireland before," he said importantly. "But this time I flew the plane."

"Did you now?" She saw her cousin in him, the pixie-like features and deep green eyes. He'd be a handful, she thought, as her mother claimed Adelia had always been. "Well, you're all grown up since I saw you last."

"I'm the oldest. Brady's the baby now."

"Erin?" She glanced over in time to see Adelia rush forward. Even heavy with child she moved lightly. And when she wound her arms around Erin, there was strength in them. The recognition came strongly—family to family, roots to roots. "Oh, Erin, it's so good to be back, so good to see you. Let me look at you."

She hadn't changed a bit, Erin thought. Adelia would be nearly thirty now, but she looked years younger. Her complexion was smooth and flawless, glowing against the glossy mane of hair she still wore long and loose. The pleasure in her face was so real, so vital, that Erin felt it seeping through her own reserve.

"You look wonderful, Dee. America's been good for you."

"And the prettiest girl in Skibbereen's become a beautiful woman. Oh, Erin." She kissed both her cousin's cheeks, laughed and kissed them again. "You look like home." With Erin's hand still held tightly in hers, she turned. "You remember Travis."

"Of course. It's good to see you again."

"You've grown up in four years." He kissed her cheek in turn. "You didn't meet Brady the last time."

"No, I didn't." The child kept an arm around his father's neck and eyed Erin owlishly. "Faith, he's the image of you. It's a handsome boy you are, Cousin Brady."

Brady smiled, then turned to bury his face in his father's neck.

"And shy," Adelia commented, stroking a hand down his hair. "Unlike his da. Erin, it's so kind of you to offer to meet us and take us to the inn."

"We don't often get visitors. I've got the minibus. You know from the last time you came that renting a car is tricky, so I'll be leaving it with you while you're here." While she spoke, Erin felt an itch at the base of her neck, a tingle, or a warning. Deliberately she turned and stared back at the lean-faced man she'd seen step off the plane.

"Erin, this is Burke." Adelia placed a hand on her skirt at the stirrings within her womb. "Burke Logan, my cousin, Erin McKinnon."

"Mr. Logan," Erin said with a slight nod, determined not to flinch at her own reflection in his mirrored glasses.

"Miss McKinnon." He smiled slowly, then clamped his cigar between his teeth again.

She still couldn't see his eyes but had the uneasy feeling that the glasses were no barrier to what he saw. "I'm sure you're tired," she said to Adelia, but kept her gaze stubbornly on Burke's. "The bus is right out front. I'll take you out, then we'll deal with the luggage."

Burke kept himself just a little apart as they walked through the small terminal. He preferred it that way, the better to observe and figure angles. Just now, he was figuring Erin McKinnon.

A tidy little package, he mused, watching the way her long, athletic legs moved beneath her conservative skirt. Neat as a pin and nervous as a filly at the starting gate. Just what kind of race did she intend to run? he wondered.

He knew snatches of the background from conversations on the trip from the States and from Curragh to this little spot on the map. The McKinnons and Cunnanes weren't first cousins. As near as could be figured, Adelia's mother and the mother of the very interesting Erin McKinnon had been third cousins who had grown up on neighboring farms.

Burke smiled as Erin looked uneasily over her shoulder in his direction. If Adelia Cunnane Grant figured that made her and the McKinnons family, he wouldn't argue.

For himself, he spent more time avoiding family connections than searching them out.

If he didn't stop staring at her like that, he was going to get a piece of her mind, Erin told herself as she slid the van into gear. The luggage was loaded, the children chattering, and she had to keep her wits about her to navigate out of the airport.

She could see him in the rearview mirror, legs spread out in the narrow aisle, one arm tossed over the worn seat—and his eyes on her. Try as she might, she couldn't concentrate on Adelia's questions about her family.

As she wound the van onto the road, she listened with half an ear and gave her cousin the best answers she could. Everyone was fine. The farm was doing well enough. As she began to relax behind the wheel, she dug deep for bits and pieces of gossip. Still, he kept staring at her.

Let him, then, she decided. The man obviously had the manners of a plow mule and was no concern of hers. Stubbornly avoiding another glance in the rearview mirror, she jabbed another loose pin back in her hair.

She had questions of her own. Erin expertly avoided the worst of the bumps on the road and trained her eyes straight ahead. The first of them would be who the hell was this Burke Logan. Still, she smiled on cue and assured her cousin again that her family was fit and fine.

"So Cullen's not married yet."

"Cullen?" Despite her determination, Erin's gaze had drifted back to the mirror and Burke. She cursed herself. "No. Much to my mother's regret, he's still single. He goes into Dublin now and again to sing his songs and play." She hit a rough patch that sent the van vibrating. "I'm sorry."

"It's all right."

Turning her head, she studied Adelia with genuine concern. "Are you sure? I'm wondering if you should be traveling at all."

"I'm healthy as one of Travis's horses." In a habitual gesture, Adelia put a hand on her rounded belly. "And I've months to go before they're born."

"They?"

"Twins this time." The smile lit up her face. "I've been hoping."

"Twins," Erin repeated under her breath, not sure whether she should be amazed or amused.

Adelia shifted into a more comfortable position. Glancing back, she saw that her two youngest were dozing and that Brendon was putting up a courageous, if failing, battle to keep his eyes open. "I've always wanted a big family like yours."

Erin grinned at her as the van putted into the village. "It looks like you're going to match it. And may the sweet Lord have mercy on you."

With a chuckle, Adelia shifted again to absorb the sights and sounds of the village she remembered from childhood.

The small buildings were still neat, if a bit rough around the edges. Patches of grass were deep and green, shimmering against dark brown dirt. The sign on the village pub, the Shamrock, creaked and groaned in a breeze that tasted of rain from the sea.

She could almost smell it, and remembered it easily. Here the cliffs were sheer and towering, slicing down to a wild sea. She could remember the times she'd stood on the rock watching the fishing boats, seeing them come in with their day's catch to dry their nets and cool dry throats at the pub.

The talk here was of fishing and farming, of babies and sweethearts.

It was home. Adelia rested a hand against the open window and looked out. It was home—a way of life, a place she'd never been able to close out of her heart. There was a wagon filled with hay, its color no brighter, its scent no sweeter than that of the hay in her own stables in America. But this was Ireland, and her heart had never stopped looking back here.

"It hasn't changed."

Erin eased the vehicle to a stop and glanced around. She knew every square inch of the village, and every farm for a hundred miles around. In truth, she'd never known anything else. "Did you expect it would? Nothing ever changes here."

"There's O'Donnelly's, the dry goods." Dee stepped out of the van. Foolishly she wanted to have her feet on the ground of her youth. She wanted to fill her lungs with the air of Skibbereen. "Is he still there?"

"The old goat will die behind the counter, still counting his last pence."

With a laugh, Dee took Brady from Travis and cuddled him as he yawned and settled against her shoulder. "Aye, then he hasn't changed, either. Travis, you see the church there. We'd come in every Sunday for mass. Old Father Finnegan would drone on and on. Does he still, Erin?"

Erin slipped the keys of the van in the pocket of her purse. "He died, Dee, better than a year ago." Because the light went out of her cousin's eyes, Erin lifted a hand to her cheek. "He was more than eighty, if you remember, and died quietly in his sleep."

Life went on, she knew, and people passed out of it whether you wanted them to or not. Dee glanced back at the church. It would never seem exactly the same again. "He buried Mother and Da. I can't forget how kind he was to me."

"We've a young priest now," Erin began briskly. "Sent

from Cork. A hell-raiser he is, and not a soul sleeps through one of his sermons. Put the fear of God into Michael Ryan, so the man comes sober to mass every Sunday morning." She turned to help with the luggage and slammed solidly into Burke. He put a hand on her shoulder as if to steady her, but it lingered too long.

"I beg your pardon."

She couldn't stop her chin from tilting forward or her eyes from spitting at him. He only smiled. "My fault." Grabbing two hefty cases, he swung them out of the van. "Why don't you take Dee and the kids in, Travis? I'll deal with this."

Normally Travis wouldn't have left another with the bulk of the work, but he knew his wife's strength was flagging. He also knew she was stubborn, and the only way to get her into bed for a nap was to put her there himself.

"Thanks. I'll take care of checking in. Erin, we'll see you and your family tonight?"

"They'll be here." On impulse, she kissed Dee's cheek. "You'll rest now. Otherwise Mother will fuss and drive you mad. That I can promise."

"Do you have to go now? Couldn't you come in?"

"I've some things to see to. Go on now, or your children will be asleep in the street. I'll see you soon."

Over Brendon's protest, Hannah bundled them inside. Erin turned to grip another pair of cases by the handles and began unloading. It passed through her mind that expensive clothes must weigh more when she found herself facing Burke again.

"There's just a few more," she muttered, and deliberately breezed by him.

Inside, the inn was dim but far from quiet. The excitement of having visitors from America had kept the small staff on their toes all week. Wood had been polished, floors had been scrubbed. Even now old Mrs. Malloy was leading Dee up the stairs and keeping up a solid stream of reminiscence. The children were cooed over, and hot tea and soda bread were offered. Deciding she'd left her charges in good hands, Erin walked outside again.

The day was cool and clear. The early clouds had long since been blown away by the westerly wind so that the light, as it often was in Ireland, was luminescent and pearly. Erin took a moment to study the village that had so fascinated her cousin. It was ordinary, slow, quiet, filled with workingmen and women and often smelling of fish. From almost any point in town you could see the small harbor where the boats came in with their daily catch. The storefronts were kept neat. That was a matter of pride. The doors were left unlocked. That was a matter of custom.

There was no one there who didn't know her, no one she didn't know. Whatever secrets there were were never secrets for long, but were passed out like small treasures to be savored and sighed over.

God, she wanted to see something else before her life was done. She wanted to see big cities where life whirled by, fast and hot and anonymous. She wanted to walk down a street where no one knew who she was and no one cared. Just once, just once in her life, she wanted to do something wild and impulsive that wouldn't echo back to her on the tongues of family and neighbors. Just once.

The van door slammed and jolted her back to reality. Again she found herself looking at Burke Logan. "They're all settled, then?" she asked, struggling to be polite.

"Looks like." He leaned back against the van. With his ankles crossed, he pulled out a lighter and lit his cigar. He never smoked around Adelia out of respect for her condition. His eyes never left Erin's. "Not much family resemblance between you and Mrs. Grant, is there?"

It was the first time he'd spoken more than two words at a time. Erin noted that his accent wasn't like Travis's. His words came more slowly, as if he saw no reason to hurry them. "There's the hair," he continued when Erin didn't speak. "But hers is more like Travis's prize chestnut colt, and yours—" he took another puff as he deliberated "—yours is something like the mahogany stand in my bedroom." He grinned, the cigar still clamped between his teeth. "I thought it was mighty pretty when I bought it."

"That's a lovely thought, Mr. Logan, but I'm not a horse or a table." Reaching into her pocket, she held out the keys. "I'll be leaving these with you, then."

Instead of taking them, he simply closed his hand over hers, cradling the keys between them. His palm was hard and rough as the rocks in the cliffs that dropped toward the sea. He enjoyed the way she held her ground, the way she lifted her brow, more in disdain than offense.

"Is there something else you're wanting, Mr. Logan?"

"I'll give you a lift," he said simply.

"It's not necessary." She clenched her teeth and nodded as two of the town's busiest gossips passed behind her. The evening news would have Erin McKinnon holding hands with a stranger in the street, sure as faith. "I've only to ask for a ride home to get one."

"You've got one already." With his hand still on hers, he pushed away from the van. "I told Travis I'd see to it." After releasing her hand, he gestured toward the door. "Don't worry, I've nearly got the hang on driving on the wrong side of the road."

"It's you who drive on the wrong side." After only a brief

hesitation, Erin climbed in. The day was passing her by, and she'd have to make every minute count just to catch up.

Burke settled behind the wheel and turned the key in the ignition. "You're losing your pins," he said mildly.

Erin reached behind her and shoved them into place as he drove out of the village. "You'll take the left fork when you come to it. After that it's only four or five kilometers." Erin folded her hands, deciding she'd granted him enough conversation.

"Pretty country," Burke commented, glancing out at the green, windswept hills. There were blackthorns, bent a bit from the continual stream of the westerly breeze. Heather grew in a soft purple cloud, while in the distance the mountains rose dark and eerie in the light. "You're close to the sea."

"Close enough."

"Don't you like Americans?"

With her hands still folded primly, she turned to look at him. "I don't like men who stare at me."

Burke tapped his cigar ash out the window. "That would narrow the field considerably."

"The men I know have manners, Mr. Logan."

He liked the way she said his name, with just a hint of spit in it. "Too bad. I was taught to take a good long look at something that interested me."

"I'm sure you consider that a compliment."

"Just an observation. This the fork?"

"Aye." She drew a long breath, knowing she had no reason to set her temper loose and every reason to hold it. "Do you work for Travis?"

"No." He grinned as the van shimmied over ruts. "You might say Travis and I are associates." He liked the smell here, the rich wet scent of Ireland and the warm earthy scent of the woman beside him. "I own the farm that borders his."

"You race horses?" She lifted a brow again, compelled to study him.

"At the moment."

Erin's lips pursed as she considered. She could picture him at the track, with the noise and the smells of the horses. Try as she might, she couldn't put him behind a desk, balancing accounts and ledgers. "Travis's farm is quite successful."

His lips curved again. "Is that your way of asking about mine?"

Her chin angled as she looked away. "It's certainly none of my concern."

"No, it's not. But I do well enough. I wasn't born into it like Travis, but I find it suits me—for now. They'd take you back with them if you asked."

At first it didn't sink in. Then her lips parted in surprise as she turned to him again.

"I recognize a restless soul when I see one." Burke blew out smoke so that it trailed through the window and disappeared. "You're straining at the bit to get out of this little smudge on the map. Though if you ask me, it has its charm."

"No one asked you."

"True enough, but it's hard not to notice when you stand on the curb and look around as though you wished the whole village to hell."

"That's not true." The guilt rose in her because for a moment, just a moment, she'd come close to wishing it so.

"All right, we'll alter that to you wishing yourself anywhere else. I know the feeling, Irish."

"You don't know what I feel. You don't know me at all."

"Better than you think," he murmured. "Feeling trapped,

stifled, smothered?" She said nothing this time. "Looking at the same space you saw the day you were born and wondering if it's the last thing you'll see before you die? Wondering why you don't walk out, stick out your thumb and head whichever way the wind's blowing? How old are you, Erin McKinnon?"

What he was saying hit too close to the bone for comfort. "I'm twenty-five, and what of it?"

"I was five years younger when I stuck my thumb out." He turned to her, but again she saw only her own reflection. "Can't say I ever regretted it."

"Well, it's happy I am for you, Mr. Logan. Now, if you'll slow down, the lane's there. Just pull to the side. I can walk from here."

"Suit yourself." When he stopped the van, he put a hand on her arm before she could climb out. He wasn't sure why he'd offered to drive her or why he'd started this line of conversation. He was following a hunch, as he had for most of his life. "I know ambition when I see it because it looks back at me out of the mirror most mornings. Some consider it a sin. I've always thought of it as a blessing."

What was it about him that made her throat dry up and her nerves stretch? "Have you a point, Mr. Logan?"

"I like your looks, Erin. I'd hate to see them wrinkled up with discontent." He grinned again and tipped an invisible hat. "Top of the morning to you."

Unsure whether she was running from him or her own demons, Erin got out of the van, slammed the door, and hurried down the lane.

Chapter 2

She had a great deal to think about. Erin sat through dinner at the inn, with her family talking on top of each other, with laughter rolling into laughter. Voices were raised to be heard over the clatter of tableware, the scrape of chair legs, the occasional shout. Scents were a mixture of good hot food and whiskey. The lights had been turned up high in celebration. The group filled Mrs. Malloy's dining room at the inn, but wasn't so very much bigger than a Sunday supper at the farm.

Erin ate little herself, not because one of her brothers seemed to interrupt constantly to have her pass this or that, but because she couldn't stop thinking about what Burke had said to her that afternoon.

She *was* dissatisfied, though she didn't like the idea that a stranger could see it as easily as her family had always overlooked it. Years before she'd convinced herself it wasn't wrong to be so. How could it be wrong to feel what was so natural? True, she'd been taught that envy was a sin, but...

Damn it all, she wasn't a saint and wouldn't choose to be one. The envy she felt for Dee sitting cozily beside her husband felt healthy, not sinful. After all, it wasn't as if she wished her cousin didn't have; it was only that she wished she had as well. She doubted a body burned in hell for wishes. But she didn't think they grew wings for them, either.

In truth, she was glad the Grants had come back to visit. For a few days she could listen to their stories of America and picture it. She could ask questions and imagine the big stone house Dee lived in now and almost catch glimpses of the excitement and power of the racing world. When they left again, everything would settle back to routine.

But not forever, Erin promised herself. No, not forever. In a year, maybe two, she would have saved enough, and then it would be off to Dublin. She'd get a job in some big office and have a flat of her own. Of her very own. No one was going to stop her.

Her lips started to curve at the thought, but then her gaze met Burke's across the table. He wasn't wearing those concealing glasses now. She almost wished he was. They'd been disturbing, but not nearly as disturbing as his eyes—dark gray, intense eyes. A wolf would have eyes like that, smoky and patient and cunning. He had no business looking at her like that, she thought, then stubbornly stared right back at him.

The noise and confusion of the table continued around them, but she lost track of it. Was it the amusement in his eyes that drew her, or the arrogance? Perhaps it was because both added up to a peculiar kind of knowledge. She wasn't sure, but she felt something for him at that moment, something she knew she shouldn't feel and was even more certain she'd regret.

* * *

An Irish rose, Burke thought. He wasn't sure he'd ever seen one, but was certain they would have thorns, thick ones with sharp edges. An Irish rose, a wild rose, wouldn't be fragile or require careful handling. It would be sturdy, strong and stubborn enough to grow through briers. It was a flower he thought he could respect.

He liked her family. They would be called salt of the earth, he supposed. Simple, but not simple-minded. Apparently their farm did well enough, as long as they worked seven days a week. Mary McKinnon had a dressmaking business on the side, but seemed more interested in discussing children with Dee than fashion. The brothers were fair, except for the oldest, Cullen, who had the looks of a Black Irish warrior and the voice of a poet. Unless Burke missed his guess, Erin had her softest spot there. Throughout the meal he watched her, curious to see what other soft spots he might discover.

By the time dinner was over, Burke was glad he'd let Travis talk him into an extra few days in Ireland. The trip had been profitable, the visit to the track at Curragh educational, and now it seemed it was time to mix business with a little pleasure.

"You'll play for us, won't you, Cullen?" Adelia was already reaching across the table to grip Erin's oldest brother's hand. "For old times' sake."

"He'll take little enough persuading," Mary McKinnon put in. "You'd best clear a space." She gestured to her two youngest sons. "It's only fitting that we dance off a meal like that."

"I just happen to have my pipe." Cullen reached in his vest pocket and drew out the slim reed. He stood, a big man with broad shoulders and lean hips. The fingers of his workingman's hands slid over the holes as he lifted the instrument to his lips.

It surprised Burke that such a big, rough-looking man could make such delicate music. He settled back in his chair, savored the kick of his Irish whiskey and watched.

Mary McKinnon placed her hand in her youngest son's and, without seeming to move at all, set her feet in time to the music. It seemed a very restrained dance to Burke, with a complicated pattern of heels and toes and shuffles. Then the pace began to pick up—slowly, almost unnoticeably. The others were keeping time with their hands or occasional hoots. When he glanced at Erin, she was standing with a hand on her father's shoulder and smiling as he hadn't seen her smile before.

Something shimmered a bit inside him—shimmered, then strained, then quieted, all in the space of two heartbeats.

"She still moves like a girl," Matthew McKinnon said of his wife.

"And she's still beautiful." Erin watched her mother whirl in her son's arms, then spin with a flare of skirt and a flash of leg.

"Can you keep up?"

With a laugh that was only slightly wistful, Erin shook her head. "I've never been able to."

"Come now." Her father slid an arm around her waist. "My money's on you."

Before she could protest, Matthew had spun her out. His grin was broad as he held her hand high and picked up the rhythm of the timeless folk dance she'd been taught as soon as she could walk. The pipe music was cheerful and challenging. Caught up in it and her family's enthusiasm,

Erin began to move instinctively. She put her hands on her hips and tossed up her chin.

"Can you manage it?"

Adelia looked up at her eighteen-year-old cousin. "Can I manage it?" she repeated with her eyes narrowed. "The day hasn't come when I can't manage a jig, boyo."

Travis started to protest as she joined her cousins on the floor, but then he subsided. If there was one thing his Dee knew, it was her own strength. The depth of it continued to surprise him. "Quite a group, aren't they?" he murmured to Burke.

"They're all of that." He drew out a cigar, but his eyes remained on Erin. "I take it you don't jig."

With a chuckle, Travis leaned back against the wall. "Dee's tried to teach me and labeled me hopeless. I'm inclined to believe you have to be born to it." He saw Brendon go out to take his place as his mother's partner. His mother's son, Travis thought with a ripple of pride. Of all their children, Brendon was the most strong-willed and hardheaded. "She needed this more than I realized."

Burke managed to tear his eyes from Erin long enough to study Travis's profile. "Most people get homesick now and again."

"She's only come back twice in seven years." Travis watched her now, her cheeks pink with pleasure, her eyes laughing down at Brendon as he copied her moves. "It's not enough. You know, she'll take you to the wall in an argument—half the time an argument no sane man can understand. But she never complains, and she never asks."

For a moment Burke said nothing. It still surprised him after four years that his friendship with Travis had become so close, so quickly. He'd never considered himself the kind of man to make friends, and in truth had never wanted the responsibility of one. He'd spent almost half his thirty-two years on his own, needing no one. Wanting no one. With the Grants, it had just happened.

"I don't know much about women." At Travis's slow smile, Burke corrected himself. "Wives. But I'd say yours is happy, whether she's here or in the States. The fact is, Travis, if she loved you less I might have made a play for her myself."

Travis continued to watch her as his mind played back the years. "The first time I saw her I thought she was a boy."

Burke drew the cigar out of his mouth. "You're joking."

"It was dark."

"A poor excuse."

His chuckle was warm and easy as he looked back. "She seemed to think so, too. Nearly took my head off. I think I fell for her then and there." He heard her laugh and looked over as she shook her head and stepped away from the dancers. She came to him, hands outstretched. The jeweled ring he'd put on her finger years before still glimmered.

"I could go for hours," she claimed, a little breathlessly. "But these two have had enough." With her free hands, she covered her babies. "Are you going to try it, Burke?"

"Not on your life."

She laughed again and put a hand on his arm with the simple generosity he'd never quite gotten used to. "If a man doesn't make a fool of himself now and again, he's not living." She took a couple of deep, steadying breaths, but couldn't keep her foot from tapping. "Oh, it's like magic when Cullen plays and all the more magic to be here, hearing it." She brought Travis's hand to her lips, then rested her cheek on it. "Mary McKinnon can still outdance anyone in the county, but Erin's wonderful, too, isn't she?"

Burke took a long sip of whiskey. "It's not a hardship to watch her."

Laughing again, Adelia rested her head against her husband's arm. "I suppose as her elder cousin I should warn her about your reputation with women."

Burke swirled the whiskey in his glass and gave her a bland look. "What reputation is that?"

With her head still nestled against Travis, she smiled up at him. "Oh, I hear things, Mr. Logan. Fascinating things. The racing world's a tight little group, you know. I've heard murmurs that a man not only has to watch his daughters but his wife when you're about."

"If I was interested in another man's wife, you'd be the first to know." He took her hand and brought it to his lips. Her eyes laughed at him.

"Travis, I think Burke's flirting with me."

"Apparently," he agreed, and kissed the top of her head.

"A warning, Mr. Logan. It's easy enough to flirt with a woman who's five months along with twins and who knows you're a scoundrel. But mind your step. The Irish are a clever lot." She stood on her toes and kissed his cheek. "If you keep staring at her like that, Matthew McKinnon's going to load his shotgun."

He glanced back as Erin stepped away from the group. "No law against looking."

"There should be when it comes to you." She snuggled against Travis again. "Looks like Erin's going outside for a breath of air." When Burke merely lifted a brow, she smiled. "You'd probably like to light that cigar, maybe take a little walk in the night air yourself."

"As a matter of fact, I would." He nodded to her, then sauntered to the door.

"Were you warning him off or egging him on?" Travis wanted to know.

"Just enjoying the view, love." She turned her mouth up for a kiss.

Erin drew her jacket tightly around her. Nights were coldest in February, but she didn't mind now. The air was bracing and the moon half-full. She was glad her father had pressured her to dance. It seemed too seldom now that there was time for small celebrations. There was so much work to be done, and not as many hands to do it now that Frank had married and started his own family. And within a year she expected Sean to marry the Hennessy girl. With Cullen more interested in his music than milking, that left only Joe and Brian. And herself.

The family was growing, but at the same time spreading out. The farm had to survive. Erin knew that was indisputable. Her father would simply wither away without it. Just as she knew she would wither away if she stayed much longer. The only solution was to find a way to ensure both.

She hugged herself with her arms to ward off the wind. It brought with it the scent of Mrs. Malloy's wild roses and rhododendrons. She wouldn't think of it now. In a short time the Grants would be gone and her own yearnings for more would fade a bit. When the time was right, something would happen. She looked up at the moon and smiled. Hadn't she promised herself that she'd make something happen?

She heard the scrape and flare of a lighter and braced herself.

"Nice night."

She didn't turn. The little jolt to her system teased her. No, she hadn't wanted him to come out, she told herself.

Why should she? Since he had, she would hold her own. "It's a bit cold."

"You look warm enough." She wouldn't give an inch. It only gave him the pleasure of taking it from her. "I liked the dancing."

She turned to walk slowly away from the inn. It didn't surprise her when he fell into step beside her. "You're missing it."

"You stopped." The end of his cigar grew bright and red as he took another puff. "Your brother has a gift."

"Aye." She listened now as the music turned from jaunty to sad. "He wrote this one. Hearing it's like hearing a heart break." Music like this always made her long, and fear, and wonder what it would be like to feel so strongly about another. "Are you a music lover, Mr. Logan?"

"When the tune's right." This one was a waltz, a slow, weepy one. On impulse he slipped his arms around her and picked up the time.

"What are you doing?"

"Dancing," he said simply.

"A man's supposed to ask." But she didn't pull away, and her steps matched his easily. The motion and the music made her smile. She turned her face up to his. The grass was soft beneath her feet, the moonlight sweet. "You don't look like the kind of man who can waltz."

"One of my few cultural accomplishments." She fit nicely into his arms, slender but not fragile, soft but not malleable. "And it seems to be a night for dancing."

She said nothing for a moment. There was magic here, starlight, roses and sad music. The flutter in her stomach, the warmth along her skin, warned her that a woman took chances waltzing under the night sky with a stranger. But still she moved with him.

"The tune's changed," she murmured, and drew out of his arms, relieved, regretful that he didn't keep her there. She turned once again to walk. "Why did you come here?"

"To look at horses. I bought a pair in Kildare." He took a puff on his cigar. He'd yet to realize himself what his horses and farm had come to mean to him. "There's no match for the Thoroughbreds at the Irish National Stud. You pay for them, God knows, but I've never minded putting my money on a winner."

"So you came to buy horses." It interested her, though she didn't want it to.

"And to watch a few races. Ever been to Curragh?"

"No." She glanced up at the moon again. Curragh, Kilkenny, Kildare, all of them might have been as far away as the white slash in the sky. "You won't find Thoroughbreds here in Skibbereen."

"No?" He smiled at her in the moonlight, and the smile made her uneasy. "Then let's say I'm just along for the ride. It's my first time in Ireland."

"And what do you think of it?" She stopped now, unwilling to pass out of the range of the music.

"I've found it beautiful and contradictory."

"With a name like Logan, you'd have some Irish in you."

Unsmiling, he glanced down at his cigar. "It's possible."

"Probable," she said lightly. "You know, you said you were a neighbor of Travis's, but you don't sound like him. Your accent."

"Accent?" His mood changed again with a grin. "I guess if you want to call it that it comes from the West."

"The West?" It took her a moment. "The American West? Cowboys?"

This time he laughed, a full, rich laugh, so that she was

distracted enough not to protest when his hand touched her cheek. "We don't carry six-guns as a rule these days."

Her feathers were ruffled. "You don't have to make fun of me."

"Was I?" Because her skin had felt so cool and so smooth, he touched it again. "And what would you say if I asked you about leprechauns and banshees?"

She had to smile. "I'd say the last to have seen a leprechaun in these parts was Michael Ryan after a pint of Irish."

"You don't believe in legends, Erin?" He stepped closer so that he could see the moonlight reflected in her eyes like light in a lake.

"No." She didn't step back. It wasn't her nature to retreat, even when she felt the warning shiver race up her spine. Whether you won or went down in defeat, it was best to do it with feet firmly planted. "I believe in what I can see and touch. The rest is for dreamers."

"Pity," he murmured, though he had always felt the same. "Life's a bit softer the other way."

"I've never wanted softness."

"Then what?" He touched a finger to the hair that curled at her cheekbones.

"I have to go back." It wasn't a retreat, she told herself. She felt cold all at once, cold to the bone. But even as she started to turn, he closed a hand over her arm. She looked at him, eyes clear, not so much angry as assessing. "You'll excuse me, Mr. Logan. The wind's up."

"I noticed. You didn't answer my question."

"No, because it's no concern of yours. Don't," she said when his fingers closed lightly over her chin, but she didn't jerk away.

"I'm interested. When a man meets someone he recognizes, he's interested."

"We don't know each other." But she understood him. When he'd brought his arms around her in the waltz, she'd known him. There was something, something in both of them that mirrored back. Whatever it was had her heart beating hard now and her skin chilling. "And if it's rude I have to be, then I'll say it plain. I don't care to know you."

"Do you usually have such a strong reaction to a stranger?"

She tossed her head, but his fingers stayed in place. "The only reaction I'm having at the moment is annoyance." Which was one of the biggest lies she could remember telling. She'd already looked at his mouth and wondered what it would be like to be kissed by him. "I'm sure you think I should be flattered that you're willing to spend time with me. But I'm not a silly farm girl who kisses a man because there's a moon and music."

He lifted a brow. "Erin, if I'd intended to kiss you, I'd have done so already. I never waste time—with a woman."

She felt abruptly as foolish as she'd claimed not to be. Damn it, she would have kissed him, and she knew he was well aware of it. "Well, you're wasting mine now. I'll say good-night."

Why hadn't he kissed her? Burke asked himself as he watched her rush back to the inn. He'd wanted to badly. He'd imagined it clearly. For a moment, when the moonlight had fallen over her face and her face had lifted to his, he'd all but tasted her.

But he hadn't kissed her. Something had warned him that it would take only that to change the order of things for both of them. He wasn't ready for it. He wasn't sure he could avoid it.

Taking a last puff, he sent the cigar in an arch into the

night. He'd come to Ireland for horses. He'd be better off being content with that. But he was a man on whom contentment rarely sat easily.

She'd come late on purpose. Erin rolled her bike to the kitchen entrance of the inn and parked it. She knew it was prideful, but she simply didn't want Dee to know she worked there. It wasn't the paperwork and bookkeeping that bothered her. That made her feel accomplished. It was her kitchen duties she preferred to keep to herself.

Mrs. Malloy had promised not to mention it. But she tut-tutted about it. Erin shrugged that off as she entered the kitchen. Let her tut-tut, as long as that was all she let out of her mouth.

Dee and her family were visiting in town through the morning. That had given Erin time to clear up her chores at home, then ride leisurely from the farm to handle the breakfast dishes and the daily cleaning. Since the books were in order, she'd be able to take a few hours that afternoon to drive out to the farm where her cousin had grown up.

It wasn't being deceitful, she told herself as she filled the big sink with water. And if it was, it couldn't be helped. She wouldn't have Dee feeling sorry for her. She was working for the money; it was as simple as that. Once enough was made, she could move on to that office position in Cork or Dublin. By the saints, the only dishes she'd have to clean then would be her own.

She started to hum as she scrubbed the inn's serviceable plates. She'd learned young when there was work to be done to make the best of it, because as sure as the sun rose it would be there again tomorrow.

She looked out the window as she worked, across the field where she'd walked with Burke the night before.

Where she'd danced with him. In the moonlight, she thought, then caught herself. Foolishness. He was just a man dallying with what was available. She might not be traveled or have seen big cities, but she wasn't naive.

If she'd felt anything in those few minutes alone with him, it had been the novelty. He was different, but that didn't make him special. And it certainly didn't warrant her thinking of him in broad daylight with her arms up to the elbows in soapy water.

She heard the door open behind her and began to scrub faster. "I know I'm late, Mrs. Malloy, but I'll have it cleared up before lunch."

"She's at the market, fussing over vegetables."

At Burke's voice, Erin simply closed her eyes. When he crossed over and put a hand on her shoulder, she began to scrub with a vengeance.

"What are you doing?"

"I'd think you'd have eyes to see that." She set one plate to drain and attacked another. "If you'll excuse me, I'm behind."

Saying nothing, he walked over to the stove and poured the coffee that was always kept warm there. She was wearing overalls, baggy ones that might have belonged to one of her brothers. Her hair was down, and longer than he'd imagined it. She'd pulled it back with a band to keep it out of her face, but it was thick and curly beyond her shoulders. He sipped, watching her. He didn't quite know what his own feelings were at finding her at the sink, but he was well aware of hers. Embarrassment.

"You didn't mention you worked here."

"No, I didn't." Erin slammed another plate onto the drainboard. "And I'd be obliged if you didn't, either."

"Why? It's honest work, isn't it?"

"I'd prefer it if Dee didn't know I was washing up after her."

Pride was another emotion he understood well. "All right."

She sent him a cautious look over her shoulder. "You won't tell her?"

"I said I wouldn't." He could smell the detergent in the hot water. Despite the years that had passed, it was still a scent that annoyed him.

Erin's shoulders relaxed a bit. "Thank you."

"Want some coffee?"

She hadn't expected him to make it easy for her. Still cautious, but less reserved, she smiled. "No, I haven't the time." She turned away again because he was much easier to look at than she wanted him to be. "I, ah, thought you'd be out by now."

"I'm back," he said simply. He'd intended to grab a quick cup and leave, take a leisurely walk around town or duck into the local pub for conversation. He studied her, her back straight at the sink, her arms plunged deep into the soapy water. "Want a hand?"

She stared at him this time, caught between astonishment and horror. "No, no, drink your coffee. I'm sure there're muffins in the pantry if you like, or you might want to go out and walk. It's a fine day."

"Trying to get rid of me again?" He strolled over and picked up a dishcloth.

"Please, Mrs. Malloy—"

"Is at the market." He picked up a dish and began to polish it dry.

He was standing close now, nearly hip-to-hip with her. Erin resisted the urge to shift away, or was it to shift closer?

She plunged her hands into the water again. "I don't need any help."

He set down the first dish and picked up another. "I've got nothing else to do."

Frowning, she lifted out a plate. "I don't like it when you're nice."

"Don't worry, I'm not often. So what else do you do except wash dishes and dance?"

It was a matter of pride, she knew, but she turned to him with her eyes blazing. "I keep books, if you want to know. I keep them for the inn and for the dry goods and for the farm."

"Sounds like you're busy," he murmured, and began to consider. "Are you any good?"

"I've heard no complaints. I'm going to get a job in Dublin next year. In an office."

"I can't see it."

She had a cast-iron skillet in her hand now and was tempted. "I didn't ask you to."

"Too many walls in an office," he explained, and lowered the pan into the water himself. "You'd go crazy."

"That's for me to worry about." She gripped the scouring pad like a weapon. "I was wrong when I said I didn't like you when you were nice. I don't like you at all."

"You know, you've only to ask and Dee would take you to America."

She tossed the pad into the water, and suds lapped up over the rim of the sink. "And what? Live off her charity? Is that what you think I want? To take what someone is kind enough to give me?"

"No." He stacked the next plate. "I just wanted to see you flare up again."

"You're a bastard, Mr. Logan."

"True enough. And now that we're on intimate terms, you ought to call me Burke."

"There's plenty I'd like to be calling you. Why don't you be on your way and let me finish here? I've got no time for the likes of you."

"Then you'll have to make some."

He caught her off guard, though she told herself later she should have been expecting it. With her arms still elbow deep in water, he curled a hand around her neck and kissed her. It was quick, but a great deal more of a threat than a promise. His lips were hard and firm and surprisingly warm as he pressed them against hers. For a second, for two. She didn't have time to react, and certainly no time to think before he'd released her again and picked up another dish.

She swallowed, and beneath the soapy water her hands were fists. "You've a nerve, you do."

"A man doesn't get very far without any—or a woman."

"Just remember this. If I want you touching me, I'll let you know."

"Your eyes say plenty, Irish. It's a pleasure to watch them."

She wouldn't argue. She wouldn't demean herself by making an issue of it. Instead, she pulled the plug on the sink. "I've the floor to do. You'll have to get your feet off it."

"Then I guess I'd better take that walk." He laid the cloth down, spread open so it would dry. Without another word or another glance, he strolled out the back door. Erin waited a full ten seconds, then gave herself the satisfaction of heaving a wet rag after him.

Two hours later, after a quick change into a skirt and sweater, Erin met the Grants in the public room of the inn.

Joe's overalls were bundled into a sack tied on the back of her bike, and she'd used some of Mrs. Malloy's precious cream to offset the daily damage she did to her hands. Burke was there. Of course he was, she thought, and deliberately ignored him as he bounced young Brady on his knee.

"Ma sent this." Erin handed Dee a plate wrapped tightly in a cloth. "It's her raisin cake. She didn't want you to think Mrs. Malloy could outcook her."

"I remember your mother's raisin cake." Dee lifted the corner of the cloth to sniff. "Now and then she'd bake an extra and have one of you bring it by the farm." The scent brought back memories—some sweet, some painful. She covered the cake again. "I'm glad you could come with us today."

"You remember it's only on the condition that you come by and visit. Ma's counting on it."

"Then we'd best be rounding up the brood. Burke, if you give the lad chocolate you deserve to have him smear it on you. Brendon, Keeley, into the van now. We're going for a ride."

They didn't have to be told twice.

First they went to the cemetery, where the grass was high and green and the stones weathered and gray. Flowers grew wild, adding the promise of life. Some of Erin's family were buried there; most she barely remembered. She'd never lost anyone close or grieved deeply. But she loved deeply when it came to her family, and thought she could understand how wrenching it would be to lose them.

Yet it had been so long ago, Erin thought as she watched her cousin stand between the graves of her parents. Didn't a loss like that begin to fade with time? Adelia had been only a child when they'd died, nine or ten. Wouldn't her memory of them have dimmed? Still, though she could imagine a world away from her family, she couldn't imagine one where they didn't exist.

"It still hurts," Dee murmured as she looked down at the stones that bore her parents' names.

"I know." Travis ran a hand down her hair.

"I remember Father Finnegan telling me after it happened that it was God's will, and thinking to myself that it didn't seem right. It still doesn't." She sighed and looked up at him. "I'll never be able to figure it out, will I?"

"No." He took her hand in his. There was a part of him that wanted to gather her up and take her away from the grief. And a part of him that understood she'd been strong enough to deal with it years before they'd even met. "I wish I'd known them."

"They'd have loved you." She let the tears come, but smiled with them. "And the children. They'd have fussed over the children, spoiled them. More than Hannah does. It comforts me that they're together. I believe that, you know. But it's painful that they missed knowing you and the babies."

"Don't cry, Momma." Keeley slipped a hand into Adelia's. "Look, I made a flower. Burke showed me. He said they'd like it even though they're in heaven."

Dee looked at the little wreath fashioned of twigs and wild grass. "It's lovely. Let's put it right in the middle, like this." Bending, she placed it between the graves. "Aye, I'm sure they'll like this."

What a strange man he was, Erin thought as she sat beside Burke in the van and listened to Brendon's chattering. She'd seen him sit in the grass and twine twigs together for Keeley. Though she'd kept herself distant enough that she hadn't heard what he'd said, she'd been aware that the girl had listened attentively and had looked at him with absolute trust.

He didn't seem to be a man to inspire trust.

She knew the road that led to the farm that had been the Cunnanes'. She remembered Dee's parents only as the vaguest of shadows, but she did remember Lettie Cunnane well, the aunt Dee had lived with when she'd been orphaned. She'd been a tough, stern-faced woman, and because of her Erin had kept her visits to the farm few and far between. That was behind them now, she reminded herself as she gestured toward the window for Brendon. "You see, just over this hill is where your mother grew up."

"On a farm," he said knowledgeably. The patches of green pasture and yellow gorse meant little to him. "We have a farm. The best one in Maryland." He grinned at Burke as if it was an old joke.

"It'll still be the second best when I'm finished," Burke answered, willing to rise to the bait.

"Royal Meadows has been around for gener...gener..."

"Generations," Burke supplied.

"Yeah. And you're still wet behind the ears 'cause Uncle Paddy said so."

"Brendon Patrick Grant." It was all the warning Hannah had to give. She turned her stern eye on Burke. "And you should know better than to encourage him."

Burke merely grinned and tousled the boy's hair. "Doesn't take much."

"Burke won his farm in a poker game," Brendon supplied as the van shuddered to a halt. "He's teaching me to play."

"That's so when Royal Meadows belongs to you, I can win that, too." He pushed open the sliding door, then grabbed the giggling boy around the waist.

"Did he really?" Erin asked in an undertone as Hannah took Keeley's hand. "Win his horse farm gambling?"

"So I'm told." Hannah stepped a bit wearily out of the van. "Rumor is he's lost and won more than that." She glanced over as Burke settled Brendon on his shoulders. "It's hard to hold it against him."

She wouldn't, Erin thought as she joined the others. She was too Irish to turn her nose up at a gambler, especially a successful one. Trailing behind Dee, she looked over the rise to the farm below.

It hadn't changed much, not in her memory. Oh, the milking parlor was new, and a fresh coat of paint had been slapped on the barn a year or so before. It was the only farm in sight. To the east, the hills rose up and blocked the view. The vegetable garden was already tilled and planted, and a smattering of the dairy cows could be seen in the strip of pasture. There was smoke spiraling out of the chimney of the little stone cottage, which was a great deal like her own. The good, rich smell of peat carried on the wind.

"The Sweeneys are a nice family," she said at length because her cousin stared down so long without speaking. "I know they wouldn't mind if you wanted to go down and look about."

"No." She said it too quickly, then softened the refusal with a touch of her hand. "I don't mind looking from here." The truth was she couldn't bear to go any closer to what had been and was no longer her own. "Do you remember, Erin, when Aunt Lettie was so sick and you and your mother came visiting?"

"Yes, you gave Ma one of the roses from the bush there." The bush had been her mother's, Erin remembered, and she linked her fingers briefly with Dee's. "The roses still bloom every summer."

She smiled at that. "Such a little place. Smaller now than even I remember. Look, Keeley, see that window there." She crouched down to show her daughter. "That was my room when I was your age."

Adelia stood again. There was only her and Travis now as the others strolled down the side of the road. "Dee, I've told you before, you can have it back if you want. We can make the Sweeneys a good offer for it."

She continued to look down, remembering. Then, with a little sigh, she slipped an arm around Travis's waist. "You know, when I left here all those years ago, I thought I'd lost everything." She tilted her head back and kissed him. "I was wrong. Let's walk a little ways. It's such a beautiful day."

Erin watched them. There was a small meadow that was green now but would be choked with wildflowers in only a matter of weeks. She heard Burke behind her and spoke without thinking.

"If I were to go, to leave here and find something else, I'd never look back."

"If you don't look over your shoulder once in a while, things catch up with you faster than you think."

"I don't understand you." She turned, and her hair fluttered around her face and shoulders, free of bonds. "One minute you sound like a man without any roots at all, and the next you sound as though you've just transplanted them where it's convenient."

"But not too deep." He caught the ends of her hair in his fingers. He was becoming more and more fascinated by it. It wasn't silk; it was too wild and untamed for silk. "Maybe that's the trick, Irish, not letting them sink too deep. You can yank yours up because you'll damn well strangle if you don't, but you'll take some of this with you."

He reached down and took up a handful of soil. "Seems like a good enough base."

"And what's yours?"

He looked down at the rich dirt in his hand. "Have you ever seen the sand in the desert, Irish? No, no, you haven't. It's thin. It'll slip right out of your hands, no matter how hard you hold on to it."

"Grains of sand have a habit of clinging to the skin."

"And are easily brushed away." He glanced around as Brady let out a squeal of laughter at a gull that had glided in from the sea.

"Why did you kiss me before?" She hadn't wanted to ask. Rather, she hadn't wanted him to know it mattered. He smiled at her again, slowly, with the amusement only a hint in his eyes.

"A woman should never wonder why a man kisses her."

Annoyed with herself, she shrugged and turned away. "It wasn't a proper one, anyway."

"You want a proper one?"

"No." She continued to walk, but the devil on her shoulder took over. She glanced around, a half smile on her face. "I'll let you know when I do."

Chapter 3

There was a storm coming. Erin could feel it brewing inside her, just as she could see it brewing in the clouds that buried the sun and hung gloomily over the hills. She worked quickly, routinely, pulling the pins off the line and dropping the dry, billowing clothes in the basket at her feet.

She didn't mind this kind of monotonous, mindless work. It left her brain free to think and remember and plan. Just now, with the wind tossing sheets away from her and the sky boiling, she liked the simple outside chore. She wanted to see the storm break, to be a part of it when the wind and rain raised hell. When it was over, things would settle back into the quiet routine she knew was slowly driving her mad.

What was wrong with her? Erin yanked one of her brother's work shirts from the line, and out of ingrained habit folded it to ward off wrinkles. She loved her family, had friends and work to keep the wolf from the door. So why was she so restless, so edgy? She couldn't blame it all on her cousin's visit or on the unexpected appearance of one Burke Logan. She'd been feeling restless before they'd come, but for some reason their presence—his presence—intensified it.

She couldn't talk to her mother about it. Erin stripped down one of her mother's aprons and buried her face in the cool, fresh scent of the material. Her mother simply couldn't understand discontent or yearnings for more, not when there was a sturdy roof over the head and food enough for everyone. Time and again Erin had wished herself as serene a heart as her mother's. But it wasn't meant to be.

She couldn't go to her father, though Erin knew he would understand the storm inside her. He wasn't a calm, easy man. From the stories she'd heard he'd been a hellion in his youth, and it had taken marriage to his Mary and a couple of babies before he'd begun to take hold. But while her father would understand, Erin knew he would also be distressed. If she wanted more, needed more, he would take it to mean he hadn't given her enough.

There was Cullen. She'd always been able to talk to Cullen. But he was so busy just now, and her feelings were so mixed, the longings so indistinct, that she wasn't sure she could articulate them in any case.

So she would wait, let the storm come and the wind blow.

He'd been watching her for some time. Burke never considered that it was rude to stand and observe people without their knowledge. You learned more about people when they thought they were alone.

She moved well. Even doing something so simple there was an innate sensuality in her movements. She had more fire than showed in her hair. Inside her there was a flame smoldering. He recognized it because he'd been born with one himself. That kind of heat, of passion, could and would break free. It only took the right elements falling into place. Time, place, circumstance.

She didn't hum as she worked now, but occasionally looked up at the sky as if daring it to open and pour its fury on her. Her hair blew back from her face, fighting against the band that held it. Just as she fought whatever held her. He'd wondered what the results would be when she finally broke free. He'd already decided he wanted to be around to see for himself.

"I haven't seen a woman do that for a long time."

Erin spun around, her heels digging into the soft ground, a pillowcase clutched in her hand. He looked so at home, she thought, with the collar of his jacket up against the wind, the buttons undone in contradiction. He had his thumbs hooked in his pockets and that damned devil smile on his face. She'd never known a man to look better or more suited to the raw air and the warring skies. She turned away to snatch another clothespin because she knew her reaction to him would bring her nothing but trouble.

"Don't women take down the wash where you come from?"

"Progress often stamps out tradition." He moved to her with the easy strides of a man used to walking toward what he wanted. He unhooked a cotton slip—her cotton slip—folded it and dropped it in the basket. Erin clamped her teeth together and told herself only a foolish chucklehead would be embarrassed.

"There's no need for you to be putting your hands on the wash."

"Don't worry, they're clean enough." As if to prove it, he held them out. For the first time she noticed a thin, jagged scar across his knuckles.

"What are you doing here?"

"I came to see you."

She said nothing for a moment. He didn't make it easy when he didn't invent comfortable excuses. "Why?"

"Because I wanted to." He took down a pair of service-able white panties, folded those, too, without a blush, then laid them on top of the slip.

Erin felt a slow, uncomfortable curling in her stomach. "Shouldn't you be with Travis and Dee?"

"I think they'll survive the afternoon without me. I liked your farm when we were here yesterday." He glanced around now at the neat buildings. The cottage was nearly half again as large as the one where Adelia Grant had grown up, but the roof had the same bleached yellow thatching and sturdy stone walls. There were flowers here as well. The Irish seemed happy to let them grow as they chose—gay, untamed and sturdy. A hedge of wild fuchsia was already blooming. It made him think of home and the snow covering the fields.

The roof of the barn showed fresh patching. The paint on the silo was peeling and no longer white, but the chickens in the coop were fat and clucking. He imagined the Mc-Kinnons worked seven days a week to maintain the place. Such was the life of a farmer. "This is a fine piece of land. Apparently your father knows what to do with it."

"It's his life," Erin said simply as she took down the last of the wash.

"What about yours?"

"I don't know what you mean."

He lifted the basket before she could. "It's a good farm, a good life for some. You weren't meant for it."

"You don't know me well enough to say what I'm meant for." She took the basket from him and walked toward the kitchen door. "But I've already told you I'm going north to an office job in a year or so." Taking a deep breath, she swung the door open. Her mother would be horrified if she didn't ask the man in and at least offer him a cup of tea. She turned to him, but before she could issue the invitation he was taking the first step.

"Let's take a walk. I have a proposition for you."

Erin leaned back against the door and studied him coolly. "Oh, I'll just bet you do."

He took the basket from her again, set it inside the door and gave it a little shove. "You're getting ahead of yourself, Irish. Let's just say when I want you in bed I won't ask."

And he wouldn't, she thought as they watched each other. He wasn't the type to court a woman with flowers and pretty words, any more than he was the type to coax a woman gently into his arms. Well, she wasn't the type who wanted to be coaxed, but neither would she be steamrollered. "Just what is it you're wanting, Burke?"

"Let's take a walk," he repeated, but this time he closed his hand over hers.

She could have refused, but then she wouldn't know what it was he had to say. Erin decided that if she shook free and shut the door in his face, he'd tuck his hands in his pockets and stroll off, leaving her the one who was fuming.

There was no harm in walking with him, she told herself as she stepped down beside him. Her mother was in the house, and her father, along with a couple of her brothers, was somewhere on the farm. Added to that was the fact that she had every confidence she could take care of herself.

"I don't have much time," she said briskly. "There's a lot more to be done today."

"This won't take long." But he said nothing more as they walked away from the house. He didn't seem to look, but he saw everything—the care, the sweat that went into the farm, the long hours and the hope. He counted thirty cows. A man could make a living off less, he imagined. It hadn't been so many years since he'd worked backbreaking hours. He hadn't forgotten, just as he never forgot that fate could take what he had just as easily as it had given it to him.

"If it was a tour of the farm you were wanting—" Erin began.

"I had one yesterday, remember?" He paused a moment to look out over a field. He knew what it was to haul rocks from them, to ride sweating over them at baling time and to curse the land as much as you worshiped it. "You grow grain here for the stock?"

"Aye. It'll be plowing time soon."

"You work the fields?"

"I've been known to."

Burke turned her hand palm-up and studied it. It wasn't raw and cracked, but toughened with a ridge of callus. The nails were trimmed short and left unpainted. "You haven't pampered them."

"What good would that do me? I'm not ashamed of the work they've done."

"No. You're too practical for that." He turned her hand over again and looked at her face. "You're not the kind of woman who daydreams about white knights."

She could smile at that, though the intensity of his eyes made her uneasy. "I've always thought white knights would be painfully dull, and the last thing I want is to be a lady in distress. I'd rather be slaying my own dragons."

"Good. I don't have much use for a woman who wants to be taken care of." He still had her hand, he still watched the wind whip furiously through her hair. "Why don't you come back to America with me, Erin?"

She stared at him, speechless. The skies opened up. They

were both soaked in a matter of seconds. She might have stood there, wide-eyed and openmouthed, but he grabbed her arm and yanked her inside a shed.

Inside it was dim and smelled of soil and damp. Tools for the vegetable garden lined the walls. Her mother's peat pots and seeds were stacked on shelves waiting for planting. Rain beat on the tin roof, and the wind snaked through the cracks in the boards and moaned.

Erin stood shivering just inside the door, her hair plastered to her head, her sweater dripping at the hem. But her senses had come back, full force.

"You're a madman, Burke Logan. By the saints, you're as mad as a hatter. Do you think I'd just bundle up my skirts and cross an ocean with you?" She still shivered, but the more she spoke, the hotter her temper became. "Sure and it's a conceited ox you are to believe all you have to do is crook your finger to have me tagging after you. I don't even know you." She swiped a hand over her face to dry it, then went one better and shoved him hard in the chest. "And it's the God's truth that I have no desire to."

She turned to the shed door and would have yanked it open if he hadn't caught her by the shoulders.

"Take your hands off me, you snake." On impulse, she grabbed a rake and turned on him with it. "Touch me again and I'll slice you into pieces, little ones that won't be put back together easily."

So she'd slay her dragons with a garden rake, he thought, lifting both hands, palms out, in a gesture of peace. "You don't have to defend your honor, Irish. I'm not after it— yet. This is business."

"What business would I be having with you?" When he took a step toward her, she gestured with the rake. "Come closer and I promise you'll be missing an ear at the very least."

"Fine." He made as if to take a step back. Then he moved quickly. Erin cursed him when he wrenched the rake out of her hands. Even as it clattered to the floor, her back was against the wall. "You'll have to learn not to drop your guard." His face was close, so close she could see his eyes, smoky and dark, and little else. She twisted, but his fingers only dug in harder. "Hold still a minute, will you? You're making a fool of yourself."

Nothing he could have said would have struck the light to her temper faster. She all but bared her teeth and snarled. "There'll come a time and there'll come a place when you'll pay for this."

"Everyone pays, Irish. Now take a deep breath, shut your mouth and listen. I'm offering you a job, that's all." She stopped wriggling to stare at him again. "I need someone sharp, someone clever with figures, to run my books."

"Your books?"

"The farm, expenses, payroll. The man I had was a little too creative. Since he's going to be a guest of the state for the next few years, I need someone else. I want someone I know, someone I can see and talk to, handling my money rather than a big shiny company that doesn't give a damn about the farm or me."

Because her head was whirling, she took one long breath before she spoke again. "You want me to come to America and keep your books?"

He smiled because she sounded almost disappointed. "I'm not offering you a free ride. You're a pleasure to look at, Erin, but at the moment all I intend to pay for is your brain."

"Move back," she ordered in a voice that was suddenly

firm. "I can't breathe with you pushing me through the wall."

"No more attacks with garden tools?"

Her chin came up. "All right. Just move aside." When he did, she took a couple of deep breaths. She had to keep a clear head now. She didn't mind taking a new road; in fact, she'd often fretted to do just that. She only wanted to study all the curves and angles of it first. "You want to hire me?"

"That's right."

"Why?"

"I've just told you."

She shook her head, still cautious. "You told me you need a bookkeeper. I imagine there're plenty of them in America."

"Let's just say I like your style." Bending, he picked up the rake and replaced it. He wondered briefly if she would have used it. Yes, indeed, he thought, grinning to himself. Oh, yes, indeed.

"For all you know, I can't add two and two."

"Mrs. Malloy and O'Donnelly at the dry goods say differently." He leaned back against a workbench. Studying her from there, he decided he'd spoken no less than the truth. Even wet and dripping, she was a pleasure to look at.

"Mrs. Malloy. You've spoken to her? You went to Mr. O'Donnelly and asked questions about me?"

"Just checking your references."

"No one told you to go poking about the town asking questions about me."

"Business, Irish. Strictly business. What I found out is that you're neat as a pin and dependable. Your figures tally and your books are clean. That's good enough for me."

"This is crazy." Struggling against a surge of excitement,

she dragged a hand through her still-dripping hair. "A body doesn't hire someone they've known only a few days."

"Irish, people are hired after a ten-minute interview."

"That's not what I mean. This isn't a matter of me giving you a résumé, then catching a bus to take a new job across town. You're talking about me coming to America and taking on a job that's bigger than the inn, the farm and the dry goods put together."

He only moved his shoulders. "It's just a matter of more figures, isn't it? You're talking about going north in a year. I'm giving you a chance to go to America now. Make the break."

"It's not so simple." Along with the excitement was a growing panic. Wasn't this what she'd always wanted? Now that it was nearly as close as a handspan, she was terrified.

"It's a gamble." He was watching her again in that quiet, intense way. "Most things worth winning are. I'll pay for your ticket as a sign of good faith. You'll start out at a weekly salary." He considered a moment, then named a figure that had her mouth dropping open. "If it works out, there'll be a ten-percent raise in six months. For that you take care of all the details, all the figures, all the bills. I'll want a weekly report. We'll leave in two days."

"Two days?" She was numb now, so numb she could only stare at him. "But even if I agreed, I could never be ready to leave by then."

"All you have to do is pack and say your goodbyes. I'll handle the rest."

"But I—"

"You have to make up your mind, Erin. Stay or go." He stepped toward her again. "If you stay, you'll be safe, and you'll always wonder what if."

He was right. The question was already nagging at her. "If I go, where will I live?"

"I've got plenty of room."

"No." On this she would have to be firm, right from the start. "I won't agree to that. I may say I'll work for you, but I won't live with you."

"It's your choice." Again he moved his shoulders as if it didn't matter. He'd already anticipated her balking there. "I don't imagine Adelia would have any problem putting you up. In fact, I think you know she'd love to have you with her. It wouldn't be charity," he said, keeping one step ahead of her. "You'd be bringing in a wage. You could get your own place, for that matter, but I think you'd be more comfortable with your cousin at first. And our farms are close enough to make it convenient."

"I'll talk to her." Sometime during the last two minutes her mind had been made up. She was going. Her bridges might not be burning behind her, but they were certainly smoking. "I'll have to speak to my family, as well, but I'd like to accept your offer."

She held out her hand. Burke took it just as casually, though he wondered about the wild surge of relief that coursed through him. "I expect a day's work for a day's pay. I don't doubt you'll give it to me."

"That I will. I'm grateful for the chance."

"I'll remind you of that after you've spent a few days sorting through the mess my last bookkeeper left me with."

She stood very still for a moment, letting it all soak in, layer by layer. Then she spun in a quick circle and laughed. "I can't believe it. America! It's like some kind of a mad dream. I've hardly been more than fifty kilometers from Skibbereen, and now I'm going thousands in the blink of an eye."

He liked to see her this way, her face flushed with pleasure, her eyes lit with it. And the rain still drummed on the roof. "It takes a bit longer than that to cross the Atlantic."

"Don't be so literal." But she was too excited to take offense. "In a matter of days I'll be in a new country, a new place, a new job. New money."

He started to reach for a cigar, then thought better of it. "The money puts a gleam in your eye."

"Anyone who's ever been poor gleams a bit when they've got enough money."

He acknowledged this with a nod. He'd been poor, but he doubted Erin would understand that degree of poverty. He appreciated money, though if he lost it, as he had before, he would simply shake the dust off his shoes and make more. "You'll earn it."

"I wouldn't be having it any other way." She stopped as reality began to seep through. "But I need a passport and the green card that allows you to work. There must be a pile of papers that have to be processed."

"I told you I'd see to it." He drew a paper out of his pocket. "Fill this out and drop it off at the inn tonight. It's an application," he explained as she studied it. "I've already arranged to have it processed tomorrow. Your passport and whatever else you need will be in Cork when we get there."

She tapped the paper slowly against her palm. "You were damn sure of yourself, weren't you?"

"It pays to be. You'll need a picture they can use, too. A recent one."

"What if I'd said no?"

He simply smiled. "Then you'd have been a fool and I'd have thrown the application away."

"I can't figure you." She tucked the application in the pocket of her baggy pants, but shook her head at him.

"You've made me a very generous offer, you're giving me the opportunity to do something I've wanted to do for as long as I can remember. But even as you're doing it, it doesn't seem to matter to you one way or the other."

He remembered the surge of relief, but chose to ignore it. "Things matter too much to people. That's how they get hurt."

"Are you saying that things don't matter to you? Nothing at all? What about your farm?"

He shifted a bit, surprised that the question, when she asked it, made him uncomfortable. "It's a place. A comfortable and fairly profitable one at the moment. But that's all it is. I don't have the ties to it that you have to the land here, Erin. That's why if I leave it I will leave without a second glance. When you leave Ireland, no matter how much you want to go, you're going to hurt."

"There's nothing wrong in that," she murmured. "It's my home. It's only right to miss your home."

"Some people don't make homes. They just live somewhere and leave it at that."

She saw more clearly now, though the light was still dim. She saw, though she'd told herself she didn't care, that there were places inside him no one, no woman, would ever touch. "That's a cold and sorry way to live."

"It's a choice," he corrected. Then he pushed the subject aside. "Make sure you get me the application tonight. I'm leaving for Cork first thing in the morning."

"But you said we weren't going for a couple of days."

"I'll meet you there."

"All right, then. I should be getting along. There's a lot to be done."

"There's something else I think we should get out of the way." He rocked back on his heels a moment, then stunned her by grabbing both her arms and dragging her against him. "This has nothing to do with business."

Infuriated, she brought her hands to his chest and gave him one hard shove. It didn't budge him an inch. Then he clamped his mouth down on hers, rough and ready and with no patience at all.

She would have ripped and clawed at him. She would have struggled and bit and cursed. That was what she told herself she would have done if she hadn't been so stunned by the heat. His lips were firm. That she already knew. But she hadn't known they could be so hot, so passionate, so tempting.

Her head filled with sounds—louder, deeper sounds than the rain that drove furiously on the roof above. Her hands were trapped between their bodies so that she could feel the pounding of a heart without knowing which of them it came from.

This is what the apple must have tasted like when Eve took the first forbidden bite, she thought giddily. Succulent, tart, unbearably delicious. Nothing else ever tasted would be as satisfying. Lost in the flavor, she parted her lips and let him take more.

He'd known what he'd wanted but hadn't been sure what to expect. If she'd hissed at him, he would have ignored her and taken his fill. If she'd struck out at him in anger, he would have taken her struggles in stride and enjoyed the fury. He'd fought or gambled for everything he'd wanted all of his life. For days he'd been trying to convince himself that Erin McKinnon was no different. But she was.

She gave. After the first stunned instant she gave passionately, with the kind of desperation that left him shaken and edgy for more. Her mouth was avid and mobile, her body taut and trembling. He could feel the raw, jagged need raging through her, rising, speeding up to meet and match his own.

He wanted to take her there, on the damp floor with the smell of rain and earth everywhere. He wanted her to touch him, to feel those capable hands on his flesh. To hear her say his name. To watch her eyes go dark as midnight as he covered her body with his. It could be now. He could feel it in the press of her body against his, in the give of her mouth.

It could be now. There had been times, and there had been women with whom he wouldn't have hesitated. Why he did so now he couldn't be sure. But he drew her away, though his hands stayed on her shoulders and his eyes stayed on hers as they slowly fluttered open.

She couldn't speak, not for a moment. The feeling was so immense it left no room for words. She'd never known that a body could be filled so quickly with sensations or that a mind could be emptied of them just as swiftly. She knew now. If anyone had told her that the world could change in the single beat of a heart, she would have laughed. Now she understood.

He didn't speak. Erin struggled to find her footing as he kept his silence. She couldn't allow herself that kind of madness, not again. If she were to travel an ocean with him, work for him, understand him just a little, she couldn't let this happen again. Not with a man like him. Taking a deep breath, she steadied herself. No, never with him. If the past few moments had taught her anything, it was that he was a man who knew women and who understood their weaknesses very well.

"You had no right to do that." She didn't unleash her temper, knowing she hadn't the energy left for it.

He was shaken, down to the bone, down to the heart, but it wasn't the time to dwell on it. "It wasn't a matter of right but of want. That was a proper kiss, Irish, and we needed to get it out of our systems whether you were coming with me or not."

She nodded, hoping she sounded as casual as he. She'd rather have died on the spot than have admitted her own inexperience. "Now that our systems are clear, there'll be no need for it to happen again."

"Don't ask me for promises. You'll be disappointed." He strolled to the door, pushing it open so that the wind and rain lashed their way in. It helped cool his head and steady his heart rate. "You can talk to Dee and Travis when you bring the papers in. Give your family my best."

Then he was gone, into the storm. Though Erin dashed to the door, he was only a quickly fading shadow in the gloom.

A shadow, she thought, who she knew nothing about. And she would be going with him to America.

Chapter 4

America. Erin wasn't naive enough to believe the streets were paved with gold, but she was determined to make it the land of opportunity. Her opportunity.

It was the speed of things that struck her first, the hurry every living soul seemed to be in. Well, she was in a bit of a hurry herself, she decided as she sat in the back of her cousin's station wagon and tried not to gawk.

The cold had surprised her, too, a numbing, bone-chilling cold she'd never experienced in the mild Irish climate. But the snow was novelty enough to make it a small inconvenience. Piles of it, more than she'd ever seen, rolling over the gentle hills and heaped on the sides of the road. It was a different sky above, different air around her. So what if she gawked, Erin thought to herself, and she smiled as she tried to see everything at once.

Burke had been true to his word. The paperwork had gone so smoothly that in a matter of days after he'd of-

fered her the job she'd been across the Atlantic. He'd left
her with her cousin's family at the airport in Virginia, with
a casual comment that he'd see her in a couple of days,
after she'd settled in. Just like that. Erin was still trying to
catch her breath.

She'd hoped he'd say more. She'd hoped—perhaps foolishly—that he would seem more pleased that she was there.
She'd even waited to see that half smile, that dark amusement in his eyes, or to feel the flick of his finger down her
cheek. But he'd only dismissed her as an employer dis-
misses an employee. Erin reminded herself that was precisely what they were now. There would be no more waltzes
or wild embraces.

Did she wish there would be? The devil of it was she'd
done just as much thinking about Burke Logan as she had
about coming to America. Something had told her that they
were both chances, the man and the country. Sometime,
somehow, she'd begun to mix them together and had discovered she wanted both. She knew she was being foolish
again and resolved to settle for the land.

It was beautiful. The mountains dark in the distance reminded her just enough of home to make her comfortable,
while the whiz of the cars beside them in three lanes was
foreign enough to add excitement. Erin found it a palatable
combination and was already hoping for more.

Adelia shifted in her seat so that she could smile back
at her cousin. "I remember my first day here, when Uncle
Paddy picked me up at that same airport. I felt like I'd been
plopped down in the middle of a circus."

"I'll get used to it." Erin smiled and took another long
look out the window. "I'll get used to it very quickly, as
soon as I believe I'm really here."

"I for one am grateful to Burke." Distracted a moment,

Dee murmured to Brady, who was fretting in his car seat, then soothed him with a stuffed dog. "It was never in my mind when we went to Ireland that we'd be bringing family back with us."

The guilt tingled a little, shadowing the pleasure. "I know it was all very sudden, and I'm beholden to you, Dee."

"Oh, what a pack of nonsense. I feel like a girl again, having my best friend come to stay. We'll have a party." The minute the thought struck, Adelia rolled with it. "A proper one, too, don't you think, Travis?"

"I think we could handle it."

"I don't want you to go to any trouble," Erin put in.

"If you don't let Dee go to any trouble, you'll break her heart," Travis said without embellishment. They crossed over the line into Maryland. "Nearly home now, love."

"I'm as excited to be back as I was to leave. Brendon, if you don't stop teasing your sister you'll be seeing nothing but the four walls of your room until morning." Dee sighed a bit and shifted.

"All right?" Travis sent her a quick, concerned glance.

"They're just active." She patted his hand to make light of the discomfort. "Probably squabbling between themselves already."

"I'd like to help with the children." The closer they came, the more Erin's nerves began to jump. "Or however else I can to pay you back for taking me in this way."

"You're family," Adelia said simply. Then she sat up straighter as they drove between the stone pillars that led to home. "Welcome to Royal Meadows, cousin. Be happy."

Erin didn't know what she'd been expecting. Something grand, surely. She wasn't disappointed. The sun shone hard on the February snow, causing the thin crust to glitter and shine. Acres of it, Erin thought. This world was white and gleaming. Even the trees were coated with it, their bare black branches mantled with snow and dripping with cold, clear ice. Like a fairyland, she mused, then called herself foolish.

When the house came into view, she could only stare. She'd never seen anything so big or so lovely. The stone rose up as sturdy as it was majestic from the white base of snow. Charm was added by the wrought-iron-trimmed balconies that graced the windows.

"It's beautiful," Erin murmured. "It's the most beautiful house I've ever seen."

"I've always thought so, too." Dee reached over to unhook Brady as Travis brought the car to a halt. "And it's so good to see it again. Come now, my lad, we're home."

"Uncle Paddy!" From the back seat, both Brendon and Keeley began to shout. Then they were out and kicking through the snow. A short, stocky man with wiry gray hair and a face like an elf spread his arms wide for them.

"Give me the baby, missy," Hannah told Dee. "You're already carrying two. And we'll let the men handle the bags while you come in for a nice cup of tea and put your feet up."

"Stop fussing," Dee said. Then she laughed as her uncle grabbed her in a fierce hug.

"How's my best girl?"

"Fit as a fiddle and glad to be home. Look what we brought back with us from Skibbereen." Still laughing, she held out a hand to Erin. "You remember Erin McKinnon, Uncle Paddy. Mary and Matthew McKinnon's daughter."

"Erin McKinnon?" His face seemed to scrunch together as he thought back. Then, with a hoot, he was beaming. "Erin McKinnon, is it? Faith, lass, the last time I saw you you were no more than a baby. I used to raise a glass with your da now and then, but you wouldn't be remembering that."

"No, but they still speak of Paddy Cunnane in the village."

"Do they now?" He grinned as if he knew exactly what was said. "Well, get inside out of the cold."

"I can help with the bags," Erin began as Adelia started to shoo her children indoors.

"I'd appreciate it if you'd go with Dee, let her show you your room." Travis was already pulling out the first of the luggage. Even as he set them in the drive, his gaze was following his wife. "She doesn't like to admit she gets tired, and having you to fuss over will keep her from overdoing."

Erin stood a moment, torn between carrying her own weight and doing what was asked of her. "All right. If you like."

"It wouldn't hurt if you told her you'd like to sit down with a cup of tea."

Quietly domineering, Erin thought again. On impulse, she leaned over and kissed Travis's cheek. "Your wife's a fortunate woman. I'll see that she rests without knowing she's been maneuvered into it." Still, she picked up one of the cases and took it inside with her.

The warmth struck her immediately, not just the change of temperature but the colors and the feel of the house itself. The children were already racing through the rooms as if they wanted to make sure nothing had changed in their absence.

"You'll want to go up first, see your room." Dee was already stripping off her gloves and laying them on an ornamental table in the hall. Hooking her arm through Erin's, she started up the stairs. "You'll tell me if it suits you or not, and if there's anything else you want. As soon as you feel settled in, I'll show you the rest."

Erin only nodded. The space alone left her speechless. Adelia opened a door and gestured her inside.

"This is the guest room. I wish we'd had time to have some flowers for you." She glanced around the room, regretting she hadn't been able to add a few more personal touches. "The bath's down the end of the hall, and I'm sorry to say the children are always flinging wet towels around and making a mess of it."

The room was done in gray and rose with a big brass bed and a thick carpet. The furniture was a rich mahogany with gleaming brass pulls and a tall framed mirror over the bureau. There were knickknacks here and there, a little china dog, a rose-colored goblet, more brass in a whimsical study of a lion. The terrace doors showed the white expanse of snow through gauzy curtains, making a dreamlike boundary between warmth and cold. Unable to speak, Erin gripped her case in both hands and just looked.

"Will it suit you? You're free to change anything you like."

"No," Erin managed to get past the block in her throat, but her hands didn't relax on the handle of the case. "It's the most beautiful room I've ever seen. I don't know what to say."

"Say it pleasures you." Gently Dee pried the case from her. "I want you to feel comfortable, Erin, at home. I know what it's like to leave things behind and come to someplace strange."

Erin took a deep breath. She wasn't able to bear it, not for another second. "I don't deserve this."

"What foolishness." Businesslike, Dee set the case on the bed with the intention of helping her cousin unpack.

"No, please." Erin put her hand over Dee's, then sat. She didn't want her cousin to tire herself, and she didn't want her to see what a pitiful amount she'd brought with her. "I have to confess."

Amused, Dee sat beside her. "Do you want a priest?"

With a watery laugh that shamed her, Erin shook her head. "I've been so jealous of you." There, it was out.

Dee considered a minute. "But you're much prettier than I am."

"No, that's not true, and that's not it, in any case." Erin opened her mouth again, then let out a long breath. "Oh, I hate confession."

"Me, too. Sinning just comes natural to some of us."

Erin glanced over, saw both the warmth and humor and relaxed. "It comes natural enough to me. I was jealous of you. Am," she corrected, determined to make a clean breast of it. "I'd think about you here in a big, beautiful house, with pretty things and pretty clothes, your family, all the things that go with it, and I'd just near die with envy. When I met you at the airport that day, I was resentful and nervous."

"Nervous?" She could pass over resentment easily. "About seeing me? Erin, we all but grew up together."

"But you moved here, and you're rich." She closed her eyes. "I've a powerful lust for money."

A smile trembled on Dee's lips, but she managed to control it. "Well, that doesn't seem like a very big sin to me. A couple of days in purgatory, maybe. Erin, I know what is it not to have and to wish for more. I don't think less of you for envying me—in truth, I'm flattered. I suppose that's a sin, too," she added after a moment's thought.

"It's worse because you're so kind to me, all of you, and I feel like I'm using you."

"Maybe you are. But I'm using you as well, to bring Ireland a little closer, to be my friend. I have a sister— Travis's sister. But she moved away about two years ago. I can't tell you how much I miss her. I guess I was hoping you'd fill the hole."

Because her conscience was soothed by the admission, Erin touched a hand to Dee's. "I guess it's not so bad if we use each other."

"Let's just see what happens. Now I'll help you unpack."

"Let's leave it. I'd really like to go down and have a cup of tea."

As Erin rose, Adelia eyed her. "Did Travis tell you to keep me off my feet?"

"I don't know what you're talking about."

"Lying's a sin, too," Dee reminded her, but she smiled as she led her downstairs.

She dreamed of Ireland that night, of the heady green hills and the soft scent of heather. She saw the dark mountains and the clouds that rushed across the sky ahead of the wind. And her farm, with its rich plowed earth and grazing cows. She dreamed of her mother, telling her goodbye with a smile even as a tear slid down her cheek. Of her father, holding her so tight her ribs had ached. She heard each of her brothers teasing her, one by one.

She cried for Ireland that night, slow, quiet tears for a land she'd left behind and carried with her.

But when she woke, her eyes were dry and her mind clear. She'd made her break, chosen her path, and she'd best be getting on with it.

The plain gray dress she chose was made sturdily and fit well. Her mother's stitches were always true. Erin started to pin her hair up, then changed her mind and tamed it into a braid. She studied herself with what she hoped was a critical and objective eye. Suitable for work, Erin decided, then started downstairs.

She heard the hoopla from the kitchen the moment she'd reached the first floor. At ease with confusion, she headed toward it.

"You'll have plenty to tell your friends at school." Hannah was at the stove, lecturing Brendon as she scooped up scrambled eggs.

"You've missed two weeks, my lad." At the kitchen table, Dee was fussing with a ribbon in Keeley's hair. "There's no reason in the world you shouldn't go back to school today."

"I have jet lag." He made a hideous face at his sister, then attacked the eggs Hannah set in front of him.

"Jet lag, is it?" With an effort, Dee kept a straight face. After kissing the top of Keeley's hair, she nudged her daughter toward her own breakfast. "Well, if that's the truth of it, I suppose we have to forget those flying lessons when you're sixteen. A jet pilot can't be having jet lag."

"Maybe it's not jet lag," Brendon corrected without missing a beat. "It's probably some foreign disease I caught when we were in Ireland."

"Bog fever," Erin said from the doorway. Clucking her tongue, she walked over to rest a hand on Brendon's brow. "Sure and that's the most horrible plague in Ireland."

"Bog fever?" Dee made sure there was a tremor in her voice. "Oh, no, Erin, it couldn't be. Not my baby."

"Young boys are the ones who catch it easiest, I'm afraid. There's only one cure, you know."

Dee shuddered and closed her eyes. "Oh, not that. Poor darling, poor little lad. I don't think I could bear it."

"If the boy has bog fever, it has to be done." Erin put a

hand on his shoulder for comfort. "Nothing but raw spinach and turnip greens for ten days. It's the only hope for it."

"Raw spinach?" Brendon felt his little stomach turn over. He wasn't sure precisely what turnip greens were, but they sounded disgusting. "I feel a lot better."

"Are you sure?" Dee leaned over to check his brow herself. "He seems cool enough, but I don't know if we should take any chances."

"I feel fine." To prove his point, he jumped up and grabbed his coat. "Come on, Keeley, we don't want to miss the bus."

"Well, if you're sure…" Dee rose to kiss his cheek, then Keeley's. "Uncle Paddy's going to drive you to the end of the lane. It's cold, so stay in the car until the bus comes."

Dee waited until the door slammed behind them before she lowered herself in the chair again and howled with laughter. "Bog fever? Where in the blue heaven did you dig that up?"

"Ma always used it on Joe. It never failed."

"You've a quick mind." Hannah chuckled as she turned around. "What can I fix you for breakfast?"

"Oh, I don't—"

"If you think Mrs. Malloy can cook, wait until you taste Hannah's muffins." Understanding her cousin's embarrassment, Dee took the cloth off a little wicker basket. "Why don't you have some eggs to go with it? I have the appetite of a hog when I'm carrying, and I hate to eat alone."

"Coffee?" Hannah was by her shoulder with the pot.

"Please. Thank you. Ah, is Travis not up yet?"

"Up and gone," Dee said comfortably. "He's been down at the stables for more than an hour. When he travels on business, I'm never sure if he misses me or the horses more." She glanced at the muffins, lectured herself, then took another anyway. After all, she was eating for three. "Brendon's in the first grade now, and Keeley goes mornings to kindergarten. So there's only Brady." She gestured to the high chair where he sat, his face covered with oatmeal as he sang to his fingers. "He's the best-tempered child in the world, if I do say so myself. Now what would you like to do today?"

"Actually, I thought I'd go over to Mr. Logan's and begin work."

"Already?" Dee smiled her thanks at Hannah as the breakfast plates were set in front of them. "You've only just got here. Surely Burke's willing to give you a day or two to get your bearings."

"I know, but I'm anxious to get started, to see what there is to be done. And to make certain I can do it."

"I can't imagine Burke Logan putting anyone on his payroll who didn't know their business."

"It's different for me. Even thinking in dollars instead of pounds is different. If I'm in the middle of it working my way out, I won't worry so much about making a mess."

Dee remembered how anxious she herself had been to begin work when she'd come to America, to prove to herself she was still competent and able to make her own way. "All right, then, I'll drive you over myself after breakfast."

"Not on your life, missy," Hannah said from the stove.

"Oh, for pity sakes, I can still fit behind the wheel of a car."

"You're not driving anywhere until you have your next checkup and the doctor clears it. Paddy can take Miss McKinnon."

Dee wrinkled her nose at Hannah's back, but subsided. "I'm a prisoner in my own house. If I go down to the stables, Travis has every hand on the place watching me like a hawk. You'd think I never had a baby before."

"Twins come early, as you know very well."

"The sooner the better." Then she smiled. "Well, I'll just stay in and plan the party. And Brady and I can build block houses, can't we, love?"

In answer, he squealed and slapped his hand into his oatmeal.

"After he has a bath."

"Why don't I take care of that?" Rising, Erin moved over to free Brady from his high chair.

"You're not going to start pampering me, too. I'll go mad."

"Nothing of the kind. I just think it's time this handsome young man and I got better acquainted."

By the time she was finished, Erin had to clean the oatmeal off herself as well. Bundled inside a cardigan and a coat, she drove with Paddy Cunnane to Burke's neighboring horse farm. The nerves were back. She could feel them tense in her fingers as she curled them together.

It was a waste of time to be nervous about the likes of him, she told herself. What had happened on that stormy morning in the shed was over and done with. Now they were nothing more than boss and employee. He'd said he expected a day's work for a day's pay, and she intended to give it to him.

Whatever other feelings she'd had had been born of the moment. Lust, she said firmly, telling herself she was mature enough to face that as a fact of life. Just as she would be strong enough to resist it.

She was a bookkeeper now. Her nerves were suddenly tinged with excitement. A bookkeeper, she repeated silently, with a good job and a good wage. Within the month she could start sending money home, with enough left over to buy... Lord, she couldn't begin to think what would be first.

Paddy turned the Jeep under an arch. The sign was large, wrought iron, strong rather than fancy with its block letters. Three Aces. Erin caught her lip between her teeth. Was that the hand he'd won it with, or the hand the former owner had lost it with?

The snow lay here as well, but the rise of hill wasn't as gentle. She saw a willow, old and gnarled, with its leaves dulled and yellow from winter. Perhaps in the summer it would look peaceful and lovely, but for now it looked fierce. Then she saw the house. She'd thought nothing could surprise her after the Grants'. She'd been wrong.

It had cupolas, like a castle, and the stone was dull and gray. The windows were arched, some of them with little parapets. Across from the steps and circled by the drive was an oval island that was now covered with untrampled snow.

"Do people really live in places like this?" she said half to herself.

"Cunningham, he'd be the owner before Logan, liked to think of himself as royalty." Paddy sniffed, but Erin wasn't entirely sure if the sound was directed at the present or the former owner. "Put more money into fancying up this place than into the stables and the stock. Got a pool right inside the house."

"You're joking."

"Indeed not. Right inside the house. Now you've only to call when you've finished here. I'll come fetch you, or one of the boys will."

"I'm obliged to you." But her fingers seemed frozen on the handle.

"Good luck to you, lass."

"Thanks." Screwing up her courage, she pushed out of

the Jeep. She was grateful it stayed parked where it was as she climbed the stone steps to the front door.

And what a door, she thought. As big as a barn and all carved. She ran a hand over it before she pulled back the knocker. Erin counted slowly under her breath and waited. It was opened by a dark-haired woman with big eyes and a small, erect figure. Erin swallowed and kept her chin up.

"I'm Erin McKinnon, Mr. Logan's bookkeeper."

The woman eyed her silently, then stepped back. Erin managed to throw a smile to Paddy over her shoulder before she stepped inside.

By the saints, she thought, tongue-tied again as she stood in the atrium. She'd never seen anything to match it, with its high ceilings and lofty windows. It seemed the sun shone in from all directions and slanted over the leaves of thick green plants. A balcony ran all the way around in one huge circle, the rail gleaming and carved as the door had been. The heels of her sensible shoes clicked on the tile floor, then stopped as she stood, uncertain what to do next.

"I'll tell Mr. Logan you're here."

Erin only nodded. The accent sounded Spanish, making her feel more out of place than ever. Erin wiped her hands on her skirt and thought she knew what Alice had felt like when she'd stepped through the looking glass.

"Are you eager to work, or did you just miss me?"

She turned, knowing she'd been caught gaping. He was in jeans and boots, and the smile was the same. The confidence she'd lost when she'd stepped inside came flooding back. It was the best defense.

"Eager to work and earn a wage."

The cold and excitement had heightened the color in her cheeks and darkened her eyes. As she stood in the center of the big open room, Burke thought she looked ready and able to take on the world.

"You could have had a day or two to settle in."

"I could, but I didn't want it. I'm used to earning my way."

"Fine. You'll certainly earn it here." He lifted a hand and gestured her to follow. "Morita, my last bookkeeper, managed to embezzle thirty thousand before the cage shut on him. In the process, he made a mess of the records. Your first priority is to straighten them out again. While you're doing that, you're to keep up the payroll and the current invoices."

"Of course." Of course, a little voice inside her said mockingly.

Burke pushed a door open and led her inside. "You'll work here. Hopefully you won't have to ask me a bunch of annoying questions, but if something comes up, you can call Rosa on the intercom and she'll pass it on to me. Make a list of whatever supplies you think you'll need, and you'll have them."

She cleared her throat and nodded. Her office was every bit as large as O'Donnelly's entire storeroom. The furniture was old and glossy, the carpet like something out of a palace. Determined not to stare again, Erin walked over to the desk. He had been right about one thing. It was a mess. For the first time since she'd approached the big stone house, she felt relief. Here was something familiar.

Ledgers and books and papers were piled together in one heap. There was an adding machine, but it was nothing like the clunky manual one she'd used before. Besides the clutter, there was a phone, a china holder stuffed with pencils and a basket clearly marked In and Out.

Burke moved behind the desk and began opening and

closing drawers. "You've got stamps, stationery, extra work sheets, checkbooks. Since Morita, nothing goes out without my signature."

"If you'd taken that precaution before, you'd be thirty thousand dollars richer."

"Point taken." He didn't add that Morita had worked for him for ten years, during lean times and better. "Set your own pace, as long as it's not sluggish. Rosa will fix you lunch. You can take it in here or in the dining room. There may be times I'll join you."

"Are you here most of the day?"

"I'm around." He settled a hip on the corner of the desk. "You didn't sleep well."

"No, I..." But her fingers had automatically lifted to the slight smudges under her eyes. "The time change, I guess."

"Are you comfortable at the Grants'?"

"Aye, they're wonderful to me. All of them."

"They're extraordinary people. You won't find many like them."

"You're not." She hadn't meant to say it, but told herself it was too late to be sorry she had. "You've an edge to you."

"Then be careful you don't get too close. Edges can be sharp."

"I've already seen that for myself." She said it lightly as she reached for the first stack of papers. He closed his hand slowly and firmly around her wrist.

"Are you trying to provoke me, Irish?"

"No, but I don't imagine it takes much."

"You're right there. It might be fair to tell you that I have a short fuse, and a dangerous one."

"I'm so warned." She looked amused, but when she tried to free her hand, his fingers only tightened.

"One more warning, then. Since you've moved into our

little community, you'll hear it from others soon enough. When I find a woman who attracts me, I find a way to have her. Fair means or foul, it doesn't mean a damn to me."

It wasn't a warning, Erin realized. It was a threat. Beneath his fingers, her pulse was beating hard and fast, but she kept her eyes even with his. "I didn't have to be told to know that, nor have I any intention of attracting you."

"Too late." He grinned but released her hand. "I find you intriguing enough to dance in the moonlight with, desirable enough to kiss in a garden shed, and passionate enough to imagine making love to."

Her stomach knotted with fear, with longing. "Well, a woman's head could be turned clear around with such flattery, Mr. Logan. Tell me, did you bring me to America to sleep with you or to fix your books?"

"Both," he said simply, "but we'll deal with business first."

"Business is all we'll deal with. Now I'd like to begin."

"Fine." But instead of leaving, he ran his hands up her arms. Erin stiffened, but didn't back away. She wouldn't play the fool and struggle. Though she braced herself for the hot passion she'd experienced before, he only brushed a kiss over her cheek.

He'd thought of her and little else since he'd come home again. He'd thought of how she'd felt in his arms, of how his system reacted when she smiled, of how her voice flowed, warm and sweet, so that a man didn't care what the words were as long as she spoke again.

He knew he could have her. Her response had been too quick and too encompassing before for either of them to pretend otherwise. He knew she wanted him, though it didn't sit well with her. Even now, as he kissed her lightly, avoiding her lips, her breath was beginning to tremble. He'd never known a woman whose passion was so close to the surface. Now that she was here, in his home, he knew he wouldn't rest until he had all of it.

But she would come to him. His pride demanded it. So he teased her with his lips, knowing he stirred her. He teased her with his lips, knowing he was slowly killing himself.

"Fair means or foul," he murmured, nipping gently at her earlobe. "I want you."

Her eyes were closed. How was it possible to be swept away so quickly, to want so desperately what you knew you shouldn't have? She put a hand to his chest, willing it to be steady. "And you're used to taking what you want. I understand that. I won't deny you move something in me, but I'm not here for the taking, Burke."

"Maybe not," he murmured. Some women were only there for the earning. "I can be patient, Irish. When a man's got the cards, he's got to know when to hold and when to lay them on the table." Thoughtfully he ran a finger down her braid. "We'll play out this hand sooner or later. I'll let you get started."

Erin waited until he'd left before she let out a long breath. How was it he could be that arrogant and still make her want to smile? With a shake of her head, she sat behind the desk in a plush leather chair that made her sigh.

Burke was right about one thing, she mused. They would play out the hand sooner or later. The problem was, Erin was afraid that even if she won, she'd lose.

Chapter 5

Within a week, Erin had developed a routine that pleased her. In the mornings she rose early enough to help Dee ready the children for school, then drove a borrowed car to the Three Aces to report to work by nine.

The mess of Burke's bookkeeping had been an enormous understatement. So had her estimate of his wealth. As she tallied figures and pored over ledgers, she tried to think of it in simple, practical terms. Numbers, after all, were just numbers.

She was rarely interrupted, and took her lunch from the silent Rosa at her desk. By the end of the first week, she'd made enough headway to feel pleased with herself. Only once or twice had she been made to feel foolish. She'd had to ask Burke for the instruction book on the adding machine. Then she'd asked him to supply her with a pencil sharpener. He'd simply picked up a cylinder with a hole in it and handed it to her.

"And what good is this?" she'd demanded. "It doesn't even have a crank."

He'd picked up a pencil and shoved it in the hole; then, damn him, had laughed when she'd jumped at the grinding. "Batteries," he'd said, "not magic."

She'd gotten over that small humiliation by burying her face in the account books. Maybe she wasn't used to gadgets, but by the saints, she'd balanced his books. Now she sat at the little electric typewriter and wrote up her weekly report. After tidying her desk, Erin picked up her report and went to find Burke.

His house was still almost completely uncharted territory to her. In the atrium, Erin hesitated. She could have called for Rosa on the intercom, but talking into the blasted thing always made her feel foolish. Instead, Erin set off in what she hoped was the general direction of the kitchen.

The place went on forever, she thought, and found it increasingly difficult not to open doors and peek inside as she went. Hearing a hum, she turned in that direction. Dishwasher, she thought, or a washing machine. With a shrug, she decided she'd find Rosa at the end of it.

The woman was a mystery, Erin thought as she walked. Rosa rarely spoke and always seemed to know precisely where to find Burke. Though the housekeeper referred to Burke as Mr. Logan, Erin sensed something less formal between them. She'd wondered, though it hadn't brought her any pleasure, if they were or had been lovers. Pushing the thought aside, she moved to the south end of the house.

But it wasn't the kitchen she found, or the laundry room. As she pushed open one of a pair of double doors, Erin entered the tropics. The pool was an inviting blue, sparkling under the sun that poured through the glass roof and walls. There were trees here the likes of which she'd never seen, planted in huge pottery urns. And flowers. She stepped in farther, overwhelmed by the heady scent when she could still see the snow through the glass. There were rich red petals, brilliant orange and yellow, exotic blues. If she closed her eyes, she imagined, she'd hear the chatter of parrots. Paradise, she thought, smiling as she walked farther.

With his eyes half-closed and his body just beginning to relax, Burke watched her. She didn't look sultry like the room, but fresh, untouched. The sun was all over her hair, drawing out the fire, licking at the layers of light. She'd pulled it back in a band as he'd seen her wear it in Ireland. And he could remember very well, too well, what it felt like to run his fingers through its mass.

He saw her reach for a flower as if her fingers itched to pick it, then draw back her hand and bury her face in the blooms instead. Her laugh was quiet, delighted, and he knew she thought herself alone.

So the Irish rose had a weakness for flowers, he thought, then watched her shake her head and look wonderingly, longingly around. And for money. At the latter, he shrugged his shoulders. It was difficult for someone in his position to blame her.

He could blame her, however, for the fact that his body was no longer even close to relaxing.

"Want a swim, Irish?"

At the sound of his voice, she whirled around. She'd forgotten about the hum. She saw its source now, and Burke in the middle of it. Another pool—no, not a pool, she corrected. She wasn't a complete dunderhead. She'd seen pictures of spas with their jets and bubbles and steamy water. And she couldn't help, for just a moment, wondering what it felt like to lower one's body into it.

"Want to join me?"

Because he grinned when he said it, Erin merely shrugged. "Thank you, but I'll be leaving for home in a few minutes. I've finished for the day and brought you your first report."

He nodded, but merely gestured to a white wicker chair beside the spa. "Have a seat."

Biting off a sigh, Erin did as he asked. "You may be a man of leisure yourself, but I've things to do."

Burke stretched his arms along the edge of the spa. He didn't mention that he'd been up and at the stables since dawn, or that he'd strained every muscle in his body overseeing the mating between a stud and a particularly high-strung mare. "You've still got a few minutes on the clock, Irish. So how are my finances?"

"You're a rich man, Mr. Logan, though how that might be with the mess your books were in amazes me. I've done a bit of studying and come up with a new system." The truth was she'd spent two nights burning the midnight oil with books on accounting. "If you like, I'll wait until you've finished and go over it with you."

"It'll keep."

"Suit yourself. By the end of next week I should have everything running smoothly enough."

"That's good to know. Why don't you tell me how?"

He stretched his shoulders. Erin watched the muscles ripple along the damp skin, then deliberately shifted her gaze above his head. This was no place for her to be, she told herself. Especially when her mind was wandering away from accounting. "It's all in this report, if you'd care to pull yourself out of the tub there and have a look at it."

"Have it your way." Burke pushed the button that shut off the jets, then stood. Erin's limbs went weak as she saw he wore no more than he'd been born with. She was grateful color didn't rise to her cheeks, though she couldn't prevent some from leaving.

Burke took a towel and swung it easily over his hips as he stepped from the spa.

"You've no shame, Burke Logan."

"None at all."

"Well, if you'd meant to shock me, I'll have to disappoint you. I've four brothers, if you'll remember, and..." She glanced over again, prepared to look at him without interest. It was then she noticed the darkening bruise just under his left ribs. "You've hurt yourself." She was up immediately and laying gentle fingers on it. "Oh, it's a nasty one." Without thinking, she took her fingers up over his ribs, carefully checking. "You didn't break anything."

"Not so far," he murmured. He was standing very still, the amusement he'd felt completely wiped out. Her fingers felt so cool, so tender on his skin. She touched him as if she cared. That was something he'd learned to live a long time without.

"It'll look worse yet tomorrow," she said with a cluck of her tongue. "You should put some liniment on it." Then she realized her fingers were spread over his chest, and his chest was hard and smooth and wet. Erin snatched her hand away and stuck it behind her back. "How'd you come by it?"

"The new colt I picked up in Ireland."

She closed her hand into a fist. It was damp from his skin. "You'll have to give him more room next time." The shudder inside her came as no surprise and was quickly controlled.

"I intend to. I have the highest respect for the Irish temper."

"And so you should. If you'd look over the report now, I could answer any questions you might have before I leave."

Burke picked up the neatly typed sheets. Erin found it necessary to clear her throat as she turned to look out through the glass, now lightly fogged from the steam of the spa. But she didn't see the snow. She could still see him—the long arms roped with muscle, the hard chest glistening with water, the narrow hips leading to taut thighs.

A fine specimen, some would have said, herself included. And she could have murdered him for making her want.

"It seems clear enough." She jolted a bit, then cursed herself. "You know your business, Erin, but then I wouldn't have hired you if I hadn't believed that." No, he wouldn't have, but he'd have found some other way to bring her back with him. "Got anything in mind for your first paycheck?"

"A thing or two." She relaxed enough to smile at him, schooling her gaze to go no lower than his neck. Half the money would be on its way to Ireland in the morning. And the rest... She couldn't begin to think of it. "If you're satisfied, I'll be going home now."

"I'm a long way from satisfied," Burke said under his breath. "Listen, did you ever think the bookkeeping would be more interesting if you knew more about the stables, the racing?"

"No." Then she moved her shoulders as the thought he'd planted took root. "I suppose it might, though."

"I've got a horse running tomorrow. Why don't you come along, see where the money comes from and where it goes?"

"Go to the races?" She caught her lip between her teeth as she thought of it. "Could I bet?"

"There's a woman after my heart. Be ready at eight. I'll take you around the stables and paddock first."

"All right. Good day to you." She started out, then glanced over her shoulder. "I'd put some witch hazel on that bruise."

Erin paced the living room. It was her first day off, and she was going to spend it at the races. There would be mobs of people she'd never met; she'd hear dozens of voices for the first time. She ran a hand down her hair and hoped she looked all right. Not for Burke, she thought quickly. For herself, that was all. She wanted to look nice, to feel she looked nice when she stood in the midst of all those people.

The minute she heard Burke's car, she was racing out of the house. She hesitated on the steps, staring down at the fire-red sports car with its long, sleek hood. She made a mental note of the make so she could write home and tell Brian.

"You're prompt," Burke commented as she climbed in beside him.

"I'm excited." It didn't seem foolish to admit it now. "I've never been to the races before. Cullen has, and he told me the horses are beautiful and the people fascinating. Faith, look at all these dials." She studied the dash. "You'd have to be an engineer to drive it."

"Want to try?"

When she glanced at him and saw he was serious, she was sorely tempted. But she remembered all the cars that had been on the highway when they'd driven from the airport. "I'll just watch for now. When does the racing start?"

"We've got plenty of time. How's Dee?"

"She's fine. The doctor gave her a clean checkup but told her she had to stay off her feet a bit. She grumbles because she can't spend as much time down at the stables, but we're keeping her busy. The snow's melting."

"A few more days like we've been having and it'll be gone."

"I hope not. I like to look at it." She settled back, deciding that riding in the sports car was like riding on the wind. "Are you going to be warm enough?" she asked, looking at his light jacket and jeans. "There's still a bite in the air."

"Don't worry. So what do you like best about America so far, besides the snow?"

"The way you talk," she said instantly.

"Talk?"

"You know, the accent. It's charming."

"Charming." He glanced over at her, then laughed until the bruise began to throb. Still chuckling, he rubbed a hand over it absently.

"Is that troubling you?"

"What, this? No."

"Did you use witch hazel?"

He knew better than to laugh again. "I couldn't put my hands on any."

"I'd imagine you'd have a case or two of horse liniment down in the stables. Oh, look at the little planes." When he turned into the airport, she looked over at him. "What are we doing here?"

"Taking a ride on one of the little planes."

Her stomach did a quick flip-flop. "But I thought we were going to the races."

"We are. My horse is racing at Hialeah. That's in Florida."

"What's Florida?"

Burke paused in the act of swinging his door closed. On

the other side of the car, Erin stared at him. "South," he told her, and held out a hand.

Too excited to think, too terrified to object, Erin found herself bundled onto a plane. The cabin was so small that even she had to stoop a bit, but when she sat the chair was soft and roomy. Burke sat across from her and indicated the seat belt. Once hers was secured, he flipped the switch on an intercom. "We're set here, Tom."

"Okay, Mr. Logan. Looks like smooth sailing. Skies are clear except for a little patch in the Carolinas. We ought to be able to avoid most of them."

When she heard and felt the engines start, Erin gripped the arms of the chair. "Are you sure this thing's safe?"

"Life's a gamble, Irish."

She nearly babbled before she caught the amusement in his eyes. Deliberately she made her hands relax. "So it is." As the plane started to roll, she looked out the window. Within minutes the ground was tilting away under them. "It's quite a sight, isn't it?" She smiled, leaning a little closer to the window. "When all of you landed in Cork, I looked at the plane and wondered what it would be like to sit inside. Now I know."

"How is it?"

She gave him a sideways smile. "Well, there's no champagne."

"There can be."

"At half past eight in the morning?" With a laugh, she sat back again. "I think not. I should have thanked you for asking me to go today. The Grants have been nothing but kind to me, so I'm really grateful to give them a day to themselves."

"Is that the only reason you should have thanked me?" He stood and went into a little alcove.

"No. I appreciate the chance to go."

"You want cream in this coffee?"

"Aye." He could have said you're welcome, she thought, then let it pass. Nothing was going to spoil her mood. When he sat, she took the cup but was too wound up to drink. "Will you give me an answer if I ask a question that's none of my business?"

Burke drew out a cigar, then lit it. "I'll give you an answer, but not necessarily the truth." He kicked out his legs, then rested his ankles on the seat beside her.

"Did you really win Three Aces in a poker game?"

He blew out smoke. "Yes and no."

"That's not an answer at all."

"Yes, I played poker with Cunningham—quite a bit of poker with Cunningham—and he lost heavily. When you gamble you have to know when to stick and when to walk away. He didn't."

"So you won the farm from him."

She'd like that, he thought, watching her eyes. He imagined she saw a smoky, liquor-scented room with two men bent over five cards each and the deed to the farm between them. "In a manner of speaking. I won money from him, more money than he had to lose. He didn't have enough cash to pay me, or for that matter to pay certain other parties who were growing tired of holding IOUs. In the end, I bought the farm from him, dirt cheap."

"Oh." It wasn't quite as romantic. "You must have been rich before then."

"You could say my luck was on an upswing at the time."

"Gambling's no way to make a living."

"It beats sweeping floors."

Since she could only agree, Erin fell silent a moment. "Did you know about horses before?"

"I knew they had four legs, but when you've got your money riding on a game, you learn fast. Where did you learn to keep books?"

"Arithmetic came easily to me. When I could I took courses in school, then I started to run the books at the farm. It was more satisfying than morning milking. Then, because everyone knows what everyone else is up to back home, I found myself working for Mrs. Malloy, then Mr. O'Donnelly. I worked for Francis Duggan at the market for a time, too, but his son Donald thought I should marry him and have ten children, so I had to let that job go."

"You didn't want to marry Donald Duggan?"

"And spend my life counting potatoes and turnips? No, thank you. It came to the point where I knew I had to either black both his eyes or give up the job. It seemed easier to give up the job. What are you smiling at?"

"I was just thinking that Donald Duggan was lucky you didn't carry a rake."

Erin tilted her head as she studied him. "It's you who're lucky I held myself back." Comfortable now, she tucked her legs under her and sipped her cooling coffee. "Tell me about the horse you're racing today."

"Double Bluff, he's a two-year-old. Temperamental and nervy unless he's running. He's proved himself from his first race, took the Florida Derby last weekend. That's the biggest purse in the state."

"Aye, I heard Travis mention it. He seems to think this horse is the best he's seen in a decade. Is it?"

"Might be. In any case, he'll be my Derby entry this year. His sire won over a million dollars in purses in his career, and his dam was the offspring of a Triple Crown winner. Likes to come from behind, on the outside." He took another puff, and again Erin noticed the scar along his knuckles.

"You sound as though you're fond of him."

He was, and that fact was a constant surprise. Burke only shrugged. "He's a winner."

"What about the one you bought in Ireland, the one who kicked you?"

"I'm going to start him off locally—Charles Town, Laurel, Pimlico, so I can keep an eye on him. If my hunch is right, he'll double what I paid for him in a year."

"And if your hunch was wrong?"

"They aren't often. In any case, I'd still consider my trip to Ireland paid off."

She wasn't completely comfortable with the way he looked at her. "Being a gambler," she said evenly, "you'd know how to lose."

"I know how to win better."

She set her coffee down. "How did you get the scar on your hand?"

He didn't glance at it as most people would, but tapped out his cigar as he watched her. "Broken bottle of Texas Star in a bar fight outside of El Paso. There was a disagreement over a hand of seven-card stud and a pretty blonde."

"Did you win?"

"The hand. The woman wasn't worth it."

"I suppose it makes more sense to gash your hand open over a game of cards than it does for a woman."

"Depends."

"On what? The woman?"

"On the game, Irish. It always depends on the game."

When they arrived, Erin stepped off the plane into another new world. Burke had told her to leave her coat on the plane, but even so she hadn't been expecting the warmth or the glare of the sun.

"Palm trees," she managed, then laughed and grabbed Burke's hands. "Those are palm trees."

"No fooling?" Before she had a chance to be annoyed, he swung an arm over her shoulders and swept her away. There was a car waiting for them. Erin slipped inside, wanting to pretend she did such things every day. "There's no handle for the window," she began. Burke leaned over and pressed the button to lower it. "Oh." After ten seconds, she gave up trying to be poised. "I can't believe it. It's so warm, and the flowers. Oh, my mother would die for the flowers. It's like that room in your house with all the glass. Two weeks ago I was scrubbing Mrs. Malloy's floor, and now I'm looking at palm trees."

He drove competently, without asking directions or checking a map. Erin realized this life wasn't new to him. Here she was babbling and sounding like a fool. She made one attempt to restrain herself, then gave it up. It didn't matter how she sounded.

He hadn't realized he'd get such enjoyment out of seeing someone take little things and make them special. For a moment he wished they could just keep driving so that she would go on talking, laughing, asking questions. He'd nearly forgotten there were people who could still find things fresh and new no matter how often they'd been used.

Traveling was a profession to him, and like most professional travelers he'd long ago stopped looking at what was around him. Now, with Erin pointing out white sand, young skateboarders and towering hotels, he began to remember what it was like to see something for the first time.

They knew him at the track. Erin noticed as they walked over the green lawn toward the spread of stables that peo-

ple nodded in his direction or greeted him as Mr. Logan.
There were jockeys and trainers and grooms already pre-
paring for the afternoon races.

"Logan."

Erin glanced over and saw a big, potbellied man in a
straw hat. She saw the flash of a diamond on his finger
and the light film of sweat the heat had already drawn on
his face. "Durnam."

"Didn't know you were coming down for a look-see."

"I like to keep an eye on things. Your horse ran well
last week."

"At Charles Town. I didn't know you were there."

"I wasn't. Erin McKinnon, Charlie Durnam. He owns
Durnam Stables in Lexington."

"Real horse country, ma'am." He took her hand and
flashed her a smile. "A pleasure, a real pleasure. Nobody
picks the fillies like Logan."

"I won't be running any races, Mr. Durnam," she told
him, but she smiled, judging him harmless.

"From Ireland, are you?"

"She's Adelia Grant's cousin." Burke spoke mildly, giving Durnam a straight look until he released Erin's hand.

"Well, ain't that something? I tell you, ma'am, any friend
of the Grants is a friend of Charlie Durnam's. Fine people."

"Thank you, Mr. Durnam."

"I'm going to go check on my horse, Charlie. See you
around."

"Take a look at Charlie's Pride while you're at it," he
called after them. "That's a real piece of horseflesh."

"What a funny man," Erin murmured.

"That funny man has one of the best stables in the country and a roving eye."

She glanced back over her shoulder and chuckled. "His

eye can rove all it pleases. I can't imagine he has much luck on a landing."

"You'd be surprised the kind of luck ten or fifteen million can buy." Burke nodded to a groom. "I'm running against him today."

"Is that so?" Erin tossed her hair back and was sure the sun had never shone brighter. "Then you'll just have to beat him, won't you?"

With a grin, Burke put his arm around her shoulders again. "I intend to." He walked by a few stalls. Erin cautiously kept on the far side of him. The smell of horse and hay was familiar, and so was the little knot in her stomach. Ignore it, she told herself, stepping up beside Burke as he stopped at a stall.

"This is Double Bluff."

She judged the dark bay to be about fifteen hands, broad at the chest and streamlined for speed. The beauty of him struck her first; then she froze when he tossed his head. "He's a big one." Her throat had gone bone-dry, but she forced herself to take one step closer.

"Ready to win?" With a laugh, Burke reached up to stroke his nose. The colt's ears came forward in acknowledgment, but he continued to prance. "Impatient. This one hates to wait. He's an arrogant devil, and I think he might just win Three Aces its first Triple Crown. What do you think of him?"

"He's lovely." Erin had taken a step backward the first time the colt had looked in her direction. "I'm sure he'll do you proud."

"Let's have a closer look, make sure the groom's done his job." Burke opened the stall door and stepped in. Erin steeled herself, and with her heart pounding walked to the opening. "You look good, fella." Burke ran his hands over the colt's flank, then dipped under him to check the other side. He lifted each hoof, then nodded in approval. "Clean as a whistle. Wait until they put a saddle on him. The minute they do, he's ready. You have to hold him back from the starting gate."

As if he understood, Double Bluff pawed the ground. He tossed up his head and whinnied as Burke laughed. Erin fainted dead away.

When she surfaced, there was an arm supporting her. Something cool and wet was being urged through her lips. She swallowed reflexively, then opened her eyes. "What happened?"

"You tell me." Burke's voice was rough, but the hand that stroked her cheek was gentle.

"Probably too much sun." Erin heard the drawled pronouncement and shifted her gaze beyond Burke's shoulder. She saw a young face and a thatch of sandy hair.

"That's right," she said, grabbing the excuse. "I'm fine now."

"Just sit still." Burke held her down as she tried to get up. "It's okay, Bobby, I'll handle it from here."

"Yes, sir, Mr. Logan. You take it easy now, miss, stay in the shade."

"Thank you. Oh…" Erin closed her eyes and cursed herself for seven kinds of a fool. "I'm sorry I caused a scene. I don't know what could have happened."

"You were fine one minute and in a heap the next." And nothing, absolutely nothing in his life, had ever scared him so badly. "You're still pale. Why don't we take Bobby's advice and get you up and into some shade?"

"Aye." She let out a breath of relief. Just as Burke started to help her up, Double Bluff stuck his head out again and shook the stall door. With a muffled cry, Erin threw her arms around Burke's neck and clung.

It took him only a moment to put one and one together. "For God's sake, Erin, why didn't you tell me you were afraid of horses?"

"I'm not."

"Nitwit," he muttered, hauling her unceremoniously into his arms.

"Don't carry me. I've had enough humiliation already."

"Shut up." When he judged they were far enough away from the stables, he set her down under a palm. "If you'd had the brains to tell me, you wouldn't have shaved ten years off my life." With another oath, he dropped down beside her. His heart had yet to resume its normal rhythm.

"The last thing I'm wanting from you is a lecture." She would have stood and stormed away, but she knew her legs weren't ready to carry her. "Besides, there was nothing to tell. I thought I was over it."

"You thought wrong." Then, because she was still pale, he relented and took her hand. "Why don't you tell me about it?"

"It's childish."

"Tell me anyway."

"We had some field horses, two good ones." She let out a long breath. He could hardly think her any more of a fool than he did now. "We had them out, and a storm was coming up. Brian unhooked the one to take him back to the barn. There was a lot of thunder and lightning, so the horses were nervous. Joe was unhooking the second, and I was at the head trying to calm him. I don't know, it happened fast, lightning spooked him and he reared. God, those hooves are big when they're over your head." She shuddered once. "I fell, and he ran right over me."

"Oh, God." Burke tightened his fingers on her hand.

"I was lucky, it wasn't that bad. A couple of broken ribs only, bruises, but I've just never been able to get too close to one without panicking."

"If you'd told me I never would have brought you."

"I thought I'd beaten it by now. It was more than five years ago. Stupid." She ran a hand over her face, then tucked back her hair. "I've been making excuses all week to Dee and Travis why I don't go down to the stables."

"Why don't you just tell them?" When she only shrugged, he shifted closer. "It's not half as stupid to be afraid as it is to be ashamed of it."

Her chin came up; then she sighed. "Maybe." Avoiding his eyes, she plucked a blade of grass. "Don't tell them."

"More secrets?" Patiently he caught her chin in his hand and turned her face to his. It was far more difficult to resist her now when her cheeks were pale, her eyes a little damp and the vulnerability like a sheen on her skin. "You shouldn't worry so much about what people think of you. I know you wash dishes and faint at the sight of horses, but I still like you."

"Do you?" A reluctant smile tugged at her mouth. "Really?"

"Well enough." Unaccustomed to resisting any desire for long, he lowered his mouth to hers, to taste, to nibble, to explore. She lifted a hand to his chest as if to hold him off, but then her fingers simply curled into his shirt and held him there.

His other kisses hadn't made her feel peaceful or secure. Anything but. Yet this one was different. Even as excitement shimmered warm in her stomach, she felt safe. Maybe it was the way his hand curved around her neck, with his fingers gentle and soothing. Or maybe it was the way his lips made hers feel soft and tingly.

He wanted to draw her close, to cuddle her, to rock her on his lap and murmur foolish things. He'd never had that urge with a woman before. It was an odd and uneasy sensation, and at the same time...comforting.

He drew away slightly, but kept her close. "I'll take you home."

"Home? But I want to see the races." For some reason she felt as though she could face anything at that moment. "I'm fine, I promise you. Besides, maybe if I can learn to watch them from a distance I won't freeze up when I'm near one." She stood, grateful that her legs were sturdy again. "Come now, Burke, we didn't fly all the way to—where are we?"

"Florida," he told her, and rose.

"Aye, Florida to turn right around and go home again. That great beast in there is going to win, isn't he?"

"I've got my money on him."

"And I've got ten more on the nose."

With a laugh, he accepted the hand she held out. "Let's go get a seat."

The stands were already filling up. In them, Erin indeed saw many faces, tanned and sunburned ones, faces with lines spreading out from the eyes and more with skin as smooth as new cream. Some people pored over racing forms, others smoked fat cigars or sipped from plastic cups.

But in the boxes was elegance, the kind that spoke of confidence and poise. Sheer summer dresses in pastels mixed well with light cotton suits and straw hats. She saw more than one tanned, slender woman tilt a head in Burke's direction. Now and then he lifted a hand, but he made no effort to mix with them.

From Burke's box in the front, she could see the wide

brown oval where the horses would run and the lush green infield filled with tropical flowers and pink flamingos. Still farther away were more stands with more people. Every minute, more were filing in.

"I've never seen so many people in one place at one time. And they're all here to watch the race."

"Want a beer?"

Erin nodded absently and continued to take in everything as Burke left her. She spotted Durnam not far away, talking to a woman in the tiniest pair of shorts Erin had ever seen. Erin passed over him and looked at the electronic board that was beginning to flash with numbers and odds for the first race.

"I want you to explain to me what it all means up there," Erin began before Burke had a chance to sit down again. "So I'll know best how to bet."

"If you want a tip, you'll wait for the third race, bet on number five."

"Why?"

"The horse is out of Royal Meadows. Sentiment aside, he's a strong runner. Record's a little shaky, but he looks good today. First race is anybody's game. So far the odds aren't spectacular."

"Are you betting on it?"

"No."

"I thought you were a gambler."

"I like to pick my own game."

Erin sat back and listened to the announcements for the first race. "Crystal Maiden sounds pretty."

"Pretty names don't win races. Hold on to your money, Irish."

She settled back and contented herself with absorbing the sounds and sights around her. By the time the horses were brought to the starting gate, she was leaning forward in her chair. "They *are* beautiful," she said, but she felt a great deal better when Burke's hand rested lightly on hers.

Her pulse was hammering. He gauged it to be almost as much from excitement as nerves. He'd been right about the contradictions in her. As the gates opened, her fingers linked hard with his, but she didn't cringe.

"What a noise," she murmured, while her heart beat almost as loudly as hooves on turf. As they rounded the first turn, she strained to keep following them. That was power, she thought, both raw and controlled. They might well have made it a business, but she could see why it had been and was still the sport of kings.

When it was over, she laid a hand on her breast. "My heart's still pounding. Don't smile at me like that," she warned, but laughed with it. "It's the most wonderful thing I've ever seen. All those colors, all that energy. Can you imagine doing this every day?"

"There are plenty who do."

But she only shook her head. Today was special, a once-in-a-lifetime day. "I want to bet on the next one."

"Third race," Burke repeated, and sipped his beer.

When her time came, she insisted on betting herself. Erin put the stub in the pocket of her shirt, then changed her mind and tucked it carefully in her billfold. Seated beside Burke again, she fretted until the horses were brought to the gate.

"I don't mind losing," she said with a quick grin, "but I'd sure as hell like to win better."

When they were off, she stood and leaned against the rail. "Which one is he?" she demanded, grabbing Burke's hand to drag him forward with her.

"Fourth back on the inside. Red-and-gold silks."

"Aye." She watched, urging him on. "He runs well, doesn't he?"

"Yes."

"Oh, look, he's moving up."

"Better hang on, Irish. They've got half a mile to go."

"But he's moving up." She gave a hoot of laughter as she pointed. "He's in second now."

There was shouting all around her, competing with the announcer and the thundering of hooves. Erin strained to hear all three as she grabbed Burke's shirt and tugged.

"He's taken the lead. Look at him!" She spun away from the rail and into Burke's arms as he finished half a length ahead. "He won! *I* won!" Laughing, she kissed Burke hard. "How much?"

"Mercenary little witch."

"It's nothing to do with mercenary and everything to do with winning. I'm going home and telling Dee I bet on her horse and won. How much?"

"The odds were five to one."

"Fifty dollars?" She gave another peal of laughter. "I'll buy the next beer." She took him by the hand. "When does your horse race?"

"In the fifth."

"Thank goodness. It'll give me time to recover."

She bought him a beer, then went one better and bought them both hot dogs. The only time she could remember spending such a frivolous day was at a fair. This seemed like one to her, with the noise and smells and colors. She had another ticket in her pocket and Burke's sunglasses on by the time the fifth race was announced.

"I really hope he wins," she told him with her mouth full. "Not just because I bet on him, either."

"That makes two of us."

"How does it feel to own one?" she wondered. "Not just a horse, but a horse from a great line."

"Most of the time it's like having an expensive lover, one you have to keep happy and lavish money on for moments of intense gratification."

Erin turned and, tipping the glasses down, looked at him over them. "You're full of blarney."

"At the very least."

He turned and watched his horse charge through the gate. How did it feel? Burke asked himself. How did it feel for a dirt-poor bastard from New Mexico to sit and watch his six-figure horse come flying by? Incredible. So incredible he couldn't begin to describe it and wasn't sure he wanted to. It could all be gone tomorrow.

And what of it?

He'd taught himself long ago that when you held on to something too tightly it squeezed through your fingers. He was giving Three Aces the best he had, though he'd never intended to get involved with the running of it. He'd certainly never intended to get attached to it. He worked better on the move. Yet he'd been in one place for four years.

Just recently he'd been telling himself that maybe it was time for him to get a manager for the place and take an extended vacation. Monte Carlo, San Juan, Tahoe. If a man stuck with one game too long, didn't he get stale? But then he'd gone to Ireland. And had come back with Erin.

The damnedest thing was, he wasn't thinking about Monte Carlo or playing the wheel anymore. It was becoming easier and easier to stay in one place. And think about one woman.

"You won!" Suddenly she was laughing and her arms were around his neck. "You won by two lengths, maybe three, I couldn't tell. Oh, Burke, I'm so pleased for you."

"Are you?" He'd forgotten the race, the horse and the bet.

"Of course I am. It's wonderful that your horse won, and he looked so beautiful doing it. And I'm happy for me, too." She grinned. "The odds were eight to five."

Then he stunned her by dragging her closer and kissing her with a power and passion that left her limp. She didn't protest but, held trapped in his arms, allowed herself to be buffeted by the storm.

"The hell with the odds," Burke muttered, and kissed her again.

Chapter 6

She didn't know what to think. No one could have been kinder than Burke the day Erin had spent with him. She'd watched the races, the strong, beautiful horses striving for speed. She'd seen women dressed in elegant clothes and jockeys in brilliant silks. She'd heard the noises that came from thousands of people in the same place. She'd seen exotic birds and flowers, had sipped champagne in a private plane. But her clearest memory of the day was of sitting on the grass in Burke's arms.

She didn't know what to think.

Since then, the days had passed routinely. Erin had to remind herself she was doing exactly what she'd set out to do—making a wage, starting a life, seeing new things. But Burke's visits to her office had become few and far between. She began to catch herself watching the door and wishing it would open.

She told herself that her feelings for him were surface

ones. He made her laugh, showed her exciting things and could be kind enough when it suited him. He was just arrogant enough to keep an edge on without alienating her. A woman could like a man like that without putting her heart at risk. Couldn't she? A woman could even kiss a man like that without falling too deep. Wasn't that right?

And yet she knew she'd come to the point where she thought of him a bit too easily and watched for him far too often.

He'd stayed away from her long enough. That was what Burke told himself as he came in through the back of the house from the stables. He'd stayed away from her since their quick trip to Florida because his feelings were mixed. He was used to clear thinking and well-defined emotions, not this jumbled mess of needs and restraint.

He couldn't stop thinking about the way she'd looked at the track, watching the horses race by. She'd been vivid, excited, exciting. The kind of woman he could handle. Yet he couldn't stop thinking about the way she'd looked when she'd fainted all but at his feet. She'd been pale and helpless, frightened. He'd needed to protect and soothe.

He'd never wanted the responsibility of a woman who needed protection or care. Yet he wanted Erin. She wasn't the kind of woman you took to bed for a night of mutual enjoyment, then strolled away from. Yet he wanted her. For all her strong talk, she was a woman who would put down roots and sink them deep. He'd never wanted the restriction or the responsibility of a home in the true sense. Yet he still wanted Erin McKinnon.

And he'd stayed away from her long enough.

When he walked into the office, she was marking in the ledger in her clear, careful hand. She knew it was him—

even without looking she knew—but made herself finish before she glanced up.

"Hello. I haven't seen much of you lately."

"I've been busy."

"That's clear from the papers on my desk. I've just paid your vet bill. Dr. Harrigan back home could live a year off what you pay a month. Are the new foals well?"

"They'll do."

"I see you've hired a new stable boy."

"My trainer sees to the hiring."

Erin lifted a brow. So he was going to play master of the estate, was he? "I see your Ante Up ran well at Santa Anita."

"Reading the sports page these days?"

"I figure living with the Grants and working for you I should keep up." Erin picked up her pencil again. "Now that we've had such a pleasant little talk I'll get back to work, unless there's something you're wanting."

"Come with me."

"What?"

"I said come with me." Before either of them had a chance to think it through, he took her arm and hauled her to her feet. "Where's your coat?"

"Why? Where are we going?"

Instead of answering, he glanced around and spotted it folded on a chair. "Put this on," he told her. Then, even as he thrust it at her, he began to walk.

"A fine thing," Erin began breathlessly as he pulled her down the hall. "Interrupting my work in the middle of the day, dragging me off without any explanation. Just because you pay me, Burke Logan, doesn't mean I have to jump at your bidding. An employee has rights in this country.

Which reminds me, I've been meaning to ask you about my paid holidays."

"You learn fast," he muttered as he pushed the door open.

"If you don't let go of my arm, I won't be able to put it in my coat." When he did, Erin rammed her arm in the sleeve but left the coat unbuttoned. "Sure and it's a fine day. The ground's a bit of a mess with the snow melting, but that's all the better for spring growing. If that was all you wanted to show me, I'll go back to work."

She managed to hiss out a protest when he grabbed her arm and began walking again.

"Burke, what the devil's got into you? If there's something you want me to do or see, fine, but there's no need to strong-arm me."

"How long have you been working for me?"

"Three weeks." Giving up, Erin matched her stride to his.

"And in three weeks you've barely poked your head out of the office."

"I work in the office," she reminded him.

"Did it ever occur to you that you can't understand the work if you've never looked at where the money comes from or where it goes?"

"I thought that's why we went to the races."

"There's more to this place than one race."

"Why do I have to understand as long as the figures tally?"

He wasn't sure of the answer himself, but he knew he wanted her to see what was his, to understand it, to move closer to it.

Pushing the hair out of her eyes, she glanced up at him.

His profile was set, and she thought she detected a shadow in his eyes. "Is there something troubling you?"

"No." He said it sharply, almost defensively, then made himself relax. "No, nothing." Except the need tethered tight inside him that strained hard at the scent of her. What the hell was happening to a man who could only think of one woman, of one voice, of one taste?

She continued to walk beside him in silence, but she noticed the crocuses—big fat purple ones that pushed their way up through the soggy ground, unmindful of the patches of snow. She saw the way the land sloped, the way the sun slanted over it. And she saw the stables, with their white wood gleaming in the sunlight. She saw the checkerboard of paddocks and the long oval track where even now a horse was being ridden.

"Why, it's lovely," she murmured. "Like something out of a book. You must be proud that it's yours."

He wasn't sure he had been, but he stopped and looked out as she did. He'd won it fairly, but then he'd won and lost a great deal in his life. It had never been his intention to stay, but rather reorganize so that the gamble paid off. He'd come into this knowing little about horses and nothing about racing or breeding, and had told himself he'd better learn in order to turn a true profit.

That had been four years ago, and he was still here. Looking out with Erin beside him, he began to understand why. It was lovely, it was his, and it was and would always be a gamble.

Keeping Erin's hand in his, he began to walk again. "We've got thirty horses, two of which are studs that do nothing but please the ladies."

"And themselves," Erin added.

"Two of the mares just foaled, and we've two more that

are due any day. Nearly half of what's left are being trained for next year. At the moment I've got five prime two-year-olds and a few veterans that have another season or two in them before they go out to stud or retirement. There, you see the horse being exercised now? That's one of the pair I picked up in Ireland."

Erin looked back at the track. The rider was up in the stirrups and bent low, but he earned no more than a glance. The horse was magnificent, a chestnut with a slash down his face like white lightning. Already his legs were spreading out in a rhythm that picked up speed and pounded on the soggy track.

"He's fast."

"And mean as hell."

"That would be the one that kicked you." Erin looked back again. Beautiful he might be, but she'd keep her distance. "If he's bad-tempered, why did you buy him?"

"I liked his style." As he started to walk again, Erin held back.

"I'd just as soon not be on closer acquaintance."

"I want to show you something else."

Erin told herself to relax as she walked with him. "If you'd told me we were going tramping around the yard, I'd have worn boots."

He glanced down but kept walking. "You could use some new shoes anyway."

"Thank you very much."

"I'd have thought you'd have gone shopping by now with a couple of paychecks under your belt."

"I'm thinking about it." They passed the stables, where the scent of horses and wet grass was strong. She could hear men talking inside. Erin braced herself, but he continued to walk. Then she saw the paddock where the mare was standing nursing a fawn-colored foal.

"That's one of the newest residents of Three Aces."

Cautiously Erin approached the fence. "They're sweet when they're little, aren't they?" She relaxed enough to curl her hands over the top rail and lean a little closer. The air was mild, with just a hint of spring. It wasn't the green or the scent of Ireland, but she found herself suddenly content. "We never had much time to think of an animal as any more than a means to an end." She smiled as the foal burrowed deeper and sucked. "Joe was always the one for animals, cooing at them and stroking. He'd love to see this."

"You miss your family."

"It's strange not seeing them every day. I hadn't realized…" She let the words trail off. "Word from home is everyone's fine. Cullen's back in Dublin playing at one of the clubs, and Brian's taken a fancy to Mary Margaret Shannesy. Ma says he's making a fool of himself, but that's to be expected."

The foal, having had his fill, began to scamper around the paddock. Erin watched him absently, thinking of home. "Frank's wife's nearly ready to have the baby. I could be an aunt already. It's funny, most mornings when I wake up I think it's time to go down to the henhouse. But there's no henhouse here."

The foal came over to the fence to sniff at her. Without thinking, Erin reached out a hand and rubbed between his ears.

"Do you wish there were?"

"I suppose I could live my life happily enough without gathering eggs again." She glanced down and, focusing on the foal, started to draw her hand back automatically. Burke set his on top of hers and rested it on the foal's head.

"Trusting little soul, isn't he?"

"Aye, but his mother—"

"Is probably relieved that he's distracted for a few minutes. Sometimes if you're afraid it's best to face it in small doses."

"I suppose." The foal was soft as butter and nuzzled its nose between the rails to nip at her coat. "Find something else to chew on," she said laughing. "It's all I brought with me." Finding nothing of interest, the foal scampered away to race around his mother. "Will he be a champion?"

"If it's in the cards."

Erin stepped away from the fence and, dipping her hands in her coat pockets, looked at him. "Why did you bring me out here?"

"I don't know." He didn't think about the men walking around the yard and going in and out of the stables. He thought only of her as he lifted a hand to her cheek. "Why should it matter?"

Had it come so far, so fast, that it only took the touch of his fingers on her skin to send her heart racing? Inside her pockets, the palms of her hands grew damp. "I think it does, and I think I should go back in."

"You've faced one fear today, why not face another?"

"I'm not afraid of you." That was true, and she felt a surge of relief that it was. Her heart might not be steady, but it wasn't in fear that it raced.

"Maybe not." He slid his hand from her cheek to the back of her neck as he drew her closer. He was afraid, afraid of what she was doing to him without his planning, without his calculations.

She yearned toward him. She strained away. "I don't think it's wise for you to kiss me that way again."

"All right. We'll try another way."

So he nibbled, teasing, tempting, tormenting. She felt the scrape of his teeth, then the moist trace of his tongue. Her hand went to his cheek and rested there as she opened herself for an emotional assault like nothing she'd ever experienced.

So he could be sweet and patient and alluring. She hadn't known. Her fingers crept into his hair as her lips parted and invited. No, she wasn't afraid, not of him. If what he brought to her was more than she'd ever imagined, then she was willing, even eager to accept it. With a sigh she tilted her head back and let him take.

He held himself back. The more generosity she showed him, the more wary he became of accepting. Burning inside him was a desire to sweep her away to some dim, private place where they could both take their fill. To touch her. He pressed his lips over hers and imagined how it would be to fill his hands with her. No barriers. While her teeth nipped gently, he imagined what it would feel like to have her flesh slide warm over his.

There was such a flavor here, warm and wild and willing. But he wanted more than her mouth. As her sigh whispered into him, he knew he needed more.

He took his hand to her hair and held her close against him. "I want you to stay with me tonight."

"Stay?" She floated up out of the dream and was stunned by the heat and passion that had turned his eyes to smoke.

"Stay," he repeated. "Tonight. Damn it, more than tonight. Get your things and bring them here."

The thrill moved through her. There was something in the command, in the look in his eyes as he gave it, that called to her even as it raised her hackles. "Move in with you?" She lifted her hands to his chest and struggled to keep her voice calm. "You want me to live under your roof, eat your food, sleep in your bed?"

"I want you with me. You know damn well I've wanted that since the first time I put my hands on you."

"Aye, maybe I did. But what I agreed to do was work for you." She tilted her head back again, but not in surrender this time. Yes, she'd been willing to accept the feelings he stirred in her, but not to compromise her principles for them. "Do you think I'd be your mistress? Do you think I'd let you keep me in your fine house?"

"No one's talking about keeping."

"No, you're not a man for keeping, are you, but for taking, enjoying and moving on. I'll tell you now, no matter how you make me feel, how you make me want, I'll not be any man's mistress."

It was foolish to be hurt, ridiculous to be insulted, but she was both. Erin jerked out of his hold and stood with her feet planted. "If I kiss you, it's because it pleasures me to do so, and nothing more. I'll not live in your house, shaming my family, until you're tired of me." She tossed back her hair and crossed her arms. "I'll be going back to work now, and you'd best keep out of my way unless you want to explain to your men why the payroll isn't done."

She turned on her heel and strode away. Burke leaned back against the paddock fence. A smart man would have folded his cards and pushed away from the table. He figured he'd stay for the next hand and see where the chips fell.

Whether she was feeling festive or not, Erin was swept along in her cousin's plans for the party. And what better day to celebrate than St. Patrick's Day? Erin decided if there'd been a dog around, she'd surely have kicked it.

No "come live with me and be my love" from the likes

of Burke Logan, she thought. She attacked a silver platter with a polishing cloth as though she could have rubbed through the metal. Oh, no, with him it was just "pack your things and be quick about it." Hah!

As if she'd want pretty words from that swine of a man. The truth of it was Erin McKinnon didn't want pretty words from anyone. What she wanted was to be left alone to pursue her new career. In six months she'd have a place of her own and a new job altogether, she decided. She'd find a job where she didn't have to put up with a man who made her laugh one minute and steam the next. And steam in more ways than one, she added as she tossed the polishing cloth aside.

Turning the platter over, she studied her own reflection. He was toying with her, he was. Hadn't she known that right from the beginning? Well, what was fine for him was fine for her. She could do some toying herself, and tonight was as good a time as any to start it. From what Dee had told her, there would be plenty of men at the party tonight. Including a certain snake in the grass.

"Have you finished scowling at yourself?" From the other side of the table, Dee set aside another tray.

"Almost."

"That's good, then, because we've only a couple more hours." Rising, she stacked the bowls and platters beside the crystal. Between Hannah and the caterers, the rest could be easily handled. "Is there anything you'd like to talk to me about?"

"No."

"Nothing that might have to do with why you've been muttering to yourself for the past week or so?"

Erin set her teeth, then dropped her chin on her hand.

"I think American men are even more rude and arrogant than Irish men."

"I've always thought it was a draw." Adelia came over to lay a hand on her shoulder. "Has Burke been troubling you?"

"To say the least."

Something in the way Erin said it caused Dee to smile. "He has a way with him."

"Not my way."

"Well, then, we won't be worrying about him anymore. We've a party to get ready for."

Erin nodded as she rose. She'd known she was in trouble as soon as she'd seen the silver and crystal. Things had only gotten worse when she'd watched the team of caterers descend to fuss over things like salmon mousse and gooseliver pâté. She'd seen the cases of champagne delivered. Cases, by God. Then there was the black caviar she'd managed to sample while no one was looking. And there were the flowers, tubs of them, that were being arranged even as she walked with Dee down the hall.

"A madhouse, isn't it?" Dee began when they started up the stairs. "Later, if you've had your fill of hearing about horses and tracks and stud fees, just send me a sign."

"I like listening. It's a bit like learning a new language."

"It's all of that." Dee moved into her room and took a large box off the bed. "Happy St. Patrick's Day."

Automatically Erin put her hands behind her back. "What is it?"

"It's a present, of course. Aren't you going to take it?"

"There's no need for you to give me presents."

"No, but I didn't think of it as a need." Pride was something Adelia understood too well. Her own had been bruised repeatedly. "I'd like you to have it, Erin, from all of us as a kind of welcome to a new place. When I came here I had only Uncle Paddy. I think I understand now how happy it made him to share with me. Please."

"I don't mean to seem ungrateful."

"Good, then you'll pretend to like it even if you don't." Dee sat on the bed and gestured with both hands. "Open it. I've never been long on patience."

Erin hesitated only another moment, then laid the box on the bed to draw off the top. Under a cushion of tissue paper was dark green silk. "Oh. What a color."

"It's expected today. Well, take it out," she demanded. "I'm dying to see if it's right on you."

Cautiously Erin touched the silk with her fingertips, then lifted the dress from the box. The material draped softly in the front and simply fell away altogether in the back to a slim skirt. Dee rose to hold the dress in front of her cousin.

"I knew it!" she said, and her face lit up. "I was sure it was right. Oh, Erin, you'll be dazzling."

"It's the most beautiful thing I've ever seen." Almost reverently she brushed her fingers over the skirt. "It feels like sin."

"Aye." Then, with a laugh, Dee stepped back for a better viewpoint. "It'll look like it, too. There won't be a man able to keep his eyes in his head."

"You're kinder to me than I deserve."

"Probably." Gathering up the box, she handed it to Erin. "Go put it on, fuss with yourself awhile."

Erin kissed her cheek. Then, letting her feelings spread, she gave her cousin a hard, laughing hug. "Thank you. I'll be ready in ten minutes."

"Take your time."

Erin paused at the door. "No, the sooner I have it on, the longer I can wear it."

* * *

The party was already underway when Burke drove up. He'd nearly bypassed it altogether. Restless and edgy, he'd thought about driving up to Atlantic City, placing a few bets, spinning a few wheels. That was his milieu, he told himself, casinos with bright lights, back rooms with dim ones. A party with the racing class, with their old money and closed circles, wasn't his style.

He told himself he was here because of the Grants. The fact that Erin would be there hadn't swayed him. So he told himself. Since their last encounter he'd nearly talked himself out of believing there was something between them. Oh, a spark, certainly, a frisson, a lick or two of flame, but that was all. That overwhelming and undesirable feeling that there was something deeper, something truer, had only been his imagination.

He hadn't come tonight to prove that, either. So he told himself.

It was Travis who let him in. Burke could hear voices raised in the living and dining rooms along with the piping Irish music that set the tone.

"Dee was worried about you." Travis closed the door on the nippy mid-March air outside.

"I had a few things to see to."

"No problems?"

"No problems," Burke assured him. But if that was true, he wondered why his shoulders were tensed, why he felt ready to jump in any direction.

"You'll know just about everyone here," Travis was saying as he led him into the living room.

"You've got quite a crowd," Burke murmured, and was already searching through it, though he didn't move beyond the doorway.

"I think you'll see that Dee's outdone herself in more ways than one." With the slightest gesture, Travis had Burke's gaze traveling to the far end of the room and Erin.

He hadn't known she could look like that, coolly sexy, polished. She was sipping champagne and laughing over the rim of her glass at Lloyd Pentel, heir to one of the oldest and most prestigious farms in Virginia. Flanking her were two more men he recognized. Third- and fourth-generation racing barons, with Ivy League educations and practiced moves. Burke felt his blood heat as one of them leaned close to murmur something in her ear.

Both amused and sympathetic, Travis laid a hand on Burke's shoulder. "Beer?"

"Whiskey."

He downed the first one easily, appreciating its bite. But it did nothing to relax his muscles. He took a second and sipped it more slowly.

Erin was perfectly aware that he was there. She doubted he'd been in the room ten seconds before she'd felt his presence. She smiled and flirted with Lloyd and the others who wandered her way, and told herself she was having a wonderful time. But she never stopped watching Burke and the women who gravitated to him.

Adelia had been right—the talk was horses. Purses, the size of which made the head reel, were discussed and the politics of racing dissected. Erin took it in, determined to hold her own, but as she nursed her single glass of champagne her gaze kept roaming.

The man didn't even have the courtesy to say "how do you do," she decided. But then he seemed more interested in the leggy blonde than in manners. Erin accepted a dance with Lloyd, and if he held her a bit too close she ignored it. And watched Burke.

It didn't appear to bother her to have the young Pentel stud pawing her, Burke noted as he swirled his whiskey. And where in the hell had she gotten that dress? Setting down his whiskey, he lit a cigar. She was nothing to get worked up over, he reminded himself. If she wanted to wear a dress that was cut past discretion and bat her baby blues at Pentel, that was her business.

The hell it was. Burke crushed out his cigar and, leaving the blonde who had snuggled up beside him staring, walked over to Erin.

"Pentel."

Annoyed, but as well-bred as his father's prize colt, Lloyd nodded. "Logan."

"I have to borrow Erin a minute. Business."

Before either of them could object, Burke had maneuvered his way between and had Erin in his arms.

"You're a rude, shameless man, Burke Logan." She was delighted.

"I wouldn't talk about shameless while you're wearing that dress."

"Do you like it?"

"I'd be interested to hear what your father would say about it."

"You're not my father." Though she smiled, there was more challenge than humor in the curve of lips. "Doesn't a man like you worry about luck, Burke? No wearing of the green on St. Patrick's Day?"

"Who says I'm not?" His eyes tossed the challenge right back.

"Money doesn't count."

"I was talking about something more personal than money. If you want to go somewhere private, I'll be happy to show you where I'm wearing my green."

"I'm sure you would," she murmured, and tried not to be amused. "Now, what business do we have?" He wasn't holding her as close, not nearly as close as Lloyd had been, but she felt the pull of him.

"You've come a long way from dancing in moonlit fields, Irish."

"Aye." Some of the pleasure went out of her as she studied him. "What does that mean?"

"You're an ambitious woman, one who wants things, big things." God, it was driving him mad to be this close, to smell her as he had once before in a dim garden shed with rain pelting the roof.

"And what of it?"

"Lloyd Pentel's not a bad choice to give it to you. He's young, rich, not nearly as shrewd as his old man. The kind of man a smart woman could twist easily around her finger."

"It's kind of you to point that out," she said in a voice that was very low and very cold. She didn't know what possessed her to go on, but whatever it was, she swore she wouldn't regret it. "But why should I settle for the colt when I can have the stallion? The old man's a widower."

Burke's mouth thinned as he smiled. "You work fast."

"And you. The skinny blonde's still pouting after you. It must be rewarding to walk into a room and have six females trip over themselves to get to you."

"It has its compensations."

"Well, why don't you get back to them?" She started to pull away, but his hand pressed into her back so that their bodies bumped. The flame that was never quite controlled flared at the contact. "Damn you," she said from the heart as he tightened his fingers on hers.

"I'm tired of playing games." He had her across the room and into the hall before she found the breath to speak.

"What are you doing?"

"We're leaving. Where's your coat?"

"I'm not going anywhere, and I—"

He merely stripped off his jacket and tossed it over her shoulders before he yanked her outside. "Get in the car."

"Go to hell."

He grabbed her then, hard and fast. "There'll be little doubt of that after tonight." When his mouth came down on hers, her first reaction was to fight free, for this was a man to fear. But that reaction was so quickly buried under desire that she moved to him.

"Get in the car, Erin."

She stood at the base of the steps a moment, knowing no matter how strong, how determined he was, the choice would be hers. She opened the door herself and got in without looking back.

Chapter 7

Had she lost her mind? Erin sat in Burke's car, watching his headlights cut through the night, and heard nothing but the sound of her own heart pounding in her ears. She must be mad to have thrown all caution, all sense, all pretense of propriety to the winds. Why had no one ever told her that madness felt like freedom?

She'd never been self-destructive. Or had she? she asked herself, almost giddy from the speed and the night and the man beside her. Perhaps that was one more thing he'd recognized in her. A need to take risks and damn the consequences. If that wasn't true, why didn't she tell him to stop, to turn back?

Erin gripped her fingers together until the knuckles turned white. She wasn't at all sure he'd listen, but that wasn't the reason she didn't speak. No, the reason she didn't speak was that she'd lost more than her mind. Her heart was lost as well.

Perhaps one was the same as the other, Erin thought. Surely it was a kind of madness to love him. But love him she did, in a way she'd never imagined she could love anyone. There was a ferocity to it, an edgy sort of desperation that didn't swell the heart so much as tighten it. Indeed, it felt like a hard, hot lump beneath her breast even now.

Was this the way love should feel? Shouldn't she know? There should be a warmth, a comfort, a sweetness—not this wild combination of power and terror. Though she searched, she could find no tenderness in her feelings. Perhaps they were a reflection of his. At a glance she could see no gentleness in the man beside her. His hands gripped the wheel tightly and he looked nowhere but straight ahead.

Erin pressed her lips together and told herself not to be a romantic fool. Love didn't have to be gentle to be real. Hadn't she known all along that her emotions when it came to Burke would never be ordinary or simple? She didn't want them to be. Still, she would have liked to have laid a hand over his, to have offered some word to show him how deep her feelings went and how much she was willing to give. But more than her heart was involved. There was pride and spirit as well. She had to be realistic enough to understand that just because she loved didn't mean he loved in return.

So she said nothing as they drove under the sign and onto his land.

Why did he feel as though his life had just changed irrevocably? Burke saw the lights of his house in the distance and tensed as though readying for a blow. He wanted her, and if the need was stronger than he wanted to admit, at least tonight it would be assuaged. She hadn't said a word. His nerves neared the breaking point as he rounded the first curve in the drive. Did it mean so little to her, could she take what was happening between them so casually that she sat in silence?

He didn't want this. He wanted it more than he'd ever wanted anything in his life.

What was she feeling? Damn it, what was going on inside her? Couldn't she see that every day, every hour he'd spent with her had driven him closer and closer to the brink? Of what? Burke demanded of himself. What line was he teetering on that he'd never crossed before? What would his life and hers be like once he'd stepped over it?

The hell with it. Burke braked at the base of the steps and without sparing her a glance, slammed the door and got out of the car.

Legs trembling, Erin got out and started up the steps. The door looked bigger somehow, like a portal to another world. With one long breath, she passed through.

Was it always so silent and angry when lovers came together? she wondered as she started up the staircase. Her hand on the banister was dry—dry and cold. She wished he'd reached for it, held it, warmed it in his own. That was nonsense, she told herself. She wasn't a child to be coddled and soothed, but a woman.

He walked into the bedroom ahead of her, waiting for her to smile, to offer her hand, to give him some sign that she was happy to be with him. But when the door closed at her back she simply stood, chin up, eyes defiant.

The hell with it, he thought again. She didn't need sweetness and neither did he. They were both adults, both aware and willing. He should have been glad she didn't want coaxing and candlelight and the promises that were so rarely kept.

So he pulled her against him. Their eyes met once, acknowledging. Then his mouth was on hers and the chance for quiet words and gentle caresses was past.

This was enough, Erin told herself as the heat rose like glory. This had to be enough, because she would never have more from him. Accepting, she pressed against him, offering her mind and body along with her heart he didn't know was already his. There was no hesitation now as her lips parted, as their tongues met in a hot, greedy kiss. When his hands roamed over her back, pressed into her hips, she only strained closer. She was prepared to trust him to show her the art of intimacy. She was prepared to risk self-destruction as long as he was part of the gamble.

Her fingers trembled only slightly as they dug into his arms. The strength was there, an almost brutal kind of strength that had her heart racing and her body yearning.

Good God, no woman had ever taken him so close to desperation so quickly. It only took a touch, a taste. When she kissed him avidly for one sweet moment he could almost believe he was the only one. That was its own kind of madness. A sane man would think of just this one night, but like a drug she was seeping into his system, making his heart race and his mind swirl.

He tugged on her dress and she moved against him, murmuring. He recognized the excitement, the tremble of anticipation, but not the modesty. When her flesh was freed for him he took, with rough hands that incited both desire and panic. No one had ever touched her like this, as if he had a right to every part of her. No one had ever caused this hard fist of need to clench inside her so that she was willing to cede to him that right.

Then she was naked, tumbling to the bed so that his body covered hers. His hands found her, sent her spiraling so that she arched against him even as the fear of the unknown began to brew. Her breath caught with the sensation of being pressed under him, vulnerable, dizzy with desire. Her own body seemed like a stranger's, filled with towering emotions and terrifying pleasures. She wanted a moment, just one moment of reassurance, one soft word, one tender touch. But she was beyond asking, and he beyond listening.

Greedy, impatient, he took his lips over her as he wrestled out of his shirt. He wanted the feel of her flesh against his. How many times had he imagined them coming together this way, urgently, without questions? She was murmuring his name in a breathy, desperate whisper that had his passion snowballing out of control. He dragged at his clothes, swearing, hardly able to breathe himself and far beyond the capacity to think.

Her body was like a furnace beneath his, and with each movement she stoked the flames higher. She dug her nails into his shoulders; he fused his mouth with hers. Past all reason, he plunged into her.

She was curled away from him, trembling. Burke lay in the dark and tried to clear his head. Innocent. Dear God, he'd taken her with all passion and no care. And he was the first. He should have known. Yet from the first time he'd held her she'd been so ripe, so ready. There had been the strength, the hotheaded passion, the unquestioning response. It had never crossed his mind that she hadn't been with anyone else.

He ran his hands over his face, rubbing hard. He hadn't seen because he was a fool. The innocence had been there in her eyes for any man to see who'd had the brains to look. He hadn't looked, perhaps because he hadn't wanted to see. Now he'd hurt her. However careless, however callous he had been with women in the past, he'd never hurt one. Because the women he'd chosen before had known the rules, Burke reminded himself. Not Erin. No one had ever taught them to her.

Searching for a way to apologize, he touched her hair. Erin only drew herself closer together.

She wouldn't cry. She squeezed her eyes tight and swore it. She was humiliated enough without tears. What a fool he must think her, sniffling like a baby. But how could she have known loving would be all heat and no heart?

The hell of it was, he was lousy at words. Burke reached down to the foot of the bed and drew a cover over her. As he tried to sort through and pick the best ones, he continued to stroke her hair.

"Erin, I'm sorry." By God, he *was* lousy with words if those were the pick of the litter.

"Don't apologize. I can't bear it." She turned her face into the pillow and prayed he wouldn't do so again.

"All right. I only want to say that I shouldn't have…" What? Wanted her? Taken her? "I shouldn't have been careless with you." That was beautiful, he thought, detesting himself. "I hadn't realized that you hadn't—that tonight was your first time. If I'd known, I would have…"

"Run for cover?" she suggested, pushing herself up. Before she could climb out of the bed, he had her arm. He felt her withdrawal like a blade in the gut.

"You've every right to be angry with me."

"With you?" She turned her head and made herself look at him. He was hardly more than a silhouette in the dark. They had loved in the dark, she thought, unable to see, unable to share. Perhaps it was best it was dark still so that he couldn't see the devastation. "Why should I be angry with you? It's myself I'm angry with."

"If you'd told me—"

"Told you?" She sniffed again, but this time there was

more than a little derision in it. "Of course. I should have told you, while we were rolling around on the bed naked as the day we were born, I might have said, *'Oh, by the way, Burke, you might be interested in knowing I've never done this before.'* That would have put a cap on it."

He was amazed to find himself smiling even as he reached for her hair again and she jerked her head away. "Maybe the timing could have been a bit better than that."

"It's done, so there's no sense pining over it. I want to go home now before I humiliate myself again."

"Don't."

"Don't what?"

"Don't go." That was a tough one. He hadn't known he'd had it in him to ask. "What happened wasn't wrong, it was just done badly. And that's my fault." He caught her chin in his hand as she started to turn away. "Look, I'm not good at asking, but I'd like you to let me make it up to you."

"There's no need." She wasn't aware that it was the gentleness in his voice that was calming her. "I told you I'm not angry with you. It's true it was my first time, but I'm not a child. I came here of my own free will."

"Now I'm asking you to stay." He took her hand and, turning it palm up, pressed his lips to the center. When he looked up at her again she was staring, her lips parted in surprise. He cursed himself again. "I'll draw you a bath."

"You'll what?"

"Draw you a bath," he said, snapping off the words. "You'll feel better."

When he disappeared into the adjoining room, Erin simply continued to stare after him. What in the world had gotten into him? she wondered. She gathered the blanket around her and stood as Burke came back in. He was wearing a robe tied loosely at the waist. The light from the bath angled out onto the floor. She could hear the sound of water running and sensed—but surely she was mistaken—a hesitation in him.

"Go ahead in and relax. Do you want something. Tea?"

Mutely she shook her head.

"Take your time, then. I'll be back in a few minutes."

Not a little baffled, Erin walked in and lowered herself into the tub. The water was steaming so that she felt the tension and the ache begin to diminish almost immediately. Sinking down, she closed her eyes.

She wished she had another woman to talk to, another woman to ask if this was all there was to lovemaking. She wished there was someone she could talk to about her feelings. She loved Burke, yet she felt no fulfillment after being with him. It had been exciting. The way he had touched her, the way his body had felt against hers, made her tremble and ache. But there had been no glorious glow, no beautiful colors, no feeling of rightness and contentment.

She was probably a fool for imagining there would be. After all, it was the poets and dreamers who promised more. Pretty words, pretty images. She was a practical woman, after all.

But Burke had been right. The bath had made her feel better. There was no reason for humiliation or for regret. If she was no longer innocent, she had brought about the change herself, willingly. One thing her parents had always told her was to follow what was in your heart and to blame no one.

Steadier, she stepped from the bath. She would face Burke now. No tears, no blushes, no recriminations.

Seeing no other cover, she wrapped the towel securely around her and stepped into the bedroom.

He'd lighted candles. Dozens of them. Erin stood in the

doorway, staring at the soft light. There was music, too, something quiet and romantic that seemed to heighten the scent of wax and flowers. The sheets on the bed were fresh and neatly turned down. Erin stared at them as all the confidence she'd newly built up began to crumble.

He saw her glance at the bed and saw the quick, unmistakable flash of panic that went with the look. It brought him guilt and a determination to erase it. There were other ways, better ways. Tonight he would show both of them. Rising, he went to her and offered a rose he'd just picked in the solarium.

"Feel better?"

"Aye." Erin took the rose, but her fingers nearly bit through the stem.

"You said you didn't want tea, so I brought up some wine."

"That's nice, but I—" The words jammed in her throat as he lifted her into his arms. "Burke."

"Relax." He pressed a kiss to her temple. "I won't hurt you." He carried her to the bed and laid her against the pillows. Taking two glasses already filled with pale wine, he offered her one. "Happy St. Patrick's Day." With a half smile, he touched his glass to hers. Erin managed a nod before she sipped.

"This is a fine room…" she began lamely. "I didn't notice…before."

"It was dark." He slipped an arm around her shoulders and settled back even as she tensed.

"Aye. I've, ah, wondered what the other rooms were like."

"You could have looked."

"I didn't want to pry." She sipped a little more wine and unconsciously brushed the rose over her cheek. Its petals were soft and just on the verge of opening. "It seems like a big place for one man."

"I only use one room at a time."

She moistened her lips. What was this music? she wondered. Cullen would know. It was so lovely and romantic. "I heard Double Bluff won his last race. Travis said he beat Durnam's colt by a length. Everybody's talking about the Kentucky Derby already and how your horse is favored." When she realized her head was resting against his shoulder, she cleared her throat. She would have shifted away, but he was stroking her hair. "You must be pleased."

"It's hard not to be pleased when you're winning."

"And tonight at the party, Lloyd told me that Bluff was the horse to beat."

"I didn't tell you how wonderful you looked tonight."

"The dress. Dee gave it to me."

"It made my heart stop."

She was able to chuckle at that. "What blarney."

"Then again, you managed to stop it wearing overalls."

She slanted a look up at him. "Aye, now I'm sure there's some Irish in you."

"I discovered I had a weakness for women taking in the wash."

"I'd say it's more a matter of a weakness for women in general."

"Has been. But just lately I've preferred them with freckles."

Erin rubbed rueful fingers over her nose. "If you're trying to flirt with me, you ought to be able to do better."

"Works both ways." Lifting the hand that still held the rose, he kissed her fingers. "You could say something nice about me."

Erin caught her lip between her teeth and waited until

he glanced up. "I'm thinking," she said, then laughed when his teeth nipped her knuckle. "Well, I suppose I like your face well enough."

"I'm overwhelmed."

"Oh, I'm picky, I am, so you should be flattered. And though you haven't Travis's build, I'm partial to the wiry type."

"Does Dee know you've had your eye on her husband?"

Erin laughed into her glass. "Surely there's no harm in looking."

"Then look here." Tilting her face up to his, he kissed her. His lips lingered softly, more a whisper than a shout.

"There's the way you do that, too," she murmured.

"Do what?"

"Make my insides curl all up."

With his lips still hovering over hers, he took the glass from her and set it aside. "Is that good?"

"I don't know. But I'd like you to do it again."

With a hand to her cheek, he nuzzled. Drawing on a tenderness he hadn't known he possessed, waiting for her lips to warm and soften beneath his. She hesitantly touched a hand to his shoulder. She knew his strength now, what it was capable of, and yet…and yet his mouth was so patient, so sweet, so beautifully gentle. When he increased the pressure, her fingers tensed. Immediately he drew back to nibble again until he felt her begin to relax.

He wanted to take care, and not just for her, he realized, but for himself. He wanted to savor, to explore, to open doors for both of them. He'd never been a man to bother with candlelight and music, had never looked for the romance of it. Now he found himself as soothed and seduced by it as she was.

The scent of her bath was on her skin, fresh, clean. On

her his soap seemed feminine, somehow mysterious. Her skin was smooth but not frail. Beneath it were firm muscles, honed by an unpampered life. He would never have found frailty as appealing. Still, he could feel the nerves jangle inside her. Now he would treat her as though she'd never been touched. Where there was innocence there should be compassion. Where there was trust there should be respect.

And somehow, wonderingly, he felt as though it was his own initiation.

She heard the rustle of the sheets as he shifted. Her body hammered with need even while her fears held her back. It was natural, she reminded herself. And now that she wasn't expecting, she wouldn't be disappointed. Then her breath caught as a new thrill coursed over her skin. Confused, she brought a hand to his chest.

"I won't hurt you again." He drew away from her to brush the hair from her face. His fingers weren't steady. God, he had to be steady now, he warned himself. He couldn't afford to lose control, to lose himself a second time. "I promise I won't hurt you."

She didn't believe him. Even as she opened her arms in acceptance, he saw she didn't believe him. So he lowered his mouth to hers again and thought only of Erin.

He'd never been a selfish lover, but he'd never been a selfless one, either. Now he found himself ignoring his own needs for hers. When he touched her, it wasn't to fulfill his own desire but to bring her whatever passion he was able. He felt the change in her start slowly, a gradual relaxation of the limbs, a dreamy murmuring of his name.

She'd waited, braced, for the speed, the pressure, the pain. Instead he gave her languidness, indulgence and pure pleasure. He moved his hands over her freely, as he had be-fore, but this time there was a difference. He stroked, ca-

ressed, lingered until she felt as though she was floating.
The sensation of vulnerability returned, but without the
panic. Light and sweet, he brought his mouth to her breast
to nibble and suckle so that she felt the response deep inside, a pull, a tug, a warmth that spread to her fingertips.

With a moan she wrapped her arms around him, no longer simply accepting but welcoming.

My God, she was sweet. With his lips rubbing over her
skin he discovered she had a taste like no other, a taste he
would never be able to do without again. Her body was
so completely responsive under his that he knew he could
have her now and satisfy them both. But he was greedy in
a different way this time. Greedy to give.

Reaching for her hand, he linked his fingers with hers.
Even that, just that, was the most intimate gesture he'd ever
made. In the candlelight he saw her face glow with pleasure, the soft, silky kind that could last for hours.

So he came back to her mouth to give them both time.

She tasted the wine, just a hint of it, on his tongue. Then
she felt his lips move against hers with words she heard
only in her heart.

Here was the glow she'd once imagined, and all the
bright, beautiful colors the poets had promised. Here was
music flowing gently and light soft as heaven. Here was everything a woman who'd given her heart could ask in return.

She'd loved him before. But now, experiencing the compassion, the completeness, she fell deeper.

Slowly, carefully, he began to show her more, finding all the pleasure he could want from her response. Her
body shuddered and strained toward him without hesitation, without restrictions. When he nudged her over the first
peak, he saw her eyes fly open with shock and dark delight.

Breathless, she clung to him. It felt as though her mind

was racing to keep pace with her body. And still he urged her on in ways she'd never dreamed existed. The next wave struck with a force that had her rearing up. There couldn't be more. The colors were almost too bright to bear now, and need and pleasure had mixed to a point that was both sharp and sweet.

She held him, moaning out his name. There couldn't be more.

But he filled her and showed her there was.

She was trembling again, but she wasn't curled away from him. This time she was turned to him, her face pressed against his shoulder, her arms holding tight. Because he was more than a little dazed himself, he kept her close and said nothing.

He was no novice at this game, Burke reminded himself. So why did he feel as though someone had just changed the rules? The candlelight flickered its shadows around the room so that he shook his head. It looked as if he'd changed them himself. Soft light, soft music, soft words. That wasn't his style. But it felt so damn right.

He was used to living hard, loving hard and moving on. Win, lose or draw. Now he felt as though he could go happily to the grave if he never moved beyond this spot. As long as Erin stayed with him.

That thought had several small shock waves moving through him. Stayed with him? Since when had he started thinking along those lines? Since he'd laid eyes on her, he realized, and let out a long, none-too-steady breath. Good God, he was in love with her. He'd gone through his life without taking more than a passing interest in any woman. Then someone had opened the chute, and he'd fallen face first in love with a woman who hadn't had time to test the waters.

He didn't have time for this. His life was unsettled, the way he wanted it. His days, his decisions, his moves were his own. He had plans, places to go. He had…nothing, he thought. Absolutely nothing without her.

Closing his eyes, he tried to talk himself out of it. It was crazy, he was crazy. How did he know what it meant to love someone? There had only been one person he'd loved in his life, and that was long ago. He was a drifter, a hustler. If he'd stayed in one place a little too long, it was only because…because there hadn't been a better game, that was all. But he knew it was a lie.

He should do them both a favor and take that trip to Monte Carlo. He should leave first thing in the morning. The hell with the farm, the responsibilities. He'd just pick up and go, the way he always had. Nothing was keeping him.

But her hand was resting on his heart.

He wasn't going anywhere. But maybe it was time he upped the stakes and played out his hand.

"You okay?" he asked her.

Erin nodded, then lifted her face to look into his. "I feel… You'll think I'm foolish."

"Probably. How do you feel?"

"Beautiful." Then she laughed and threw her arms around his neck. "I feel like the most beautiful woman in the world."

"You'll do," he murmured, and knew in that moment that no matter how hard he struggled he was already caught.

"I never want to feel any different than this." She drew him closer to press kisses along his jawline and throat.

"You will, but there's no reason you can't feel like this as often as possible. We'll bring your things over tomorrow."

"What things?" Still smiling, her arms still around his neck, she drew back.

"Whatever things you have. There's no reason to bother moving tonight. Tomorrow's soon enough."

"Moving?" Slowly she unwound her arms. "Burke, I told you once before I won't live here with you."

"Things have changed," he said simply, reaching for the wine. He wished it was whiskey.

"Aye, but that hasn't. What happened tonight..." Had been beautiful, the most beautiful experience of her life, and she didn't want it spoiled by talk of sharing a life with him that wouldn't be a true one. "I want to remember it. I'd like to think that there may be a time when we might—when we might love each other this way again, but that doesn't mean I'll toss my beliefs aside and move in as your mistress."

"Lover."

"The label doesn't really matter." She started to move away, but he grabbed her shoulders. The glass tilted to the floor and shattered.

"I want you, damn it, don't you understand? Not just once. I don't want to have to drag you away from the Grants every time I want an hour with you."

"You'll drag me nowhere." The afterglow of love was replaced by angry pride. "Do you think I'll move in here so it'll be convenient for you when you have an urge to wrestle in bed? Well, I won't be a convenience to you or any man. The hell with you, Burke Logan."

She pushed away and had swung her legs off the bed when she went tumbling backward to find herself pinned under him. "I'm getting tired of you wishing me to hell."

"Well, get used to it. Now take your hands off me. I'm going home."

"No, you're not."

Her eyes narrowed. "You'll not keep me here."

"Whatever it takes." Then she twisted under him. Before

he realized her intent, her teeth were sunk into his hand. He swore, and they rolled from one end of the bed to the other before he managed to pin her again.

"I'll draw blood next time, I swear it. Now let me go."

"Shut up, you crazy Irish hothead."

"Name-calling, is it?" Erin sucked the breath between her teeth. The words she uttered now were Gaelic.

This was hardly the time to be amused, he reminded himself. But there was no help for it. "What was that?"

"A curse. Some say my granny was a witch. If you're lucky, you'll die fast."

"And leave you a widow? Not a chance."

"Maybe you'll live, but in such pain you'll wish... What did you say?"

"We're getting married."

Because her mouth went slack and her bones limp, he released her to suck on his wounded hand.

"It's a relief to know you've got good teeth." He reached to the bedside table for a cigar. "Nothing to say, Irish?"

"Getting married?"

"That's right. We could fly to Vegas tomorrow, but then Dee would give me grief. I figure we can get a license and do it here in a few days."

"A few days." She shook her head to clear it, then sat up. "I think the wine's gone to my head." Or he had, she thought. "I don't understand."

"I want you." He lit the cigar, then spoke practically, deciding it was the style she'd relate to best. "You want me, but you won't live with me. It seems like the logical solution."

"Solution?"

Calmly, as if his life wasn't on the line, he blew out smoke. "Are you going to spend the rest of the night repeating everything I say?"

Again she shook her head. Trying to keep calm, she watched him, looking for any sign. But his eyes were shuttered and his face was closed. He'd played too many hands to give away the most important cards he'd ever held.

"Why do you want marriage?"

"I don't know. I've never been married before." He blew out another stream of smoke. "And I don't intend to make a habit of it. I figure once should do me."

"I don't think this is something you can take lightly."

"I'm not taking it lightly." Burke studied the end of his cigar, then leaned over to tap it out. "I've never asked another woman to marry me, never wanted one to. I'm asking you."

"Do you..." Love me? she wanted to ask. But she couldn't. Whatever answer he gave wouldn't be the right one, because she'd posed the question. "Do you really think that what we had here is enough for marriage?"

"No, but we're good together. We understand each other. You'll make me laugh, keep me on my toes, and you'll be faithful. I can't ask for more than that." And didn't dare. "I'll give you what you've always wanted. A nice home, a comfortable living, and you'll be the most important person in my life."

She lifted her head at that. It could be enough. If she was indeed important to him. "Do you mean that?"

"I rarely say what I don't mean." Because he needed to, he reached for her hand. "Life's a gamble, Irish, remember?"

"I remember."

"Most marriages don't make it because people go into them thinking that in time they'll change the other person. I don't want to change you. I like you the way you are."

He took her fingers to his lips, and her heart simply spoke louder than her head. "Then I guess I'll have to take you the way you are as well."

Chapter 8

"This is all happening so fast." Dee sat in Erin's bedroom, where even now a dressmaker was pinning and tucking a white satin gown on her cousin. "Are you sure you don't want a little more time?"

"For what?" Erin stared out the window, wondering whether if one of the dressmaker's pins slipped and pierced her skin she would discover it was all a dream.

"To catch your breath, think things through."

"I could have another six months and still not catch my breath." She lifted a hand to her bodice and felt the symphony of tiny freshwater pearls. Who would have thought she'd ever have such a dress? In another two days she would put it on to become Burke's wife. Wife. A chill ran up her spine, and at her quick shudder the dressmaker murmured an apology.

"Have a look, Miss McKinnon. I think you'll be pleased

with the length. If I do say so myself, the dress is perfect for you. Not every woman can wear this line."

Holding her breath, Erin turned to the cheval mirror. The dress was the real dream, she thought. Thousands of pearls glimmered against the satin, making it shimmer in the late-afternoon light. She thought it was something a medieval princess would wear, with its snug sleeves coming to points over her hands and its miles of snowy skirts.

"It's beautiful, Mrs. Viceroy," Adelia put in when her cousin only continued to stare. "And it's a miracle indeed that you could have it ready for us in such a short time. We're beholden to you."

"You know you've only to ask, Mrs. Grant." She eyed Erin as she continued to stare into the glass. "Is there something you'd like altered, Miss McKinnon?"

"No. No, not a stitch." She touched the skirt gingerly, just a fingertip, as if she was afraid it would dissolve under her hand. "I'm sorry, Mrs. Viceroy, it's only that it's the most beautiful thing I've ever seen."

More than placated, Mrs. Viceroy began to fuss with the hem. "I think your new husband will be pleased. Now let me help you out of it."

Erin surrendered the dress and stood in the plain cotton slip Burke had once unhooked from the clothesline. As the wedding gown was packed away, she slipped into her shirtwaist and thought she understood what Cinderella must have felt like at midnight.

"If I might suggest," the dressmaker continued, "the dress and veil would be most effective with the hair swept up, something very simple and old-fashioned."

"I'm sure you're right," Dee murmured as she continued to watch her cousin. Erin was staring out the window as if she was looking at a blank wall.

"And, naturally, jewelry should be kept to the bare minimum."

"She'll have my pearl earrings for something borrowed."

"What a sweet thought."

"Thank you again, Mrs. Viceroy," Dee said, rising. "I'll show you out."

"No need for you to go up and down those stairs in your condition. I know the way. The dress will be delivered by ten, day after tomorrow."

Day after tomorrow, Erin thought, and felt the chill come back to her skin. Would it always be now or never when it came to Burke?

"A lovely lady," Dee said after she closed the bedroom door.

"It was kind of her to come here."

"Kind is one thing, business another." Since the weight of the twins seemed to grow heavier every day, she sat again. "She would hardly pass up the opportunity to please the future Mrs. Burke Logan. Erin... I'm happy for you, of course. Oh, I feel like a mother hen. Are you sure this is what you want?"

"I'm not sure of anything," Erin blurted out, then sank onto the bed. "I'm scared witless, and I keep thinking I'll wake up and find myself back on the farm and this all something I dreamed up."

"It's real." Dee squeezed her hand. "You have to understand that everything happening now is as real as anything can be."

"I do, and that only scares me more. But I love him. I wish I knew him better. I wish he'd talk to me about his family, about himself. I wish Ma was here and my father and the rest of them. But..."

"But," Dee coaxed as she moved over to sit beside her.

"But I love him. It's enough, isn't it?"

"Enough to start." She remembered that in the beginning all she'd had was a blind, desperate love for Travis. Time had given her the rest. "He's not an easy man to know."

"But you like him?"

"I've always had a soft spot for Burke. He's got a kind heart, though he'd rather no one noticed. He's a tough one, but I believe he'd do his best not to hurt someone he loved."

"I don't know if he loves me."

"What's this?"

"It doesn't matter," Erin said quickly, and rose to pace. "Because I love him enough for the two of us."

"Why would he want to marry you if he didn't love you?"

"He wants me." Better to face it now, head-on, she told herself as she turned back to Dee.

"I see." And because she did, she chose her words with care. "Marriage is a mighty big step for a man to take only for a want, a bigger step yet for a man like Burke. If the words are hard to come by, it might be that he hasn't learned how to say them."

"It doesn't matter. I don't need words."

"Of course you do."

"Aye, you're right." She turned back with a sigh. "But they can wait."

"Sometimes a person needs to feel safe before he can speak what's in his heart."

"You're good for me." Erin reached out both hands and grasped Dee's. "I'm happy, and despite the both of us I'm going to make him happy."

Brave words aside, when she stood at the top of the stair-case two days later, clinging to Paddy's arm, Erin wasn't sure she could walk as far as the atrium, where the ceremony would take place. The music had begun. In truth, she could hear nothing else. She took one step and stopped. Then she felt Paddy's comforting pat on her hand.

"Come now, lass, you look beautiful. Your father would be proud of you today."

She nodded, took two slow, easy breaths, then descended.

Burke thought the tux would strangle him. If he'd had his way, they would have walked into the courthouse, said a few words and walked out again. Mission accomplished. It had been Dee who had browbeaten him into a wedding. Just a simple one, she'd said, Burke thought with a grimace. A woman was entitled to white lace and flowers once in her life. She herself hadn't been given the choice, but she wanted it for Erin. He'd relented because he'd been certain she couldn't pull it off in the two weeks he'd given her. Of course, she had.

The simple wedding she'd promised had swelled into what he considered a sideshow, with two hundred people eager to watch him juggle. The house was full of white and pink roses, and he'd been forced to pull himself into a tux. She'd ordered a five-tiered wedding cake and enough champagne to fill his pool. Wasn't it enough that he was about to make a lifetime commitment without having a trio of violins behind him?

Burke stood with his hands at his side and his face carefully blank and wondered what in the hell he was doing.

Then he saw her.

Her hair was glowing, warm and vibrant under layers of white tulle. She seemed pale, but her eyes met his without hesitation. How was it he'd never noticed how small she was, how delicate, until now, when she was about to become a permanent part of his life? Permanent. He felt the quick sliver of panic. Then she smiled, slowly, almost questioningly. He held out a hand.

Her fingers were icy. It was a relief to find his equally cold. She held tight and turned to face the priest.

It didn't take long to change lives. A few moments, a few words. She felt the ring slip onto her finger, but she was looking at him. Her hand was steady when she took the gold band from Dee and placed it on Burke's finger.

And it was done. He lifted the veil and touched the warm skin beneath. He brought his lips to hers, lightly, then more strongly. With a laugh, Erin threw her arms around his neck and held him. And it was sealed.

Then, almost from the moment she became his wife, she was spun away to be congratulated, complimented and envied.

It became like a dream, full of music and strangers and frothy wine. She was toasted and fussed over. Cameras flashed. There was caviar and elegant little hors d'oeuvres and sugared fruit that sparkled like diamonds under the lights. Erin found herself answering questions, smiling and wishing herself a hundred miles away.

Then she was dancing with Burke, and the world snapped back into focus.

"This didn't seem real. Until now." She rested her cheek against his and sighed. "I always dreamed of a day like this. Are we really married, or am I still imagining?"

He lifted her hand, running a finger over her ring. "Looks real to me."

Smiling, she looked down, then caught her breath. "Oh, Burke, it's beautiful." Stunned, she turned her hand so that the layers of diamonds and sapphires glittered. "I never expected anything like this."

"You've had it on for an hour. Haven't you looked?"

"No." It was foolish to cry now, but she felt the tears sting her eyes. "Thank you." She was grateful the music stopped while she still had control. "I'll be back in just a minute."

"You'd better be. I'll be damned if I'll deal with this crowd alone."

She tucked her thumb into her fist so that she could run it along the ring as she hurried upstairs. She just needed a minute, Erin told herself. To compose, to adjust, to believe.

Stepping inside the bedroom, she leaned back against the door and caught her breath. Tonight, she thought, this would be her room, just as Burke would be—was—her husband. She would sleep in this bed, wake in it, tidy the sheets, fuss with the curtains. And one day it would become usual.

No, she thought with a laugh, and hugged herself. It would never become usual. She wouldn't let it. From this day on her life would be special. Because she loved and belonged.

Touching her cheeks to be certain they were cool and dry, she started to open the door. A trio of women were passing on their way downstairs.

"Why, for his money, of course." This from a woman Erin recognized from Adelia's party, one with beautiful white hair and a watered-silk suit. "After all, she hardly knew the man. Why else would she marry him? You don't think she came all the way from Ireland to settle for keeping his books."

"It seems strange that Burke would marry her, a nobody, when he could have had his pick of some of the most acceptable women in the area." The leggy blonde from the party fussed with the snap of her purse.

"I thought they made a lovely couple." The third woman

merely shrugged as the white-haired matron looked down her nose. "Really, Dorothy, a man hardly marries without reason."

"No doubt she's got a few tricks up her sleeve. It's one thing to get a man into bed, after all, and another to get him to the altar. Men are charmed easily enough, and bore just as easily. I imagine he'll be finished with her in a year. If she's as smart as I think she is, she'll tuck away a nice settlement—starting with that ring he gave her. Ordered it from Cartier's, you know. Ten thousand. Not a bad start for a little farm girl from nowhere."

The blonde fussed with her hair as they approached the head of the stairs. "It should be interesting to see her struggle to climb the social ladder in the next few months."

"She's not one of us," the white-haired woman announced with a flick of the wrist.

Erin stood with her hand on the knob and watched them descend the stairs. Not one of them? Through the first shock came the tremble of anger. Well, damned if she wanted to be. They were nothing but a bunch of gossiping old broody hens with nothing better to do than make cruel remarks and speculate on the feelings of others.

For his money? Did everyone really believe she'd married Burke for his money? Did he? she wondered with a sudden and very new shock. Anger drained as she let her hand slip off the knob. Oh, sweet God, did he? Was that what he'd meant when he'd said he could give her what she wanted?

She put her hands to her cheeks again, but they were no longer cool. Could he believe that her feelings were tied up in what he had instead of what he was? She hadn't done anything to show him otherwise, Erin realized with a sinking heart.

But she would. Lifting her head, she started out of the

room. She would show him, she would prove to him that it was the man she had married, not his fine house or his rich farm. And to hell with the rest of them.

When she descended the steps this time, she didn't look like the pale, innocent bride. Her color was high, her eyes dark. She might not be one of them, she thought, but she would find a way to fit in. She would make Burke proud of her. Forcing a smile, she walked directly to the woman in watered silk.

"I'm so glad you could come today."

The woman gave Erin a gracious nod as she sipped champagne. "Wouldn't have missed it, my dear. You do make a lovely bride."

"Thank you. But a woman's only a bride for a day, and a wife for a lifetime. If you'll excuse me." She crossed the room, her dress billowing magnificently. Though Burke was surrounded, she moved directly to him and, putting her arms around him, kissed him until the people around them began to murmur and chuckle. "I love you, Burke," she said simply, "and I always will."

He hadn't known he could be moved by words, at least not such well-used ones. But he felt something shift inside him as she smiled. "Is that a conclusion you just came to?"

"No, but I thought it past time I told you."

He thought he'd never nudge the last guest out the door. No one loved a party and free champagne like the privileged class.

Erin stood in the center of the atrium with her hands clasped together. "It's going to take an army to put this place to rights."

"No one's walking through that door for twenty-four hours."

She smiled, but the fatigue and nerves were beginning to show. "I should go up and change."

"In a minute." Before she could move, he took both her hands. "I should have told you how beautiful you are. I can't remember ever being as nervous as I was when I stood down here waiting for you."

"Were you?" Her smile came fully now as she pressed against him. "Oh, I was scared to death. I nearly picked up my skirts and bolted."

"I'd have caught you."

"I hope so, because there's no place I want to be but here with you."

He framed her face with his hands. "You haven't had much chance to compare."

"It doesn't matter."

But he wondered. He was the only man she'd ever known. Now he'd done his best to be certain he was the only one she ever would. Selfish, yes, but a desperate man takes desperate measures. He kissed her again and then, while his lips were on hers, lifted her into his arms. "There's no threshold to carry you over."

Her eyes laughed at him. "There's one in the bedroom."

"I told you that you were a woman after my heart," he said, and carried her up the stairs. Rosa had champagne chilling in a bucket and two glasses waiting.

"Burke, I wonder, would you mind giving me ten minutes?"

"Who's going to help you out of that dress?"

"I can manage. I'm sure it's bad luck for the bridegroom to do so. Just ten," she repeated when he set her down. "I'll be quick."

With a shrug, he pulled a robe out of his closet. "I suppose I can get out of this straitjacket somewhere else."

"Thank you."

He didn't give her a minute more than that, but she was ready. She was still in white, but this gown was like a cloud, wisping down, shifting with each breath she took. Her hair was loose over the shoulders, fire against snow. He closed the door quietly behind him and looked his fill.

"I didn't think you could be more beautiful than you were this afternoon."

"I wanted tonight to be special. I know we've already... we've already been together, but—"

"This is the first time I'll make love to my wife."

"Aye." She held out her hands. "And I want you to love me. I want you more now than I did before. If you could—" It was foolish to blush now. She was a married woman. "If you could teach me what to do."

"Erin." He didn't know what to say. He simply didn't have the words. But he took her hand and pressed a kiss to her brow. "I have something for you."

When he took a box out of his pocket and handed it to her, she moistened her lips. "Burke, I don't want you to feel obliged to buy me things."

"If I don't, how am I going to please myself by looking at you wear them?" So he opened the box himself. Inside was a rope of diamonds holding one perfect sapphire.

"Oh, Burke." She wanted to cry because it was so lovely. She wanted to cry because she was afraid he thought she required it. "It matches my ring," she managed.

"That was the idea." But he was watching her, frowning at the look in her eyes. "Don't you like it?"

"Of course I do, it's like something out of a palace. I think I'm afraid to wear it."

He laughed at that and turned her toward the mirror. "Don't be silly. It's made to be worn. See?" He held it up around her throat. The sapphire gleamed dark against her skin and the wink of diamonds. "What good are pretty stones if a woman doesn't wear them? You'll need more than this before it's done. We can pick up some things on our honeymoon." He kissed the curve of her throat. "Where do you want to go? Paris? Aruba?"

Ireland, she thought, but was afraid he'd laugh at her. "I was thinking maybe we should wait awhile for that. After all, this is one of the busiest times of year for you, with the Derby coming up. Could we wait a few months before we go away?"

"If you like." He placed the necklace back in the box before turning her to face him. "Erin, what's wrong?"

"Nothing. It's just all so new and… Burke, I swear to you I won't do anything to cause you shame."

"What the hell is this?" Patience gone, he took her by the arm and set her on the bed. "I want to know what you've got into your head and how it got there."

"It's nothing," she said, furious with herself that she was always an open book to him while she could never dig beneath the top layer. "It's just that I realized today that I don't really fit in with your people and life-style."

"My people?" His laugh wasn't amused and had her tensing. "You don't know anything about my people, Irish, and you can consider yourself fortunate. If you mean the people who were here today, two-thirds of them aren't worth the snap of your fingers."

"But I thought you liked them. You've friends among them, and associates."

"Associates, for the most part. And that can change at any time. We can go to parties, and you can join any clubs or committees you like. But if you want to thumb your nose at the lot of them, it wouldn't matter to me."

"You're part of the racing world," she insisted. "And married to you, so am I. I won't have anyone saying you married some little nobody who can't fit in."

"And someone did," he murmured. She didn't have to confirm with words what he could see so clearly in her eyes. "You listen to me. It only matters what we think. I married you because you were what I wanted."

"I'm going to be." She lifted her hands to his face. "I swear to you." She brought her mouth to his with all the passion, love and longing she had.

She wanted the night to be special, but that meant more than champagne and white lace. It meant showing him what was in her heart, what she was just beginning to understand for herself. That she loved him unrestrictedly. With her arms around him, her mouth on his, she lowered onto the bed. Their marriage bed.

He had shown her what loving could be. Now she hoped she could give some of that beauty back to him. Since experience wasn't hers, she could only act on what was in her heart. She had no idea if a man could feel more than need and satisfaction, but she wanted to try to give him some of the sweetness, some of the comfort he had given to her.

Hesitant, unsure, she pressed her lips to his throat. His taste was darker there, potent, and she could feel the beat of his pulse beneath her mouth. Its rhythm quickened. She smiled against his skin. Yes, she could give him something.

She liked the way he felt under her hands, the muscles that bunched and flowed as she moved her fingers over them. Tentatively she parted his robe. When she felt him tense, she retreated immediately, an apology forming on her lips.

"No." With a half laugh, he took her hand and brought it back to him. "I want you to touch me."

He kept his own hands gentle, though each hesitant stroke of her fingertips drove him mad. He was already caught in the innocence and passion of her, in her willingness to be taught, her eagerness to please and be pleased.

So they loved slowly, taking time to teach, to learn. There was no shyness on her part when he drew the lace from her shoulders, but rather a wonder that he found her so desirable. In answer, she slipped his robe away and let herself marvel at the strength and beauty that was her husband.

Perhaps it didn't make sense, but it was more exciting now that he belonged to her. The hard fist of need hadn't lessened, the trembles of anticipation and anxiety were just as sharp. But now, along with desire, was the simple joy that the man who held her was the man who would hold her night after night. This was only the beginning, she thought. Laughing, she rolled over him.

"Something funny?" he managed. He felt as though his body was stretched beyond the breaking point.

"I'm happy." She brought her mouth down hard on his, then, incredibly, felt her bones liquify. With a soft moan, she took him into her. When the whirlwind started, she could only hold her breath and grip his hands tight. Her body took control now, moving with his instinctively as pleasure built and crested and built again.

Her head was thrown back. He thought she looked like a goddess, red hair streaming over white shoulders, her slender body strong and agile as it merged with his. He wanted to hold her like this, to see her like this again and again in his mind's eye. Then the pleasure was so complete that it blinded him.

Erin woke on her first day as Mrs. Logan to a gray morning lashed by spring rain. She thought it was beautiful.

Smiling, she shifted over to reach for Burke. And found him gone. Terrified she'd dreamed it all, she sat straight up.

"Do you always wake up like that?" Across the room, Burke hooked his belt and watched her.

"No, I thought…" It wasn't a dream. Of course, it wasn't. She laughed at herself and shook her head. "Never mind. Where are you going?"

"Down to the stables."

"So early?"

"It's seven."

"Seven." She rubbed her hands over her eyes as she struggled up. "I'll fix your breakfast."

"Rosa'll see to it. You should get some more sleep."

"But I—" She wanted to fix his breakfast. It was one of the small and very vital things a wife could do for her husband. She wanted to sit in the kitchen with him, talking of the day to come and remembering the night that had passed. But he was already pulling on his boots. "I'm not tired. I could go down and start on the books."

"You've gotten them in good enough shape to take a couple of days off. In fact, we haven't talked about it, but you don't have to continue with that if you don't like."

"Well, of course I'll continue with it. That's why I came here."

He lifted a brow as she tugged on a robe. "Things have changed. I don't want my wife to have to close herself up in an office all day."

"If it's all the same to you, I'd like to work." Uncomfortable, she began to tug on the sheets. "If you don't want me to be doing your books anymore, I'll find another job."

"I don't care if you work on them or not, I just want you to know you have a choice. What are you doing?"

"I'm making the bed, of course."

Crossing over, he caught her hand in his. "Rosa takes care of the bed-making, as well."

"There's certainly no need for her to make mine—ours."

"That's her job."

He kissed her brow, then changed his mind and drew her close against him. "Good morning," he murmured against her lips.

Hers curved just slightly. "Good morning."

"I'll be back in a few hours. Why don't you take a swim?"

When the door closed behind him, Erin crossed her arms. Take a swim? On her first day as a wife, she wasn't supposed to cook breakfast or make a bed but to take a swim? Walking over to the mirror, she stared at herself. She didn't look so very different. But feelings didn't always show. Wasn't it odd that she'd refused to be Burke's mistress, but now she was feeling more like that than a wife?

Married him for his money.

Erin pushed away from the mirror. The hell with that. It was past seven and she had work to do.

Rosa wasn't any more cooperative than Burke. There was no reason for the *señora* to do that. There was no reason for the *señora* to do this. Perhaps the *señora* would like to take a book into the solarium. In other words, Erin thought, you're of no use here. That was going to change, she decided.

She threw herself into her paperwork. When Burke didn't return for lunch, Erin took matters into her own hands. Filling a pail with hot water and detergent, she took it and a mop to the atrium. Glasses and plates had already been cleared away, but Rosa hadn't yet gotten to the tiles. Erin felt a stab of satisfaction at having beaten her to it.

This is my house, she told herself as she sloshed out soapy water. My floor, and I'll damn well wash it if I like.

Burke strode through the streaming rain, thinking that the horse he had entered at Charles Town that night would have an edge on the muddy track. His second thought was that Erin might get a kick out of taking the trip to West Virginia to see the run. It would give him a chance to show her off a bit.

God, she'd looked beautiful that morning, all heavy-eyed and dewy-skinned. He was far from certain he'd done the right thing for her by rushing her into marriage, but he was more certain than ever that he'd done the right thing for himself. He couldn't remember ever being at peace before or ever feeling as though each day had a solid purpose to it.

He could give her the things in life she'd always wanted. The money didn't matter to him, so he didn't give a hang how she spent it. In turn she was giving him a solid base, something he hadn't known he'd wanted.

Inside, he shook the rain out of his hair and went to look for her. When he entered the atrium, he stopped. She was on her hands and knees, scrubbing. Even as she heard his steps and glanced up, he was dragging her to her feet.

"What in hell are you doing?"

"Why, I'm washing the floor. It took a beating yesterday. You'd be amazed what people can drop and what they don't bother to pick up again. Burke, you're hurting my arm."

"I don't ever want to see you down on your knees again. Understand?"

"No." Studying him, she rubbed her arm. She knew real anger when she looked it in the face. "No, I don't."

"My wife doesn't scrub floors."

"Now wait a minute." As he turned on his heel, she

caught him. "She'll scrub them if she pleases, and she won't be called *my wife* as though she were something shiny to be kept in a box. What's the matter with you?"

"I didn't marry you so you could scrub floors."

"No, nor that I could cook your breakfast or make the bed, that's plain. Just why did you marry me, then?"

"I thought I'd made that clear."

"Aye." She dropped her hand from his arm. "I suppose you did. So I'm to be your mistress after all, it's just a matter of being a legal one."

He made an effort, an enormous one, to block off the anger. It didn't work. "Don't be a fool. And leave that damn bucket where it is."

"You'll remember the word in the ceremony was changed from obey to cherish." Scowling at him, she gave the bucket a kick and sent soapy water pouring over the tiles. "But I'll be happy to leave it just where it is."

"Where the hell are you going?"

"I don't know," she said over her shoulder. "Surely I can walk through the house even though I'm not allowed to touch anything in it."

"Stop it." He caught her as she stormed down the hall, but she only shook him off and kept going. "Damn it, Erin, you can touch whatever you like, just don't clean it."

"I can see it's time we had the rules straight." She pushed through the doors into the solarium. The heat was like a wall and suited her mood perfectly. "Touching and looking are allowed."

"Stop acting like an idiot."

"Me?" She turned on him and nearly upset a pot of geraniums. "It's me who's an idiot, is it? Out there it's a fool I am and in here an idiot. Well, it wasn't me who went into a rage because the floor was getting washed."

"I thought you came here to get away from that, because you wanted more out of life than washing dishes."

Slowly she nodded. "Aye, I came to America for that, but it's not why I married you. Maybe I can handle others thinking I married you because of your money and your fine house, but not you. I told you yesterday that I loved you. Don't you believe me?"

"I don't know." He ran a hand over his face and struggled for calm, for clear thinking, for the kind of controlled logic that had always brought him out on top of any game he chose. "Why does it matter?"

She had to turn away because it hurt too much to face him. "I didn't lie when I said it, but you can think whatever you like. It doesn't matter at all." Very deliberately she picked up a pottery bowl and sent it crashing to the tiles. "You needn't worry, I won't clean it up."

"Are you finished?"

"I haven't decided." Crossing her arms, she stared at the clear water of the pool.

He put his hand on her shoulder. Perhaps she did love him a little. It would take a bigger fool than he to push her away. "My mother spent more than half of her life on her knees scrubbing other people's floors. She was barely forty when she died. I don't want you on your knees for anyone, Erin."

When he started to draw his hand away, she clasped it in her own. "That's the first thing you've trusted me with." She turned to put her arms around him. "Don't you see you'll drive me mad if you shut me out?"

"You agreed to take me for what I am."

"I have. I will. I do love you, Burke."

"Then let me see you enjoy yourself."

"But I am." Tilting her head back, she grinned at him. "I like to fight."

He ran a finger down her nose. "Then I'm glad to oblige you. Did you take that swim?"

"No, I had the books, and then I argued with Rosa for a while."

"Busy day. Let's take one now."

"I can't."

"More arguing to do?"

"No, I've done with that, but I don't want to swim."

"Can't you?"

Her chin angled as he'd expected. "Of course I can, but I don't have a suit."

"That's okay." Lifting her up, he walked to the edge as she giggled and shoved against him.

"You wouldn't, and if you try, by God, you'll go in with me."

"I never intended it any other way." They went in together, fully dressed.

Chapter 9

Before she had been married a full month, Erin had taken trips to New York and Kentucky and back to Florida. She grew used to the look and feel of the racetracks, whether they were earthy or glamorous. She grew used to, but never less fascinated by, the people who inhabited them, from the young grooms still shiny with ambition to the older hands who lived from race to race and bet to bet.

The contrasts were a constant curiosity. From her box she could watch the other owners, their families and friends. Seersucker suits and picture hats. While against the rail, elbow to elbow, were the masses who came for the fun or the money. She learned that wagering had its own scent, often a desperate one, always a little sweaty. Away from the stands were the horses, the scales, the tack and the riders. Only a few who watched knew the thrill and the anxiety of ownership.

In Lexington she visited horse farms with Burke and

saw stables grander than she had ever thought any house could be. She saw the races of the Thoroughbred world, grew to know the people whose lives were tied to them, and she learned.

At cocktail parties, dinner parties and small celebrations she listened to discussions on breeding, on training, on strategy. She grew to understand that owners often thought of their horses as possessions, while trainers more often than not thought of a horse in their care as an athlete to be disciplined and pampered in the peculiar way of the sportsman. But above all the horse was the focus, for envy or for pride.

After a time she drew together the courage to go as far as the paddocks, where she could watch the horses being examined and saddled for the races. Though the scent and sounds of horses still disturbed her, she was determined that Burke's associates would never twitter about his wife being afraid.

She grew more accustomed to the parties, the lavish ones, that only the successful and the privileged could attend. The talk there was of horses and the people who owned them. Not so different from Skibbereen, she began to think. Certainly this life was more glamorous, but at home the talk had often been just as narrow.

She studied, poring over books on Thoroughbreds, racing and the history of both. She learned that every Thoroughbred descended from three Arabian studs and that the most expensive horseflesh in the world was to be found in Ireland at the Irish National Stud. She'd had to smile at that, not only from home pride but because two such horses were in Burke's stables.

She learned to wager wisely and to win, a skill that never failed to amuse her husband. He'd been right when he'd said she would make him laugh. Erin found more pleasure in that than in all the pretty stones he bought her or the new clothes that hung in her closet. She'd discovered something in a month of marriage. The things she'd thought she'd always wanted weren't important after all.

And she was pregnant.

The knowledge both thrilled and terrified her. She was carrying a child, Burke's child, one that had been conceived on their first night together. In a matter of months they would no longer be just husband and wife but a family. She couldn't wait to tell him. She was afraid of what he would say.

They'd never discussed children. But then, there had been time to discuss little. She hardly knew more of him now than she had when she'd married him. True, she had come to understand that unlike many of his associates his horses were neither possessions nor pets. Nor were they the game of chance he claimed them to be. They had his pride and his affection, and Erin came to see that they had his admiration for simply being what they were. It wasn't just the winning but the heart that made champions.

There was this and little more she had learned of him. He'd never spoken of his mother or his family again. Though she'd tried to question him gently, he'd simply ignored her. Not evaded, Erin thought now, just ignored.

It didn't matter, she told herself as she went to find him. She'd seen him with Dee's children, and he'd been gentle and kind and caring. Surely he would be only more so with a child of his own. She would tell him and he would hold her tight and tell her how happy he was. They would laugh and she would show him all the pamphlets the doctor had given her on childbearing classes and diet. Then they would plan the nursery, all pinks and blues like a sunrise.

She found him in the library and had to bite back an impatient oath when she saw he was on the phone.

"I'm not interested in selling," he said as he gestured her in. "No, not at that price, not at any. If you want to get back to me in a few years and talk stud fees... Yes, that's a firm no. Tell Durnam none of my stock's for sale at the moment. Yeah, you'll be the first to know." He hung up and pulled a hand through his hair.

"Problems?" Erin crossed over to kiss his cheek.

"No. Charlie Durnam's interested in buying one of the new foals. Makes me think he's the one with problems. So what did you buy?"

"Buy?"

"You said you were going shopping."

"Oh, yes. I didn't buy anything." She rested her cheek against his hair a moment. "Burke, I've something I want to tell you."

"In a minute. Sit down, Erin."

It was the tone that had her retreating. He used that odd flat voice when she'd annoyed him. "What's wrong?"

"I've had a letter from your father."

"From Da?" She was up again almost before she sat. "Is something wrong? Is someone sick?"

"No, nothing's wrong. Sit down." He swiveled in his chair, and for the first time in a month she felt as though they were back on terms of business. "He wrote to welcome me into the family and to express what I suppose is fatherly concern that I take good care of you."

"What nonsense. He knows very well I can take care of myself." She relaxed again, unconsciously resting a hand low on her stomach. "Was that all?"

"He also thanked me for the money you've been sending over. He says it's been a great help." Burke paused a moment as he flipped through the papers on his desk. "Why didn't you tell me you've been sending more than half your money over to Ireland?"

"I never thought of it," she began. Then she stopped. "How do you know how much I'm sending?"

"You keep excellent and very clear books, Erin." He pushed away from the desk to pace to the window.

"I don't understand why you're angry. The money's mine, after all."

"It's yours," he murmured. "Damn it, Erin, there's a checkbook in the office. If you'd felt the need to send money home, why didn't you just take what you wanted and be done with it?"

"There's more than enough out of my wages."

"You're my wife, damn it, and that entitles you to whatever you want. You're past the point where you have to draw wages."

She was silent a moment, and when she spoke, she spoke carefully. "That's it, isn't it? You still believe that I'm here because of your fat checkbook."

He didn't know what he thought, Burke admitted as he stared out of the window. She was perfect, warm, loving. And the longer she was with him, the more he was certain there had to be a catch. No one gave unconditionally. No one gave without wanting something back. "Not entirely," he said after a moment. "But I don't believe you'd have married me if I didn't have one. I told you before it doesn't matter. We suit well enough."

"Do we?"

"The point is the money's there and you may as well make use of it. You never know how long it'll last." With a half smile, he lit a cigar. "That's a bridge we'll cross when we come to it. Enjoy it, Irish, it's all part of the bargain."

She thought of the child inside her and could have wept. Instead she stood. "Is there anything else?"

"I want you to go write out a check for whatever your family needs."

"All right. Thank you."

"We'll be leaving for Kentucky in a few days. The Bluegrass Stakes and the Derby." He turned and leaned back against the sill. "You should enjoy it. It's quite a show."

"I'm sure it's wonderful." She took a long breath and watched him carefully. "It's a pity Dee's too far along to travel so she and Travis won't be there."

"That's the price you pay for having a family." He shrugged and moved back to his desk.

"Aye," she said quietly, but the light had gone out of her eyes. "I'll let you get back to work."

"Wasn't there something you wanted to tell me?"

"No. It was nothing." Erin closed the door behind her, then covered her face with her hands. Hadn't she told him she loved him? Hadn't she showed him in every way she knew? And now she was carrying physical proof of her feelings, but none of it mattered to him.

Then it would have to matter to her even more. Erin straightened her shoulders and walked away from the door, unaware that Burke stood on the other side, hesitating, his hand on the knob.

He hadn't meant to be angry. She'd looked so happy when she'd come into the room. She'd smiled at him as though...as though she loved him. Why couldn't he get past the block and just accept? Because he didn't believe in that kind of love, not even when he felt it himself.

He did believe that she would stay with him, happily enough, as long as he continued to provide her with what she needed. When he'd met her, he'd recognized the hunger for more he himself had always felt. He'd recognized the need to see new things, climb new mountains and win. It was just fortunate for both of them that he was in a position to show her those things, to provide her with the means to taste and hear and see the fantasies she'd had.

She could love him for that, and that he could understand.

But what about the man who had come from nothing? What about the man who could be back to nothing at the toss of the dice? What would her feelings be for him? He couldn't afford to find out, because the man who thought love only existed for convenience was desperately in love with his wife.

She was far from aware of it. As Erin walked into the kitchen, she was certain Burke only wanted her as long as she did nothing to upset the balance of his life-style. Sooner or later, he would be aware that together they already had.

Rosa was washing crystal in the sink but stopped the moment Erin walked in the room.

"Is there something you want, *señora*?"

"I'm just going to fix some tea."

"I'll heat the water."

"I can do it myself," Erin snapped as she slammed the kettle onto the stove.

"As you like, *señora*."

Erin leaned her palms against the stove. "I'm sorry, Rosa."

"De nada."

As Rosa went back to her crystal, Erin found a cup and saucer. What kind of wife was it, she wondered, who didn't even know which cupboard held her dishes? How could she be so happy and so unhappy at the same time?

"Rosa, how long have you worked for Mr. Logan?"

"Many years, *señora*."

"Before he came here to this house?"

"Before that."

Like pulling teeth, she thought, determined to pull harder. "Where did you work with him before that?"

"In another house."

Erin turned from the stove. "Where, Rosa?"

She saw the housekeeper's lips tighten. "In Nevada. In the West."

"What did he do there?"

"He had much business. You should ask Mr. Logan yourself."

"It's you I'm asking. Rosa, don't you think I have a right to know who my husband is?"

She saw the brief hesitation before Rosa began to polish glasses. "It's not my place, *señora*."

"I need something." With an angry flick of her wrist, she shut off the flame. "I don't care what he did, what he was. If he's done something wrong it doesn't matter. How can I get through to him if I don't understand him?"

"Señora." Carefully Rosa set down the first glass and picked up another. "I'm not sure you would understand even if you knew."

"Tell me, and let me try."

"Some things are better left alone."

"No!" She wanted to throw something, anything, but managed to hold the need back. "Rosa, look at me. I love him." When the housekeeper turned, Erin spoke again. "I love him and I can't stand being kept apart from who he is. I want to make him happy."

Rosa stood silently a moment. Her eyes were very dark and very clear. For a moment Erin felt a stab of recognition. Then it passed. "I believe you."

"It's Burke who needs to believe."

"For some, believing such things doesn't come easily."

"Why? Why for Burke?"

"Do you know what it's like to be hungry? Truly hungry? For food, for knowledge, for love?"

"No."

"He grew up with nothing, less than nothing. When there was work, he worked. When there was not, he stole." She moved her shoulders and picked up the next glass. "Not such a bad life for some. Hell for others. He never knew his father. His mother was not married, you understand?"

"Yes." Erin sat and made no objection when Rosa moved over to the stove to fix her tea.

"His mother worked very hard, though she was never well. But in such places a person always owes much more than they could ever have. At times he went to school, but more often he worked in the fields."

"On a farm?" she asked, remembering the way Burke had looked over hers.

"*Sí.* He lived on one for a while so that he could give his mother his pay."

"I see." And she was beginning to.

"He hated the life, the dirt and the stench of it."

"Rosa, how did you know him when he was a child?"

She set the tea down in front of Erin. "We had the same father."

Erin stared. Then, when Rosa would have walked away, she grabbed her arm. "You're Burke's sister?"

"Half sister. My father took me to New Mexico when I was six. He met Burke's mother. She was pretty, frail and very innocent. After Burke was born he left me with her, promising to send for us all when he had a job. He never did."

"Something might have happened to him. He might—"
She stopped when she saw the look in Rosa's eyes.

"Burke's mother discovered he'd met another woman in
Utah. That was his way. So she worked, washing up other
people's dirt, for twenty years. Then she died. She had done
her best for him, but Burke was always wild and restless.
The day she was buried, he left. It was five years before I
saw him again."

"He found you?"

"No, I found him." Rosa went back to her glasses.
"Burke is not a man who looks for anyone. He owned part
of a casino in Reno. Because I wouldn't take the money he
offered, I went to work for him. He's never been comfortable with it, but he doesn't send me away."

"He couldn't. You're his sister."

"Not to him. Because to him our father never existed.
There is no family in Burke's life, no roots, no home."

"That can change."

"Only Burke can change it."

"Aye." Nodding, she stood. "Thank you, Rosa."

She didn't tell him about the baby. Over the next few
days she fretted over the secret but didn't speak it. There
were races to prepare for. Important ones. Now, as she
watched Burke handle his business and deal with his horses,
she watched from a different perspective.

How had his early life shaped him? She took note of the
way he treated those who worked for him. He was firm
and demanding but never unreasonable. Not once had she
heard him raise his voice to any of his men. Because he
knew what it was like to be abused by an employer? she
wondered. Because he understood how it felt to be depen-
dent for your existence on another?

He loved the horses. She wasn't sure he was aware of it himself, but she could see it in the way he watched them take to the track, the way he supervised their grooming. Perhaps it was true that when he'd won the farm it had been only another game, but he'd made a life out of it whether he realized it or not. That alone gave Erin hope.

The time came for them to fly to Kentucky. Erin vowed she would tell him about the baby when they returned.

There was something different about her, Burke thought as he fixed himself a drink in the parlor of their hotel suite. He just couldn't quite put his finger on it. Her moods were like a roller coaster—up, down and sideways as quick as a wink. Not that he didn't find them interesting. He'd never been one who wanted to settle in too comfortably, and a man would hardly do that with a wife who was raging one minute and smiling sweetly the next. She was always doing the unexpected these days, cuddling up against him and falling into long, thoughtful silences or racing down to the stables to drag him back for a picnic under the willow.

She was the same in public, playing the dignified wife one moment and a flirtatious woman the next. And she didn't always flirt with only him. He couldn't deny it made him jealous, but he was fully aware that was her intent.

He found her daydreaming one minute and rushing around talking about redecorating the next. At times he worried that she was becoming restless again, but then she would reach for him at night, and no one had ever seemed so content.

He'd noticed she seemed to have lost her taste for champagne, though they attended the spring parties with regularity. She'd taken to sipping plain juice and discussing bloodlines and the pros and cons of certain tracks.

Then there had been the day he'd given her the earrings, sapphires to match her necklace. She had opened the box, burst into tears and fled, only to come back an hour later to gather him close and thank him.

The woman was driving him crazy, and he was enjoying every minute of it.

"Are you almost ready, or do you want to be fashionably late?" he asked as he strolled toward the bedroom.

"Almost ready. Since we're going to win the race tomorrow, I thought I should look my best for the pictures they'll be taking tonight. I've never known people with such love for taking pictures at parties."

"You didn't complain about having yours in the paper," he began, then stopped to stand in the doorway. She smiled when she saw him and turned a slow circle.

She'd chosen the dress carefully, knowing that before too many more weeks she would be showing and wouldn't feel proper wearing something daring. The midnight blue was shot through with silver threads so that she shimmered even standing still. It left her shoulders bare, then slithered down her body without drape or fold. Without the slit up the skirt, she wasn't sure she could have moved in it.

"Well, do you like it? Mrs. Viceroy said I should have something to show off my necklace."

"Who's going to notice the necklace?" He came to her and, in the way he had of making her heart stop, took both her hands to kiss them. "Irish, you're gorgeous."

"It's sinful for me to want the other women to be jealous, isn't it?"

"Probably."

"But I do. I want them to look at you and think he's the most wonderful man here. And she has him." Laughing, she spun another circle. "Then I can just look at them and smile, sort of pitying."

"It's a shame I won't be able to notice, because I won't be able to take my eyes off you."

She turned back to touch his cheek. "You know, when you say things like that, it still makes my insides curl up. Burke…" She wanted to tell him she loved him, but she knew he would only smile and kiss her forehead. Then her heart would break a little because he wasn't able to give the words back to her. "Did you ever think these parties are a little—slow?"

"I thought you liked them."

"Well, I do." She moved closer to run a finger down his lapel. "But sometimes, sometimes I find myself in the mood for something that takes a little more energy." She smiled as she looked up at him under her lashes. "A lot more energy. You smell very nice."

"Thanks." He lifted a brow as she loosened his tie. "Are you trying to start something?"

"And what if I am?" She pushed his jacket off his shoulders.

"Just checking," he murmured while she unbuttoned his shirt. "This isn't going to make all those women jealous."

With a laugh she ran her hands up his chest. "That's what you think." Grinning, she shoved him onto the bed and jumped in after him.

For the first time since she'd fainted, Erin insisted on going down to the stables with Burke. She told him it was a matter of pride, and it was. Pride in him.

She wasn't able to bring herself to go in, but urged him to as she stood in the sun and watched the people.

A long way from Skibbereen indeed, she thought. The

air was warm with springtime, and flowers were already in bloom. Trainers and exercise boys she'd come to know by sight nodded or tipped their hats as they passed her and greeted her as Mrs. Logan.

There was excitement in the air as well, the kind that hummed before an important race. Before long, it would be *the* race. The Derby. But for now everyone's attention was on today and the Bluegrass Stakes. A win here added to Double Bluff's record would make him the favorite. Erin smiled as she thought that would lower the odds, but odds didn't matter. She wanted Burke to win, today and at Churchill Downs. She could almost taste the satisfaction of having Double Bluff named Horse of the Year. More than she'd wanted anything, she wanted that for Burke, for him to know he'd done something special, something only the best could accomplish.

"Good day to you, Mrs. Logan."

"Paddy." Pleased to see him, Erin opened her arms for a hug. "Oh, it's a fine day, isn't it? How's Dee?"

"Right as right and mean as a bear. She told me to tell you if Travis's Apollo doesn't win, Burke's Double Bluff better."

"And who are you betting on?"

"Now who do you think? I trained Apollo myself. But if I was hedging my bets, I'd lay some money on the colt out of Three Aces."

"A smart man would put his money down on Charlie's Pride." Durnam came up behind them and slapped Paddy on the shoulder.

"Well, now, it's a fine colt you have there, Mr. Durnam, and that's the truth. But I think I'll stick with my own."

"That's your choice. Hello there, Mrs. Logan. You're looking as pretty as ever."

"Thank you. Good luck to you today."

"You don't need luck when you've got the best." He pulled at the brim of his straw hat and moved on.

"We'll see who's the best," Erin said under her breath.

"Got the fever, do you?" Chuckling, Paddy slipped an arm around her shoulders. "There's a powerful competition in this business. Can't be otherwise when money and prestige change hands in a matter of minutes."

"How do you know when you've got a winner?"

"Well, now, there's breeding and training and a matter of attitude. There's feed and grooming. There's the jockey that sits on top and finding the right man for the right mount. But what it comes down to, darling, is blood. It's in the blood or it isn't, just like with people."

"Aye, the blood." She looked toward the stables and thought of Burke. "So you think that someone could be denied the proper care and feeding, the training, and still be a winner?"

"We talking horses or people?"

"Does it matter?"

"Not much." He gave her shoulder a quick squeeze. "It's in the blood and it's in the heart. I've got to tend to my boy now."

"I'll wave to you from the winner's circle, Paddy Cunnane," she called after him.

"You sound sure of yourself," Burke commented as he crossed to her.

"Sure of you." She gripped his hands as they headed for the stands. "You don't have to walk me up. I know you want to stay to see your jockey weighed in and watch Double Bluff saddled."

"The last time I didn't go with you I found you surrounded by reporters."

"I know how to handle them now. Besides, I did like seeing my picture in the paper."

"You're a vain woman, Irish."

"Aye, and why not?" She brushed a finger over his cream-colored shirt and found herself pleased he didn't go in for the seersucker of his associates. "Whether it's pride or vanity, I find it exciting to see my picture on the society page. Did you know, Mr. Logan, you're a very important man?"

"Is that so?"

"Aye, 'tis so, and so I'm told often enough. Then, by rights, I have to be an important woman."

"You could pass for one today," he decided, taking a quick study of her pale blue suit and pearls. She'd added a plain wide-brimmed straw hat, then had tilted it at an angle so it could no longer be called demure.

"I decided the day called for dignified." Then she laughed and touched the brim of her hat. "Sort of. Burke, I'll be fine, really. I know you want to stay close to the horse."

"I'd rather stay close to you. Mind?"

"No." She hooked her arm through his and grinned. "Why don't I buy you a beer?"

She thought it was a perfect day. The most perfect day of her life. The sky was cloudless, a soft spring blue that made her smile just to look at it. She noticed the woman from her wedding as she stepped into the box, and made sure she tilted her head and smiled coolly in greeting.

"Why do I feel you're always sticking pins in Dorothy Gainsfield?"

"Because I am, darling." She stood on tiptoe and kissed him. "Long, sharp ones. I didn't know until the other day that the skinny blonde who was hanging all over you on

St. Patrick's Day was Mrs. Gainsfield's favorite niece." She laughed again, figuring it meant another day in purgatory. "Life can be sweet."

"You'll have to fill me in on all this later."

"In ten or twenty years, perhaps. Look, Burke, television cameras. Can you imagine?"

Delighted with the world in general, she took her seat. Now and then she spotted someone she knew and waved, to Lloyd Pentel, to Honoria Louis, to the elderly Mrs. Bingham.

"Do you know, I've met as many people in a month's time as I've known all of my life. It's an odd and wonderful feeling." She turned to see he was smiling at her. "Why do you look at me like that?"

"It's an education to watch you in a place like this, soaking it all up, storing it away. I wonder what you'll look like when we go to Paris or Rio."

"Probably stand around with my mouth hanging open the whole time and humiliate you."

"There's that." He only laughed when she jabbed him with her elbow. "Try to behave yourself. It's almost post time."

"Oh, Lord save us, so it is, and I haven't bet."

"I bet for you while you were buying my beer and trying to decide if you were going to eat a cheeseburger or two hot dogs. Living in America's improved your appetite."

It wasn't only that that was increasing her appetite, she thought, and wondered when she would work up the nerve to tell him. "It wasn't my fault we missed breakfast," she reminded him. "Where's my ticket?"

Watching the horses being led to the starting gate, he reached in his pocket. Erin took the stub and was about to tuck it away when she noticed the amount.

"A thousand dollars?" Her voice squeaked so that a few interested heads turned. "Burke, where would I be getting a thousand dollars to bet on a horse?"

"Don't be ridiculous." He didn't spare her a glance. His trainer had moved to Double Bluff's head as the colt reared and danced. "Seems a little more wired than usual," he murmured as two grooms stepped up to help.

"But, Burke, a thousand dollars."

"Afraid you'll lose?"

"No." She stopped. Then, closing the ticket tight in her hand, she said a quick prayer. "No, of course not."

The bell sounded. The gate was released. The horses plunged forward.

She recognized the Pentel colt in the lead. He was a fast starter, she remembered, but he didn't have stamina. With the ticket still clutched in her hand, she put a fist to her breast. The pack was hardly more than a blur, but she could see the green-and-white silks of Burke's jockey. Rounding the first turn he was in fourth, with Travis's colt on his left. The crowd was already shouting so that she could no longer hear the announcer. It didn't matter. With her free hand she gripped the sleeve of Burke's linen shirt and held on.

"He's making his move," Burke murmured.

She saw the whiz of crops, the strain of speed as the jockeys leaned low. Double Bluff moved to the outside. His stride lengthened, eating up distance. It seemed that before her eyes he grew bigger, his coat glossier, his legs longer.

A champion, she thought again, was in the heart. Hers was with the colt. It was more than a race, she knew, more than prestige and certainly more than money. It was Burke's pride. She understood what it was like to come from little, then to have a chance for everything.

The Pentel colt began to lag. As they came down the

stretch it was a race between three, leaving the pack behind. Charlie's Pride held first, with Travis's colt and Double Bluff vying for second. She could see the dirt flying and the sweat. All around her there was one huge, bellowing roar.

"He's going to do it!" She didn't even realize she was shouting as she watched Double Bluff gain on Charlie's Pride. They were nose to nose for what seemed forever. And then he was ahead, by a neck, by half a length, by a length, with his speed only increasing. He was two lengths ahead at the wire.

"Oh, Burke, he did it. You did it!" She hadn't been aware of standing, but found herself on her feet as she turned to throw her arms around him. "Sure and he's the most beautiful horse ever born. I'm so proud of you."

"I wasn't racing."

She drew back to caress his cheek. "Yes, you were."

"Maybe I was," he murmured as he kissed the tip of her nose. He continued to watch as his jockey took the horse around for the victory lap. "Can you manage to stand in the winner's circle with me?"

"I think so." People were congratulating them, and though Erin acknowledged them, her thoughts were already moving forward to standing beside Burke as he accepted the win.

Her arms were still around him when the official winner was declared. Charlie's Pride. Double Bluff had been disqualified.

"Disqualified? What do they mean?"

"We'll find out." Taking her hand, Burke moved out of the stands. The murmurs had already started.

"Burke, they can't say he didn't win. For heaven's sake, I saw it with my own eyes. He was well in the lead. There's a mistake."

"Wait here." Leaving her, he walked over to the paddock area where Double Bluff was being held. She saw a bald man in a suit approach Burke, then two other men join them. It looked so official, she thought. The bald man was talking calmly, pointing to the horse, then to a piece of paper. As he spoke, both the jockey and the trainer began to argue furiously, but Burke simply stood, listening.

She began to feel the heat as she stood there, so she moved over into the shade. It was a mistake, of course, she told herself as she removed her hat to stir air into her face. No one would take away what Burke had earned, what he needed, what she needed for him.

"What is it?" she demanded as Burke strode back.

"Amphetamines. Someone gave the horse amphetamines."

"Drugs? But that's ridiculous."

"Apparently not." His eyes were narrowed as he looked over at the paddock. "Someone wanted him to win very badly. Or to lose."

Chapter 10

"What do you mean you're sending me home? I'm not a package to be wrapped and stamped." Erin rushed after Burke as he strode from the parlor to the bedroom of the suite. "You've barely said a word to me since we left the track, and now all you can say is you're sending me home."

"There's nothing else to say, not at the moment."

"Nothing to say?" Because she was breathless after struggling to keep pace with him, she sat. "Double Bluff was just disqualified from one of the most important races of the year because someone gave him drugs. That's plenty to talk about to start."

"It's not your concern." He pulled a suitcase out of the closet, then set it open on the bed. "Pack."

She kept her seat and, just barely, her temper, but her eyes narrowed. "Oh, I see. So this is one more thing I'm not to touch."

Pausing only a moment, Burke studied her. He could see

the temper beginning to brew. As far as he was concerned, she was better off angry than dealing with the tempest of the next few days. He'd never considered himself a man of great virtues, but he'd protect his wife.

"You can look at it that way or any other way you like. I've got some calls to make. Pack your things, I'll see that your flight's changed."

"Just one bloody minute." She was up and after him again as he walked into the next room. "I'm sick to death of orders from you. Almost as sick as I am of talking to your back. If you don't put down that phone, Burke Logan, it'll pleasure me to wrap the cord around your neck."

"Erin, I've got enough to deal with at the moment without you adding one of your tantrums."

"Tantrums." Her hands clenched into fists as she walked toward him. "Oh, I've a flash for you, I do. You haven't seen a tantrum yet. Now sit." Taking both hands, she shoved him into a chair. "And it's time you unplugged your ears and listened for a change."

He could have risen again and struck back with his own temper. He decided against it, in the same way he might have decided to bluff his way to a pot with a pair of deuces. The quickest way to have her out and on her way was to show disinterest. "Is this going to take long?"

"As long as needs be."

"Then would you mind if I had a drink?"

Seething, she went behind the bar and grabbed a bottle and a glass. She slammed them down on the table beside him. "Go ahead, have the whole bottle. Drown yourself in it."

"Just one'll do." He poured two fingers, then lifted the glass in a half salute. "Say what's on your mind, Irish. I have a few things to see to before your flight."

"If I said half what was on it, your ears would be ringing from now till Gabriel blew his horn. Answer me this, are you going to take this business lying down?"

He lifted the glass and sipped, watching her steadily over the rim. "What do you think?"

"I think you're going to fight, and I think you won't be resting until you find out who's behind this. Then I think you're going to carve them up in little pieces."

He toasted her again, then downed the rest of the whiskey. "That about covers it."

"And I'm not going home to twiddle my thumbs while you're about it."

"That's exactly what you're going to do."

"Did it ever occur to you that I could help?"

"I don't want your help or need it, Erin."

"No, you don't need anyone." She swung away to pace the room, wishing she knew a better way than shouting to handle an argument. "All you need are a few paid servants to deal with the little details while you go on your merry way. You certainly don't need a wife, a partner, to tend to your shirts or hold your hand when there's trouble."

The urge to get up, to hold on to her, was so strong he had to press his fingers into the glass until his knuckles whitened. Because she was wrong. She was very, very wrong about what and whom he needed. "I didn't marry you to do my laundry."

"No, you married me to sleep with, and I know it well enough. But you got more than you bargained for, because I'm not running back home like some weakhearted, whiny female who can't face a spot of trouble."

Pride, he thought, and nearly laughed. It always seemed to be his pride or hers on the line. "No one's insulting your valor, Erin. It would simply make things easier if I didn't have you to deal with."

"You won't have to deal with me. In private I'll stay out of your way and you can do your business however you please. But in public I'm going to be there."

"The loyal and trusting wife?"

"What's wrong with that?"

"Nothing." He sat back, determined to study her calmly. She looked like a comet about to go into orbit. "It matters to you what these people think, what they say?"

"And why shouldn't it?"

Why shouldn't it indeed? he thought as he stared into his empty glass. She was worried about her position, and hers walked hand in glove with his own. "Have it your way, then, I can hardly drag you to a plane and tie you on. But I warn you, it won't be pretty."

"You've said you understand me, almost from the first moment we met you said it, and I believed you. Now I see that you really don't understand me at all." There was no more anger. It had been smothered by a rising despair. If they'd really been married, in the true sense, they would have been able to talk about what had happened, they would have been able to fight together, rage together instead of at each other. "You can make your calls, I'm going for a walk."

But he didn't pick up the phone when she left. It was more than being unused to having someone stand beside him, more than his own penchant for handling his own in his own way. He'd wanted her to go, away from the murmurs and sly looks. He didn't want her to be a part of the suspicion that had already fallen over him and his.

She'd never even asked. Burke scrubbed his hands over his face and tried to get beyond his own fury. It wasn't losing the purse or the race so much as knowing that someone had violated what was his. And she'd never asked if he'd arranged it himself. Could she really believe so blindly in him, or was it a matter of her not caring how he won?

However she felt, he couldn't shield her from the gossip. And gossip there would be, he thought grimly. Once she had a taste of it, he figured she'd be happy enough to go back to the quiet of Three Aces. In the meantime, he was going to find out who'd messed with him. Pushing the bottle aside, Burke picked up the phone.

The action moved to Churchill Downs and Derby week. Erin made certain she attended each function and every qualifying race. She held her head up and, when she heard a whisper, only held it higher.

Not everyone seemed inclined to believe that Burke had had a hand in the drugging of his horse. For every snub and murmur there was someone else to offer support. But the only one who mattered had closed himself off from her. She didn't try to break through the barrier. It took all the energy she had to hold up the pretense of a united couple. The strain was taking its toll, all the more because she worked hard to make sure Burke didn't see it.

He rose early, so she rose early. He went to the track to oversee Double Bluff's morning exercise, so she spent her mornings at the track. There were days when by noon she was so weary she wanted to crawl off into a corner and sleep. But there were races and luncheons and functions, often back-to-back. She refused to miss even one.

Erin McKinnon Logan wasn't hiding in some dim corner until the trouble passed. She would face it, shoulders straight, and dare even one person to look her in the eye and make an accusation. It was hard, and grew harder, so that every day she had to force herself to put in an appearance. There were whispers and knowing looks behind smiles. There were eyes that turned away rather than meet hers. And there were a few who preferred to cloak their insults in manners.

She dressed carefully for a formal dinner party near the end of Derby week. Erin had always felt that a strong outer appearance helped tap the inner strength. Attending alone was only more difficult, but Burke had been called to a meeting at the last minute.

She could have stayed at the hotel, just as Burke had asked. The truth was that a quiet evening, a tray in bed and a good book was exactly what she would have preferred. But that would have been cowardly. So she wore her midnight-blue silk and hung her sapphire around her neck like a badge.

While others sipped cocktails, she nursed orange juice and made conversation. More than ever she was grateful for Paddy. He stayed close, keeping her spirits up and her mind busy with stories of Ireland. But he couldn't shield her from everything, nor from everyone.

"My dear, what a pretty dress." Dorothy Gainsfield swept toward her, her eyes as cold as her diamonds.

"Good evening, Mrs. Gainsfield."

"Tell me, are you enjoying your first Derby week? It is your first, isn't it?"

"Aye, it's my first." If Erin had learned one thing, it was how to return a meaningless smile. "I'm sure you've been coming here for many years."

"Indeed," she said repressively, refusing to be insulted by one so beneath her station. "I don't see your husband."

"He couldn't make it."

"That's understandable, isn't it?"

Erin felt Paddy start forward, and laid a hand on his arm. "With the race only a couple of days away, Burke is busy."

"I'm sure he is." The older woman gave a dry laugh and sipped her champagne. "You know, I'm rather surprised he's being allowed to enter after that...mishap, shall we say, at the Bluegrass Stakes."

"The racing commission feels Double Bluff's record speaks for itself and for Burke. Once the investigation's complete, that, too, will speak for itself."

"Oh, I don't doubt it, my dear, not for a minute. It isn't unusual for someone to get a bit too enthusiastic about winning. This wouldn't be the first time the method's been used to lower the odds."

"Burke doesn't cheat. He doesn't have to."

"I'm sure you're right." Mrs. Gainsfield smiled again. "But then, I wasn't speaking of your husband... Mrs. Logan." Satisfied with the dig, Mrs. Gainsfield moved away.

"That dough-faced old cow," Paddy began as he fired up. "I'll give her a piece of my mind."

"No." Again Erin put a hand on his arm. "She's not worth it." Erin watched her mingle with the crowd. "When Double Bluff wins, it'll be enough."

Erin was determined that by the end of the week they would have discovered who was responsible for Double Bluff's disqualification and the cloud on Burke's reputation would be gone. She was even more determined that on Sunday, when Churchill Downs opened for the Derby, Burke would win what was rightfully his.

Once that was done, she would face the cracks and scars on her marriage. Perhaps Burke had been wrong when he'd said most marriages didn't work because one person tried to change the other. She knew now that if changes weren't made—in both of them—their marriage would never survive.

She watched him now as he stood near the oval with his trainer. It was barely dawn, with a light so sweet and fragile that it turned the white steeples pink. The air was cool, quiet enough to carry voices to her, if not the words. All around her the stands were empty. In twenty-four hours they would be filling, section by section, until they and the infield grass were packed with bodies. The race would last only a matter of minutes, but for those few minutes, every square inch would be crammed with excitement, with pumping hearts and with hope.

"It has its own magic, this time of day."

"Travis." Erin was up and swinging her arms around him. She hadn't realized until that moment how badly she'd needed someone to hold on to. "Oh, it's so glad I am to see you. But you shouldn't be here." She drew away just as quickly. "What about Dee? Is she all right?"

"All right enough to throw me out. She told me she could use a couple of days without my hovering over her."

"That's nonsense and I know it, but I'm grateful to both of you." She looked beyond his shoulder to her husband. "He needs his friends now."

"How about you?"

She gave a quick laugh and a shake of her head. "Oh, he doesn't seem to need me."

"I don't believe that, but it isn't what I meant. How are you holding up?"

"I'm tough enough to get through a few rough spots yet."

"You're a bit pale," he murmured, then took her chin in his hand. "More than a bit."

"I'm fine, really. Could use a bit more sleep, that's all."

Then she swayed against him. Before she could pull herself back, he was settling her into a seat.

"Just sit back. I'll get Burke."

"No." She gripped his hand and held hard. "I'll be all right in a second. I just need to close my eyes."

"Erin, if you're ill—"

"I'm not ill." She laughed and unconsciously laid a hand on the child that was growing inside her. "I promise you."

He lifted his brow as he studied her. "Then congratulations."

Erin opened her eyes slowly. "You're a sharp one."

"I've been through it a few times." He stroked her hand until a hint of color returned to her face. "How does Burke feel about starting a family?"

"He doesn't know." Steadier, she sat up and was relieved to see Burke's back was still to them. "He has enough to worry about right now."

"Don't you think this would more than balance the scales?"

"No." Letting out a sigh, she faced Travis again. "No, I don't, because I'm not sure he wants children at all. And right now he doesn't want anything more than for me to leave him alone."

"You're underestimating him."

"You're his friend."

"And yours."

"Then stand up with him until this is over. Let me tell him about the baby when the time's right."

"All right. If you promise to take better care of yourself."

She smiled and kissed his cheek. "After tomorrow, I'll sleep for a week."

"Travis." Burke slipped under the rail. "I didn't expect to see you down here."

"Hate to miss a Derby. How are things going?"

Burke glanced over his shoulder to where the horse was being walked and cooled. "The colt's in top form. You can say we're both ready to put things right."

"The investigation?"

"Slow." That was true, at least of the official one. His own was moving quite a bit faster. Now that Travis was here, he would have someone he could trust to listen to his theory. Though he wore his tinted glasses, Erin felt his eyes on her. With a nod of acknowledgment, she rose.

"I'll leave you to discuss business."

"She's worried about you," Travis murmured as Erin walked away from the stands.

"I'd prefer she didn't. What I'd prefer is that she went back to the Three Aces until this is cleared up."

"If you'd wanted a quiet, obedient wife, you shouldn't have picked an Irish one."

Burke pulled out a cigar and contemplated it. "How many times have you been tempted to throttle Dee?"

"In the last seven years, or in the last week?"

For the first time in days, Burke smiled and meant it. "Never mind. Do me a favor and keep an eye on her, will you? I don't think she's feeling well."

"You could try talking to her yourself."

"I'm not much good at talk. I'd like you to take her back with you after the race tomorrow."

"Aren't you coming back?"

"I might have to stay in Kentucky a few more days."

"Got a lead?"

"A hunch." He lit the cigar and blew out smoke. "Trouble is, the racing commission likes proof."

"Want to talk about it?"

He hesitated, only because it still seemed unnatural to confide in another. "Yeah. You got a few minutes?"

Erin wasn't sure why she felt the sudden need, but she walked toward the stables. Maybe if she could prove to herself that she was strong and capable, Burke would begin to believe it. She'd faced the gossip, she'd stood tall against the innuendos. She'd held her own. But there was one thing she'd yet to face, one fear she'd yet to vanquish. So she would do it. Then, tomorrow, she would walk easily beside Burke into Double Bluff's stall, and she would stand beside him without a quiver in the winner's circle.

Three yards from the stables, she stopped to give herself another lecture. It was foolish to be afraid after all this time. It was useless to cling to a feeling that had been caused years before by an accident. She'd been around animals all her life. Married to Burke, she would continue to be around them. And the child... She rested a hand on her stomach. Her child would be raised without fear of his inheritance.

She would walk in alone. Then, tomorrow, even if Burke wished her to hell and back, she would walk in beside him.

She went closer. The scents were there—the hay, the sweet smell of grain, the pungent smell of horse and sweat. The sounds, too—hooves scraping over concrete, harness jingling, the sighs and lazy whinnies of horses at rest. She'd be quiet and go carefully, remembering that each step was one step closer.

The light changed almost from the moment she stepped inside. It was dimmer, softer, and now there was the scent of leather as well.

Most of the horses had already been exercised, and the grooms were indulging in their own breakfasts before it came time to brush and rub and wrap. She'd chosen this time, the least busy time, so that if she bolted no one would see.

But she didn't bolt. One of the horses dipped its head over the gate and she jumped a little, but she stood her ground. She could touch him, Erin told herself. The gate was latched. She could lay her hand on him just as easily as she had with Burke's foal.

Her fingers trembled a little, but she laid them gingerly against the horse's cheek. He eyed her, but when he shifted his weight she jerked back.

"I'll have to do better than that," she muttered, then laid her hand more firmly on his neck. Her palm was damp and she didn't move a muscle, but she felt a little thrill of victory.

He was a fine-looking animal, she told herself as she made her hand move just a little over his neck. It was the Pentel colt, one she'd seen race nearly as often as she'd seen Bluff.

"There, now," she managed with a sigh. "It's not so bad. My heart's thumping, but I'm here." I'm here, she repeated silently, and I'm coming back every day. Each time it would be a little easier. She drew her hand back, then made herself reach out again. And it was easier. Just as it would become easier to face and overcome her insecurities with Burke. She wasn't going to go through life being cowed and miserable because her husband was too stubborn to accept her love and her support. She might have taken him the way he was, but there would be some changes made. And soon.

When she heard voices, she drew her hand back again, embarrassed. She didn't want one of the grooms wandering in to find her. She didn't think she was quite ready to stand in the stables and hold a conversation. Erin wiped her damp palm on her slacks and fixed a casual smile on her face.

She'd started out when the tone of the voices stopped her. There was anger in them and, though they remained quiet, more than a little desperation. Because she hesitated, she had time to recognize one of them.

"If you want your money, you'll find a way."

"I tell you the horse isn't alone for five minutes. Logan's got him locked up like the crown jewels."

Erin's lips parted, then firmed. She took a step back into the shadows and listened.

"You've got a job to do, one you're paid well for. If you can't get to the horse, get to his feed. I want him out of the running for tomorrow."

"I ain't poisoning no horse, and I'm tired of taking all the risks."

"You didn't have any qualms about using a hypodermic or taking ten percent of the purse from the Bluegrass Stakes."

"Amphetamines is one thing, cyanide's another. That horse dies and Logan's not going to rest until somebody hangs for it. It ain't going to be me."

"Then use the drugs." The voice was impatient, dismissive. Erin found her hands balled into fists. "Find a way, or you won't see a penny. If the colt's found drugged in the Derby, he's out for the season. I need this race."

And she needed to get to Burke. Erin stayed still and waited for them to pass on. But luck wasn't with her. As she saw the two figures enter the stables, she straightened her shoulders and moved forward. It was a gamble, but the best she could hope for was a bluff.

"Good day to you, Mr. Durnam." She made her lips curve even when she saw the shock come into his eyes. She glanced at the groom, too, one of the new ones Burke's trainer had hired.

"Mrs. Logan." Durnam smiled in return but was already calculating. "We didn't see you in the stables."

"Just thought I'd look over the competition. If you'll excuse me, Burke's waiting."

"I think not." He took her arm as she tried to pass. Because she'd been half expecting it, Erin was already primed to scream. With surprising speed, his hand clamped over her mouth.

"Good God almighty, what are you doing?" the groom demanded. "Logan'll have your head."

"He'll have yours as well if she goes to him and blabs. She heard everything, you idiot." Because Erin's struggles were making him pant, Durnam thrust her at the groom. "Hold on to her. Let me think."

"We've got to get the hell out of here. If someone comes in—"

"Shut up. Just shut up." Durnam's face was already sheened with sweat. He took out a white handkerchief and mopped it. He was a desperate man who had already taken desperate measures. Now it was time to take another. "We'll put her in the van until the race is over tomorrow. By then I'll have thought of something." Taking the handkerchief, he pulled it around her mouth. As an extra precaution, he took the groom's grimy bandanna and tied it over her eyes. "Get some rope. Hurry, tie her hands and feet."

Erin choked on the gag and struggled against both of them, but she was already aware she'd lose. On a desperate impulse she worked her wedding ring off her hand and let it fall to the ground. Then ropes bit into her wrist and she was smothered inside a blanket.

She felt herself being lifted but could do no more than squirm. Even that was futile as the more she resisted, the harder it was to breathe. She heard a door open just before she was lifted up and set inside on a hard floor.

"What the hell are we going to do with her?" the groom demanded as he stared down at the heap inside the blanket. "The minute we let her go, she'll talk."

"Then we won't let her go." Durnam leaned against the side of the van and this time mopped his brow with his sleeve. Everything was going to go his way, he told himself. He'd come too far, risked too much to have one woman destroy it.

"I ain't having no part in murdering a woman."

Durnam dropped his arm and gave the groom a long, narrow look. "You just take care of the horse and leave the woman to me."

They were going to kill her. Erin struggled to work the blanket from her face as she heard them shut the van door and walk away. She'd heard that in his voice. Even if he'd promised the groom that he'd cause her no harm, she would have known. Whatever had pushed Durnam to this point, he wouldn't hesitate to do away with any obstacle.

Her baby. With a half sob, Erin twisted her wrists and fought against the rope. Mother of mercy, she had to protect her baby. And Burke.

The panic welled up, and for a moment she lost herself in it completely. Before she'd regained control, her wrists were raw and her shoulders bruised. Panting, Erin lay quiet in the dark and tried to think. If she could get up somehow and find the door, she might find a way of forcing it open. She inched her way over to the wall; then, using it as a brace, she managed to get to her knees. She was soaked with sweat by the time she'd struggled to her feet. Keeping her back to the wall, she slid along it, groping with her fingers.

She almost wept when she found the knob. She twisted,

straining on her toes before she could fit her fingers around it. Locked. She had to shake her head to keep the tears from coming. Of course it was locked. Durnam might be a brute, but he wasn't a fool. She tried thudding against the door, hoping to draw some attention, but trussed up tightly she was unable to get the momentum to make more than a quiet bump. Erin slid to the floor again and, closing her mind to both panic and pain, continued to work at the ropes.

"Have you seen Erin?"

Travis continued to run his hands down his colt's leg as he looked up at Burke. "Not since this morning. I assumed she'd gone back to the hotel."

"Maybe. She could have taken a cab." It was logical, Burke reminded himself. There was no reason for the sick feeling in his stomach. "We came in together this morning. She usually waits."

"She was looking a little tired." Travis straightened. "She could have gone back to get some rest before tonight."

"Yeah." It made sense. She was probably soaking in a hot tub right now, thinking about the party that night. "I think I'll drive back and check on her."

"Ask her if she'll take pity on a lonely man and save a few dances for me."

"Sure."

"Burke?"

"Yeah?"

"Something wrong?"

His hands were cold. Ice-cold. "No, nothing. See you in a couple hours."

They stayed cold as he drove from the track toward the hotel. It wasn't like Erin to simply go off without a word. But then, they hadn't been exchanging a great many words lately. His fault. He accepted that with a shrug. He didn't feel right about her being there. And he hated seeing her brace herself against the gossip that would certainly swell before it diminished.

If she wasn't so damn stubborn about maintaining a social position...but then, that was one of the things he'd promised her when they'd married. He couldn't help but be grateful that she was sticking by him, whatever her reasons, but with gratitude came only more guilt and responsibility.

He was no fonder of responsibility now than he'd ever been. Maybe it would be a relief to head the car west and keep going. To start from scratch as he'd done so many times before. Nothing had ever held him back before. But then, there hadn't been an Erin before.

Once the race and the scandal were behind them, they would talk. The air had to be cleared, the rules had to be reset. Maybe, just maybe, after it was all done, he'd tell her about his past. The way he'd grown up, the things he'd filled his life with. It was better to have it out, to make it clean now and let her walk away, than to continue waiting for her to find out for herself.

He'd never thought of his past as anything to be ashamed of. That was something else she'd done to him. She'd forced him to look back at his past a little too hard. And he didn't like what he saw.

His mood hadn't improved by the time he reached the hotel. He knew it was ridiculous for him to be angry with her for leaving the track when he'd demanded she leave altogether. But, damn it, she'd made him depend on her. The days were easier to get through when he knew he could look around and see her. He didn't care for that, either.

By the time he walked into their suite, he was primed for a fight. It had been too long since they'd developed a polite veneer and no substance. He was going to shout at her and let her shout back. Then they'd both vent the rest of their frustrations in bed.

"Erin?" He slammed the door behind him, but had gone no farther than the center of the parlor before he knew she wasn't there. And his hands were cold again.

Cursing himself, he walked into the bedroom. Had she left him? Had he pushed her away far enough, consistently enough, that she'd decided to take that final step? He didn't want to lose her. That admission left him shaken as he reached for the closet door. No, he didn't want to lose her any more than he wanted to need her.

He had to make himself pull open the door of the closet, and was nearly dizzy with relief when he saw her clothes undisturbed.

She'd gone shopping, he told himself. Or to have her hair done. But those thoughts didn't relieve his mind as he closed the closet door.

He was pacing the suite nearly thirty minutes later when the phone rang. Burke pounced on it, ready to rail at her no matter what her explanation.

"Burke, it's Travis."

"Yeah?"

"Is Erin back at the hotel?"

"No." And now his mouth was dry. "Why?"

"Lloyd Pentel just brought me her wedding ring. He found it on the floor in the stables."

"What? The stables?" He was lowering himself into a chair, unaware that he'd moved at all. "That's not right. She wouldn't go in the stables. She's afraid of horses."

"Burke." Travis kept his voice calm. "Has she been back to the hotel?"

"No, she hasn't been here. I want to talk to Pentel."

"I already have. He hasn't seen her. Burke, we may be jumping the gun, but I think you should call the police."

She'd lost track of the time. Once she'd thought the ropes had loosened, but had had to accept it as wishful thinking. More than her wrists hurt now. There were bumps and bruises all over from a fall she'd taken while trying to maneuver standing up. Because the fall had scared her badly with the thought of what might have happened to the baby, she no longer tried to stand. For a time she closed herself off and thought of Burke, as if she could will him to find her.

Would he be worried? Had enough time passed that he would begin to wonder where she was? Would he care? She may have prayed, then slept a little while, dreaming first of Ireland and the farm. Why had she wanted to leave so badly what had been safe and secure? Then she dreamed of Burke and knew that part of the answer was that she'd been meant for him.

"Mrs. Logan."

Her body jackknifed as a hand touched her shoulder. The blindfold was loosened, and she had to blink and struggle to focus. In the dim light she made out the face of the groom, and panic flooded back. He'd come to kill her. And her baby.

"I brought you some food. You gotta promise to be quiet. Durnam would have my hide for coming in here like this. If you promise not to scream, I'll take the gag off so you can eat. If you make noise, I put it back and you get nothing."

She nodded, then drew in fresh air when her mouth was free. It wasn't easy to smother the instinct to cry out, but she could still taste the gag he'd pulled from her mouth. "Please, why are you doing this? If it's money you want, you can have it."

"I'm in too deep." He had a sandwich that was rapidly going stale. "Eat some or you'll get sick."

"What difference does it make?" Just the smell of the meat between the bread made her stomach turn. "You're going to kill me anyway."

"Now, I don't have nothing to do with that." She saw the panic in his eyes and the sweat beading on his lip. He was as afraid as she was. If she could use that, she might yet have a chance.

"You know what Durnam's going to do. He can't let me go."

"He just wants to win, that's all. He needs to. Got himself in some financial trouble, and his stable isn't as good as it was. Charlie's Pride is his best shot, but Logan's colt is better. That's why he had me hire on at Three Aces, so I could keep an eye on things and make sure the race went wrong. But that's it," he added, glancing around. He was talking too much. He always talked too much when he got nervous. And he wanted a drink. The saliva in his mouth had dried to nothing. "I just sweetened the horse some. That's what Durnam wanted. He just needs to put him out of the running. You gotta understand, this is business. Just business."

"You're talking about races. I'm talking about murder."

"I don't want to hear about it. I got nothing to do with that. Now you eat."

"Mr.... I don't know your name."

"It's Berley, ma'am. Tom Berley." Ridiculous as it was, he lifted his fingers to his cap.

"Mr. Berley, I'm begging you for my life. And not just for mine, but for the baby I'm carrying. You can't let him kill my baby. Now you'll only be in trouble about the horse, but this is murder. An innocent child, Mr. Berley."

"I'm not going to hear no more talk about killing." His voice had roughened, but his hands weren't steady when they pulled the gag up again. He no longer wanted a drink, he needed one desperately. He started to replace the blindfold, but the look in her eyes had him hesitating. There was nothing for her to see anyway, he told himself. The back of the van was windowless, and the cab was blocked off by a wooden partition.

"You don't want to eat, that's your business. I've got my own to see to." He stuffed the sandwich in his pocket. Erin saw him look both ways before he stepped out the door again and left her in the dark.

Chapter 11

"I'd prefer if you'd go out and look for my wife, Lieutenant, rather than sitting here asking me questions."

Lieutenant Hallinger was nearly sixty, and after thirty-seven years on the force he figured he'd seen it all and heard twice as much. He'd certainly experienced more than his share of frustrated and angry spouses. It seemed to him that the man in front of him was both.

"Mr. Logan, we have an APB out on your wife right now, and several officers are asking questions at the track." Though he envied Burke his cigar, he didn't mention it. "It would help clear things up, and give us a better chance of locating your wife, if you'd fill me in."

"I've already told you Erin hasn't come back to the hotel. No one's seen her since this morning, and her wedding ring was found at the stables at Churchill Downs."

"Some people are careless with jewelry, Mr. Logan."

Some people. What the hell was this business about some

people? They were talking about Erin, his Erin. Where the hell was she? He looked back at Hallinger again and spoke precisely. "Not Erin. And not with her wedding ring."

"Um-hmm." He made a notation in his book. "Mr. Logan, occasionally this sort of thing comes down to a simple misunderstanding." He could have written a book, Hallinger thought. Yeah, he could've written a book on misunderstandings alone. "Did you and your wife quarrel this morning?"

"No."

"It's possible she rented a car and decided to do a little sight-seeing."

"That's ridiculous." He glanced up as Travis handed him a cup of coffee. Burke accepted it but set it aside. "If Erin had wanted to go for a drive, she would have taken the car we've already rented. She would have told me she was leaving and she would have been back two hours ago. We had plans for this evening."

He'd had plans himself, which had included a nice quiet evening with his own wife. And a footbath. Hallinger wriggled his aching toes inside his shoes. "Derby week can be chaotic. It might have slipped her mind."

"Erin's the most responsible person I know. If she's not here, it's because she can't get here." He thought again of the hateful and terrifying calls he'd already made to the hospitals. "Because someone's keeping her from getting here."

"Mr. Logan, kidnapping usually prompts a ransom call. You're a wealthy man, yet you tell me you haven't been contacted."

"No, I haven't been contacted." But he still broke out in a sweat every time the phone rang. "Look, Lieutenant, I've told you everything I know. And I'm damn sick of going over the same ground when you should be out doing your job. I'd go out and look myself, but I feel it's more important for me to stay here and…" Wait. Endlessly.

Hallinger glanced over his notes. He was a thin man with small, aching feet and a quiet voice. He was a man who took his appearance as seriously as he took his job. It was possible for him to admire Burke's casually expensive shoes while noting his nerves and anxiety.

"Mr. Logan, you had some trouble at the Bluegrass Stakes. How did your wife feel about that?"

"She was upset, naturally." Crushing out his cigar, he rose to pace.

"Upset enough to want to avoid the crowds tonight and tomorrow? Upset enough to want to escape from it, and you?"

There was a flat and dangerous look in Burke's eyes when he turned. "Erin wouldn't run from anything or anyone. The fact is I asked her to go back home until this thing was settled. She wouldn't do it. She insisted on staying and seeing it through."

"You're a fortunate man."

"I'm aware of that. Now why don't you get the hell out of here and find my wife?"

Hallinger simply made a note in his book and turned to Travis. "Mr. Grant, you're the last person we know of who spoke with Mrs. Logan this morning. What was her mood?"

"She was anxious about the race, about Burke. A little tired. She told me she intended to sleep a week when the Derby was over. The last thing on her mind was missing the race or leaving her husband. She's only been married a few weeks, and she's very much in love."

"Um-hmm," the lieutenant said again with maddening calm. "Her ring was found in the stables. You tell me she didn't go in the stables, Mr. Logan, yet she was seen walking toward them early this morning."

"To prove a point to herself, maybe, I can't be sure." His patience was stretching thinner by the second. If she'd waited for him to go with her…if she'd asked him to take her in, stand with her… He'd been the one who'd pulled away, far enough that she'd stopped asking him for anything.

"What sort of point, Mr. Logan?"

"What?"

Patience was an integral part of Hallinger's job. "You said she might have gone inside the stables to prove a point."

"She had an accident a few years ago and was afraid of horses. Over the past few weeks she's been trying to win out over it. Damn it, what difference does it make why she went in? She was there, and now she's missing."

"I work better with details."

When the phone rang, Burke jumped. His face was gray with strain when he lifted the receiver. "Yes?" With a muttered oath, he offered it to Hallinger. "It's for you."

"They're going to find her, Burke." Travis touched a hand to Burke's shoulder as he passed. "You've got to hold on to that."

"It's wrong. It's very wrong, I can feel it." It was welling up inside him; beyond the first panic, beyond the lingering fear, was a dread, a certainty. "If they don't find her soon, it's going to be too late. I've got to get out of here. Will you stay in case a call comes in?"

"Sure."

Hallinger watched Burke walk to the door and simply gestured for one of his men to follow.

* * *

She must have slept. Erin woke from the nightmare soaked with sweat and shivering with cold. She murmured for Burke and tried to reach out, but her arms wouldn't move.

It wasn't just a dream, she realized as she closed her eyes and took deep breaths to stem another wave of panic. How long? Oh, God, how long? Perhaps they were just going to leave her here to go mad or slowly starve to death.

She wouldn't go mad, because she would think of Burke. She would close her eyes and remember how it felt to lie beside him at night with the moonlight coming through the windows and his body warm against hers. She would think about the way he would kiss her in that way he had—that slow, devastating way that made her bones melt and her mind go dim. She could taste him. Even now she could taste him and feel the way his hand felt as he brushed it over her cheek and into her hair.

He had such wonderful hands, so strong and hard. They were always so steady, always so sure. Sometimes at night she'd reach for his hand and hold it against her cheek just to have it there. She didn't think he ever knew.

If she concentrated hard enough, she could almost feel his hand against her cheek now. She could hold it there as long as she wanted.

When her eyes grew accustomed to the dark, she could see his head on the pillow beside hers. His profile was such a handsome one, with its firm jaw and the sharp planes of his cheeks. She liked it when it was shadowed just a bit with beard. Had she ever told him that? He was such a pleasure to look at.

And if she was careful, she could cuddle close, not waking him. The scent of his skin would lull her to sleep. He always smelled as she'd thought a man should, without the sweetening of colognes. So she could cuddle close, and sometimes he would shift closer, his arm stretching lazily over her waist. Those were the best times, when she could murmur that she loved him. She'd told herself that if he heard it enough times in his sleep he would begin to believe it.

So Erin kept her eyes closed and thought only of Burke. After a time, she slept again.

It was nearly three, but Burke sat in the same chair. He'd gone out for only an hour, driving to the track with some wild hope that he would find Erin waiting for him. He'd prowled the stables and badgered the stable boys and grooms with the same questions the police had already asked.

But there was no Erin, nor any sign of her.

So he'd come back, to pace the parlor, haunt the bedroom and ignore the coffee that Travis poured for him. For the past hour he'd sat unmoving, staring at the phone.

He'd told Travis to go, to get some sleep, and had been ignored. It reminded him that there had only been one other person in his life who had stuck by him. If he lost her... He couldn't think of that. He knew that luck could change, could turn cruel like a change in the wind. But not with Erin.

She hadn't had her chance yet, not a real one, to see everything there was. Maybe he'd been wrong to lock her in so quickly, to bind her to him. But she still had so much life, so much energy. Why was it he couldn't get past that one sick thought that whatever was happening to her now was because of him?

When the phone rang, he grabbed the receiver with both

hands. "Logan." The voice in his ear was thick with liquor, but he understood. And his heart began to thud. "Where is she?"

"I don't want no trouble. Spiking the horse was one thing, but I don't want no trouble."

"Fine. Tell me where she is." He glanced up to see Travis beside him, waiting.

"I didn't want no part of it. He'll kill me if he finds out I'm talking to you."

"Just tell me where she is and I'll take care of it."

"Kept her at the track, in the van. I don't know what he's going to do. Kill her, maybe."

"What van? What van, damn it?"

"I ain't having no part in murder."

When the phone went dead, Burke simply dropped it and rose. "She's at the track. They're holding her in a van."

"I'll call the police and be right behind you."

He drove like a maniac, ignoring red lights and speed limits. *Kill her, maybe.* Those three words drummed in his head over and over so that he didn't notice the speedometer hovering at a hundred and ten. The streets were deserted. People were asleep, anticipating the race tomorrow. Some would already be camped on the infield grass.

He prayed that Erin was asleep as well. And when she woke he would be there.

Gravel spit from under the tires as he braked behind the stables. Vans were parked there for trainers, for owners who preferred to stay close to their horses, for grooms and hands who could afford a little luxury.

He only needed to find one.

He started across the lot when he heard steps behind him. Fists clenched and murder on his mind, he whirled.

"Easy, lad," Paddy told him. "Travis called me."

He nodded briefly, though in the moonlight he could see that the old man hadn't slept, either. "Durnam's van. Which is it?"

"Durnam? Travis said you didn't know which."

"Call it a hunch. Which one is Durnam's?"

"The big black one there." Paddy turned as he heard the whine of sirens. "The police are coming." But Burke was already racing to the black van.

"Erin!" The door held fast. For a moment he thought he could tear it off with his bare hands.

"Use this." Paddy handed him a crowbar. "When Travis called and filled me in, I thought we'd have use for it."

Without hesitation, Burke began to pry the door open, all the time calling to her. He wanted her to know it was him. He couldn't stand the thought of her having one more instant of fear. The metal groaned, fought back, then gave. Burke gripped the crowbar like a weapon as he jumped inside. He shoved away the plywood partition that separated the back of the van from the cab.

"Erin?" There was no answer, no sound. What if he was too late? Burke turned the crowbar in his hands, wiping sweat on metal. "Erin, it's all right. I've come to take you out of here." He cursed the lack of light and dropped to his hands and knees. He saw her then, curled in a corner in the rear.

He was with her in an instant, but he was almost afraid to touch her. His hand went to her cheek first. So cold, so still. "Erin." In a fit of rage, he tore the gag away. When her eyes fluttered open, he nearly wept with relief. "Erin, it's all right."

But when he reached for her she cringed, making small sounds in her throat.

"It's all right," he murmured. "I'm not going to let anyone hurt you. It's Burke, darling, it's okay now."

"Burke." Her eyes were still glazed with shock, but she said his name.

"That's right, and I'm going to take you out of here." He shifted her, cursing under his breath each time she whimpered. Her trembles became shudders that none of his soothing words could halt.

He found the ropes, but when he started to loosen them she cried out. "I'm sorry. I have to get them off. I don't want to hurt you. Can you stay very still?"

She simply turned her face to the wall.

The van shook as men entered, and she pressed back in the corner. "I need a knife." He looked up and saw Lieutenant Hallinger. "Give me a damn knife, then get out. She's terrified."

Hallinger reached in his pocket with one hand and signaled his men back with the other.

"Just hold on, Irish, it's all over now." He hurt her. He could feel each jerk and tremble inside his own body as he cut through the bonds. Both his skin and hers were damp before he had freed her feet as well. "I'm going to pick you up and carry you out. Just stay still."

"My arms." She bit her lip, as even the gentlest touch sent the pain throbbing.

"I know." As carefully as he could, he lifted her up. She moaned and pressed her face against his shoulder.

When they stepped outside, the lot was bright with lights. Erin squeezed her burning eyes shut. She couldn't think beyond the pain and fear, and concentrated on the sound of Burke's voice.

"You stay the hell away from her," he said very quietly, his eyes on Hallinger.

"I called an ambulance." Travis stepped between Burke and the police. "It's here now. Paddy and I will follow you."

As if in a dream, Erin felt herself laid down. The light was still too bright, so she kept her eyes closed. There were voices, too many voices, but she focused in on the only one that mattered. She jolted as she felt something cool over the raw skin of her wrist, but Burke stroked her hair and never stopped talking to her.

He didn't know what he said. Promises, vows, nonsense. But he could see the dried blood on her wrists and ankles and the bruises that ran up her arms. Each time she winced, he thought of Durnam. And how he would kill him.

"In the stables," she murmured. "I heard them in the stables, talking about drugging the horse."

"It doesn't matter." Burke kept stroking her hair.

"In the stables," she repeated in a voice that was thin and tended to float. "I couldn't get away. I tried."

"You're safe now. Just lie still."

They wouldn't let him go with her. Erin was wheeled away the moment they reached the hospital, and Burke was left helpless and hurting in the hallway.

"She's going to be all right." Travis laid a hand on his shoulder.

Burke nodded. The ambulance attendants had already assured him of that. Her wrists were the worst of her physical injuries. They would heal, just as the bruises would fade. But no one knew how badly she'd been scarred emotionally.

"Stay with her. There's something I have to do."

"Burke, you'll do her more good here. And yourself."

"Just stay with her," he repeated, then strode out through the wide glass doors.

He kept his mind carefully blank as he drove out to Durnam's farm. The rage was there, but he held it, knowing it would cloud his thinking. So he thought of nothing, and his mind stayed as cool as the early-morning air.

The thirty-minute drive took him fifteen, but still the police were faster. Burke slammed out of his car in front of Durnam's palatial stone house and faced Hallinger once again.

"Thought I'd see you here tonight." Hallinger lit one of the five cigarettes he allowed himself—which was five more than his wife knew about. "Figured a sharp man like you would have already put it together that Durnam was the one who had your horse drugged."

"Yeah, I put that together. Where is he?"

"He's my guest tonight." Hallinger blew out smoke, then leaned against the hood of Burke's car. If the footbath didn't work, he was going to have to go see the damned podiatrist. "You know, sometimes cops have brains, too. We were here questioning Durnam when the call came in that you were on your way to the track to get your wife."

"Why?"

"Well, assuming that your wife's disappearance had something to do with the trouble last week, which was a big assumption, I had to figure out who had the most to gain. That would be Durnam. I take it you'd already worked that out."

"I had everything but proof."

"We've got that now, too. The man was already on the edge. Our call coming in was all it took to push him over. He'd cleaned out his bank account, what was left of it. Knew that, did you?"

"Yeah, I knew that."

"Had his bags packed. But he wasn't going to miss that race tomorrow. Today," Hallinger corrected with a glance up at the lightening sky. "He wanted that Derby win bad.

Funny how people can set their minds on one thing and forget about the consequences. How's your wife?"

"She's hurt. Where are you keeping him?"

"That's police business now, Mr. Logan." He examined his cigarette thoughtfully before taking another drag. "I know how you feel."

Burke cut him off with a look. "You don't know how I feel."

Hallinger nodded slowly. "You're right. And I doubt you're in the mood for advice, but here it is. You haven't been a Boy Scout, Logan." He smiled, a little sourly, when Burke only continued to stare at him. "I make it my business to check details. You've had a few scrapes in your time. Some bad luck and some good. Right now I'd say you've got yourself a good woman and a chance to make things click. Don't blow it on something as pitiful as Charles Durnam. He lost a hell of a lot more than a horse race. Isn't that enough?"

"No." Burke pulled open the door of his car, then paused to turn back. "He gets out in a year, in twenty years—he's dead."

With some regret, Hallinger flipped the butt of his cigarette away. "I'll keep that in mind."

When Erin awoke, she opened her eyes cautiously. The hospital. The wave of relief came as it did every time she awoke to find herself safe. The light beside her bed was still burning. She'd hated to be weak, but had insisted the nurse leave it on even when the sun was coming up.

Burke hadn't been there. She'd fretted and asked for him, but they'd wheeled her to a private room and tucked her into bed, promising he'd be with her soon. She was to sleep, to relax, she wasn't to worry.

But she wanted him.

Listless, she turned her head. There were already flowers in the room. She imagined Travis or Paddy had seen to that. They'd been so kind.

But she wanted Burke.

Shifting in search of comfort, she pushed herself up in bed. And she saw him. He was standing by the window, his back to her. Everything fled but the pleasure of knowing he was there with her.

"Burke."

He turned immediately. His first thought was that she was sitting up and her cheeks were no longer pale. His second thought was that if it hadn't been for him she wouldn't be in a hospital bed with bandages on her wrists. Because she was holding out a hand, he went to her and touched it lightly.

"You're looking better," he said inadequately.

"I'm feeling better. I didn't know you were here."

"I've been around awhile. Do you want anything?"

"I could eat." She smiled and reached for his hand again, but his was in his pocket.

"I'll get the nurse."

"Burke." She stopped him as he reached the door. "It can wait. Look at you, you haven't slept."

"Busy night."

She tried another smile. "Aye, it was all of that. I'm sorry."

His eyes went hard and flat. "Don't. I'll get the nurse."

Alone, Erin lay back on the pillows. Maybe she was still confused and disoriented. He couldn't really be angry with her. With a half sigh, she closed her eyes. Of course he could. There was no telling with men, and with Burke in particular. Whether it was her fault or not, she'd put him through hell. And now she was tying him to a hospital room on the most important day of his life.

When the door opened again she made sure her smile was cheerful, and her voice, though her throat still tended to ache, mirrored it. "You should be at the track. I had no idea it was so late. Did anyone think to bring me a change of clothes? I can be ready in ten minutes."

"You're not going anywhere."

"You don't expect me to miss my first Derby? I know what the doctor said, but—"

"Then you'll know you're not getting up from that bed for twenty-four hours. Don't be stupid."

She opened her mouth, then firmly shut it again. She wouldn't argue with him. She'd been close to death, and that made a person think about how much time was wasted on pettiness. "You're right, of course. I'll just sit here and be pampered while I watch on television." Why didn't he come to her? Why didn't he hold her? Erin kept her lips curved as he turned again to stare out of the window. "You'd better be on your way."

"Where?"

"To the track, of course. It's nearly noon. You've already missed the morning."

"I'm staying here."

Her heart did a quick flip, but she shook her head. "Don't be silly. You can't miss this. If I'm to be shut up here it's bad enough. At least I can have the pleasure of watching you step into the winner's circle. There's nothing for you to do here."

He thought of how helpless he'd felt through the night. Of how helpless he felt now. "No, I suppose there isn't."

"Then off with you," she told him, forcing her voice to be light.

"Yeah." He rubbed his hands over his face.

"And I don't want to see you back here until you've had some rest."

She lifted her face for a kiss, but his lips only brushed over her brow. "See you later."

"Burke." He was already out of reach. "You're going to win."

With a nod, he closed the door behind him. He leaned against the wall, almost too exhausted to stand, far too exhausted to think. He didn't give a damn about the Derby or any other race. All he could see, playing over and over in his mind, was Erin curled in the corner of that van, cringing away from him.

She'd bounced back, smiling and talking as though nothing had happened. But he could still see the white bandages on her wrists.

He was afraid to touch her, afraid she'd cringe away again. Or, if she didn't, that he'd hurt her. He was afraid to look at her too long because he'd see that glazed shock in her eyes again. He was afraid that if he didn't gather her close, keep her close, that she'd slip away from him, that he would lose her as he'd nearly lost her only hours before.

But she was urging him to go, telling him she didn't need him beside her. All she needed was a win, a blanket of red roses and a trophy. He'd damn well give them to her.

She hadn't realized she would be nervous. But even watching the preliminaries, the interviews, the discussions on television, kept her pulse racing. When she saw Burke caught by the cameras as he stepped out of the stables, she laughed and hugged her pillow. Oh, if she could just be there with him, holding on. But he avoided the reporter, leaving Erin disappointed.

She'd wanted to hear him, to see his face on the screen so that they could laugh about it later.

Then it was the reporter facing the camera, recounting the story that had unfolded since the Bluegrass Stakes. It pleased her to hear that Burke's name had been cleared absolutely and that Double Bluff was considered the favorite in the Run for the Roses.

She listened, trying to be dispassionate as he talked about her kidnapping and Durnam's arrest. The groom had been picked up sleeping off a bottle in a stall. Apparently it hadn't taken much encouragement for him to spill the entire story. There were pictures of the van, with its broken door and police barriers, that she had to force herself to look at.

It almost amused her to be told that she was resting comfortably. Somehow the reporter made it all sound like a grand adventure, something out of a mystery novel—the lady in distress, the villain and the hero. She wrinkled her nose. However much she might consider Burke a hero, she didn't care to think of herself as a lady in distress.

She let it pass as she watched the horses being spotlighted as they were led from the paddock. There was Double Bluff, as big and as handsome as ever. Double Bluff, the three-year-old from Three Aces. Owners Burke and Erin Logan. She smiled at that. Though of course it was Burke's horse and the news people had made a mistake, it still gave her a good feeling to see her name flash on the screen with Burke's.

She laughed at herself again because her palms were getting sweaty. The track was just as she'd known it would be, filled to capacity. The camera panned over Dorothy Gainsfield. Erin gave herself the satisfaction of sticking out her tongue.

Then it focused on Burke, and her heart broke a little.

He looked so tired. Worn to the bone. That was why he'd been so distant before. The man was exhausted. When he'd rested and had time to get his bearings, things would be right again.

"I love you, Burke," she told him, rubbing her cheek against the pillow. "Loving you is what got me through."

Then the screen flashed back to the horses. It was nearly post time.

There was the blare of the trumpet and the roar of the crowd. Again Erin found herself tempted to jump out of bed and hurry to the track. If it hadn't been for the baby, she would have ignored the doctor and done just that. Instead she forced herself to be patient.

"We'll go to our first Derby together," she murmured as she placed a hand on her stomach. "Next year, the three of us will go."

The bell sounded, and for the next two minutes she didn't take her eyes off the screen. It seemed to her that Double Bluff was running with a vengeance. And perhaps he was. Perhaps Burke had transformed some of his emotions to the horse, for the colt ran like fury.

When he broke from the pack early, Erin held her breath. It was too soon. She knew the jockey had been instructed to hold him back the first half mile. There was no holding back today. Her first concern evaporated in pure excitement as she watched him run. He was glorious, angry and unstoppable. It was as if the horse himself wanted vindication and perhaps revenge.

He clung to the rail, taking the turns hard and close. Travis's Apollo held back by a length. The Pentel colt, under a new rider, was coming up fast on the outside. And the crowd was on its feet. Erin was shouting, but was unaware of it even after the nurse came in.

As he came down the backstretch he poured on more speed, impossibly more, so that even the announcer's voice cracked with excitement. Two lengths, then three, then three and a half. He went under the wire as if he was alone on the oval.

"He never gave up the lead." Erin brushed her palms over her cheeks to dry them. "Not once."

"Congratulations, Mrs. Logan. I'd say you've just had some of the best medicine on the market."

"The very best." But her fingers curled into the sheets as she waited for the official announcement. In her mind she could picture it, the weighing in, the certification. It seemed to take forever, but then the numbers flashed on the board. "The very, very best. There's Burke." She gripped the nurse's hand. "He's worked so hard for this, waited so long. Oh, I wish I could be with him."

She watched the cameramen and reporters vie for angles as Burke and his trainer grouped in the winner's circle. Why wasn't he smiling? she wondered as she wiped another tear away. She saw him reach up and shake his jockey's hand but couldn't hear whatever it was he said.

"It's a good day for Three Aces." A reporter stuck a microphone in Burke's face. "This must make up for the disqualification last week, Mr. Logan."

"It doesn't begin to make up for it." He patted the colt's neck. "I think Double Bluff proved himself a champion here today and proved my trust in his team, but this race was run for my wife." He pulled a rose from the blanket covering his horse. "Excuse me."

"That was a lovely thing to say," the nurse murmured.

"Aye." Still, as Erin watched the jockey hold the cup over his head, she wondered why she felt so lost.

Chapter 12

They flew home as soon as Erin was released from the hospital, but she didn't feel like celebrating. Everything should have been right. Burke's reputation had been cleared, his prize colt had won the Derby with a track record, and she was safe. So why was it everything was wrong?

She knew Burke could be aloof, that he could be arrogant and hardheaded. Those were three ridiculous reasons to love a man, but they were reasons nonetheless. What she hadn't known was that he could be both withdrawn and distant. He never touched her. In fact, as the first few days passed, Erin realized he was going out of his way to avoid any opportunity to touch her. He came to bed late and rose early. He spent a great deal more time out of the house and away than he spent at home.

She tried to tell herself he was just gearing up for the Preakness—the second jewel of the Triple Crown—but she knew it wasn't true.

With too much time left to herself to think, she began to remember the words she'd heard on her wedding day. *Men are easily charmed, and just as easily bored.*

Was that it? Was he bored with her? Trying to find the answer, she took stock of herself. Her face was the same. Maybe she was a little hollow-eyed, but those things came with worry and restless nights. Her body was still firm, though she knew that would change in a matter of weeks.

And what then? she wondered. When she told him about the baby, would he turn away completely? No, she couldn't believe that of him. Burke would never turn his back on his own child. But on her? If he was tired of her now, how would he feel when she began to round and swell?

She wanted to look forward to the changes in her body, to the signs that her baby was growing and healthy. But would those same changes push Burke only farther away? How could they not, if they didn't reestablish their intimacy? Since the physical change couldn't be avoided, Erin decided she'd better do something about seducing her husband now.

She chose the wine herself. That was something she was pleased to have developed a knack for. She wouldn't do any more than play at drinking it herself, but it was the atmosphere that mattered.

And candles. She set dozens of them around the bedroom, lighting them so that their scent would be as much a part of the mood as the flames. She chose the same gown she'd worn on her wedding night, the white lace that made her feel like a bride. He'd thought her lovely once, desirable once. He would again. She picked the Chopin he'd played on their first night together and wondered if he would remember.

Tonight would be another first, another beginning. When

they'd loved each other, when they'd finally come back together as they were meant to be, she would tell him about
the baby. Then they would talk about the future.

He'd taken himself to the wire before he climbed the
stairs. Burke found it easiest to wear himself out before he
slipped into bed beside her. That way it wasn't as difficult
to stop himself from pulling her against him. It wasn't as
difficult to ignore the fact that she was right there next to
him, soft and lovely and incredibly sweet. It wasn't as difficult to will himself to sleep and pretend he didn't want her.

But it was all a lie.

It was killing him to be with her and yet not to be with
her. Still, he knew no other way to wean her away, to give
her time to make a choice. She had secrets she was keeping from him. He could see them in her eyes. There were
times he wanted to take her by the shoulders and shake her
until she told him. Then he would remember what she had
gone through because of him, and he didn't touch her at all.

She'd been the perfect wife since they'd come back.
Never demanding, never questioning, never arguing. He
wanted Erin back.

Then he stepped into the bedroom and his limbs went
weak.

"I thought you'd never come up." She crossed to him,
holding out a hand. "You're working too hard."

"There's a lot to be done."

When he didn't take her hand, she curled her fingers
into her palm but made herself take the final step. "There's
more to living than horses and the next race."

Involuntarily he reached up to touch her hair. "I thought
you'd gone to bed."

"I've been waiting for you." She brought a hand to his

cheek as she rose on her toes to kiss him. "I've missed you. Missed being alone with you. Come to bed, Burke. Make love with me."

"I haven't finished downstairs."

"It can wait." Smiling, she began to unbutton his shirt. She was sure, almost sure, that she felt his response, his need. "We haven't had an evening alone in a long time."

It only took the feel of her bandages rubbing against his skin. "I'm sorry. I only came up to see if you were all right. You should get some rest."

The rejection stung her, and she stepped back even as he did. "You don't want me anymore, do you?"

Not want her? He was nearly eaten up with wanting. "I want you to take care of yourself, that's all. You've been through a lot of strain."

"Aye, and you. That's why we need some time together."

He touched his fingers lightly to her cheek. "Get some sleep."

She stared at the closed door before turning away blindly to blow out the candles.

Erin closed herself in the office and buried herself in columns of figures. Those, at least, she could understand. With numbers, when you added two and two, you could be assured of a logical answer. Life, she'd discovered, and Burke in particular, wasn't quite that simple.

When the call came from Travis that Dee was in labor, she found herself not only pleased for her cousin but for herself and the diversion. Scribbling a hasty note, she left it on her desk. If Burke bothered to look for her, he'd find it. If he didn't…then it didn't matter where she was.

She'd learned something else about marriage. Both husband and wife should stand on their own. In the best of worlds this was offset by an interdependence—a sharing, a love of each other and a contentment in each other's company. In the not-so-best, it simply meant survival. She was and always had been a survivor.

Still, she watched the house retreat as she drove toward the main road. Such a special place it was, the kind she'd always dreamed of living in. The grass was green now, and the flowers were in bloom. It was hard to believe she could finally have something so beautiful and still be unhappy. But it could be so much more than a place to live, she thought, just as her marriage could be so much more than an agreement between two logical adults. In time, Burke would have to decide how much more he would permit it to be.

He was dealing with his own devils when he came into the house. All morning and half the afternoon he'd been unable to erase from his mind how lovely Erin had looked the night before, how hard it had been to walk away from her and from his own feelings. He was no longer sure he was doing her a favor, and he knew for a fact he was killing himself.

Maybe the time had come for them to talk. Plain words, plain thinking. He didn't believe himself capable of much else. It hadn't taken him long to realize he was useless without her. How that had come to be, and why, didn't seem to matter. It simply was. But nagging at him, gnawing at him, was the question of what she would be without him. He'd never given her a chance to find out.

So they'd face off. That was something he understood. Now was as good a time as any.

He glanced in her office and, finding it empty, passed it by. In the atrium, Rosa was watering geraniums. He paused there, wishing he didn't continually find himself uncomfortable when he caught her going about her household duties.

"Rosa, is Erin upstairs?"

Rosa glanced up but continued her watering. "The *señora* went out a few hours ago."

"Out?" The panic was absurd. So he told himself even as it choked him. "Where?"

"She didn't tell me."

"Did she take her car?"

"I believe so." When he swore and turned away, Rosa moved to a pot of asters. "Burke?"

"Yes?"

She smiled a little and set down her watering can. "You have little more patience now than you did when you were ten."

"I don't want her left alone."

"Yet you do so continually." She lifted her brow at his look. "It's difficult to pretend not to see what's under my nose. Your wife's unhappy. So are you."

"Erin's fine. And so am I."

"You would say the same when you came home with a black eye."

"That was a long time ago."

"It's foolish to think either of us have forgotten. To have a future, it's necessary to face the past."

"What's the point in this, Rosa?"

She did something she hadn't done since they'd been children. Crossing to him, she touched a hand to his face. "She's stronger than you think, my brother. And you, you aren't nearly as tough."

"I'm not ten anymore, Rosa."

"No, but in some ways you were easier then."

"I was never easy."

"It was the life that wasn't easy. You've changed that."

"Maybe."

"Your mother would be proud of you. She would," Rosa insisted when he started to back away.

"She never had a chance."

"No, but you do. And you gave one to me."

He made a quick gesture of dismissal. "I gave you a job."

"And the first decent home I've ever known," Rosa added. "Before you go, answer one question. Why do you let me stay? The truth, Burke."

He didn't want to answer, but she'd always had a way of looking straight and waiting for as long as it took. Maybe he owed her the truth. Maybe he owed it to himself. "Because she cared about you. And so do I."

She smiled, then went back to watering. "Your wife won't wait as long for an answer. She's impatient, like you."

"Rosa, why do you stay?"

She fluffed the leaves of a fern. "Because I love you. So does your wife. If you don't mind, I would like to pick some flowers for the sitting room."

"Yeah, sure." He left Rosa there, watering plants, and went back to Erin's office. It was the first time he'd asked himself or allowed himself to ask why he'd permitted Rosa to stay. Why he'd provided her with a job in order that she could keep her pride. She was family. It was just that simple, and just that hard to accept. She'd been right, too, when she'd said that Erin wouldn't wait so long for an answer.

He wanted Erin there, where they could sit down together. There where he could talk to her about his feelings. That would be a first, he admitted.

Restless, he began to push through the papers on her desk. She was a hell of a bookkeeper, he thought ruefully.

Everything in neat little piles, all the figures in tidy rows. A man could hardly complain about having a conscientious wife. It certainly shouldn't make him want to gather up all the books and papers and dump them in the trash.

It was the doctor bill that made him frown. All medical expenses from her stay in Kentucky should have been addressed to him. Yet this one was clearly marked to her. Annoyed, he picked it up with the intention of dealing with it himself. He wanted her to have no reminders. But the doctor's address wasn't in Kentucky; it was in Maryland. And the doctor was an obstetrician.

Obstetrician? Burke lowered himself very carefully in her chair. The words "pregnancy test" seemed to jump out at him. Pregnant? Erin was pregnant? That couldn't be, because he would have known. She would have told him. Yet he had the paper in his hand. The paper stated "positive" clearly enough, and the test was dated almost a month earlier.

Erin was pregnant. And she hadn't told him. What else hadn't she told him? He sprang up again to push through the other papers as if he'd find the answers there. It was then he found her note, hastily scribbled. *Burke, I've gone to the hospital. I don't know how long it will take.*

As he stared at the note, he felt all the blood drain out of his face.

"Oh, I don't see how Dee can be so calm and patient!"

Paddy turned a page in the magazine he was pretending to read. "You can't hurry babies into the world."

"It seems to be taking forever." Erin paced the waiting room again. "My palms are sweating, and she looked like she could take a walk in the park. It's scary."

"Having babies?" He chuckled a little and sneaked a

peek at his watch while Erin wasn't looking. "Dee's an old hand at this."

Erin laid a hand on her stomach. "Was she this way when she had the first one? I mean, the first one would be the scariest. It's like taking everything on faith that nothing's going to go wrong."

"Dee's a trouper."

"Aye." She prayed she would be as well when her time came. "It must make a difference, having Travis with her through it all." She'd seen the way he'd been with Dee, standing beside the bed, holding her hand, talking, making her laugh, timing her contractions. Total support, total commitment. "I wonder, Paddy, do you think most men would do that?" Would Burke?

"I'd say when a man loves a woman the way Travis loves Dee he wouldn't be anywhere else right now. Lass, you're going to wear a rut in the floor."

"I can't sit still," she muttered. "I'm going to go downstairs and see if I can buy some flowers. Have them waiting for her."

"That's a fine idea."

"I could bring you some tea."

"You do that. Won't be long now."

He waited until she was out of sight to get up and pace himself.

Downstairs, Burke burst into the hospital like a man possessed. In seconds he had pounced on the admissions clerk. "Where's my wife?"

The clerk swiveled her chair over to her computer. "Name?"

"Logan, Erin Logan."

"When was she admitted?"

"I don't know. A couple of hours ago."

The clerk began to punch buttons. "For what purpose?"

"I—" He wasn't sure he could deal with the purpose. "She's pregnant."

"Maternity?" The clerk continued to punch. "I'm sorry, Mr. Logan. We don't have your wife."

"I know she's here, damn it. Where—" Continuing to swear, he pulled the paper out of his pocket. "Dr. Morgan. I want to see Dr. Morgan."

"Dr. Morgan's in delivery with another patient. You can check at the nurse's station on the fifth floor, but—"

She shrugged when Burke raced away. Expectant fathers, she thought. They were always crazy.

Burke jammed a fist against the elevator button. He hated hospitals. He'd lost his mother in one. Only days before, he'd watched Erin lie in one, and now...

"Burke, I didn't expect you."

He turned to see Erin walking toward him with a huge arrangement of rosebuds and baby's breath. Her hair was pulled back and her cheeks were glowing. The flowers nearly tipped to the floor when he grabbed her shoulders.

"What the hell are you doing?" he demanded.

"Burke, you're crushing them."

"I'll crush more than a bunch of flowers. I want you to tell me what you're doing."

"I'm taking them upstairs. If they survive. I think Dee will appreciate them more if they're not mangled."

"Dee?" He shook his head but didn't manage to clear it. "What are you talking about?"

"What are *you* talking about?" she countered. "It doesn't seem so strange to me to buy flowers for someone who's having babies."

"Dee? You came here because Dee's delivering?"

"Well, of course. Didn't you see my note?"

"I saw your note," he muttered. Taking her arm, he pulled her into the elevator. "It wasn't very clear."

"I was in a hurry. I wish they'd had more roses," she murmured. "Seems when you're having twins you should have twice as many flowers." She buried her face in them a moment, then smiled at him. "I'm glad you came. It'll mean a lot to Dee."

Struggling for calm, he stepped out when the doors opened again. "How is she?"

"She's perfect. Paddy and I are a wreck, but she's perfect."

"You shouldn't be on your feet." He took the flowers because he was abruptly afraid for her to carry anything. "You shouldn't be getting yourself worked up."

"Don't be silly." She turned into the waiting room, not to find Paddy pacing but to find him dancing.

"One of each!" he shouted to both of them. "She's gone and had one of each."

"Oh, Paddy!" Laughing, she flung herself at him and let him whirl her around. "She's all right? And the babies? Everyone's all right?"

"Everyone's fit as a fiddle, so the nurse told me. They'll be bringing them all out in a minute so we can have a peek. A fine day to you, Burke. A fine, fine day."

"Paddy. Erin, why don't you sit down?"

"Sit?" She shook her head with another laugh and hooked her arm through Paddy's. "I couldn't sit if my legs fell off. Paddy and I are going dancing, aren't we, Paddy?"

"That we are." He put his chin up and began to hum. Recognizing the tune, Erin joined in as their feet began to move.

Burke stood holding a bushel of roses and watched them. He hadn't heard her laugh like that for too long. He hadn't seen her smile just that way. He wanted to toss the flowers aside and gather her up. Snatch her away, take her home. Hold her for hours.

"Here she is!" Paddy did another quick jig as Dee was wheeled out. "Here's my little girl. Look at this." He had to pull out his handkerchief and wipe his eyes. "They're beautiful, lass. Just like you."

"What am I?" Travis wanted to know. "Chopped liver?"

"You did a fine job." Erin moved over to kiss his cheek. "A boy and a girl." She looked down at the two bundles beside her cousin. "And so tiny."

"They'll grow quick enough." Dee turned her head to the right, then the left, to nuzzle them. "The doctor said they have everything they should have. Lord, they came out squalling, both of them. Didn't they, Travis?"

"They have their mother's disposition."

"It's lucky you are I've my hands full. Burke, it's good of you to come. This is the best time to have family around."

"Are you okay?" He felt both foolish and awkward as he passed the flowers to Travis. "Is there anything you want?"

"A ham sandwich," she said with a sigh. "A huge one. But I'm afraid they'll make me wait just a little while yet."

"I'm sorry, we'll have to take Mrs. Grant now. Evening visiting hours start at seven."

"Paddy, bring the children back tonight."

"No children under twelve are allowed, Mrs. Grant," the nurse said as she began to push her away. Dee merely smiled and mouthed the request again.

"She looked wonderful, didn't she?" Erin mused.

"She's a Thoroughbred, my Dee. Always has been." Paddy stuffed his handkerchief back in his pocket. "Well, I'd better get home and think up a way to smuggle that brood in here tonight."

"Let me know if you need any help."

"That I will, lass." He kissed both her cheeks. As he walked down the hall, he jumped up and clicked his heels.

"You've been on your feet long enough," Burke said tersely. "I'll drive you home."

"I've got my car."

"Leave it." He took her arm again.

"That's silly. I'll just—"

"Leave it," he repeated, pulling her into the elevator.

"Fine." She bit the word off. "Since you're sure you can bear to be in the same car with me." She crossed her arms and stared at the doors. Burke stuck his hands in his pockets and scowled.

Neither of them spoke again until Erin stormed into the atrium. "If it's all the same to you, I'm going upstairs. And you, you can take your foul mood out to the stables with the rest of the dumb animals."

He wondered that her neck didn't break from holding her head that high. Burke gave himself thirty seconds to calm down. When it didn't work, he strode up the stairs after her.

"Sit down." He spit out the order as he slammed the bedroom door behind him. Erin simply narrowed her eyes and crossed her arms. "I said sit down."

"And I say to hell with you."

That was all it took. Before she could evade him, he had scooped her up and plunked her down on the bed.

"All right, now I'm sitting. Don't tell me you actually want to have a conversation with me?" She tossed her hair back, then slowly crossed her legs. "I'm all aflutter." She saw his hand close into a fist and angled her chin. "Go ahead, pop me one. You've been wanting to for days."

"Don't tempt me."

"It was quite clear last night I couldn't even do that."

She pulled her shoes off and tossed them aside. "If you're so fired up to talk to me, then talk."

"Yeah, I want to talk to you, and I want some straight answers." But instead of asking, he shoved his hands back into his pockets and circled the room. Where to start? he wondered. His fingers brushed over the ring he'd carried for days. Perhaps that was the best place. Burke pulled it out and held it in the palm of his hand.

"You found it." Erin's first burst of pleasure was almost blanked out by the look in his eyes. "You didn't tell me."

"You didn't ask."

"No, I didn't, because I was sick about it. Dropping it in the stables was stupid."

"Why did you?"

"Because I couldn't think of anything else. I knew I couldn't get away from them. They were already tying my hands." She was looking at her ring and didn't see him wince. "I guess I thought someone would find it and take it to you, and you'd know. Though I don't know what I expected you could do about it. Why haven't you given it back to me?"

"Because I wanted to give you time to decide if you wanted it or not." He took her hand and dropped the ring in it. "It's your choice."

"Always was," she said slowly, but she didn't put the ring on. "You're still angry with me because of what happened?"

"I was never angry with you because of what happened."

"You've been giving a champion imitation of it, then."

"It was my fault." He turned to her then, and for the first time began to let go of the rage. "Twenty hours. You lay in the dark for twenty hours because of me."

The words could still bring on a cold flash, but she was more intrigued by Burke's reaction. "I thought it was because of Durnam. You've never seemed willing to talk it through, to let me explain to you exactly what happened. If you'd—"

"You could have died." There was really nothing else but that. No explanations, no calm recounting, could change that one fact. "I sat in that damn hotel room, waiting for the phone to ring, terrified that it would and there was nothing, nothing I could do. When I found you, saw what they'd done to you...your wrists."

"They're healing." She stood to reach out to him, but he withdrew immediately. "Why do you do this? Why do you keep pulling away from me? Even at the hospital you weren't there. You couldn't even stay with me."

"I went to kill Durnam."

"Oh, Burke, no."

"I was too late for that." The bitterness was still there, simmering with a foul taste he'd almost grown used to. "They had him by then, where I couldn't get to him. All I could do was stand in that hospital room and watch you. And think of how close I'd come to losing you. The longer I stood there, the more I thought about the way I'd dragged you in with me right from the beginning, never giving you a choice, never letting you know what kind of man you were tied to."

"That's enough. Do you really believe I'm some weak-minded female who can't say yes or no? I had a choice and I chose you. And not for your bloody money."

It was her turn to rage around the room. "I'm sick to death of having to find ways to prove that I love you. I'll not be denying that I wanted more out of life than a few acres of dirt and someone else's dishes to wash. And I'm not ashamed of it. But hear this, Burke Logan, I'd have found a way to get it for myself."

"I never doubted it."

"You think I married you for this house?" She threw up her arms as if to encompass every room. "Well, set a match to it, then, it doesn't matter to me. You think it's for all those fine stocks and bonds? Take them all, take every last scrap of paper and put it on one spin of the wheel. Whether you win or lose makes no difference to me. And these?" She pulled open her dresser and yanked out boxes of jewelry. "These pretty shiny things? Well, take them to hell with you. I love you—God himself knows why, you thickheaded, miserable excuse for a man. Not know what kind of man I married, is it?" She tossed the jewelry aside and stormed around the room. "I know well enough who and what you are. More fool I am for not giving a damn and loving you anyway."

"You don't know anything," he said quietly. "But if you'd sit down I'll tell you."

"You won't tell me anything I don't know. Do you think I care you grew up poor without a father? Oh, you don't need to look that way. Rosa told me weeks ago. Do you think I care if you lied or cheated or stole? I know what it is to be poor, to need, but I had my family. Can't I feel sorry for the boy without thinking less of the man?"

"I don't know." She rocked him, but then it seemed she never failed to do so. "Sit down, Erin, please."

"I'm sick to death of sitting. Just like I'm sick to death of walking on eggs with you. I *did* nearly die. I thought I was going to die, and all I could think was how much time we'd wasted being at odds. I swore if we were back together there'd be no more fighting. Now for days I've held my temper, I've said nothing when you turn away from me. But no more. If you've any more questions, Burke Logan, you'd best out with them, because I've plenty more to say myself."

"Why didn't you tell me you were pregnant?"

That stopped her cold. Her mouth fell open, and for all her talk about not sitting, she lowered herself onto the bed. "How do you know?"

Burke drew out the paper he'd found and handed it to her. "You've known for a month."

"Aye."

"Didn't you intend to tell me, or were you just going to take care of it yourself?"

"I meant to tell you, but… What do you mean, take care of it myself? I could hardly keep it a secret when—" She stopped again as the realization hit like a wall. "That's what you thought I'd gone to the hospital for today. You thought I'd gone there to see that there would be no baby." She let the paper slip to the floor as she rose again. "You *are* a bastard, Burke Logan, that you could think that of me."

"What the hell was I supposed to think? You've had a month to tell me."

"I'd have told you the day I found out. I came to tell you. I could hardly wait to get the words out, but you started in on me about the money and the letter from my father. It always came down to the money. I put my heart on a platter for you time after time, and you keep handing it back to me. No more of that, either." She was ashamed of the tears, but more ashamed to wipe them away. "I'll go back to Ireland and have the baby there. Then neither of us will be in your way."

Before she could storm out of the room he asked, "You want the baby?"

"Damn you for a fool, of course I want the baby. It's our baby. We made it our first night together in this bed. I loved you then, with my whole heart, with everything I had. But I don't now. I detest you. I hate you for letting me love you this way and never giving it back to me. Never once taking me in your arms and telling me you loved me."

"Erin—"

"No, don't you dare touch me now. Not now that I've made as big a fool of myself as any woman could." She'd thrown up both hands to ward him off. She couldn't bear to have his pity. "I was afraid you wouldn't want the baby, and me with it when you found out. That wasn't part of the bargain, was it? You wouldn't be so free and easy to come and go if there was a baby to think of."

He remembered the day she'd come to tell him about the baby, and the look in her eyes. Just as he remembered the look in her eyes when she'd left without telling him. He chose his words carefully now, knowing he'd already made enough mistakes.

"Six months ago you'd have been right. Maybe even six weeks ago, but not now. It's time we stopped moving in circles, Irish."

"And do what?"

"It's not easy for me to say what I feel. It's not easy for me to feel it." He approached her cautiously, and when she didn't back away he rested his hands on her shoulders. "I want you, and I want the baby."

She closed her fingers tightly over the ring she still had in her hand. "Why?"

"I didn't think I wanted a family. I swore when I was a kid that I'd never let anyone hurt me the way my mother had been hurt. I'd never let anyone mean so much that the life went out of me when they left. Then I went to Ireland and I met you. I'd still be there if you hadn't come back with me."

"You asked me to come here to keep your books."

"It was as good an excuse as any, for both of us. I didn't want to care about you. I didn't want to need to see you just to get through the day. But that's the way it was. I pulled you into marriage so fast because I didn't want to give you a chance to look around and find someone better."

"Seems to me I'd had chance enough."

"You'd never even been with a man before."

"Do you think I married you because you had a talent in bed?"

He had to laugh at that. "How would you know?"

"I doubt a woman has to bounce around between lovers to know when she's found the right one. Sex is as sorry an excuse to marry someone as money. Maybe we've both been fools, me for thinking you married me for the first, and you for thinking I married you for the second. I've told you why I married you, Burke. Don't you think it's time you told me?"

"I was afraid you'd get away."

She sighed and tried to make herself accept that. "All right, then, that'll do." She held her wedding ring out to him. "This belongs on my finger. You should remember which one."

He took it, and her hand. The choice had been given, to her and to him. It wasn't every day a man was given a second chance. "I love you, Erin." He saw her eyes fill and cursed himself for holding that away from both of them for so long.

"Say it again," she demanded. "Until you get used to it."

The ring slipped easily onto her finger. "I love you, Erin, and I always will." When he gathered her into his arms, he felt all the gears of his life click into place. "You mean everything to me. Everything." Their lips met and clung. It was just as sweet, just as powerful as the first time. "We're going to put down roots."

"We already have." Smiling, she took his face in her hands. "You just didn't notice."

Cautiously he laid his palm on her stomach. "How soon?"

"Seven months, a little less. There will be three of us for Christmas." She let out a whoop when he lifted her into his arms.

"I won't let you down." He swore it as he buried his face in her hair.

"I know."

"I want you off your feet." As he started to lay her on the bed, she grabbed his shirt.

"That's fine with me, as long as you get off yours as well."

He nipped her lower lip. "I've always said, Irish, you're a woman after my heart."

* * * * *

IRISH REBEL

To Nancy Jackson and Karen Solem,
who took a chance on a very green writer
and made her part of the Silhouette family.

And to readers who took the story
of a young Irish woman into their hearts.

Chapter 1

As far as Brian Donnelly was concerned, a vindictive woman had invented the tie to choke the life out of man so that he would then be so weak she could just grab the tail of it and lead him wherever she wanted him to go. Wearing one made him feel stifled and edgy, and just a little awkward.

But strangling ties, polished shoes and a dignified attitude were required in fancy country clubs with their slick floors and crystal chandeliers and vases crowded with flowers that looked as if they'd been planted on Venus.

He'd have preferred to be in the stables, or on the track or in a good smoky pub where you could light up a cigar and speak your mind. That's where a man met a man for business, to Brian's thinking.

But Travis Grant was paying his freight, and a hefty price it was to bring him all the way from Kildare to America.

Training racehorses meant understanding them, working

with them, all but living with them. People were necessary, of course, in a kind of sideways fashion. But country clubs were for owners, and those who played at being racetrackers as a hobby—or for the prestige and profit.

A glance around the room told Brian that most here in their glittery gowns and black ties had never spent any quality time shoveling manure.

Still, if Grant wanted to see if he could handle himself in posh surroundings, blend in with the gentry, he'd damn well do it. The job wasn't his yet. And Brian wanted it.

Travis Grant's Royal Meadows was one of the top thoroughbred farms in the country. Over the last decade, it had moved steadily toward becoming one of the best in the world. Brian had seen the American's horses run in Kildare at Curragh. Each one had been a beauty. The latest he'd seen only weeks before, when the colt Brian had trained had edged out the Maryland bred by half a neck.

But half a neck was more than enough to win the purse, and his own share of it as trainer. More, it seemed, it had been enough to bring Brian Donnelly to the eye and the consideration of the great Mr. Grant.

So here he was, at himself's invitation, Brian thought, in America at some posh gala in a fancy club where the women all smelled rich and the men looked it.

The music he found dull. It didn't stir him. But at least he had a beer and a fine view of the goings-on. The food was plentiful and as polished and elegant as the people who nibbled on it. Those who danced did so with more dignity than enthusiasm, which he thought was a shame, but who could blame them when the band had as much life as a soggy sack of chips?

Still it was an experience watching the jewels glint and

crystal wink. The head man in Kildare hadn't been the sort to invite his employees to parties.

Old Mahan had been fair enough, Brian mused. And God knew the man loved his horses—as long as they ended by prancing in the winner's circle. But Brian hadn't thought twice about flipping the job away at the chance for this one.

And, well, if he didn't get it, he'd get another. He had a mind to stay in America for a while. If Royal Meadows wasn't his ticket, he'd find another one.

Moving around pleased him, and by doing so, by knowing just when to pack his bag and take a new road, he'd hooked himself up with some of the best horse farms in Ireland.

There was no reason he could see why he couldn't do the same in America. More of the same, he thought. It was a big and wide country.

He sipped his beer, then lifted an eyebrow when Travis Grant came in. Brian recognized him easily, and his wife as well—the Irish woman, he imagined, was part of his edge in landing this position.

The man, Grant, was tall, powerfully built with hair a thick mixture of silver and black. He had a strong face, tanned and weathered by the outdoors. Beside him, his wife looked like a pixie with her small, slim build. Her hair was a sweep of chestnut, as glossy as the coat of a prize thoroughbred.

They were holding hands.

It was a surprising link. His parents had made four children between them, and worked together as a fine and comfortable team. But they'd never been much for public displays of affection, even as mild a one as handholding.

A young man came in behind them. He had the look of his father—and Brian recognized him from the track in Kildare. Brendon Grant, heir apparent. And he looked comfortable with it—as well as the sleek blonde on his arm.

There were five children, he knew—had made it his business to know. A daughter, another son and twins, one of each sort. He didn't expect those who had grown up with privilege to bother themselves overly about the day-to-day running of the farm. He didn't expect that they'd get in his way.

Then she rushed in, laughing.

Something jumped in his belly, in his chest. And for an instant he saw nothing and no one else. Her build was delicate, her face vibrant. Even from a distance he could see her eyes were as blue as the lakes of his homeland. Her hair was flame, a sizzling red that looked hot to the touch and fell, wave after wave, over her bare shoulders.

His heart hammered, three hard and violent strokes, then seemed simply to stop.

She wore something floaty and blue, paler, shades paler than her eyes. What must have been diamonds fired at her ears.

He'd never in his life seen anything so beautiful, so perfect. So unattainable.

Because his throat had gone burning dry, he lifted his beer and was disgusted to realize his hand wasn't quite steady.

Not for you, Donnelly, he reminded himself. Not for you to even dream of. That would be the master's oldest daughter. And the princess of the house.

Even as he thought it, a man with a well-cut suit and pampered tan went to her. The way she offered her hand to him was just cool enough, just aloof enough to have Brian sneering—which was a great deal more comfortable than goggling.

Ah yes, indeed, she was royalty. And knew it.

The other family came in—that would be the twins, Brian thought, Sarah and Patrick. And a pretty pair they were, both tall and slim with roasted chestnut hair. The girl, Sarah—Brian knew she was just eighteen—was laughing, gesturing widely.

The whole family turned toward her, effectively—perhaps purposely—cutting out the man who'd come to pay homage to the princess. But he was a persistent sort, and reaching her, laid his hand on her shoulder. She glanced over, smiled, nodded.

Off to do her bidding, Brian mused as the man slipped away. A woman like that would be accustomed to flicking a man off, Brian imagined, or reining him in. And making him as grateful as the family hound for the most casual of pats.

Because the conclusion steadied him, Brian took another sip of his beer, set his glass aside. Now, he decided, was as good a time as any to approach the grand and glorious Grants.

"Then she whacked him across the back of his knees with her cane," Sarah continued. "And he fell face first into the verbena."

"If she was my grandmother," Patrick put in, "I'd move to Australia."

"Sure Will Cunningham usually deserves a whack. More than once I've been tempted to give him one myself." Adelia Grant glanced over, her laughing eyes meeting Brian's. "Well then, you've made it, haven't you?"

To Brian's surprise, she held out both hands to him, clasped his warmly and drew him into the family center. "It appears I have. It's a pleasure to see you again, Mrs. Grant."

"I hope your trip over was pleasant."

"Uneventful, which is just as good." As small talk wasn't one of his strengths, he turned to Travis, nodded. "Mr. Grant."

"Brian. I hoped you'd make it tonight. You've met Brendon."

"I did, yes. Did you lay any down on the colt I told you of?"

"On the nose. And since it was at five-to-one, I owe you a drink, at least. What can I get you?"

"I'll have a beer, thanks."

"What part of Ireland are you from?" This was from Sarah. She had her mother's eyes, Brian thought. Warm green, and curious.

"I'm from Kerry. You'd be Sarah, wouldn't you?"

"That's right." She beamed at him. "This is my brother Patrick, and my sister Keeley. Our Brady's already on campus, so we're one short tonight."

"Nice meeting you, Patrick." Deliberately he inclined his head in what was nearly a bow as he turned to Keeley. "Miss Grant."

She lifted one slim eyebrow, the gesture as deliberate as his own. "Mr. Donnelly. Oh, thank you, Chad." She accepted the glass of champagne, touched a hand briefly to the arm of the man who'd brought it to her. "Chad Stuart, Brian Donnelly, from Kerry. That's in Ireland," she added with an irony dry as dust.

"Oh. Are you one of Mrs. Grant's relatives?"

"I don't have that privilege, no. There are a few of us scattered through the country who are not, in fact, related."

Patrick snorted out a laugh and earned a warning look from his mother. "Well now, we're cluttering up the place as usual. We'll move this herd along to our table. I hope you'll join us, Brian."

"How about a dance, Keeley?" Chad asked, standing at her elbow in a proprietary manner.

"I'd love to," she said absently and stepped forward. "A little later."

"Have a care." Brian put a hand lightly on Keeley's elbow as they walked away. "Or you'll slip on the pieces of the heart you just broke."

She slid a glance over and up. "I'm very surefooted," she told him, then made a point of taking a seat between her two brothers.

Because he'd caught the scent of her—subtle sex, with an overlay of class—*he* made a point of sitting directly across from her. He sent her one quick grin, then settled in to be entertained by Sarah, who was already chattering to him about horses.

She didn't like the look of him, Keeley thought as she sipped her champagne. He was just a little too much of everything. His eyes were green, a sharper tone than her mother's. She imagined he could use them to slice his opponent in two with one glance. And she had a feeling he'd enjoy it. His hair was brown, but anything but a quiet shade, with all those gilded streaks rioting through it, and he wore it too long, so that it waved past his collar and around a face of planes and angles.

A sharp face, like his eyes, one with a faint shadow of a cleft in the chin and a well-defined mouth that struck her as being just a little too sensuous.

She thought he was built like a cowboy—long-legged and rangy, and looking entirely too rough-and-ready for his suit and tie.

She didn't care for the way he stared at her, either. Even when he wasn't looking at her it *felt* as if he were staring. And as if he'd read her thoughts, he shifted his eyes to hers again. His smile was slow, unmistakably insolent, and made her want to bare her teeth in a snarl.

Rather than give him the satisfaction, Keeley rose and walked unhurriedly to the ladies' lounge.

She hadn't gotten all the way through the door when Sarah bulleted in behind her. "God! Isn't he gorgeous?"

"Who?"

"Come on, Keel." Rolling her eyes, Sarah plopped down on one of the padded stools at the vanity counter and prepared to enjoy a chat. "Brian. I mean he is so *hot*. Did you see his eyes? Amazing. And that mouth—makes you just want to lap at it or something. Plus, he's got a terrific butt. I know because I made sure I walked behind him to check it out."

With a laugh, Keeley sat down beside her. "First, you're so predictable. Second, if Dad hears you talk that way, he'll shove the man on the first plane back to Ireland. And third, I didn't notice his butt, or anything else about him, particularly."

"Liar." Sarah propped her elbow on the counter as her sister took out a lipstick. "I saw you give him the Keeley Grant once-over."

Amused, Keeley passed the lipstick to Sarah. "Then let's say I didn't much like what I saw. The rough-edged and proud of it type just doesn't do it for me."

"It sure works for me. If I wasn't leaving for college next week, I'd—"

"But you are," Keeley interrupted, and part of her was torn at the upcoming separation. "Besides that, he's much too old for you."

"It never hurts to flirt."

"And you've made a career of it."

"That's just to balance your ice princess routine. 'Oh

hello, Chad.'" Sarah put a distant look in her eye and grace-fully lifted a hand.

Keeley's comment was short and rude and made Sarah giggle. "Dignity isn't a flaw," Keeley insisted, even as her own lips twitched. "You could use a little."

"You've got plenty for both of us." Sarah hopped up. "Now I'm going to go out and see if I can lure the Irish hunk onto the dance floor. I just bet he's got great moves."

"Oh, yeah," Keeley muttered when her sister swung out the door. "I bet he does."

Not, of course, that she was the least bit interested.

At the moment she wasn't particularly interested in men, period. She had her work, she had the farm, she had her family. The combination kept her busy, involved and happy. Socializing was fine, she mused. An interesting compan-ion over dinner, great. An occasional date for the theater or a function, dandy.

Anything more, well, she was just too busy to bother. If that made her an ice princess, so what? She'd leave the heart melting to Sarah. But, she decided as she rose, if their father hired Donnelly, she was keeping an eye on him and her guileless sister over the next week.

She'd barely taken two steps out of the lounge when Chad appeared at her side again, asking for a dance. Be-cause the ice princess crack was still on her mind, she of-fered him a smile warm enough to dazzle his eyes and let him draw her into his arms.

Brian didn't mind dancing with Sarah. It would be a pitiful man who couldn't enjoy a few moments of holding a pretty young girl in his arms and listening to her bubble over about whatever came into her head.

She was a sweetheart as far as he was concerned, mirac-ulously unspoiled and friendly as a puppy. After ten minutes, he knew she intended to study equine medicine, loved Irish music, broke her arm falling out of a tree when she was eight, and that she was an innate and charming flirt.

It was a pure pleasure to dance with Adelia Grant, to hear his own country in her voice and feel the easy welcome of it.

He'd heard the stories, of course, of how she'd come to America, and Royal Meadows, to stay with her uncle Patrick Cunnane, who was trainer in those days for Travis Grant. It was said she'd been hired on as a groom as she had her uncle's gift with horses.

But guiding the small, elegant woman around the dance floor, Brian dismissed the stories as so much pixie dust. He couldn't imagine this woman ever mucking out a stall—any more than he could picture her pretty daughters doing so.

The socializing hadn't been so bad, he acknowledged, and he couldn't say he minded the food, though a man would do better with a good beef sandwich. Still it was plentiful, even if you did have to pick your way through half of it to get to something recognizable.

But despite the evening not being quite the ordeal he'd imagined it would be, he was glad when Travis suggested they get some air.

"You've a lovely family, Mr. Grant."

"Yes, I do. And a loud one. I hope you still have your hearing left after dancing with Sarah."

Brian grinned, but he was cautious. "She's charming— and ambitious. Veterinary medicine's a challenging field, and especially when you specialize in horses."

"She's never wanted anything else. She went through stages, of course," Travis continued as they walked down a wide white stone path. "Ballerina, astronaut, rock star. But under it all, she always wanted to be a vet. I'm going to miss her, and Patrick, when they leave for college next week. Your family will miss you, I imagine, if you stay in America."

"I've been coming and going for some time. If I settle in America, it won't be a problem."

"My wife misses Ireland," Travis murmured. "A part of her's still there, no matter how deep she's dug her roots here. I understand that. But…" He paused and in the backwash of light studied Brian's face. "When I take on a trainer, I expect his mind, and his heart, to be in Royal Meadows."

"That's understood, Mr. Grant."

"You've moved around quite a bit, Brian," Travis added. "Two years, occasionally three at one organization, then you switch."

"True enough." Eyes level, Brian nodded. "You could say I haven't found the place that wants to hold me longer than that. But while I'm where I am, that farm, those horses, have all my attention and loyalty."

"So I'm told. The boots I'm looking to fill are big. No one's managed to fill them to my satisfaction since Paddy Cunnane retired. He suggested I take a look at you."

"I'm flattered."

"You should be." Travis was pleased to see nothing more than mild interest on Brian's face. He appreciated a man who could hold his own thoughts. "I'd like you to come by the farm when you're settled."

"I'm settled enough. I prefer moving right along if it's all the same to you."

"It is."

"Fine. I'll come round tomorrow, for the morning work-out, and have a look at how you do things, Mr. Grant. After I've seen what you have, and you've heard what I'd have in mind to do about it, we'll know if it works for both of us. Will that suit you?"

Cocky young son of a bitch, Travis thought, but didn't smile. He, too, knew how to hold his thoughts. "It suits me fine. Come on back inside. I'll buy you a beer."

"Thanks just the same, but I think I'll go on back to my hotel. Dawn comes early."

"I'll see you tomorrow." Travis held out a hand, shook Brian's briskly. "I'll look forward to it."

"So will I."

Alone, Brian took out a slim cigar, lighted it, then blew out a long stream of smoke.

Paddy Cunnane had recommended him? The idea of it had both nerves and pleasure stirring in his gut. He'd told Travis he'd been flattered, but in truth, he'd been staggered. In the racing world, that was a name spoken of with reverence.

Paddy Cunnane trained champions the way others ate breakfast—with habitual regularity.

He'd seen the man a few times over the course of years, and had spoken to him once. But even with a well-fed ego, Brian had never thought that Paddy Cunnane had taken notice of him.

Travis Grant wanted someone to fill Paddy's boots. Well, Brian Donnelly couldn't and wouldn't do that. But he'd damn well make his mark with his own, and he'd make sure that would be good enough for anyone.

Tomorrow morning they would see what they would see.

He started down the path again when the light and shadows in front of him shifted briefly. Glancing over, he saw Keeley come out of the glass doors and walk across a flagstone terrace.

Look at her, Brian thought, so cool and solitary and perfect. She was made for moonlight, he decided. Or perhaps it was made for her. What breeze there was fluttered the layers of the filmy blue dress she wore as she crossed over to sniff at the flowers that grew out of a big stone urn in colors of rust and butter.

On impulse, he snapped off one of the late-blooming roses from its bush, and strode onto the terrace. She turned at the sound of his footsteps. Irritation flickered first in her eyes, so quickly here and gone he might have missed it if he hadn't been so focused on her. Then it was smoothed away, coated over with a thin sheen of cool politeness.

"Mr. Donnelly."

"Miss Grant," he said in the same formal tone, then held out the rose. "Those there are a bit too humble for the likes of you. This suits better."

"Really?" She took the rose because it would have been rude not to, but neither looked at it nor lifted it to sniff. "I like simple flowers. But thank you for the thought. Are you enjoying your evening?"

"I enjoyed meeting your family."

Because he sounded sincere she unbent enough to smile. "You haven't met them all yet."

"Your brother in college."

"Brady, yes, but there's my aunt and uncle. Erin and Burke Logan, and their three children, from the neighboring Three Aces farm."

"I've heard of the Logans, yes. Seen them round the tracks a time or two in Ireland. Don't they come to functions here?"

"Often, but they're away just now. If you stay in the area, you'll see quite a bit of them."

"And you? Do you still live at home?"

"Yes." She shifted, glanced back toward the light. "That's why it's home."

Which was where she wanted to be right now, she realized. Home. The thought of going back inside that overwarm and overcrowded room seemed unbearable.

"The music's better from a distance."

"Hmm?" She didn't bother to look at him, wished only that he would go away and give her back her moment of solitude.

"The music," Brian repeated. "It's better when you can barely hear it."

Because she agreed, wholeheartedly, she laughed. "Better yet when you can't hear it at all."

It was the laugh that did it. There'd been warmth then. The way smoke brought warmth even as it clogged your brain. He reached for her before he let himself think. "I don't know about that."

She went rigid. Not with a jerk as many women would, he noted, but by standing so absolutely still she stiffened every muscle.

"What are you doing?"

The words dripped ice, and left him no choice but to tighten his grip on her waist. Pride rammed against pride and the result was solid steel. "Dancing. You do dance, I saw you. And this is a better spot for it than in there, where you're jammed elbow to ass, don't you think?"

Perhaps she agreed. Perhaps she was even amused. Still, she was accustomed to being asked, not just grabbed. "I came out here to get away from the dancing."

"You didn't, no. You came out to get away from the crowd."

She moved with him because to do otherwise was too much like an embrace. And Sarah had been right, he had some lovely moves. Her heels brought her gaze level with his mouth. She'd been right, she decided. Entirely too sensuous. Deliberately she tilted her head back until their eyes met.

"How long have you been working with horses?" It was a safe topic, she thought, and an expected one.

"All my life, one way or another. And you? Are you one for riding, or just for looking from a distance?"

"I can ride." The question irritated her, and nearly had her tossing her collection of blue ribbons and medals in his face. "Relocating, if you do, would mean a big change for you. Job, country, culture."

"I like a challenge." Something about the way he said it, about the way his hand was spread over her back, had her eyes narrowing.

"Those that do often wander off looking for the next when the challenge is met. It's a game, lacking substance or commitment. I think more of people who build something worthwhile where they are."

Because it was no more than the truth, it shouldn't have stung. But it did. "As your parents have."

"Yes."

"It's easy, isn't it, to have that sensibility when you've never had to build something from the ground up with nothing but your own hands and wits?"

"That may be, but I respect someone who digs in for the long haul more than the one who jumps from opportunity to opportunity—or challenge."

"And that's what you think I'm doing here?"

"I couldn't say." She moved her shoulder, a graceful little shrug. "I don't know you."

"No, you don't. But you think you do. The rover with his eye on the prize, and stable dirt under his nails no matter how he scrubs at them. And less than beneath your notice."

Surprised, not just by the words but the heat under them,

she started to step back, would have stepped back, but he held her in place. As if, she thought, he had the right to.

"That's ridiculous. Unfair and untrue."

"Doesn't matter, to either of us." He wouldn't let it matter to him. Wouldn't let her matter, though holding her had made him ache with ideas that couldn't take root.

"If your father offers me the job, and I take it, I doubt we'll be running in the same circles, or dancing the same dance, once I'm an employee."

There was anger there, she noted, just behind the vivid green of his eyes. "Mr. Donnelly, you're mistaken about me, my family, and how my parents run their farm. Mistaken, and insulting."

He raised his eyebrows. "Are you cold or just angry?"

"What do you mean?"

"You're trembling."

"It's chilly." She bit off the words, annoyed that he'd upset her enough to have it show. "I'm going back in."

"As you like." He eased away, but kept her hand in his, then angled his head when she tugged at it. "Even the stable boy learns manners," he murmured and walked her to the door. "Thank you for the dance, Miss Grant. I hope you enjoy the rest of your evening."

He knew it could cost him the offer of the job, but he couldn't resist seeing if there was any fire behind that wall of ice. So he lifted her hand, and with his eyes still on hers, brushed his lips over her knuckles. Back, forth, then back again.

The fire, one violent flash of it, sparked. And there it simmered while she yanked her hand free, turned her back on him and walked back into the polished crowd and perfumed air.

Chapter 2

Dawn at the shedrow was one of the magic times, when fog was eating its way along the ground and the light was a paler, purer gray. Music was in the jingle of harness, the dull thud of boot and hoof as grooms, handlers and horses went about their business. The perfume was horses, hay and summer.

Trailers had already been loaded, Brian imagined, and the horses picked by the man Grant had left in charge already gone to track for their workout or preparation for today's race. But here on the farm there was other work to be done.

Sprains to be checked, medication to be given, stalls to be mucked. Exercise boys would take mounts to the oval for a workout, or to pony them around. He imagined Royal Meadows had someone to act as clocker and mark the time.

He saw nothing that indicated anything other than first-class here. There was a certain tidiness not all owners insisted upon—or would pay for. Stables, barns, sheds, all were neatly painted, rich, glossy white with dark green trim. Fences were white too, and in perfect repair. Paddocks and pastures were all as neat as a company parlor.

There was atmosphere as well. It was a clever man, or a rich one, who could afford it. Trees in full leaf dotted the hillside pastures. Brian spotted one, a big beauty of an oak, that rose from the center of a paddock and was fenced around in white wood. In the center grass of the brown oval was a colorful lake of flowers and shrubs. Back away, curving between stables and track, were trim green hedges.

He approved of such touches, for the horses. And for the men. Both worked with more enthusiasm in attractive surroundings in his experience. He imagined the Grants had glossy photos of their pretty farm published in fancy magazines.

Of the house as well, he mused, for that had been an impressive sight. Though it had still been more night than day when he'd driven past it, he'd seen the elegant shape of the stone house with its juts of balconies and ornamental iron. Fine big windows, he thought now, for standing and looking out at a kingdom.

There'd been a second structure, a kind of miniature replica of the main house that had nestled atop a large garage. He'd seen the shapes and silhouettes of flowers and shrubberies there as well. And the big, shady trees.

But it was the horses that interested him. How they were housed, how they were handled. The shedrow—should he be offered this job and take it—would be his business. The owner was simply the owner.

"You'll want a look in the stables," Travis said, leading Brian toward the doors. "Paddy'll be along shortly. Between us we should be able to answer any questions you might have."

He got answers just from looking, from seeing, Brian mused. Inside was as tidy as out, with the sloped concrete floors scrubbed down, the doors of the box stalls of strong and sturdy wood each boasting a discreet brass plaque engraved with its tenant's name. Already stableboys were pitching out soiled hay into barrows or pitching in fresh. The scent of grain, liniment and horse was strong and sweet.

Travis stopped by a stall where a young woman carefully wrapped the foreleg of a bay. "How's she doing, Linda?"

"Coming along. She'll be out causing trouble again in a day or two."

"Sprain?" Brian stepped into the box to run his hands over the yearling's legs and chest. Linda flicked a glance up at him, then over at Travis, who nodded.

"This is Bad Betty," Linda told Brian. "She likes to incite riots. She's got a mild sprain, but it won't hold her back for long."

"Troublemaker, are you?" Brian put his hands on either side of Betty's head, looked her in the eye. A quick, hot thrill raced through him at what he saw. What he sensed. Here, he thought, was magic, ready to spring if only you could find the right incantation.

"It happens I like troublemakers," he murmured.

"She'll nip," Linda warned. "Especially if you turn your back on her."

"You don't want a bite of me, do you, darling?"

As if in challenge, Betty laid her ears back, and Brian grinned at her. "We'll get along, as long as I remember you're the boss." When he ran his fingertips down her neck, back again, she snorted at him. "You're too pretty for your own good."

He murmured to her, shifting without thought to Gaelic as Linda finished the bandage. Betty's ears pricked back up, and she watched him now with more interest than malice.

"She wants to run." Brian stepped back, scanning the filly's form. "Born for it. And more, born to win."

"One look tells you that?" Travis asked.

"It's in the eyes. You won't want to breed this one when she comes into season, Mr. Grant. She needs to fly first."

Deliberately he turned his back, and as Betty lifted her head, he glanced back over his shoulder. "I don't think so," he said quietly. They eyed each other another moment, then Betty tossed her head in the equine equivalent of a shrug.

Amused, Travis moved aside to let Brian out of the box. "She terrorizes the stableboys."

"Because she can, and is likely smarter than half of them." He gestured to the opposite box. "And who's this handsome old man here?"

"That's Prince, out of Majesty."

"Royal Meadows' Majesty?" There was reverence in Brian's voice as he crossed over. "And his Prince. You had your day, didn't you, sir?" Gently Brian stroked a hand down the dignified nose of the aged chestnut. "Like your sire. I saw him race, Mr. Grant, at the Curragh, when I was a lad, a stableboy. I'd never seen his like before, nor since for that matter. I worked with one of the stallions this one sired. He didn't embarrass his breeding."

"Yes, I know."

Travis showed him through the tack room, the breeding shed and birthing stalls, past a paddock where a yearling was going through his paces on a longe line, and then to the oval where a handsome stallion was being ponied around in the company of a well-behaved gelding.

A wiry little man with a blue cap over a white fringe of hair turned as they approached. He had a stopwatch dangling from his pocket and a merry grin on his weathered leprechaun's face.

"So you've had your tour then, have you? And what do you think of our little place here?"

"It's a lovely farm." Brian extended a hand. "I'm pleased to meet you again, Mr. Cunnane."

"Likewise, young Brian from Kerry." Paddy gave Brian's hand a firm shake. "I told them to hold Zeus until you got here, Travis. I thought you and the lad would like a look at his morning run."

"King Zeus, out of Prince," Travis explained. "He's running well for us."

"He took your Belmont Stakes last year," Brian remembered.

"That's right. Zeus likes a long run. Burke's colt snatched the Derby from him, but Zeus came back for the Breeder's Cup. He's a strong competitor, and he'll sire champions."

At Paddy's signal, an exercise boy trotted over mounted on a magnificent chestnut. The horse gleamed dark red in the strengthening sun, with a blaze like a lightning bolt down the center of his forehead. He pranced, sidestepping, head tossing.

Brian knew, at one glance, he was looking at poetry.

"What do you think of him?" Paddy asked.

"Beautiful form" was all Brian said.

Twelve hundred pounds of muscle atop impossibly long and graceful legs. A wide chest, sleek body, proud head. And eyes, Brian saw, that glinted with ferocious pride.

"Take him around, Bobbie," Paddy ordered. "Don't rate

him. We'll let him show off a bit this morning." Whistling between his teeth, Paddy leaned on the fence, pulled out the stopwatch.

With his thumbs hooked in his pockets, Brian watched Zeus trot back onto the track, prance in place until the boy controlled him. Then the rider rose up in the stirrups, leaned over that long, powerful neck. Zeus shot forward, a bright arrow from a plucked bow. Those long legs lifted, stretched, fell, flew, shooting out clumps of dirt like bullets as he rounded the first curve.

The air roared with the thunder.

Inside Brian's chest, his heart beat the same way, at a hard and joyful gallop. The boy's hat flew off as they turned into the backstretch. When they streaked by, Paddy gave a grunt and flicked his timer.

"Not bad," Paddy said dryly and held out the watch.

Brian didn't need to see it. He had a clock in his head, and he knew he'd just watched a champion.

"I think I've seen the like of your Prince at last, Mr. Grant."

"And he knows it."

"You want your hands on that one, boy?" Paddy asked him.

There was a time, Brian thought, to hold your cards close, and a time to lay them out. "I do, yes." Struggling not to dance with eagerness, he turned to Travis again. "If the job's being offered, Mr. Grant, I'll take it."

Travis inclined his head, extended a hand. "Welcome to Royal Meadows. Let's go get some coffee."

Brian simply stared as Travis walked off. "Just like that?" he murmured.

"He'd already made up his mind," Paddy said, "or you wouldn't be here in the first place. Travis doesn't waste time—his or anyone else's. After you're done with your coffee and such, come over to my place—above the garage. You'll want a look at the condition book, and have a little conversation."

"Yes, I will. Thanks." A bit dazed, Brian headed off after Travis.

He caught up, surprised, and a little embarrassed, to find his palms were sweaty. A job was only a job, he reminded himself. "I'm grateful for the opportunity, Mr. Grant."

"Travis. You'll work for it. We have high standards at Royal Meadows. I expect you to meet them. I'd like you to start as soon as possible."

"I'll start today."

Travis glanced over. "Good."

Scanning the area, Brian gestured toward another small building, with the paddock set up with jumps. "Do you train jumpers, show horses, as well?"

"That's a separate enterprise." Travis smiled slightly. "You'll work the racehorses. You can move your things into the trainer's quarters when you're ready." Travis flicked a glance toward the garage house.

Brian opened his mouth—then shut it again. He hadn't expected housing to be part of the package, but wasn't about to argue it away. If it didn't suit him, they'd deal with it later.

"You have a beautiful home. Someone likes their flowers."

"My wife." Travis turned onto a slate path. "She's particularly fond of flowers."

And Brian imagined they had a staff of gardeners, landscapers, whatever it was, to deal with them. "The horses appreciate a pretty setting."

Travis stepped onto a patio, turned. "Do they?"

"They do."

"Did Betty tell you that when you were speaking to her?"

Brian met Travis's amused eyes levelly. "She indicated she was a queen and expected to be treated as such."

"And will you?"

"I will, until she abuses the privilege. Even royalty needs a bit of a yank now and again."

So saying, he stepped through the door Travis held open.

Brian didn't know what he'd been expecting. Something sleek and sophisticated. Something grand, certainly.

He hadn't been expecting to walk into the Grants' kitchen, nor to find it big and cluttered and despite the gleam of snazzy appliances and fancy tiles, homey.

Certainly the last thing he'd expected was to see the lady of the manor herself in an old pair of jeans, bare feet and a faded T-shirt standing at the stove with a skillet while she rang a peal over the head of her youngest son.

"And I'll tell you another thing, Patrick Michael Thomas Cunnane, if you think you can come and go at all hours as you damn please just because you're going off to college, you'd best get that thick head of yours examined in a hurry. I'll be happy to do it myself, with the skillet I have in my hand, just as soon as I'm done with it."

"Yes, ma'am." At the table Patrick sat with his shoulders hunched, wincing at his mother's back. "But since you're using it, maybe I could have some more French toast. No-body makes it like you do."

"You won't get around me that way."

"Maybe I will."

She shot a look over her shoulder that Brian recognized as one only a mother could conjure to wither a child.

"And maybe I won't," Patrick muttered, then bright-ened when he saw Brian at the door. "Ma, we've got company. Have a seat, Brian. Had breakfast? My mother makes world-famous French toast."

"Witnesses won't save you," Adelia said mildly, but turned to smile at Brian. "Come in and sit. Patrick, get Brian and your father plates."

"No, thank you. There's no need to trouble."

"Ma, I can't find my brown shoes." Sarah came bursting in. "Hello, Brian, morning, Dad."

"Sure I had my eyes right on them for weeks," Adelia said as she flipped sizzling bread in the pan. "I can't think how those shoes slipped out of my sight."

Sarah rolled her eyes and yanked open the refrigerator. "I'm going to be late."

"You could wear one of the other six thousand pairs of shoes jammed in your closet," her brother suggested.

Sarah rapped him on the back with the carton of juice she held and otherwise ignored him. "I don't have time for breakfast." She poured juice, glugged it down. "I'll be home by five."

"Take a muffin," Adelia ordered.

"We don't have any blueberry."

"Take what we do have."

"Okay, okay." She grabbed a muffin off a plate, gave her mother a smacking kiss on the cheek, rounded the table to give her father one in turn, crossed her eyes at her brother, then dashed out again.

"Sarah works at the vet's office during the summer," Adelia explained. "The pair of you wash up here now, and we'll get you something hot to eat."

Since the scent of that fried bread was impossible to resist, Brian started toward the sink. And saw the huge old dog stretched out by the stove. He resembled a long, black and outrageously shaggy floor mat.

"And who's this?" Automatically Brian crouched down.

"That's our Sheamus. He's an old man now, and likes to tuck himself at my feet while I'm cooking."

"My wife's fond of mutts," Travis said as he ran water in the sink.

"And they of me. He spends most of his time sleeping," she told Brian. "And isn't much for anyone but family now." Even as she said it her brows rose up. Brian had no more than stroked the old dog's head before Sheamus opened his eyes, thumped his ragged tail, and with a moan rolled over onto his back for a belly rub.

"Would you look at that? He's taken to you."

"Well mutts and I, we understand each other. You're a good old boy, aren't you? Fat and happy."

"Someone feeds him table scraps." Adelia slanted a look at her husband.

"I don't know what you're talking about." All innocence, Travis held out the soap when Brian stood up again.

"Hah" was all she said to that. "Would you have coffee, Brian, or tea?"

"Tea, thank you."

"Sit." She pointed to a chair, then shifted the finger to her son. "You, go. I'll finish with you later."

"I'll be at the stables, doing penance." With a heavy sigh, Patrick rose, then he wrapped his arms around his mother's waist, laid his chin on top of her head. "Sorry."

"Get."

But Brian saw her lay a hand over Patrick's, and squeeze. With a quick grin tossed to the room in general, he bolted.

"That boy's responsible for every other line on my face," Adelia muttered.

"What lines?" Travis asked, and made her laugh.

"That's the right answer. So, Brian, does Royal Meadows suit you?"

After drying his hands, he crossed to the table to sit. "Yes, ma'am."

"Oh, we're not so very formal around here. You don't have to ma'am me. Unless you're in trouble." She poured tea for him, and coffee for Travis, then stayed where she was, her free hand resting on her husband's shoulder.

"How did Zeus do this morning?"

"Took the oval in a minute-fifty flat."

"I'm sorry I missed it." She turned back to the stove to heap golden bread onto a platter.

"I'll offer you a one-year contract," Travis began.

"Can't you let the boy eat before you.talk business?"

"The boy wants to know."

Brian took the platter, transferred three slices to his plate. "Yes, he does."

"You'll have a guaranteed annual salary." Travis named an amount that had Brian struggling not to bobble the syrup. "And, after two months, a two-percent share of each purse. In six months, we'll renegotiate that percentage."

"We'll negotiate it up." Steady again, Brian cut into his breakfast. "Because I promise you, I'll have earned it."

They discussed—haggled a bit for form sake—responsibilities, benefits, bonuses, duties.

Brian was on his second serving of toast, and Travis the last of his coffee, when Keeley came in.

She wore buff colored jodhpurs. Elegant and form-fitting. Her high black boots were shined like dark mirrors. Her white blouse draped soft with its wide collar buttoned high. She had tamed her hair into a sleek twist that left her face unframed. Small, complicated twists of gold glinted at her ears.

Her brow lifted at the sight of Brian eating breakfast in her kitchen, and her mouth thinned before it moved into a cool, practiced smile. "Good morning, Mr. Donnelly."

"Miss Grant."

"I'm pressed for time this morning." She walked to her father, bent down, rubbed her cheek against his.

"You should eat," her mother told her.

"I'll get something later." She went to the refrigerator, took out a soft drink. "I'll be done in a couple of hours." She went to her mother, bending first to scratch Sheamus on the top of the head, then in the same manner she'd used with her father, rubbed cheeks with Adelia before she headed out the back door.

"I'll come down in a bit," Adelia called after her. "I'd like to watch."

Twenty minutes later, Brian walked from the house toward the trainer's quarters. He saw Keeley in the paddock in front of the small building. She sat astride a black gelding. As she walked the horse, a man photographed her from various angles.

Brian paused to watch, hands on hips. She was getting her picture in some fancy magazine, he imagined. Royal Meadows Princess. No doubt she'd look fine and glossy in it.

She set the horse into a trot, then a canter, swinging in to sail over a jump. Brian's lips pursed. She had good form, he had to admit it. When she repeated that jump, then another, for the camera, he heard her laugh float out over the air.

He turned away, dismissing her. Trying to.

He climbed the stairs to the trainer's quarters, knocked.

"Come in, and welcome. In here," Paddy called out.

He sat at a desk in a room set up as an office. File cabinets lined one wall, and photographs of horses lined them all. The window was open, and on a shelf beside it sat a computer. If the dust on its cover was any indication, it was rarely, if ever, used.

Paddy's glasses balanced on the end of his nose as he gestured to a chair. "You and Travis worked out your details."

"We did. He's a fair man."

"Did you expect otherwise?"

"I don't expect anything from owners, and that way they don't often surprise me."

With a chuckle Paddy shoved up his glasses, scratched his nose. "This one might."

"I want to thank you for putting my name in so Mr. Grant would consider me."

"I've kept my eye and ear on things, though I've retired. Well, retired twice now, if the truth be known, and come out of it again as Travis and Dee haven't been satisfied with the trainers who've come along. This time I mean it to stick. I mean you to stick, boy."

When his glasses slid down again, Paddy grunted in annoyance and took them off. "We'll be bunking here together, if you have no objection, for the next week. After that, I'll be off, and the place is yours."

"Where are you going?"

"Home. Back to Ireland."

"After all these years?"

"I was born there. I've a mind to die there—though I've life left in me, no mistake. I've a yearning to spend the last years of it at home."

"What'll you do there?"

"Oh, go to the pub to tell lies," Paddy said with a twinkling grin. "Drink a pint of decent Guinness. You'll miss that here, I can tell you. It's just not the same built out of a Yank tap."

Brian had to laugh. "It's a long way to go for a pint, even for Guinness."

"Well now, there's a little farm in the south of Cork, not far from Skibbereen. Do you know Skibbereen, Brian?"

"Aye. It's a pretty town."

"Sloping streets and painted doorways," Paddy said, a bit dreamily. "Well, the farm's a bit of a ways from that pretty town. My Dee was raised there, by my sister after Dee's parents died. When my sister got sickly, the farm fell on hard times with Dee trying to run it and tend to her aunt Lettie. In the end, Lettie passed and the farm was lost, and Dee came here to me. A few years ago, the farm came up for sale, and though she told him not to, Travis bought it for her. The man knows her heart."

"So that's where you're going?" Brian asked, though he didn't have a clue why Paddy was telling him. "To be a farmer?"

"That's where I'm going, but I don't think I'll make much of a farmer. I'll have myself a few horses for company."

He shifted, turned his gaze to the window and the hills beyond where horses grazed in the late-morning sunshine.

"I'll miss my little Dee, and Travis, and the children. The friends I've made here. But I've a need to go. An itch, if you follow me."

"I do." There was little Brian understood more than an itch to be going.

"I imagine I'll be flying back and forth across the pond quite a bit—and they'll come to me as well. I've seen Dee married to a man I respect, and love like my own son. I've watched her children grow into fine young men and women. That's a rare thing. And I've had a hand in turning out champions. A man who has a thoroughbred put into his hands is a fortunate man."

"Have you no wish for your own place, your own champions?"

"I toyed with it—but in the end no, it wasn't for me." He turned his attention back to Brian. "Is that what you're after in the end?"

"No. Your own place means you're rooted, doesn't it? And there's no moving on if moving on strikes you. In any case, most owners leave the work and the decisions to the trainer, so you don't own, but you run."

"Travis Grant knows how to work." Paddy inclined his head. "He knows his horses. He loves them. If you earn his trust, he'll trust you, but he'll know every move you make. He's not one for strolling into the winner's circle after the day is done. Shedrow business will be his business, and Dee's, as much as it is yours. Whether you like it or not."

"His wife?"

Amused now, Paddy sat back. "You met her last night when she was done up fancy. I like seeing her looking fine that way. You're more like to see her down in the stables lancing an abscess or soothing a colicky mare. She's no delicate flower. My Dee's a thoroughbred. And she's bred true. Not one of her children would back away from a hard day's work when it's needed. You'll learn for yourself how things go around here, and you'll find it's not such a far distance from main house to shedrow as it is in some places."

"It's usually better all around if it is," Brian muttered, and Paddy cackled with laughter.

"Right you are, lad, in most cases. Owners can be a fly in your ointment without a doubt. You'll make up your own mind about this place, and these owners. And I hope you'll let me know what you think after a bit of time's passed. Now, let's take a look at the condition book to start off."

When Brian left Paddy, he was satisfied with the world in general. Or what, he thought as he trooped down the stairs, was soon to become his world in general. He'd make his mark at Royal Meadows, and live well doing it. His quarters were first-rate. The truth was, he'd have been willing to live in a hovel for the chance to work with Travis Grant's stable.

Everything he'd ever wanted was at his fingertips. He didn't intend to let it slip through.

He turned toward the stables where he'd parked his rental car. Paddy had told him to have a look at the little red lorry down that way, as he'd be selling it before leaving for Ireland. If the thing ran, it would do, Brian thought. He didn't require anything but the most elemental means of transportation. And time to get used to driving on the wrong damn side of the road.

As he rounded the garage he was scowling over that one sticking point, and nearly ran into Keeley.

She looked as fresh and perfect as she had that morning. Not a hair out of place, not a speck of dust on her boots. He wondered how the hell she managed it.

"Good day to you, Miss Grant. I saw you in the paddock earlier. That's a fine horse."

She was hot, irritable and very close to flash point since the photographer had hit on her. The photo shoot had been necessary. She needed the exposure, the publicity, but she damn well didn't need the hassle.

"Yes, he is." She made to move by, and Brian shifted to block her.

"Begging your pardon, princess. Did I neglect to pull my forelock?"

She held up a hand. Her temper was a vile thing when loose, and the drumming in her head warned her it was very close to springing free.

"I'm already annoyed. It won't take much to push me to furious." But she drew a deep breath. If the scene in the kitchen earlier meant anything, Brian Donnelly was now part of Royal Meadows. She didn't make a habit of sniping at a member of the team.

"Sam's a nine-year-old. Hunter. A thoroughbred, Irish Draught horse cross. I've had him since he was four." She lifted the bottle she carried and sipped her soft drink.

"Is that all you put in you?" He tapped a finger on the bottle. "Bubbles and chemicals?"

"You sound like my mother."

"Maybe that's why you have a headache."

Keeley dropped the hand she'd pressed to her temple. Those eyes of his, she thought, were entirely too keen. "I'm fine."

"Turn around."

"I beg your pardon."

Brian merely stepped around her, laid his hands on the nape of her neck. Her already stiff shoulders jerked in protest. "Relax. I'm not after grabbing you in a fit of passion when any member of your family might come along. I'd like to put in at least one day on the job before I get the boot."

As he spoke he was kneading, pressing, running those strong fingers over the knots. He hated seeing anything in pain. "Blow out a breath," he ordered when she stood rigid as stone. "Come on, *maverneen,* don't be so hardheaded. Blow out a nice long breath for me."

Out of curiosity she obeyed and tried not to think how marvelous his hands felt on her skin.

"Now another."

His voice had gone to croon, lulling her. As he worked, murmured, her eyes fluttered closed. Her muscles loosened, the knots untied. The threatening throbbing in her head faded away. She all but slid into a trance.

She arched against his hands, just a little. Moaned in pleasure. Just a little. He kept his hands firm, professional, even as he imagined skimming them down over her, slipping them under that soft white blouse. He wanted to touch his lips to her nape, just where his thumb was pressing. To taste her there.

And that, he knew, would end things before they'd begun. Wanting a woman was natural. Taking one, where the taking held such risks, was suicide.

So he let his hands drop away, stepped back. She nearly swayed before she caught herself. When she turned toward him, it felt almost like floating. "Thank you. You're very good at that."

Magic hands, she thought. The man had magic in his hands.

"So I've been told." He shot her a cocky grin. "I've a feeling you need regular loosening up." He snatched the bottle out of her hand. "Go drink some water, and change. You're dressed too warmly for the heat of the day."

She angled her head and was just annoyed enough now to give him a long, thorough look. His hair, all that mass of gold streaked brown, was windblown. That wonderfully sculpted mouth just quirked at the corners.

"Any other orders?"

"No, but an observation."

"I'm fascinated."

"No, you're irritated again, but I'll tell you anyway. Your mouth's more appealing naked as it is now than when it's painted as it was this morning."

"So you don't approve of lipstick?"

"Not at all. Some women need it. You don't, so it's just a distraction."

Baffled, nearly amused, she shook her head. "Thanks so much for the advice." She started for the house—where she'd been going to change into something cooler in the first place.

"Keeley."

She stopped, but instead of turning merely glanced over her shoulder to where he stood, thumbs in the pockets of ancient jeans. "Yes?"

"It's nothing. I just wanted to try out your name. I like it."

"So do I. Isn't that handy?"

This time he blew out a breath as she strode off—long legs in tight pants and tall boots. He lifted her soft drink, took a deep sip. Playing with fire with that one, Donnelly, he warned himself. Since he was damned sure singed fingers wouldn't be all he would get if he risked a touch, it was best to back away before the heat became too tempting to resist.

Chapter 3

"Heels down, Lynn. Good. Hands, Shelly. Willy, pay attention." Keeley scanned each one of her afternoon students' form. They were coming along.

Six horses mounted with six children circled the paddock at a sedate walk. Two months before three of those children had never seen a horse firsthand, much less ridden one. Royal Meadows Riding Academy had changed that. It was making a difference.

"All right. Trot. Heads up," she ordered, hands on hips as she watched her students change gaits with varying degrees of success. "Heels down. Knees, Joey. That's the way. You're a team, remember. Looking good. Much better."

She moved closer, tapped the heels of one of her two boys. He grinned and turned them down. Oh, yes, much better, she thought. A month before Willy had jerked like a puppet every time she'd touched him.

It was all about trust.

She had them change leads, reverse, then attempt a wide figure eight.

It was a little messy, but she let them giggle their way through it.

It was also all about fun.

Brian watched her from a distance. He hadn't seen her for a couple of days. Nearly all of his time had been spent at the stables, or at one of the tracks where the Grants' horses ran. Apparently Keeley didn't spend much time at any of those locations.

He'd looked for her.

And had assumed she whiled away her time having lunch in some trendy spot, or shopping. Having her hair done or her fingernails painted. Whatever it was rich daughters did with their days.

But here she was, circling the paddock with a bunch of kids, obviously instructing them. He supposed it was a kind of hobby, teaching the privileged children of country club parents how to ride in proper English style.

Hobby or not, she looked good doing it. She'd chosen an informal look of jeans and a cotton shirt the color of blueberries. She'd pulled her hair back in some sort of band so that it fell in a wildly curling ponytail. Her boots appeared old, scuffed and serviceable.

She seemed to be enjoying herself. He didn't believe he'd seen her smile like that before. Not so quick and open and warm. Unable to resist, he walked closer as she stopped one of her students, stroked a hand over the horse's neck as she and the little girl had what appeared to be an earnest conversation.

By the time he'd reached the fence, Keeley had lined up all but the girl. Teaching them to control their mounts, he decided, to keep them quiet while something was going on around them.

The single rider posted prettily around the paddock, while Keeley turned a circle to keep her in sight. And circling, she saw Brian leaning on the fence.

The smile vanished, and he thought that was a true shame. But there was something almost as appealing about that cool, suspicious look she often aimed in his direction. He answered it with a grin, and settled in to watch the rest of the lesson.

Keeley didn't mind an audience. Often her parents or one of her siblings or one of the hands stopped by to watch. She'd certainly carried on her lessons with a parent or two of a student looking on. But since she didn't care for this particular observer, she ignored him.

One by one she selected a student to go through the day's routine solo. She corrected form, encouraged, pushed a little when it was needed for more effort or concentration. When she called for dismount, every one of them groaned.

"Five more minutes, Miss Keeley. Can't we ride for five more minutes?"

"I already let you ride five more minutes." She patted Shelly's knee. "Next week we're going to try a canter."

"I'm getting a horse for Christmas," Lynn announced. "And next spring, my mother says we'll enter shows."

"Then you'll have to work very hard. Cool off your mounts."

"That's a fine-looking group you have there. Miss Keeley."

Ingrained manners had her acknowledging Brian, walking over to the fence as she kept her eye on her students. "I like to think so."

"That boy there?" He nodded toward the dark-eyed, thin-faced Willy. "He's in love with that horse. Dreams of him at night, of racing over fields and hills and adventuring."

It made her smile again. "Teddy loves him, too. Teddy Bear," she explained. "A big, gentle sweetheart."

"This lot's lucky to have the wherewithal for lessons with a good instructor, and smart mounts. You stable them here? I haven't seen any of these down in my area."

"They're mine. I stable them here." Her horses, her school, her responsibility. "Excuse me. The lesson's not over until the horses are groomed."

Here's your hat, what's your hurry? Brian thought. Well, he had a few things to see to. But that didn't mean he couldn't wander back this way in a bit.

He bothered her. There was no real explanation for it, Keeley thought. It just was. She didn't like the way he looked at her. And why was she the only one who seemed to notice that edge in his eyes when they landed on her?

She didn't like the way he talked to her. And again, she seemed to be the only one aware of that sly little lilt in his voice when he said her name.

Everyone else thought Brian Donnelly was just dandy, she mused as she ran her hands up a gelding's legs to check for heat. Her parents considered him the perfect man to replace Uncle Paddy—and Uncle Paddy had nothing but praise for him.

Sarah thought he was hot. Patrick thought he was cool. And Brendon thought he was smart.

"Outnumbered," she muttered, and lifted the horse's foreleg to check the hoof.

Maybe it was some chemical reaction. Something that caused her hackles to rise when he was in the vicinity. After all, he appeared to be perfectly competent in his work.

More than, she admitted, from what she'd heard. And as they were both busy, they would rarely bump up against each other. So it shouldn't matter.

But she didn't like the fact that she was avoiding the stables and shedrow. That she was deliberately foregoing the pleasure of wandering down that way and watching the workouts, or lending a hand in grooming. She didn't like knowing that about herself.

She certainly didn't care for the fact that she suspected *he* knew it. Which gave him entirely too much importance.

Which, she admitted, she was doing even now just by thinking of him.

The horse wickered. Keeley's shoulders stiffened.

"You've a good eye for horses," Brian said.

It didn't surprise her that she hadn't heard him come in. And it didn't surprise her that despite not hearing she'd known he was there. The air changed, she thought, when he was in it.

"I come by it naturally."

"You do. Teddy Bear." He murmured it, causing her to look up as she lowered the gelding's leg. His eyes were on the horse's, his skilled and clever hands already moving over head and throat. Keeley heard the gelding blow out a soft breath. Pure pleasure.

"You've a kind and patient heart, don't you?" Brian moved into the box, those wide palmed hands still skimming, stroking, checking. "And a fine broad back for carrying small, dreamy boys. How long have you had him?"

She blinked, nearly flushed. There was something hypnotic about those hands, about that voice. "Nearly two years."

Brian ran his hands down the flank. Stopped. His eyes narrowed as he stepped closer and examined a crosshatch of scarring. "What's this?" But he knew, and turned on

Keeley so quickly she backed up to the wall before she could stop herself. "This horse has been whipped, and whipped bloody."

"His previous owner," she said, icily as a defense against that first spurt of alarm, "had a heavy hand with a whip. He wanted to show Teddy, but Teddy shied at the jumps. This was his way of showing he was the boss."

"Bloody bastard." And though his eyes still glinted with heat, his voice went soft again. "You're in a better place now, aren't you, boy. A fine home with a pretty woman to rub you down. Rescued him, did you?" he said to Keeley.

"I wouldn't go that far. There are different methods of breaking a horse. I don't happen to—"

"I don't break horses." Brian ducked under Teddy's belly, then his eyes met Keeley's over the wide back. "I make them. Any idiot can use a bat or a whip and break both spirit and heart. It takes skill and patience and a gentle hand to make a champion, or even just a friend."

She waited a moment, surprised her knees wanted to shake. "Why do you expect me to disagree with you?" she wondered aloud. She stepped out of the box, moved to the next.

The aging mare greeted her with a snort and a bump of head on shoulder. Keeley snatched up a body brush to finish off her student's sketchy grooming.

"I can't stand seeing anything mistreated." Brian spoke quietly from behind her. Keeley didn't turn, didn't answer. Now that the first spurt of anger had passed, he had just enough room for shame at the way he'd turned on her. "Especially something that has so little choice. It makes me sick, and angry."

"And you expect me to disagree, again?"

"I snapped at you. I'm sorry." He touched a hand to her

shoulder, left it there even when she stiffened—as he would with a nervous horse. "You look into eyes like that one has over there, and you see inside them that huge, generous heart. Then the scars where someone beat him—because he could. It scrambles my brain."

With an effort she relaxed her shoulders. "It took me three months to get him to trust me enough not to shy every time I lifted my hand. One day, he stuck his head out when I came in and called to me the way they do when they're happy to see you. I fed him carrots and cried like a baby. Don't tell me about mistreatment and scrambled brains."

Shame wasn't something he felt often, but it was easy to recognize. He took a deep breath and hoped to start again. "What's this pretty mare's story?"

"Why do you think there's a story? She's a horse. You ride her."

"Keeley." He laid a hand over hers on the brush. "I'm sorry."

She moved her hand, but gave in and rested her cheek on the mare's neck. Rubbing, Brian noted, as she did when she hugged her parents.

"Her crime was age. She's nearly twenty. She'd been left stabled, and neglected. She was covered with nettle rash and lice. Her people just got bored with her, I suppose."

He didn't think when he stroked her hair. His hands were as much a part of his way of communicating as his voice. "How many do you have?"

"Eight, counting Sam, but he's too much for the students at this point."

"And did you save them all?"

"Sam was a gift for my twenty-first birthday. The others…well, when you're in the center of the horse world, you hear about horses. Besides, I needed them for the school."

"Some would expect you to stock thoroughbreds."

"Yes." She shifted. "Some would. Sorry, I have to feed the horses, then I have paperwork."

"I'll give you a hand with the feeding."

"I don't need it."

"I'll give you one anyway."

Keeley moved out of the box, rested a hand on the door. Best, she decided, to deal with this clean and simple. "Brian, you're working for my family, in a vital and essential role, so I think I should be straight with you."

"By all means." The serious tone didn't match the glint in his eye as she leaned back.

"You bother me," she told him. "On some level, you just bother me. It's probably because I just don't care for cocky, intense men who smirk at me, but that's neither here nor there."

"No, that's here and it's there. What kind do you care for?"

"You see—that's just the sort of thing that annoys me."

"I know. It's interesting, isn't it, that I find myself compelled to do just the thing that gets a rise out of you? You bother me as well. Perhaps it's that I don't care for regal, cool-eyed women who look down their lovely noses at me. But here we are, so we should try getting on as best we can."

"I don't look down my nose at you, or anyone."

"Depends on your point of view, doesn't it?"

She turned on her heel and marched away, focusing intensely on measuring out grain.

"Why don't we talk of something safe?" he suggested. "Like what I think about Royal Meadows. I've worked on farms and around tracks since I was ten. Stableboy, exercise boy, groom. Working my way up, hustling my way through. Twenty years means I've seen all sides of training, racing and breeding. The bright and the dark. And in twenty years, I've never seen brighter than Royal Meadows."

She paused, and her gaze shifted to his face before she began to add supplements to the grain.

"To my way of thinking, there aren't many people as worthy as one good horse. Your parents are admirable people. Not just for what they have, but much more for what they've done, and what they do with it. I'm honored to work for them. And," he said when she turned to him again, "they're lucky to have me."

She laughed. "Apparently they agree with you." Shaking her head, she moved by to start the feeding, and as she passed him he breathed in the scent of her hair, of her skin.

"But you're not sure you do. Though you don't seem to have much interest in the workings of the farm itself."

"Don't I?"

He studied the neatly typed list on the wall that indicated which supplements in what amounts were added for each particular horse for the evening feed. "I see your sisters and your brothers on a daily basis," he commented as he began to fix Teddy's meal. "Everyone in your family, down at the shedrow, or at the track, but you."

She could have told him the time and placement of every horse they'd run that past week. Which were being medicated, which mares were breeding. Pride kept her silent. She preferred thinking of it as pride, and not sheer stubbornness.

"I suppose your little school keeps you busy."

Her teeth clamped together, wanted to grind, but she spoke through them. "Oh, yes, my little school keeps me busy."

"You're a good teacher." He moved to Teddy's box.

"Thank you so much."

"No need to be snotty about it. You are a good teacher. And one of those rich kids might stick it out, rather than getting bored once horse fever's passed."

"One of my rich kids," she murmured.

"It takes skill, endurance, and money, doesn't it, to compete in horse shows. I don't follow show jumping myself, though I've found it pretty enough to watch. You might be training yourself a champion. The Royal International or Dublin Grand Prix. Maybe the Olympics."

"So, let's see if I get this. Rich kids compete in horse shows and win blue ribbons and those who aren't so privileged do what? Become grooms?"

"That's how the world works, doesn't it?"

"That's how it can work. You're a snob, Brian."

He looked up, flabbergasted. "What?"

"You're a snob, and the worst kind of snob—the kind who thinks he's broad-minded. Now that I know that, you don't bother me at all."

The stable phone rang, delighting her. Whoever was on the other end not only had perfect timing but they had her gratitude. It gave her great pleasure to see the absolute shock on Brian's face as she walked to the phone.

"Royal Meadows Riding Academy. Would you hold one moment, please." With a friendly smile, she laid a hand over the receiver. "Really, I can finish up here. I'm keeping you from your work."

"I'm not a snob," he finally managed to say.

"Of course you wouldn't see it that way. Can we discuss this another time? I need to take this call."

Irked, he shoved the scoop back in the grain. "I'm not the one wearing bloody diamonds in my ears," he muttered as he stalked out.

It put him out of humor for the rest of the day. It stuck in his craw and festered there. A nasty little canker sore on the ego.

Snob? Where did the woman get off calling him a snob?

And after he'd made the effort to be friendly, even compliment her on her snooty little riding academy.

He did the evening check himself, as was his habit, and spent considerable time going over the prime filly who was to head down to Hialeah to race there. Travis wanted Brian to go along for this one, and he was more than happy to oblige.

It would do him a world of good to put a thousand miles or so between himself and Keeley.

"Shouldn't be looking in that direction, even for a blink," he muttered, then nuzzled the filly. "Especially when I've got a darling like you in hand. We'll have us a time in Florida, won't we, you and me?"

"Poker game tonight," one of the grooms called out as Brian left the stables. He added an eyebrow wiggle and a grin to the announcement.

"I'll be back then. And it'll be my pleasure to empty your pockets." But for now, he thought, he had paperwork of his own.

When he returned from Florida they'd separate the foals from their mothers. The weanlings would cause a commotion the first day or so. And the yearling training would begin in earnest. He had charts to make, schedules to outline, plans to ponder.

And he wanted to put a great deal of personal time into the forming of Bad Betty.

He had no business detouring toward Keeley's stable. Still it would only take a minute, Brian told himself, to set the woman straight.

But instead of Keeley, he found her sister. Sarah stopped her dash past him and waved. "Hi. Wonderful evening, isn't it? I'm going to take advantage of it and sneak in a ride before sunset. Want to join me?"

It was tempting. She was good company, and he hadn't

felt a horse under him in weeks. But there was work. "I'd love to, another time. You riding one of Keeley's?"

"Yeah. She's always up for someone to exercise one of her babies. The kids don't give them much of a workout, so they can get stale. Or bored. Her Saturday class is a little more advanced, but still."

He fell into step beside her. "I don't suppose an hour of posture and posting does much for the horses."

"Oh, she lets them out to pasture, and rides herself whenever she can fit it in. Which isn't as much as she'd like, but the kids are the priority. And that hour of posture and posting does a lot for them."

He made a noncommittal sound as they rounded the building. He hoped Keeley was still inside what he supposed was an office. He wanted a word with her. "I saw part of her class today."

"Did you? Aren't they cute? Today's what...oh, yeah, Willy. Did you notice the little guy, dark hair and eyes? He rides Teddy."

"Aye. He has good form, and he's cheerful about it."

"He is now. He was a scared little rabbit when Keeley took him on." Sarah swung into the stables, headed directly for the tack room.

"Afraid of horses?"

"Of everything. I don't know how people can do that to a child. I'll never understand it."

"Do what?"

She chose her tack, murmuring a thanks when Brian took the saddle from her. "Hurt them." She glanced back. "Oh, I thought since you'd seen the class, Keeley would have told you the whole deal about the school."

"No." He took the saddle blanket as well. "We didn't get to that. Why don't you tell me the whole deal?"

"Sure." She went to the old mare, cooed. "There's my girl. Want to go for a ride? Sure you do." She slipped the bridle on, fixed the bit, then led the mare out. "I don't know if it started with the horses or the kids. It all seemed to happen at the same time. She bought Eastern Star first. He was a thoroughbred, five years old, and he hadn't lived up to his potential. According to the owners. They pumped him up before a race."

"Drugged him."

"Amphetamines." Her pretty face went hard. "They got caught, but they'd damaged Star's heart and kidneys in the process. She bought him. We nursed him, did everything we could. He didn't last a year. It still gets me," Sarah murmured.

She shook her head and began to saddle her mount. "After that it was like a mission to Keeley. So I guess the horses came first. She put this place together, and got the word out that she was opening a small academy. The ones who can pay, pay a very stiff fee to have her teach their kids—and she's worth it. Those stiff fees help subsidize the other students."

"What other students?"

"Ones like Willy." Sarah cinched the saddle, checked the stirrups. "Underprivileged, abused, circling the system kids. She takes them for nothing—no, she hunts them up, sponsors them, outfits them, works with a child psychologist. It's why she doesn't have as much time to ride as she used to. Our Keeley doesn't do anything halfway. She'd take more on, but she wants to keep the classes small so each kid gets plenty of attention. So she's campaigning for other academies, other owners to start similar programs."

Sarah patted the mare's neck. "I'm surprised she didn't

mention it. She rarely misses an opportunity to talk some-one into getting involved."

With a cheerful smile, she vaulted into the saddle. "Listen, would you like to come up for dinner? I hear Dad's grilling chicken."

"Thanks all the same, but I've plans. Enjoy your ride."

He had plans all right, he thought as Sarah trotted off. To eat crow. He wasn't sure what it tasted like, but he already knew he wasn't going to enjoy it.

He walked around to the office, knocked. He supposed if he'd been wearing a hat, he'd have held it in his hands. When she didn't answer, he opened the door, glanced in.

Neat, organized, as expected. The air smelled of her—just the faintest echo of scent.

But everything inside was designed for business. A desk—with a computer he imagined was a great deal more in use than Paddy's—a two-line telephone and a little fax machine. File cabinets, two trim chairs and a small fridge. Curious, he walked in and opened it. Then had to grin when he saw it was stocked with bottles of the soft drink she seemed to live on.

A scan of the walls had the grin turning to a wince. Blue ribbons, medals, awards were all neatly framed and displayed. There were photographs of her in formal riding gear flying over jumps, smiling from the back of a horse or standing with her cheek pressed to her mount's neck.

And in a thick frame was an Olympic medal. A silver.

"Well, hell. We'll make that two portions of crow," he murmured.

Chapter 4

It was his fault. She could put the blame for this entirely on Brian Donnelly's shoulders. If he hadn't been so insufferable, if he hadn't been there *being* insufferable when Chad had called, she wouldn't have agreed to go out to dinner. And she wouldn't have spent nearly four hours being bored brainless when she could've been doing something more useful.

Like watching paint dry.

There was nothing wrong with Chad, really. If you only had, say, half a brain, no real interest outside of the cut of this year's designer jacket and were thrilled by a rip-roaring debate over the proper way to serve a triple latte, he was the perfect companion.

Unfortunately, she didn't qualify on any of those levels.

Right now he was droning on about the painting he'd bought at a recent art show. No, not the painting, Keeley thought wearily. A discussion of the painting, of art, might have been the medical miracle that prevented her from slipping into a coma. But Chad was discoursing—no other word for it—on The Investment.

He had the windows up and the air conditioning blasting as they drove. It was a perfectly beautiful night, she mused, but putting the windows down meant Chad's hair would be mussed. Couldn't have that.

At least she didn't have to attempt conversation. Chad preferred monologues.

What he wanted was an attractive companion of the right family and tax bracket who dressed well and would sit quietly while he pontificated on the narrow areas of his interest.

Keeley was fully aware he'd decided she fit the bill, and now she'd only encouraged him by agreeing to this endlessly tedious date.

"The broker assured me that within three years the piece will be worth five times what I paid for it. Normally I would have hesitated as the artist is young and relatively unknown, but the show was quite successful. I noticed T.D. Giles considering two of the pieces personally. And you know how astute T.D. is about such things. Did I tell you I ran into his wife, Sissy, the other day? She looks absolutely marvelous. The eye tuck did wonders for her, and she tells me she's found the most amazing new stylist."

Oh God, was all Keeley could think. Oh God, get me out of here.

When they swung through the stone pillars at Royal Meadows, she had to fight the urge to cheer.

"I'm so glad our schedules finally clicked. Life gets much too demanding and complicated, doesn't it? There's nothing more relaxing than a quiet dinner for two."

Any more relaxed, Keeley thought, and unconsciousness

would claim her. "It was nice of you to ask me, Chad." She wondered how rude it would be to spring out of the car before it stopped, race to the house and do a little dance of relief on the front porch.

Pretty rude, she decided. Okay, she'd skip the dance.

"Drake and Pamela—you know the Larkens of course—are having a little soirée next Saturday evening. Why don't I pick you up at eightish?"

It took her a minute to get over the fact he'd actually used the word *soirée* in a sentence. "I really can't, Chad. I have a full day of lessons on Saturday. By the time it's done I'm not fit for socializing. But thanks." She slid her hand to the door handle, anticipating escape.

"Keeley, you can't let your little school eclipse so much of your life."

Her hand stiffened, and though she could see the lights of home, she turned her head and studied his perfect profile. One day, someone was going to refer to the academy as *her little school,* and she was going to be very rude. And rip their throat out. "Can't I?"

"I'm sure it amuses you. Hobbies are very satisfying."

"Hobbies." She bared her teeth.

"Everyone needs an outlet, I suppose." He lifted a hand from the wheel and gracefully waved away over two years of hard work. "But you must take time for yourself. Just the other day Renny mentioned she hadn't seen you in ages. After all, when the novelty wears off, you'll wonder where all this time has gone."

"My school is not a hobby, an amusement, or a novelty. And it is completely my business."

"Naturally. Of course." He gave her a patronizing little pat on the knee as he stopped the car, shifted toward her. "But you must admit, it's taking up an inordinate amount of your time. Why it's taken us six months to have dinner together."

"Is that all?"

He misinterpreted the quiet response, and the gleam in her eyes. And leaned toward her.

She slapped a hand on his chest. "Don't even think about it. Let me tell you something, pal. I do more in one day with my school than you do in a week of pushing papers in that office your grandfather gave you between your manicures and amaretto lattes and soirées. Men like you hold no interest for me whatsoever, which is why it's taken six months for this tedious little date. And the next time I have dinner with you, we'll be slurping Popsicles in hell. So take your French tie and your Italian shoes and stuff them."

Utter shock had him speechless as she shoved open her door. As insult trickled in, his lips thinned. "Obviously spending so much time in the stables has eroded your manners, and your outlook."

"That's right, Chad." She leaned back in the door. "You're too good for me. I'm about to go up and weep into my pillow over it."

"Rumor is you're cold," he said in a quiet, stabbing voice. "But I had to find out for myself."

It stung, but she wasn't about to let it show. "Rumor is you're a moron. Now we've both confirmed the local gossip."

He gunned the engine once, and she would have sworn she saw him vibrate. "And it's a British tie."

She slammed the car door, then watched narrow-eyed as he drove away. "A British tie." A laugh gurgled up, deep from the belly and up into the throat so she had to stand, hugging herself, all but howling at the moon. "That sure told me."

Indulging herself in a long sigh, she tipped her head back, looked up at the sweep of stars. "Moron," she murmured. "And that goes for both of us."

She heard a faint *click,* spun around and saw Brian lighting a slim cigar. "Lover's spat?"

"Why yes." The temper Chad had roused stirred again. "He wants to take me to Antigua and I simply have my heart set on Mozambique. Antigua's been done to death."

Brian took a contemplative puff of his cigar. She looked so damn beautiful standing there in the moonlight in that little excuse of a black dress, her hair spilling down her back like fire on silk. Hearing her long, gorgeous roll of laughter had been like discovering a treasure. Now the temper was back in her eyes, and spitting at him.

It was almost as good.

He took another lazy puff, blew out a cloud of smoke. "You're winding me up, Keeley."

"I'd like to wind you up, then twist you into small pieces and ship them all back to Ireland."

"I figured as much." He disposed of the cigar and walked to her. Unlike Chad, he didn't misinterpret the glint in her eye. "You want to have a pop at someone." He closed his hand over the one she'd balled into a fist, lifted it to tap on his own chin. "Go ahead."

"As delightful as I find that invitation, I don't solve my disputes that way." When she started to walk away, he tightened his grip. "But," she said slowly, "I could make an exception."

"I don't like apologizing, and I wouldn't have to— again—if you'd set me straight right off."

She lifted an eyebrow. Trying to free herself from that big, hard hand would only be undignified. "And are you referring to my little school?"

"It's a fine thing you're doing. An admirable thing, and not a little one at all. I'd like to help you."

"Excuse me?"

"I'd like to give you a hand with it when I can. Give you some of my time."

Off balance, she shook her head. "I don't need any help."

"I don't imagine you do. But it couldn't hurt, could it?"

She studied him with equal parts suspicion and interest. "Why?"

"Why not. You'll admit I know horses. I have a strong back. And I believe in what you're doing."

It was the last that cut through her defenses. No one outside of family had understood what she wanted to do as easily. She flexed her hand in his, and when he released her, stepped back. "Are you offering because you feel guilty?"

"I'm offering because I'm interested. Feeling guilty made me apologize."

"You haven't apologized yet." But she smiled a little as she began to walk. "Never mind. I might be able to use a strong back from time to time." She glanced over as he fell into step beside her. It looked like he had one, she mused, skimming her gaze over the rough jeans and plain white T-shirt he wore.

A strong, healthy body, good hands and an innate understanding of horses. She could do a great deal worse, she supposed. "Do you ride?"

"Well, of course I ride," he began, then caught her smirky little smile. "Having me on again, are you?"

"That one was easy." She turned to wander along a path that meandered through late-blooming shrubs and an arbor of gleaming moonflowers. "I won't pay you."

"I've a job, thanks."

"The kids handle a lot of the chores," she told him. "It's

part of the package. This isn't just about teaching them to post and change leads at a canter. It's about trust—in themselves, in their horse, in me. Making a connection with their horse. Shoveling manure makes quite a connection."

He grinned. "I can't argue with that."

"Still they're kids, so fun is a big part of the program. And they're learning so they don't always do the best job mucking out or grooming. And there isn't always enough time to have them deal properly with the tack."

"I started my illustrious career with a pitchfork in my hand and saddle soap in my pocket."

Idly he tugged a white blossom from the vine, tucked it into her hair. The gesture flustered her—the easy charm of it—and made her remember they were walking in the moonlight, among the flowers.

Not, she reminded herself, a good idea.

"All right then. If and when you've time to spare, I've got an extra pitchfork."

When she veered toward the house he took her hand again. "Don't go in yet. It's a pretty night and a shame to waste it with sleeping."

His voice was lovely, with a soothing lilt. There was no reason she could think of why it made her want to shiver. "We both have to be up early."

"True enough, but we're young, aren't we? I saw your medal."

Distracted, she forgot to pull her hand away. "My medal?"

"Your Olympic medal. I went looking for you in your office."

"The medal lures parents who can afford the tuition."

"It's something to be proud of."

"I am proud of it." With her free hand she brushed her

hair as the breeze teased it. Her fingertips skimmed over the soft petals of the flower. "But it doesn't define me."

"Not like, what was it? A British tie?"

The laugh got away from her, and eased the odd tension that had been building inside her. "Here's a surprise. With a great deal of time and some effort, I might begin to like you."

"I've plenty of time." He released her hand to toy with the ends of her hair. She jerked back. "You're a skittish one," he murmured.

"No, not particularly." Usually, she thought. With most people.

"The thing is, I like to touch," he told her and deliberately skimmed his fingers over her hair again. "It's that... connection. You learn by touching."

"I don't..." She trailed off when those fingers ran firmly down the back of her neck.

"I've learned you carry your worries right there, right at the base there. More worries than show on your face. It's a staggering face you have, Keeley. Throws a man off."

The tension was slipping away from under his fingers as he touched her, and building everywhere else. A kind of gathering inside her, a concentration of heat. The pressure in her chest was so sudden and strong it made her breath short. The muscles in her stomach began to twist, tighten. Ache.

"My face doesn't have anything to do with what I am."

"Maybe not, but that doesn't take away the pure pleasure of looking at it."

If she hadn't trembled, he might have resisted. It was a mistake. But he'd made them before, would make them again. There was moonlight, and the scent of the last of summer's roses in the air. Was a man supposed to walk away from a beautiful woman who trembled under his hand?

Not this man, he thought.

"Too pretty a night to waste it," he said again, and bent toward her.

She jerked back when his mouth was a whisper from hers, but his fingers continued to play over her neck, keeping her close. His gaze dropped to her lips, lingered, then came back to hers.

And he smiled. *"Cushla machree,"* he murmured, and as if it were an incantation, she slid under the spell.

His lips brushed hers, wing-soft. Everything inside her fluttered in response. He drew her closer, gradually luring her body to fit against his, curves to angles, as his hand played rhythmically up and down her spine.

A light scrape of teeth, and her lips parted for him.

Her head went light, her blood hot, and her body seemed balanced on the brink of something high and thin. It was lovely, lovely to feel this soft, this female, this open. She brought her hands to his shoulders, clung there while she let herself teeter on that delicious edge.

He knew how to be gentle, there had always been gentleness inside him for the fragile. But her sudden and utter surrender to him, to herself, had him forcing back the need to grab and plunder. Resistance was what he'd expected. Anything from cool disdain to impulsive passion he would have understood. But this…giving destroyed him.

"More," he murmured against her mouth. "Just a little more." And deepened the kiss.

She made a sound in her throat, a low purr that slipped into his system like silk. His heart shook, then it stumbled, then God help him, it fell.

The shock of it had him yanking her back, staring at her

with the edgy caution of a man suddenly finding himself holding a tiger instead of a kitten.

Had he actually thought it a mistake? Nothing more than a simple mistake? He'd just put the power to crush him into her hands.

"Damn it."

She blinked at him, struggling to catch up with the abrupt change. His face was fierce, and the hands that had shifted to her arms no longer gentle. She wanted to shiver, but wouldn't permit another show of weakness.

"Let me go."

"I didn't force you."

"I didn't say you did."

Her lips still throbbed from the pressure of his, and her stomach quaked. Rumor was she was cold, she thought dimly. And she'd believed it herself. Finding out differently wasn't cause for celebration. But for panic.

"I don't want this." This vulnerability, this need.

"Neither do I." He released her to jam his hands into his pockets. "That makes this quite the situation."

"It's not a situation if we don't let it be one." She wanted to rub a hand over her heart, to hold it there. It amazed her that he couldn't hear it hammering. "We're both grown-ups, able to take responsibility for our own actions. That was a momentary lapse on both our parts. It won't happen again."

"And if it does?"

"It won't, because each of us have priorities and a... situation would complicate matters. We'll forget it. Good night."

She walked to the house. She didn't run, though part of her wanted to. And another part, a part that brought her no pride, simply wanted him to stop her.

* * *

He'd hoped the time away in Florida with work at the center of his world would help him do just what she'd said to do. Forget it.

But he hadn't, and couldn't, and finally decided it had been a ridiculous thing for her to expect. Since he was suffering, he saw no reason why he should let her off so damn easy.

He knew how to handle women, he reminded himself. And princess or not, Keeley was a woman under it all. She was going to discover she couldn't swat Brian Donnelly aside like a pesky fly.

He walked up from the stables, his bag slung over his shoulder. He'd yet to go to his quarters, and had slept very little on the drive back from Hialeah. He could have flown back, but the choice to stay with the horses and make the drive had been his.

His horses had done all he'd asked of them, made him proud at heart and plumper in the pocket. Seeing that they were delivered home and settled back again was the least he could do.

But right now he wanted nothing more than a hot shower, a shave and a decent cup of tea.

Though he'd have traded all of that for one more taste of Keeley.

Knowing it irritated him had him scowling in the direction of her paddock. The minute he was cleaned up, he promised himself, the two of them would have a little conversation. Very little, he decided, before he got his hands on her again. And when he did, he was going to—

The erotic image he conjured in his head burst like a bubble when he rounded the house and saw Keeley's mother kneeling at the flower bed.

It was not the most comfortable thing to come across the mother when you'd been picturing the daughter naked. Then Adelia looked over at him, and he saw the tears on her cheeks. And his mind went blank.

"Ah… Mrs. Grant."

"Brian." Sniffling, she wiped her cheeks with the back of her hand. "I was doing some weeding. Just tidying up the beds here." She tugged at the cap on her head, then she lowered her hands, dropped back on her heels. "I'm sorry."

"Ah…" Said that already, he thought, panicked. Say something else. He was never so helpless as he was with female tears.

"I'm missing Uncle Paddy. He left yesterday." She didn't quite muffle a sob. "I thought if I came by here and fiddled, I'd feel some better, but it's knowing he's not down at the stables, or up there. I know he had to go. I know he wanted to go. But…"

"Ah…" Oh hell. Frantic, Brian dug in his back pocket for his bandanna. "Maybe you should…"

"Thanks." She took the cloth as he crouched beside her. "You'll know what it's like, I think, being away from family."

"Well, mine's not close, so to speak."

"Family's family." She dried her face, blew out a breath.

She looked so young, he thought, and not like a mother at all, with her cap crooked on her head and her eyes drenched. He did what came natural for him, and took her hand.

For a moment, she leaned her head on his shoulder, sighed. "He changed everything for me, Paddy did, when he brought me here. I was so nervous coming all this way. New place, new people. A new country. And I hadn't seen Paddy outside pictures for years, or even been face-to-face since I was a baby, but as soon as I saw him, it was all right again. I don't know what I'd have done without him."

It loosened the fist around her heart to talk. Soothed her that he gave her the quiet that was an offer to listen.

"I didn't want to blubber in front of Travis and the children because they're missing him, too. And I was holding on pretty well until I came down here. This is where I lived when I first came to Royal Meadows. In a pretty room with green walls and white curtains. I was so young."

"I guess you're old and decrepit now," Brian said and was relieved when she laughed.

"Well, perhaps not quite decrepit, but I was greener then. I'd never seen a place like this in all my life, and I was going to be living right in the middle of it thanks to Paddy. If it hadn't been for him, I don't think Travis would ever have taken the likes of me on as a groom."

"A groom." Brian's brows lifted. "I thought that was a made-up story."

"Indeed it's not," she said with some heat—and an unmistakable touch of pride. "I earned my keep around here, make no mistake. I was a damn fine groom in my time. Majesty was mine."

Brian lowered himself until he was sitting on the ground beside her. "You groomed Majesty?"

"That I did, and was there to watch him take the Derby. Oh, I loved that horse. You know what it's like."

"I do, yes."

"We lost him only last year. A fine long life he had. I think that was when Paddy decided it was time for him to go home again. He's there by now, and I know what he sees when he stands out in front of the house, and that's a comfort. As you've been just now, Brian. Thank you."

"I didn't do anything. I fumble with tears."

"You listened." She handed him back his bandanna.

"Mostly because tears render me speechless. You've a bit of garden dirt here."

Keeley came down the path just in time to see Brian gently wipe her mother's face with a blue bandanna. The tearstains had her leaping forward like a mama bear to her threatened cub.

"What is it? What did you do?" Hissing at Brian, she wrapped an arm around Adelia's shoulder.

"Nothing. I just knocked your mother down and kicked her a few times."

"Keeley." With a surprised laugh, Adelia patted her daughter's hand. "Brian's done nothing but lend me his hankie and his shoulder while I had a little cry over Uncle Paddy."

"Oh, Mama." Keeley pressed her cheek to Adelia's, rubbed. "Don't be sad."

"I have to be, a little. But I'm better now." She leaned over, surprising Brian with a kiss on the cheek. "You're a nice young man, and a patient one."

He got to his feet to help her up. "I don't have much of a reputation for either, Mrs. Grant."

"That's because not everyone looks close enough. You should be able to call me Dee easy enough now that I've cried on you. I'm going down to the stables, do some work."

"She never cries," Keeley murmured when her mother walked away. "Not unless she's very happy or very sad. I'm sorry I jumped at you that way, but when I saw she'd been crying, I stopped thinking."

"Tears affect me much the same way, so we'll let it be."

She nodded, then cast around for something to say that would help relieve the awkwardness. She'd been so sure she'd be controlled and composed when she saw him again. "So, I heard you did well at Hialeah."

"We did. Your Hero runs particularly well in a crowd."

"Yes, I've seen him. He lives to run." She noted the bag Brian had set down. "And here you are not even really back yet, and you've had one woman crying on your shoulder and another swiping at you. I really am sorry."

"Sorry enough to make me some tea while I clean up?"

"I...all right, but I've got less than an hour."

"Takes a good deal less to brew a pot of tea." Satisfied, he started up the steps. "You've a class this afternoon then?"

"Yes." Trapped, Keeley shrugged and followed him up and inside. He'd been kind to her mother, she reminded herself. She was obliged to repay that. "At three-thirty. I have some things to do before the students arrive."

"Well, I won't be long. You know where the kitchen is, I expect."

She frowned after him as he strolled off into the bedroom.

Making him cozy pots of tea wasn't how she'd expected to handle the situation, she thought. She'd given it a great deal of consideration and had decided the best thing all around would be to maintain a polite, marginally friendly distance. That business the other night had been nothing but a moment's foolishness. Harmless.

Incredible.

She gave herself a shake and got down the old teapot Paddy had favored. No, it was nothing to worry about. In fact, on one level she really should be grateful to Brian. He'd shown her she wasn't as indifferent to men as she'd believed. It had bothered her a little that she'd never felt that spark so many of her friends had spoken of.

Well, she'd certainly felt a whole firestorm of sparks when he'd put his hands on her. And that was good, that was healthy. Someone had finally caught her at the right time and the right place and the right mood. If it could happen once, it could happen again.

With someone else, of course. When she decided it was time.

She set the tea aside to steep, then opening a cupboard stretched high for a cup.

"I'll get that." He moved in behind her, handily trapping her between his body and the counter. Closed his hand over hers on the cup.

She could smell the shower on him, feel the heat of it. And her mouth went dry.

"I decided I don't care to forget it."

She had to concentrate on regulating her breathing. "I beg your pardon?"

"And that I'm not going to let you forget it, either."

She needed to swallow, but her throat wouldn't cooperate. "We agreed—"

"No, we didn't." He brought the cup down, set it aside. "We agreed we didn't want this." The ponytail she wore left a lovely curve of her neck bare. He nuzzled there. "And I'd say there's been an unspoken agreement that despite that, we want each other."

The firestorm was back, a burst at the base of her neck that showered heat down her spine. "We don't know each other."

"I know how you taste." He nipped lightly at flesh. "And feel, and smell. I see your face in my mind whether I want to or not." He spun her around, and his eyes were dark and restless. "Why should you have a choice when I don't?"

His mouth crushed down on hers, a hot and dangerous

thrill. With his hands gripped in her hair, he pressed his body to hers.

And this time she felt as much anger as passion in the embrace. Now, wrapped around the thrill, was a thin snake of fear. The combination was unbearably exciting.

"I'm not ready for this." She struggled back. "I'm not ready for this. Can you understand?"

"No." But he understood what he saw in her eyes. He'd frightened her, and he'd no right to do so. "But then again, I don't want to." So he backed away. "Your mother said I was a patient man. I can be, under some circumstances. I'll wait, because you'll come to me. There's something alive between us, so when you're ready, you'll come to me."

"There's a thin line between confidence and arrogance, Brian. Watch your step," she suggested as she started for the door.

"I missed you."

Her hand closed over the knob, but she couldn't turn it. "You know all the angles," she murmured.

"That may be true. But still I missed you. Thanks for the tea."

She sighed. "You're welcome," she said, and left him.

Chapter 5

Bad Betty had more than earned her name. She didn't just make trouble, she looked for it. Nothing seemed to please her more than nipping at grooms. Unless it was kicking exercise boys. She chased other yearlings when out in pasture, then reared and kicked and snorted bad-temperedly when it was time to be stabled for the night.

For all those reasons, and more, Brian adored her.

There was a communal sigh of relief in the shedrow when he opted to deal with her personally. She tested him, and though she rarely got by Brian's guard he had an impressive rainbow of bruises with her name on them.

There were mutters that she was a man-eater, but Brian knew better. She was a rebel. And she was a winner. It was only a matter of teaching her how to start winning without damaging that wild spirit.

On the longe line he circled her into a walk while she pretended to ignore him. Still, when he spoke to her, her ears twitched, and now and then she sent him a sidelong glance. And days of hard work were rewarded when he lengthened the line and she broke into a canter.

"Ah, that's the way. What a beauty you are." He'd liked to have captured that moment—the gorgeous filly cantering gracefully in a circle, while green hills rolled up to a blue sky.

It would make a picture, and look to some like a frolic. But those who knew would see this moment—a racehorse learning to take commands from signals transmitted through her mouth—was another step toward the finish line.

He saw one more thing as he looked at her, as he studied lines and form and that unmistakable gleam in her eyes.

He saw his destiny.

"We'll go, you and I," he said quietly. "We were meant to go together. Rebels we are, or so people say who can't see where we're headed. We've races to win, don't we?"

He shortened the line, and she dropped into a trot. Shortened it still further and her gait changed to a walk. Sweat gleamed on her coat, trickled down his back. Summer wasn't just clinging to September. It was pummeling it.

They ignored the heat, and watched each other.

Again and again he used the line to signal her as she circled, and all the while he praised her.

Watching was irresistible. She had work to do, chores piled up. But if she couldn't take a few moments out on a brilliant September day to watch a little magic, what was the point?

She leaned on the paddock fence, enjoying the view as Brian put Betty through her paces. Her father had been right in hiring him, she thought. There was a connection between man and horse that was stronger, and even more tangible than the line between them. She could feel it. Amusement, affection, challenge.

This wasn't something that could be taught. It simply was.

She knew Brian took time for every weanling on the farm when he wasn't out of town at a race. That wasn't an easy task in an operation as large as Royal Meadows. But it was the kind of touch that made a difference. A smart and caring horseman knew that the more a horse was handled, touched, communicated with during its youth, the better it would respond to later training.

"Looks good, doesn't she?" Brian said as he let out the line for one last canter.

"Very. You've made considerable progress with her."

"We've made progress with each other, haven't we *a ghra.* She's ready to feel a rider on her."

Knowing Betty's reputation, Keeley tucked her tongue in her cheek. "And who are you bribing—or threatening—to get up on her?"

Gradually Brian shortened the line, and Betty moved into an even trot. "Want the job?"

"I have a job, thanks." But it was tempting.

Brian knew when a seed planted needed to be left alone to sprout. "Well, she'll have her first weight on her tomorrow morning." He shortened the line again, moving Betty toward him, and both of them toward Keeley.

He liked the look of her there against the fence, with her hair as glossy as the filly's coat, and her eyes as cautious. "This one won't be placid and eager to please. But she'll come round, won't you, *maverneen?*"

He stroked the filly's neck, and she sniffed at the pouch on his belt, then turned her head away.

"She wants to let me know she doesn't care that I've apples in here. No, doesn't matter a bit to her." He looped the line around the fence and took an apple and his knife from his pocket. Idly he cut it in half. "Maybe I'll just offer this token to this other pretty lady here."

He held out the apple to Keeley, and Betty gave him a solid rap with her head that rammed him into the fence. "Now she wants my attention. Would you like some of this then?"

He shifted, held the apple out. Betty nipped it from his palm with dignified delicacy. "She loves me."

"She loves your apples," Keeley commented.

"Oh, it's not just that. See here." Before Keeley could evade—could think to—he cupped a hand at the back of her neck, pulled her close and rubbed his lips provocatively over hers.

Betty huffed out a breath and butted him.

"You see?" Brian let his teeth graze lightly before he released Keeley. "Jealous. She doesn't care to have me give my affection to another woman."

"Next time kiss her and save yourself a bruise."

"It was worth it. On both counts."

"Horses are more easily charmed than women, Donnelly." She plucked the apple out of his hand, bit in. "I just like your apples," she told him, and strolled away.

"That one's as contrary as you are." He nuzzled Betty's cheek as he watched Keeley walk to her stables. "What is it that makes me find contrary females so appealing?"

She hadn't meant to go down to the yearling stalls. Really. It was just that she was up early, her own morning chores were done. And she was curious. When she stepped inside the stables, out of the soft gray dawn, the first thing she heard was Brian's voice.

It made her smile. At least the exasperation in it made her smile.

"Come on now, Jim, you lost the draw. You can't be welshing on me."

"I'm not. I'm gearing up."

The young exercise boy was gritting his teeth and rolling his shoulders when Keeley stepped up to the box. "Good morning. I heard you drew the short straw, Jim."

"Yeah, just my luck." He shot a mournful look at Betty. "This one wants to eat me."

"Chew you up and spit you out more like," Brian said in disgust. "You're just giving her cause now by letting her know she intimidates you. You'll go down in history today—the first weight the next winner of the Triple Crown feels on her back."

As if reacting to the prediction, Betty snorted, tried to dance as Brian firmed his grip on the shortened reins. And Jim's eyes went big as moons in a pale face.

"I'll do it." Keeley wasn't sure if it was the challenge of it, or compassion for the terrified boy. "If it's an historic moment, it should be a Grant up on a Royal Meadows champion." She smiled at Jim as she said it. "Let me have the jacket and hat."

"You sure?" With more hope than shame, Jim looked from Keeley to Brian.

"She's the boss. In a manner of speaking," Brian told him. "Your loss here, Jim."

"I'll take the loss and save all my skin." A little too eagerly, he started out of the box. As if sensing her opening, Betty bunched, kicked out. Swearing, Brian shoved Jim aside with his shoulder and took the hoof in the ribs.

The air went blue, and every curse was in an undertone that only added impact. Without a second thought, Keeley moved into the box and laid her hand over his on the reins to help control the filly.

A thousand pounds of horse fought to plunge. Keeley felt the heat from her, and from Brian when their bodies bumped together. "How bad did she get you?"

"Not as bad as she'd like." But enough, he thought, to steal his breath and have the pain shooting up until he saw stars dancing.

He tossed the hair out of his eyes, blinked at the sweat stinging in them and muscled the filly down.

"Man, Bri, I'm sorry."

"You should have more sense than to turn your back on a skittish filly," Brian snapped out. "Next time I'll let her take a shot at your head. Go on out. She knows she's bested you. Stand back," he ordered Keeley in the same cold tone of command, then he jerked the reins just enough to bring Betty's head down.

"So this is how it's to be? You want all the temper and none of the glory? Am I wasting my time with you? Maybe you don't want to run. We'll just wait until you come into season and bring a stallion in to mount you, and set you out to pasture to breed. Then you'll never know, will you, what it is to win."

Just outside the box, Keeley slipped on the padded jacket and hat. And waited. There was a line of damp down the back of his shirt, his hair was a wild tangle of brown and gold. Muscles rippled in his arms, and his boots were scarred and filthy.

He looked, she decided, exactly how a horseman should look. Powerful. Confident. And just arrogant enough to believe he could win over an animal more than five times his weight.

He kept talking, but he'd switched to Gaelic now. Slowly, the rhythm of the words smoothed out, and warmed. Almost like a song, they played in the air, rising, falling. Mesmerizing.

The filly stood quiet now, her dark brown eyes focused on Brian's green ones.

Seduced, Keeley thought. She was watching a kind of seduction. She'll do anything for him, Keeley realized. Who wouldn't if he touched you that way, looked at you that way, used his voice on you that way?

"Come in here," he told Keeley. "Let her get your scent. Touch her so she can feel you."

"I know how it's done," she murmured. Though she'd never seen it done quite like this.

She slipped into the stall, ran her hands gently over Betty's neck, her side. She felt the muscles quiver under her hand, but the filly looked at nothing and no one but Brian.

"I've seen countless people work in countless ways with countless horses." Keeley spoke quietly as she stroked Betty. But like the horse, her eyes were on Brian. "I've never seen anyone like you. You have a gift."

His eyes shifted, met hers, held for a moment. One timeless moment. "She has the gift. Talk to her."

"Betty. Not-so-bad Betty. You scared poor Jim, didn't you, but you don't scare me. I think you're beautiful." She saw the filly's ears lay back, felt the slight shift under her hands, but kept talking. "You want to race, don't you? Well, you can't do it alone. I'd tell you this isn't going to hurt, but you don't care about that anyway. It's all pride with you."

Once again she looked at Brian. "It's all pride," she repeated, understanding both horse and man. "But you can't have the pride of winning without this step."

When Brian tightened the saddle, everyone seemed to hold their breath. Then Keeley let hers out, and put her knee in Brian's hands for a leg up.

She bellied over the saddle, lay still as Betty shied. She knew just what could happen if the filly wasn't controlled.

A wrong move on anyone's part and she could find herself under several hundred pounds of agitated horse.

But Brian's voice whispered, soft and dreamy, and the light began to go pale gold. Slowly Keeley eased herself up until she sat, her feet sliding into the stirrups.

The new sensation had Betty fighting to toss her head, dancing back and kicking out. Now Keeley leaned forward, stroking, and added her voice to Brian's.

"Get used to it," she ordered in a no-nonsense tone directly opposed to his crooning. "You were born for this."

"There now, *cushla*." His lips twitched at the corners as he soothed Betty. "She's not so scary now, is she? She's hardly much of a thing at all up there on your big, beautiful back. She's only a princess, but you, you're a queen, aren't you?"

"So, I'm outranked?" Keeley wasn't sure if she was amused or insulted.

Gradually the restless movements stilled. Brian took a chunk of apple from his pocket, fed it to Betty with murmured praise and reassurance. "She's doing well."

"She'd like to bounce me off the ceiling."

"Oh aye, that she would, but she's not trying it at the moment. You're doing well, too." His gaze lifted until his eyes met Keeley's. "As natural at this as she is. Blue bloods, both of you."

"Are we making history, Brian?"

"Bet on it," he told her and kissed Betty just above the nose.

She gave him most of the morning. Dismounting, remounting, sitting quietly while he led them around the stall. Betty gave a couple of bucks, but everyone knew it was only for show.

"Will you try the walking ring with her?"

Keeley started to decline. She had work, and was already

behind for the day. But the feel of the young, fresh horse under her was too much of a pleasure, too much of a challenge. She'd put in a few hours on paperwork that night.

"If you think she's ready."

"Oh, she's ready. It's the rest of us who have to catch up." He opened the box and led them out.

The walking ring was surrounded by a high wall, to give the student privacy and prevent distractions as she took her first steps under the control of a rider. As Brian led them toward it, several of the hands stopped work to watch. Money changed hands.

"Some of them bet we wouldn't manage her this morning," Brian said casually. "You just earned me fifty dollars."

"If I'd known there was a pool, I'd have bet myself."

He glanced up. "Which way?"

"I always bet to win."

He stopped inside the ring, handed Keeley the reins. "She's yours now."

Keeley angled her head. "In a manner of speaking," she said and nudged Betty into a walk.

They made a picture, Brian mused. A stunning one. The long-legged thoroughbred with her regal head and gleaming coat, and the delicate woman riding her.

If he'd ever wanted one horse for his own—and he didn't, hadn't—it would be this one.

If he'd ever wanted one woman for his own…

Well, that was the same. He'd never wanted the responsibilities that came from having. And neither of these could ever be his in any case. But he'd have something of each of them, and that was better all around.

For the horse, he'd have the knowledge that part of what he was went into the making of a champion. And the woman, before long he'd have the pleasure of knowing what it was to have her wrapped around him in the night. Maybe only once, but once would be enough.

Whatever the risks of that were, there was no stopping it. They came a bit closer to it every time they looked at each other. Today, he'd come to understand she knew it, too. Now it was only a matter of the time and place. And that would be up to her.

"They look good."

Brian didn't wince, but he wanted to. It was definitely inconvenient to have the father of the woman you were fantasizing about interrupt that particular image. Especially inconvenient when the man was also your employer.

"That they do. Betty needs a steady hand, and your daughter has one."

"Always has." Travis slapped a hand on Brian's shoulder and brought on instantaneous guilt. "I ran into Jim, who confessed all. You took a kick."

"It's nothing." He imagined his ribs would be sore for weeks.

"Have it looked at." The tone was casual, and carried command.

"I will shortly. Jim was spooked. I shouldn't have pushed him into it."

"He's young," Travis agreed. "But this is part of his job. At the moment, he feels bad enough that you could ask him to let Betty sit on him. I'd take advantage of it."

"And so I will. He's a good lad, Travis. Just a bit green yet. I'm thinking of taking him with me to the track more, letting him get some seasoning."

"That's a good idea. You have a number of them. Good ideas," Travis added.

"That's what you pay me for." Brian hesitated, then plunged. "Betty's not just your best shot at your Derby, she's the one who'll do it for you. And I'll wager my full year's contract pay she'll wear the Triple Crown."

"That's a leap, Brian."

"Not for her. I say she'll break records, smash them to bits. And when it comes time to breed her, it should be Zeus. I've done the charts," Brian continued. "I know you and Brendon manage the breeding end of the farm yourselves, but—"

"I'll look at your charts, Brian."

Brian nodded, shifted to watch Betty. "It's not the charts so much, though they'll bear me out. It's that I know her. Sometimes..." Despite himself, he found himself staring at Keeley. "You just recognize it all."

"I know it." Eyes narrowed in consideration, Travis scanned Betty's form. "Work out the race schedule you think will work for her—once she's ready. We'll talk about it."

Keeley walked Betty toward them, pulling her up with a tug of the reins and a quiet vocal command. "She's decided to tolerate me."

"What do you think?" Travis stroked the filly's neck, ignoring her first instinctive feint at nipping.

"She's not common," Keeley began, "though she has some behavioral problems that would make her so if they aren't corrected. She's smart. A fast learner. Which means you have to stay a step ahead of her. It's early days yet, of course, but I'd say this isn't a horse that's going to loaf. She'll work hard, and she'll race hard, under the right hand. If I were still competing, I'd want her."

"She's not meant for the show ring." Brian took out another chunk of apple. "She's for the oval."

Betty took the reward, then as if to show he was the only one of the three humans who mattered, bumped her head lightly against his shoulder.

"She still has to prove she can run in a crowd," Keeley pointed out. "You might want to put blinders on her."

"Not with this one, I'm thinking. The other horses won't be distractions to her. They'll be competitors."

"We'll see." Keeley dismounted, started to hand Brian the reins, but her father took them.

"I'll walk her back."

And that, Brian thought, absurdly bereft, was the difference between training and owning.

"No need to look so annoyed." Keeley cocked her head as Brian scowled after Betty. "She did very well. Better than I'd expected."

"Hmm? Oh, so she did, yes. I was thinking of something else."

"Ribs hurting?" When he only shrugged, she shook her head. "Let me take a look."

"She barely caught me."

"Oh, for heaven's sake." Impatient, Keeley did what she would have done with one of her brothers: She tugged Brian's T-shirt out of his jeans.

"Well, darling, if I'd known you were so anxious to get me undressed, I'd have cooperated fully, and in private."

"Shut up. God, Brian, you said it was nothing."

"It's not much."

His definition of not much was a softball-size bruise over the ribs in a burst of ugly red and black. "Macho is tedious, so just shut up."

He started to grin, then yelped when she pressed her fingers to the bruise. "Hell, woman, if that's your idea of tender mercies, keep them."

"You could have a cracked rib. You need an X ray."

"I don't need a damned—ouch! Bollocks and bloody hell, stop poking." He tried to pull his shirt down, but she simply yanked it up again.

"Stand still, and don't be a baby."

"A minute ago it was don't be macho, now it's don't be a baby. What do you want?"

"For you to behave sensibly."

"It's difficult for a man to behave sensibly when a woman's taking his clothes off in broad daylight. If you're going to kiss it and make it better, I've several other bruises. I've a dandy one on my ass as it happens."

"I'm sure that's terribly amusing. One of the men can drive you to the emergency room."

"No one's driving me anywhere. I'd know if my ribs are cracked as I've had a few in my time. It's a bruise, and it's throbbing like a bitch now that you've been playing with it."

She spotted another, riding high on his hip, and gave that a poke. This time he groaned.

"Keeley, you're torturing me here."

"I'm just trying…" She trailed off as she lifted her head and saw his eyes. It wasn't pain or annoyance in them now. It was heat, and it was frustration. And it was surprisingly gratifying. "Really?"

It was wrong, and it was foolish, but a sip of power was a heady thing. She trailed her fingers along his hip, up his ribs and down again, and felt his muscles quiver. "Why don't you stop me?"

His throat hurt. "You make my head swim. And you know it."

"Maybe I do. Now. Maybe I like it." She'd never been deliberately provocative before. Had never wanted to be. And she'd never known the thrill of having a strong man turn to putty under her hands. "Maybe I've thought about you, Brian, the way you said I would."

"You pick a fine time to tell me when there's people everywhere, and your father one of them."

"Yeah, maybe that's true, too. I need that buffer, I guess."

"You're a killer, Keeley. You'd tease a man to death."

He didn't mean it as a compliment, but to her it was a revelation. "I've never tried it before. No one's ever attracted me enough. You do, and I don't even know why."

When she dropped her hand, he took her wrist. It surprised him to feel the gallop of her pulse there, when her eyes, her voice had been so cool, so steady. "Then you're a quick learner."

"I'd like to think so. If I come to you, you'd be the first."

"The first what?" Temper wanted to stir, especially when she laughed. Then his mind cleared and the meaning flashed through like a thunderbolt. His hand tightened on her wrist, then dropped it as though she had turned to fire.

"That scared you enough to shut you up," she observed. "I'm surprised anything could render you speechless."

"I've…" But he couldn't think.

"No, don't fumble around for words. You'll spoil your image." She couldn't think just why his dazed expression struck her as so funny, or why the shock in his eyes was endearing somehow.

"We'll just say that, under these circumstances, we both have a lot to consider. And now, I'm way behind in my work, and have to get ready for my afternoon class."

She walked away, as easily, as casually, Brian thought numbly, as she might have if they'd just finished discussing the proper treatment for windgalls. She left him reeling.

He'd gone and fallen in love with the gentry, and the gentry was his boss's daughter. And his boss's daughter was innocent.

He'd have to be mad to lay a hand on her after this.

He began to wish Betty had just kicked him in the head and gotten it all over with.

* * *

Served her right, Keeley decided. Spend the morning indulging herself, spend half the night doing the books. And she hated doing the books.

Sighing, she tipped back in her chair and rubbed her eyes. In another year, maybe two, the school would generate enough income to justify hiring a bookkeeper. But for now, she just couldn't toss the money away for something she could do herself. Not when she could use it to subsidize another student, or buy one of them a pair of riding boots.

It was tempting, particularly at times like these, to dip into her own bank account. But it was a matter of pride to keep the school going on its own merit, as much as she possibly could.

Ledgers and forms and bills and accounts, she thought, were her responsibility. You didn't have to like your responsibilities, you just had to deal with them.

She had two full-tuition students on her waiting list. One more, she calculated—two would be better—but one more and she could justify opening another class. Sunday afternoons.

That would give her eighteen full tuitions. Two years before, she'd had only three. It was working. And so, now, should she.

She swiveled back to the computer and focused on her spreadsheet program. Her eyes were starting to blur again when the door behind her opened.

She caught the scent of hot tea before she turned and saw her mother.

"Ma, what are you doing out here? It's midnight."

"Well, I was up, and I saw your light. I thought to myself, that girl needs some fuel if she's going to run half the night." Adelia set a thermos and a bag on the desk. "Tea and cookies."

"I love you."

"So you'd better. Darling, your eyes are half shut. Why don't you turn this off and come to bed?"

"I'm nearly done, but I can use the break—and the fuel." She ate a cookie before she poured the tea. "I'm only behind because I played this morning."

"From what your father tells me you weren't playing." Adelia took a chair, nudged it closer to the desk. "He's awfully pleased with how Brian's bringing Betty along. Well, he's pleased with Brian altogether, and so am I from what I've seen. But Betty's quite the challenge."

"Hmm." So was Brian, Keeley thought. "He has his own way of doing things, but it seems to work." Considering, she drummed her fingers on the desk. She'd always been able to discuss anything with her mother. Why should that change now?

"I'm attracted to him."

"I'd worry about you if you weren't. He's a fine-looking young man."

"Ma." Keeley laid a hand over her mother's. "I'm very attracted to him."

The amusement faded from Adelia's eyes. "Oh. Well."

"And he's very attracted to me."

"I see."

"I don't want to mention this to Dad. Men don't look at this sort of thing the way we do."

"Darling." At a loss, Adelia sighed out a breath. "Mothers aren't likely to look at this sort of thing the same way their daughters do. You're grown up, and you're a woman who answers to herself first. But you're still my little girl, aren't you?"

"I haven't been with a man before."

"I know it." Adelia's smile was soft, almost wistful. "Do you think I wouldn't know if that had changed for you? You think too much of yourself to give what you are to something unless it matters. No one's mattered before."

Here the ground was boggy, Keeley thought. "I don't know if Brian matters in the way you mean. But I feel different with him. I want him. I haven't wanted anyone before. It's exciting, and a little scary."

Adelia rose, wandered around the little office looking at the ribbons, the medals. The steps and the stages. "We've talked about such matters before, you and I. About the meaning and the precautions, the responsibilities."

"I know about being responsible and sensible."

"Keeley, while it is true that all that is important, it doesn't tell you—it can't tell you—what it is to be with a man. There's such heat." She turned back. "There's such a force you make between you. It's not just an act, though I know it can be for some. But even then it's more than just that. I won't tell you that giving your innocence is a loss, for it shouldn't be, it doesn't need to be. For me it was an opening. Your father was my first," she murmured. "And my only."

"Mama." Moved, Keeley reached for her hands. Her mother's hands were so strong, she thought. Everything about her mother was strong. "That's so lovely."

"I only ask you to be sure, so that if you give yourself to him, you take away a memory that's warm and has heart, not just heat. Heat can chill after time passes."

"I am sure." Smiling now, Keeley brought her mother's hand to her cheek. "But he's not. And, Ma, it's so odd, but the way he backed off when I told him he'd be the first is why I'm sure. You see, I matter to him, too."

Chapter 6

It was amazing, really, how two people could live and work in basically the same place, and one could completely avoid the other. It just took setting your mind to it.

Brian set his mind to it for several days. There was plenty of work to keep him occupied and more than enough reason for him to spend time away from the farm and on the tracks. But he found avoidance scraped his pride. It was too close a kin to cowardice.

Added to that, he'd told Keeley he wanted to help her at the school and had done nothing about it. He wasn't a man to break his word, no matter what it cost him. And, he reminded himself as he walked to Keeley's stables, he was also a man of some self-control. He had no intention of seducing or taking advantage of innocence.

He'd made up his mind on it.

Then he stepped into the stables and saw her. He wouldn't have said his mouth watered, but it was a very close thing.

She was wearing one of those fancy rigs again—jodhpurs the color of dark chocolate and a cream sort of blouse
that looked somehow fluid. Her hair was down, all tumbled
and wild as if she'd just pulled the pins from it. And indeed,
as he watched she flipped it back and looped it through a
wide elastic band.

He decided the best place in the universe for his hands
to be were in his pockets.

"Lessons over?"

She glanced back, her hands still up in her hair. Ah, she
thought. She'd wondered how long it would take him to
wander her way again. "Why? Did you want one?"

He frowned, but caught himself before he shifted his
feet. "I said I'd give you a hand over here."

"So you did. As it happens I could use one. You did say
you could ride, didn't you?"

"I did, and I do."

"Good." Perfect. She gestured toward a big bay. "Mule
really needs a workout. If you take him, I'll be able to give
Sam some exercise, too. Neither of them has had enough
the last couple of days. I'm sure I have tack that'll suit you."
She opened a box door and led out the already saddled Sam.
"We'll wait in the paddock."

As they clipped out, Brian eyed Mule, Mule eyed Brian.
"She's a bossy one, isn't she now?" Then with a shrug,
Brian headed to the tack room to find a saddle that suited
him.

She was cantering around the paddock when he came
out, her body so tuned to the horse they might have been
one figure. With the slightest shift in rhythm and angle, she
took her mount over three jumps. Cantering still, she started
the next circle, then spotted Brian. She slowed, stopped.

"Ready?"

For an answer, he swung into the saddle. "Why are you all done up today?"

"It was picture day. We take photographs of the classes. The kids and the parents like it. Mule's up for a good run, if you are."

"Then let's have at it." With a tap of his heels he sent the horse out of the open gate at an easy trot.

"How are the ribs?" she asked as she came up beside him.

"They're all right." They were driving him mad, because every time he felt a twinge he remembered her hands on him.

"I'm told the yearling training's coming along well, and Betty's one of the star pupils—as predicted."

"She has the thirst. All the training in the world can't give a horse the thirst to race. We'll be giving her a taste of the starting gate shortly, see how she does with it."

Keeley headed up a gentle slope where trees were still lush and green despite the encroaching fall. "I'd use Foxfire with her," she said casually. "He's a sturdy one, with lots of experience. He loves to charge out of the gate. She sees him do it a couple of times, she won't want to be left behind."

He'd already decided on Foxfire as Betty's gate tutor, but shrugged. "I'm thinking about it. So…have I passed the audition here, Miss Grant?"

Keeley lifted a brow, and a smile ghosted around her mouth as she looked Brian over. She'd been checking his form, naturally. "Well, you're competent enough at a trot." With a light tap, she sent Sam into a canter. The minute Brian matched her pace, she headed into a gallop.

Oh, she missed this. Every day she couldn't fly out across the fields, over the hills, was a sacrifice. There was nothing to match it—the thrill of speed, the power soaring under her, through her, the thunder of hooves and the whip of wind.

She laughed as Brian edged by her. She'd seen the quick grin of challenge, and answered it by letting Sam have his head.

It was like watching magic take wing, Brian thought. The muscular black horse soared over the ground with the woman on his back. They streaked over another rise, moving west, into the dying sun. The sky was a riot of color, a painting slashed with reds and golds. It seemed to him she would ride straight into it, through it.

And he'd have no choice but to follow her.

When she pulled up, turned to wait for him, her face flushed with pleasure, her eyes gleaming with it, he knew he'd never seen the like.

And wanting her was apt to kill him.

"I should've given you a handicap," she called out. "Mule runs like a demon, but he's no match for this one." She leaned over the saddle to pat Sam's neck. She straightened, shook her hair back. "Gorgeous out, isn't it?"

"Hot as blazes," Brian corrected. "How long does summer last around here?"

"As long as it likes. Mornings are getting chilly, though, and once the sun dips down behind the hills, it'll cool off quickly enough. I like the heat. Your Irish blood's not used to it yet."

She turned Sam so she could look down at Royal Meadows. "It's beautiful from up here, isn't it?"

The buildings spread out, neat, elegant, with the white fences of the paddocks, the brown oval, the horses being led to the stable. A trio of weanlings, all legs and energy, raced in the near pasture.

"From down there, too. It's the best I've ever seen."

That made her smile. "Wait till you see it in winter, with snow on the hills and the sky thick and gray with more—or so blue it hurts your eyes to look at it. And the foalings start and there are babies trying out their legs. When I was little, I couldn't wait to run down and see them in the morning."

They began to walk again, companionably now, as the light edged toward dusk. She hadn't expected to be so comfortable with him. Aware, yes, she always seemed aware of him now. But this simple connection, a quiet evening ride, was a pleasure.

"Did you have horses when you were a boy?"

"No, we never owned them. But it wasn't so far to the track, and my father's a wagering man."

"And are you?"

He tilted his face toward her. "I like playing the odds, and fortunately, have a better feel for them than my father. He loved the look of them, and the rush of a race, but never did he gain any understanding of horses."

"You didn't gain any, either," Keeley said and had him frowning at her. "What you've got you were born with. Just like them," she added, gesturing toward the weanlings.

"I think that's a compliment."

"I don't mind giving them when they're fact."

"Well, fact or fiction, horses have been the biggest part of my life. I remember going along with my da and seeing the horses. When he could manage it, he liked to go early, check out the field, talk with the clockers and the grooms, get himself a feel for things—or so he said. He lost his money more often as not. It was the process that appealed to him."

That, and the flask in his pocket, Brian thought, but with tolerance. His father had loved the horses and the whiskey. And his mother had understood neither.

"One of the first times I went along, I saw an exercise boy, very young lad, ponying a sorrel around the track. And I thought, there, that's it. That's what I want to do, for there can't be anything better than doing that for your life and your living. And while I was still young enough, and small enough, I slid out of going to school as often as it could be managed and hitched rides to the track to hustle myself. Walk hots, muck stalls, whatever."

"It's romantic."

He caught himself. He hadn't meant to ramble on that way, but the ride, the evening, the whole of it made him sentimental. When he started to laugh at her statement, she shook her head.

"No, it is. People who aren't a part of the world of it don't understand, really. The hard work, the disappointments, the sweat and blood. Freezing predawn workouts, bruises and pulled muscles."

"And that's romantic."

"You know it is."

This time he did laugh, because she'd pegged him. "As a boy, when I hung around the shedrow, I'd see the horses come back through the mist of morning, steam rising off their backs, the sound of them growing louder, coming at you before ever you could see them. They'd slip out of the fog like something out of a dream. Then, I thought it the most romantic thing in the world."

"And now?"

"Now, I know it is."

He broke into a canter, riding with her until the lights of Royal Meadows began to flicker on and glow. He hadn't expected to spend a comfortable, contented hour in her company, and found it odd that underlying all the rest that buzzed between them they'd seemed to have formed a kind of friendship.

He'd been friends with women before, and was well on the way to being convinced he'd do just fine keeping it all on a friendly level with Keeley. He was the one who'd initiated the sexual charge, so it seemed reasonable and right that he be the one to dampen it again.

The logic of it, and the ride, relaxed him. By the time they reached the stables to cool down the horses, he was in an easy mood and thinking about his supper.

Since she was interested, he told her of the yearling training, the progress, the five-year-old mare with colic, and the weanling with ringbone.

Together they watered the horses, and while Brian took the saddles and bridles to the tack room, Keeley set up the small hay nets and set out the grooming kits.

They worked across from each other, in opposite boxes.

"I heard you and Brendon are heading off to Saratoga next week," she commented.

"Zeus is running. And I think Red Duke is a contender, and your brother agrees. Though I've only seen that track on paper and in pictures. We're off to Louisville as well. I want to be well familiar with that course before the first Saturday in May."

"You want Betty to run the Derby."

"She will run it. And win it." He picked up the curry comb to scrape out the body brush. "We've conversed about it."

"You've talked to Brendon about the Derby?"

"No, Betty. And your father as well. I expect Brendon and I will talk it through while we're away."

"What does Betty have to say?"

"Let's get on with it." He glanced over, saw she was

running her fingers over Sam's coat, checking for lumps or irregularities. "Why aren't you still competing? With that one under you you'd need a vault for all your medals."

"I'm not interested in medals."

"Why not? Don't you like to win?"

"I love to win." She leaned gently against Sam, lifted his leg and sent Brian a long look that had his stomach jittering before she gave her attention to picking out the hoof. "But I've done it, enjoyed it, finished with it. Competing can take over your life. I wanted the Olympics, and I got it."

She shifted to clean out the next hoof. "Once I had, I realized that so much of what I was, what I felt and thought had been focused on that single goal. And then it was over. So I wanted to see what else there was out there, and what else I had in me. I like to compete, but I found out it doesn't always have to be done, and won, in the show ring."

"With the kind of school you've got going here, you should have someone working with you."

She shrugged and began to rub in hoof oil. "Up until now I'd been able to draft Sarah or Patrick into giving me a hand. Ma helps out when she can, and so does Dad. Brendon and Uncle Paddy put in hours with each one of my horses as I got them. And the cousins—Burke and Erin's kids from Three Aces—they're always willing to pitch in if I need extra hands."

"I haven't seen anyone working here but you."

"Well, that's very simple. Patrick and Sarah are off to college—and Brady, who's another I can browbeat into shoveling boxes when he's here. Brendon's doing a lot more traveling now than he used to. Uncle Paddy's in Ireland, and the cousins are just back from a holiday and in school. Either my mother or father, sometimes both, show up here at dawn half the time. Whether I ask them or not."

She got to her feet. "And now that I've got you interested, I've come up with a part-time groom/exercise boy/stable-hand. That's a pretty good deal for a small riding academy."

She strolled out to start the evening feeding.

"You could get an eager young boy or girl to come in before and after school—pay them in lessons."

"Before school, eager young boys and girls should be eating breakfast, and after they should be playing with friends and doing homework."

"That's very strict."

She chuckled and mixed some sliced carrots into the feed as an extra treat. "That's what all my students say. I want them well-rounded. My family saw to it that I had interests and friendships outside the stable, that I got an education, that I saw something of the world besides the track and the barn. It matters."

They divvied up the horses, and the stables filled with the sounds of whickers and whinnies as the meal was served.

"If you don't mind my saying so, you don't seem to be getting out and about much now."

"I'm compulsive. Goal oriented. I see what I want and well, it's like putting on blinders and heading down the backstretch. All I see is the finish line."

She leaned in to rub a gelding's neck as if he were a pet dog. "Which is why my parents wouldn't let me spend my entire childhood around or on a horse. I took piano lessons, and as soon as I started I was determined to be the best student at the recital. If it was my job to clean the kitchen after dinner, then that damn kitchen was going to sparkle so bright you'd need sunglasses for your midnight snack."

"That's frightening."

Responding to the humor in his eyes, she nodded. "It

can be. Focusing on the school means, even though it's still a single goal, that my compulsion to succeed is spread out to encompass so many elements—the kids, the horses as well as the academy itself. Once it's firmly established, I can delegate a bit more, but I need to learn from the ground up. I don't like to make mistakes. Which is why I haven't been with a man before now."

He was thrown off balance so quickly and completely, he could hear his own brain stumble. "Well, that's…that's wise."

He took one definite step back, like a chessman going from square to square.

"It's interesting that makes you nervous," she said, countering his move.

"I'm not nervous, I'm…finished up here, it seems." He tried another tactic, stepped to the side.

"Interesting," she continued, mirroring his move, "that it would make you nervous, or uneasy if you prefer, when you've been… I think it's safe to use the term 'hitting on me' since we met."

"I don't think that's the proper term at all." Since he seemed to be boxed into a corner, he decided he was really only standing his ground. "I acted in a natural way regarding a physical attraction. But—"

"And now that I've reacted in a natural way, you've felt the reins slip out of your hands and you're panicked."

"I'm certainly not panicked." He ignored the terror gripping claws into his belly and concentrated on annoyance. "Back off, Keeley."

"No." With her eyes locked on his, she stepped in. Checkmate.

His back was hard up against a stall door and he'd been maneuvered there by a woman half his weight. It was mortifying. "This isn't doing either of us any credit." It took a lot of effort when the blood was rapidly draining out of his head, but he made his voice cool and firm. "The fact is I've rethought the matter."

"Have you?"

"I have, yes, and—stop it," he ordered when she ran the palms of her hands up over his chest.

"Your heart's pounding," she murmured. "So's mine. Should I tell you what goes on inside my head, inside my body when you kiss me?"

"No." He barely managed a croak this time. "And it's not going to happen again."

"Bet?" She laughed, rising up just enough to nip his chin. How could she have known how much *fun* it was to twist a man into aroused knots? "Why don't you tell me about this rethinking?"

"I'm not going to take advantage of your—of the situation."

That, she thought, was wonderfully sweet. "At the moment, I seem to have the advantage. This time you're trembling, Brian."

The hell he was. How could he be trembling when he couldn't feel his own legs? "I won't be responsible. I won't use your inexperience. I *won't* do this." The last was said on a note of desperation and he pushed her aside.

"I'm responsible for myself. And I think I've just proven to both of us, that if and when I decide you'll be the one, you won't have a prayer." She drew a deep, satisfied breath. "Knowing that's incredibly flattering."

"Arousing a man doesn't take much skill, Keeley. We're cooperative creatures in that area."

If he'd expected that to scratch at her pride and cut into her power, he was mistaken. She only smiled, and the smile was full of secret female knowledge. "If that was true between us, if that were all that's between us, we'd be naked on the tack room floor right now."

She saw the change in his eyes and laughed delightedly. "Already thought of that one, have you? We'll just hold that thought for another time."

He swore, raked his hands through his hair and tried to pinpoint the moment she'd so neatly turned the tables on him, when the pursued had become the pursuer. "I don't like forward women."

The sound she made was something between a snort and a giggle, and was girlish and full of fun. It made him want to grin. "Now that's a lie, and you don't do it well. I've noticed you're an honest sort of man, Brian. When you don't want to speak your mind, you say nothing—and that's not often. I like that about you, even if it did irritate me initially. I even like your slightly overwide streak of confidence. I admire your patience and dedication to the horses, your understanding and affection for them. I've never been involved with a man who's shared that interest with me."

"You've never been involved with a man at all."

"Exactly. That's just one reason why. And to continue, I appreciate the kindness you showed my mother when she was sad, and I appreciate the part of you that's struggling to back away right now instead of taking what I've never offered anyone before."

She laid a hand on his arm as he stared at her with baffled frustration. "If I didn't have that respect and that liking for you, Brian, we wouldn't be having this conversation no matter how attracted I might be to you."

"Sex complicates things, Keeley."

"I know."

"How would you know? You've never had any."

She gave his arm a quick squeeze. "Good point. So, you want to try the tack room?" When his mouth fell open, she laughed and threw her arms around him for a noisy kiss on his cheek. "Just kidding. Let's go up to the main house and have some dinner instead."

"I've work yet."

She drew back. She couldn't read his eyes now. "Brian, neither of us have eaten. We can have a simple meal in the kitchen—and if you're worried, we won't be alone in the house so I'll have to keep my hands off you. Temporarily."

"There's that." He couldn't stand it. How could he be expected to? She'd thrown her arms around him with such easy affection. And his heart was balanced on a very thin wire. Trying to keep the movement casual, he set her aside. "Well, I could eat."

"Good."

She would have taken his hand, but his were already in his pockets. It amused and touched her how restrained he was determined to be. And if it made her naturally competitive spirit kick in, well, she couldn't help it, now could she?

"I'm hoping to get down to Charles Town and watch some of the workouts once you take Betty and some of the other yearlings to the track."

"She'll be ready for it soon enough." Relief was like a cool wave through his blood. Talking of horses would make it all easier. "I'd say she'll surprise you, but you've been up on her. You know what she's made of."

"Yeah, good stock, good breeding, a hard head and a hunger to win." She flashed him a smile as they approached the kitchen door. "I've been told that describes me. I'm half Irish, Brian, I was born stubborn."

"No arguing with that. A person might make the world

a calmer place for others by being passive, but you don't get very far in it yourself, do you?"

"Look at that. We have a foundation of agreement. Now tell me you like spaghetti and meatballs."

"It happens to be a favorite of mine."

"That's handy. Mine, too. And I heard a rumor that's what's for dinner." She reached for the doorknob, then caught him off guard by brushing a light kiss over his lips. "And since we'll be joining my parents, it would probably be best if you didn't imagine me naked for the next couple of hours."

She sailed in ahead of him, leaving Brian helplessly and utterly aroused.

There was nothing like an extra helping of guilt to cool a man's blood. And it was guilt as much as the hot food and the glass of good wine that got Brian through the evening in the Grant kitchen. The size of it left little room for lust, considering.

There was Adelia Grant giving him a warm greeting as if he was welcome to swing in for dinner anytime he had the whim, and Travis getting out an extra plate himself—as if he waited on employees five days a week—and saying that there was plenty to go around as Brendon had other plans for dinner.

Before he knew it, he was sitting down, having food heaped in front of him and being asked how his day had been. And not in a way that expected a report.

He didn't know what to do about it. He liked these people, genuinely liked them. And there he was lusting after their daughter. An alley mutt after a registered purebred.

And the hell of it was, he liked her as well. It had been so simple at first, when there'd been only heat. Or he'd been able to tell himself that's all there was. For a time it had been possible to tolerate being in love with her—or at least talking himself out of believing it. But *caring* for her made it all a study in frustration.

He could certainly convince himself that he was in love with the *idea* of her rather than the woman. The physical beauty, the class, the sheer inaccessibility of her. That was all a kind of challenge, a risk he enjoyed taking. But she'd gone and opened herself up to him, so every time he was around her, she showed him more of herself.

The kindness, the humor, the strength of purpose and sense of self he admired.

And now this teasing, this sexual flirt in an innocent's body was driving him mad. And God help him, he liked it.

"Have some more, Brian."

"I'll be sorry if I do." But he took the big bowl Adelia offered him. "Sorrier if I don't. You're a rare cook, Mrs. Grant."

"Dee, I told you. And rare was just what I was for a number of years. Before Hannah retired—that was our housekeeper. She was with Travis longer than I've been with him. When she retired a few years back I just didn't want another woman, a stranger, you know, in the house day and night and so on. I figured I'd better learn to cook something more than fish and chips or we'd all starve to death."

"Nearly did the first six months," Travis commented and earned a narrow-eyed stare from his wife.

"Well, sure and the experience made you get a handle on that fancy grill outside, didn't it? The man was spoiled rotten. I wager you could even put a meal together for yourself, Brian."

Idly he rubbed Sheamus—who was snoring under the

table—with the side of his boot. "If I've no choice in the matter."

Brian caught the lazy look Keeley sent him as she sipped her wine. Heat balled in his belly. In defense he turned to Travis. "I'm told you enjoy a hand or two of poker from time to time."

"I've been known to."

"The lads're talking about a game tomorrow night."

"I might come down—I've heard you're a hard man to beat."

"If you're going to play cards, you should ask Burke to join you," Adelia put in. "Then maybe Keeley, Erin and I can find something equally foolish to do with our evening."

"Good idea. More wine, Brian?" Keeley lifted the bottle, cocked a brow. The purr in her voice was subtle, but he heard it. And suffered.

"No, thanks. I've work yet."

"I'll walk down with you when you're ready," Travis told him. "I'd like a look at that colicky mare."

"The two of you go ahead. We'll see to the dishes."

Travis grinned like a boy. "No KP?"

"There's not that much to be done, and you can make up for it tomorrow." She got up to clear, and kissed his temple. "Go on, I know you've been worrying about her."

"Thank you for the fine meal, Dee," Brian added when she angled her head.

"And you're very welcome."

"Good night, Keeley."

"Good night, Brian. Thanks for the ride."

Adelia waited until the men were out, then turned to her daughter. "Keeley, I never would've thought it of you. You're tormenting the poor man."

"There's nothing poor about that man." Delighted with

herself, Keeley broke off a piece of bread and crunched down on it. "And tormenting him is so rewarding."

"Well, there's not a woman with blood in her could argue with that. Mind you don't hurt him, darling."

"Hurt him?" Seriously shocked, Keeley rose to help with the dishes. "Of course I won't. I couldn't."

"You never know what you will or you can do." Adelia patted her daughter's cheek. "You've a lot to learn yet. And however much you learn you'll never really understand everything that goes on inside a man."

"I've good a pretty good idea about this one."

Adelia opened her mouth, then shut it again. Some things, she knew, couldn't be explained. They had to be lived.

Chapter 7

Brian came to know the roads leading from Maryland into West Virginia as well as he knew those in the county of Kerry. The highways where cars flashed by like little rockets, and the curving back roads where everything meandered were all part of his life now, and what some people would say led to a feeling of home.

There were times the green of the hills, the rise of them, reminded him of Ireland. The pang he felt at those moments surprised him as he didn't consider himself a sentimental man. At others, he'd drive along a winding road that followed a winding creek and the land was all so very different with its thick woods and walls of rock. Almost exotic. Then he'd feel a sense of contentment that surprised him nearly as much.

He didn't mind contentment. It just wasn't what he was looking for.

He liked to move. To travel from place to place. It was all to the good that his position at Royal Meadows gave him that opportunity. He figured in a couple of years, he'd have seen a great deal of America—even if the oval was in the foreground of each view.

He told himself he didn't think of Ireland as home—or Maryland as home, either. Home was the shedrow, wherever it might be.

Still, he felt a sense of welcome and ease when he drove between the stone pillars at Royal Meadows. And he felt pleasure when he saw Keeley in her paddock with one of her classes. He stopped to watch as she took her group from trot to canter.

It was a pretty sight, not despite the clumsiness and caution of some of the children, but because of it. This was no slick and choreographed competition but the first steps of a new adventure. Fun, she'd said, he remembered. They would learn, take responsibility, but she didn't forget they were children.

And some of them had been hurt.

Seeing her with them, looking at what she'd built herself when she could have spent her days exactly as he'd once imagined she did, brought him more than respect for what she was. It brought admiration that was a little too bright for comfort.

He could hear the squeals, and Keeley's calm, firm voice—a pretty sight and a pretty sound. He climbed out of the truck and walked over for a closer view.

There were grins miles wide, and eyes big as platters. There were giggles and there were gasps. As far as Brian could see, the mood ran from screaming nerves to wild delight. Through it all, Keeley gave orders, instruction, encouragement, and used each child's name.

Her long fire-fall of hair was roped back again. Her jeans were faded to a soft blue-gray like the many-pocketed vest she topped over it. Under that she wore a slim sweater the color of spring daffodils. She liked her bright tones, Keeley did, Brian mused. And her glitters as well, he mused as the light caught the dangle of little stones at her ears.

She'd be wearing perfume. She always had some cagey female scent about her. Sometimes just a drift that you had to get right up beside her to catch. And other times it was a siren call that beckoned you from a distance.

Never knowing which it would be was enough to drive a man mad.

He should stay away from her, Brian told himself. God knew he should stay away from her. And he figured he had as much chance of doing so as one of her riding hacks had of winning the Breeder's Cup.

She knew he was there. The ripple of heat over her skin told her so. She couldn't afford to be distracted with six children depending on her full attention. But oh, the awareness of him, of herself and that quick trip of the pulse, was a glorious sensation.

She began to understand why women so often made fools of themselves for men.

When she ordered the class to switch back to a trot, there were a few groans of disappointment. She had them change directions, then took them through all their paces, and back down to walk. Brian waited until she instructed them to stop, then applauded.

"Nicely done," he said. "Anyone here looking for a job, you just come see me."

"We have an audience today. This is Mr. Donnelly. He's head trainer at Royal Meadows. He's in charge of the race-horses."

"Indeed I am, and I've always got my eyes open for a new jockey."

"He talks pretty," one of the girls whispered, but Brian's ears were keen. He shot her a grin and had her blushing like a rosebud.

"Do you think so?"

"Mr. Donnelly's from Ireland," Keeley explained. Amazing, she thought, he even makes ten-year-old girls moon.

"Miss Keeley's mother's from Ireland. She talks pretty, too."

Brian glanced up and saw the boy he remembered as Willy studying him. "No one talks prettier than those from Ireland, lad. It's because we've all been kissed by the fairies."

"You're supposed to get money from the Tooth Fairy when you lose a tooth, but I never did."

"That's just your mother." The girl behind Willy rolled her eyes. "There aren't real fairies."

"Maybe they don't live here in America, but we've plenty where I come from. I'll put a word in for you, Willy, next time you lose a tooth."

His eyes rounded. "How did you know my name?"

"A fairy must've told me."

Keeley struggled to compose her features as Willy goggled. "Class. Dismount. Cool and water your mounts."

There was a great deal of chatter and movement now. Though Willy dismounted, he stood, holding the reins and studying Brian. Too cautious a look for one so young, Brian thought. And it tugged at his heart.

Willy took a breath, seemed to hold it. "I have one that's loose. A tooth."

"Do you?" Unable to resist, Brian climbed over the fence, hunched down. "Let's have a look."

Willy obliged by baring his teeth and poking his tongue against a wobbly incisor. "That's a good one. You'll be able to spit through where that was in a day or two."

"You're not supposed to spit." Willy slanted a look up at Brian as he began to walk.

"Who says?"

"Ladies." Bobby added a shrug. "They don't like you to burp, either."

"Ladies can be fussy about certain things. It's best to spit and burp among the men, I suppose."

"You're not supposed to run like a wild animal, either." Peeking around to make certain Keeley wasn't frowning in his direction, Willy shoved up the sleeve of his shirt. "This is from running like a wild animal on the playground at school. I skidded for*ever* and scraped lots of skin right off so it got really bloody."

Understanding his role, Brian pursed his lips, nodded. "That's very impressive, that is."

"I've got an even better one on my knee. Have you got any?"

"I've got a pretty good bruise." To play the game properly, Brian glanced around first, then tugged his shirt up to display the yellowing bruise on his ribs.

"Wow! That musta really hurt. Did you cry?"

"I couldn't. Miss Keeley was watching. Here she comes," he added in a conspirator's whisper and pulled his shirt down, whistled idly.

"Willy, you need to water Teddy."

"Yes, ma'am. I had a dream about Teddy last night."

"You tell me about it when we're grooming him, okay?"

"Okay. Bye, mister."

"Now that's a taking little creature," Brian murmured as Willy led his horse out to the water trough.

"Yes, he is. What were you talking about?"

"Man business." Brian hooked his thumbs in his pockets. "I've got to get down to the shedrow or I'd help you with the grooming. I could send you up a hand if you like."

"Thanks, but it's not necessary."

"Just ring down if you change your mind." He needed to go, let them both get on with work. But it was so nice to stand here and smell her. Today, the scent was subtle, just a hint of heat. "They looked good at the canter."

"They'll look better in a few weeks." It was time to get the horses inside, start the grooming session. But... What would another minute hurt? "I heard you took a few pots in the poker game last night."

"I came away about fifty ahead. Your cousin Burke's a slick one. I'd say he whistled home with double that."

"And my father?"

Brian's grin flashed. "I like thinking that's where I got the fifty. I told him he's better off sticking with the horses."

Keeley's brow rose. "And his response to that?"

"Isn't something I can repeat in polite company."

She laughed. "That's what I thought. I've got to get the horses inside. Parents will be trickling along soon."

"Don't they ever come to watch?"

"Sometimes. Actually I've asked them to give us a few weeks so the kids aren't distracted or tempted to show off. You were a good test audience."

"Keeley." He touched her arm as she turned away. "The little boy. Willy. He's got a tooth he'll be losing in a couple of days. It'd be nice if someone remembered to put a coin under his pillow."

Her heart, which had leaped at his touch, quieted. Melted. "He's with a very good foster family right now. Very nice and caring people. They won't forget."

"All right then."

"Brian." This time it was her hand on his arm. Despite

the curious eyes of her students, she rose to her toes to brush her lips over his cheek. "I have a soft spot for a man who believes in fairies," she murmured, then walked away to gather her students.

A very soft spot, she thought, for a man with a cocky grin and a kind heart. She opened the terrace doors of her room, stepped out into the night. There was a chill in the air, and a sky so clear the stars flamed like torches. She could smell the flowers, the spice of the first mums, the poignancy of the last of the roses.

A breeze had the leaves whispering.

The three-quarter moon was pale gold, shedding light that gilded the gardens and shimmered over the fields. It seemed she could cup her hands, let that light pour into them and drink it like wine.

How could anyone sleep on so perfect a night?

Slowly she shifted and looked toward Brian's quarters. Light gleamed in his windows. And her pulse fluttered in her throat.

She told herself if his lights were off, she would close the doors again and try to sleep. But there they were, bright against dark, beckoning.

She closed her eyes on a shiver of anticipation and nerves. She'd prepared herself for this step, this change in her life, in her body. It wasn't an impulse, it wasn't reckless. But she felt impulsive. She felt reckless.

She was a grown woman, and the decision was hers.

Quietly she stepped back and closed the doors.

Brian closed the condition book, pressed his fingers to his tired eyes. Like Paddy, he wasn't quite sure he trusted the computer, but he was willing to fiddle with it a bit.

Three times a week he spent an hour trying to figure the damn thing out with the notion that eventually he could use it to generate his charts.

Graphics, they called it, he thought, shifting to give the machine a suspicious glare. Timesaving and efficient, if you believed all the hype. Well, tonight he was too damn tired to spend an hour trying to be timesaving and efficient.

He hadn't had a decent night's sleep in a week. Which had nothing to do with his job, he admitted. And everything to do with his boss's daughter.

It was a good thing he had that trip to Saratoga coming up, he decided as he pushed away from his desk and rose. A little distance was just what was needed. He didn't care for this unsteady sensation or this worrying ache around the heart.

He wasn't the type to fret over a woman, he thought. He enjoyed them, and was happy for them to enjoy him, then each moved on without regrets.

Moving on was always the end plan.

New York, he remembered, was a fair distance away. It should be far enough. As for tonight, he was going to have a shot of whiskey in his tea to help smooth out the edges. Then by God, he was going to sleep if he had to bash himself over the head to accomplish it.

And he wasn't going to give Keeley another thought.

The knock on the door had him cursing under his breath. Though she'd been doing well, his first worry was that the mare with bronchitis had taken a bad turn. He was already reaching for the boots he'd shed when he called out.

"Come in, it's open. Is it Lucy then?"

"No, it's Keeley." One brow lifted, she stood framed in the door. "But if you're expecting Lucy, I can go."

The boots dangled from his fingertips, and those fingertips had gone numb. "Lucy's a horse," he managed to say. "She doesn't often come knocking on my door."

"Ah, the bronchitis. I thought she was better."

"She is. Considerably." She'd gone and let her hair loose, he thought. Why did she have to do that? It made his hands hurt, actually hurt with wanting to slide into it.

"That's good." She stepped in, shut the door. And because it seemed too perfect not to, audibly flipped the lock. Seeing a muscle twitch in his jaw was incredibly satisfying.

He was a drowning man, and had just gone under the first time. "Keeley, I've had a long day here. I was just about to—"

"Have a nightcap," she finished. She'd spotted the teapot and the bottle of whiskey on the kitchen counter. "I wouldn't mind one myself." She breezed past him to flip off the burner under the now sputtering kettle.

She'd put on different perfume, he thought viciously. Put it on fresh, too, just to torment him. He was damn sure of it. It snagged his libido like a fishhook.

"I'm not really fixed for company just now."

"I don't think I qualify as company." Competently she warmed the pot, measured out the tea and poured the boiling water in. "I certainly won't be after we're lovers."

He went under the second time without even the chance to gulp in air. "We're not lovers."

"That's about to change." She set the lid on the pot, turned. "How long do you like it to steep?"

"I like it strong, so it'll take some time. You should go on home now."

"I like it strong, too." Amazing, she thought, she didn't feel nervous at all. "And if it's going to take some time, we can have it afterward."

"This isn't the way for this." He said it more to himself than her. "This is backward, or twisted. I can't get my mind around it. No, just stay back over there and let me think a minute."

But she was already moving toward him, a siren's smile on her lips. "If you'd rather seduce me, go ahead."

"That's exactly what I'm not going to do." Though the night was cool and his windows were open to it, he felt sweat slither down his back. "If I'd known the way things were, I'd never have started this."

That mouth of his, she thought. She really had to have that mouth. "Now we both know the way things are, and I intend to finish it. It's my choice."

His blood was already swimming. Hot and fast. "You don't know anything, which is the whole flaming problem."

"Are you afraid of innocence?"

"Damn right."

"It doesn't stop you from wanting me. Put your hands on me, Brian." She took his wrist, pressed his hand to her breast. "I want your hands on me."

The boots clattered to the floor as he went under for the third time. "It's a mistake."

"I don't think so. Touch me."

His hand closed over her. She was small, delicate, and through some momentary miracle, his. "Doesn't matter if it's a mistake," he said, giving up entirely.

"We won't let it be one." Her head fell back as his hands began to move.

"Doesn't matter. But I'll be careful with you."

Her eyes were blue and brilliant as she lifted her arms, slid her hands into his wildly waving hair. "Not too careful, I hope."

When he swept her up in his arms she let out a shuddering sigh. "Oh, I was hoping you'd do that." Thrilled, she pressed her lips to the side of his neck. "I was really hoping you'd do that."

He turned his face into her hair, drew in the scent, held it inside him. "You've only to tell me what you like."

She tipped her head back to look at him as he carried her into the bedroom. "Show me what I like."

With moonlight and cool breezes shimmering through the open windows, he laid her on the bed. There had been moonlight the first time he'd kissed her, soft fingers of it then, as there were now. He'd never forget the look of it, or of her.

There had been few gifts in his life that had mattered, that had stayed in him, in his heart and memory. She would, he knew. She was a gift he would cherish.

"This," he murmured, nibbling at her lips till they parted for him.

She opened, willing, wanting to be touched and tasted and taken. Even as he sensed her eagerness he led her slowly, patiently, thoroughly through the layers of sensations.

He caressed, his fingertips, palms, light as the air, then lingering at some secret place that had her breath catching on little jolts of pleasure. His mouth cruised lazily over her skin, sliding her into warmth, then it would come back to hers again, with a hungry bite that shot her into the heat.

Instinctively, avidly, she arched against him.

He was murmuring to her, lovely, stirring words in the old tongue, each like a tender kiss on the soul. Her heart fluttered, wings spreading wide for flight.

There were no nerves, no doubts as she raised herself to him, wrapped herself around him. When he slipped off her shirt, the breeze and his fingertips whispered over her. She felt beautiful.

Her skin was white silk, her hair rich flame. Every tremble was a gift, every sigh a treasure. In his life he'd never held anything as lovely as Keeley discovering herself.

She never shied when he undressed her, but embraced each new moment, welcomed each fresh sensation. Her curious hands moved over him, undressing him in turn. He'd never known how arousing it could be to be someone's first.

Her heart hammered under his mouth, and the scent she'd dabbed on that fragile flesh swirled into his senses until they were as clouded as hers. He took more, just a little more, and she began to move under him in mindless invitation.

So much. There was so much, was all she could think. Her body was flooded with sensations, her flesh quivering from them. She could hear her own moans, her own ragged breaths but could do nothing to control them. The very loss of control was thrilling.

Everything inside her was tangled and straining. And desperate. Her nails bit into his back, her teeth found his shoulder. Then his hand closed over her.

She cried out from the shock of it, all that pulsing, pumping pleasure, the sheer heat of it that washed in one huge wave that crashed over her, inside her, and left her shuddering. She reared up, eyes blind, her fingers diving into his hair.

Then his mouth was on hers again, hotter now, hungrier, giving her no chance to catch her breath or her sanity.

"Give yourself to me," he whispered, the blood pounding in his head as her eyes, heavy, stunned, looked into his. "Take me in."

With her eyes on his, she opened and arched, and gave.

It was like rising into the air, each stroke another beat of wings. Pleasure climbed higher and higher still, lifting through her body, sweeping through her mind. All she could see were his eyes, dark and green and focused on her, even as his body was focused on hers. Mated and matched and moving with her.

Staggered by the beauty of it, she lifted a hand to his cheek, murmured his name.

And he was lost. Love and passion, dreams and desire stabbed through his heart. Helpless, he buried his face in her hair and let himself go.

With her eyes closed she absorbed the delights of being a well-loved woman. Her body felt gloriously heavy, her mind wonderfully muffled. There was no need to wonder or worry if she had given Brian the same pleasure. She had seen it in his face, and felt it as he lay over her with his heart still thundering.

There was a change inside her, she thought. Awareness, understanding. And a soaring kind of triumph.

Smiling to herself, she traced a finger down his back. "How are the ribs?"

"What?"

And didn't it feel grand to hear that sleepy slur in his voice? "Your ribs. That's still a nasty bruise you have there."

"I can't feel anything." His head was still spinning. "What's this scent you've put on? It's devious."

"Just one of my many secrets."

He lifted his head, started to grin at her, then it swamped him again. The look of her, the love of her. Lowering his head he brought his lips to hers in a long, dreamy kiss that came out of his soul and stirred hers.

Her hand slid limply to the mattress. "Brian."

"I'm crushing you." He said it briskly. He'd terrified himself.

He shifted away and shattered the moment. "There's not really very much of you." Suddenly aware that the breeze fluttering in the windows he left open was cold, he tugged at the bedspread until he could wrap it around her. "Are you all right then?"

"I'm fabulous, thank you." Laughing, she sat up, without a shrug for modesty as the spread slid to her waist. She caught his face in her hands and gave him a quick, affectionate kiss. "Are you all right then?" she said, mimicking his brogue.

"That I am, but I've had a bit of practice."

"I'll bet. But let's not bring up all your conquests just now. I'd hate to be obliged to punch you when I'm feeling so friendly."

"I wouldn't say they were conquests precisely. But we'll let that be."

"Wise choice."

"Let me close the windows. You're cold."

She angled her head as he rose. "There's nurturing in that bruised body of yours, Donnelly."

"I beg your pardon?"

"I'd say it comes from the horses." She pursed her lips, considered while he *thunked* a window down and scowled. "You look after them, worry about them, make plans for them, see to their needs and their comfort—oh and their training, of course. Then if you don't watch yourself you start to do it with people, too."

"I don't nurture people." He found the idea mildly insulting. "People can look after themselves. I don't even like people very much." He stalked over and shut the other window. "Present company excepted, as you're sitting naked in my bed and it would be rude to say otherwise."

"You didn't phrase that quite right. You don't like very many people. Do you have a robe?"

"No." He wasn't sure if it was the truth in what she said, or her understanding of him that irked him.

"Figures." She spied one of his work shirts tossed over a chair, and though it smelled of horses, slipped it on. "I'd say that tea's probably strong enough to hammer nails by now. Do you still want it?"

She looked...interesting in his shirt. Interesting enough that his blood began to churn again. "What are my options?"

"On my schedule, we have a cup of tea, a little conversation, then you get to seduce me back into bed and make love to me again before I go home."

"That's not bad, but I think it bears improving."

"Oh, and how's that?"

"We cut out the tea and conversation."

She ran her tongue over her top lip—his taste was still there—as he walked toward her. "That would take us straight to you seducing me? Correct?"

"That's my plan."

"I can be flexible."

His grin flashed. "I'd like to test that out."

They never got around to the tea.

And when she'd left him, he stood at the door and watched her run along the path. Love-struck idiot, he told himself. You can't keep her. You've never kept anything in your life that you couldn't fit in the bag you toss over your shoulder.

It was a bad turn of luck, that was all, that he would slip up and fall in love. It was bound to hurt like blazes before it was done. He'd get over it, of course. Over her and over this slippery feeling inside his heart. He wasn't so far gone as to believe this sort of madness lasted.

So best to enjoy it, he decided, and turned away when Keeley disappeared in the dark.

When he climbed into bed, her scent was on his pillow. For the first time in a week he slept deep and slept well.

Chapter 8

She missed him. It was the oddest thing to find herself thinking about Brian off and on during the day, and thinking of a dozen things she wanted to tell him, or show him when he got back from Saratoga.

She wasn't the only one.

During his next lesson Willy asked if Mr. Donnelly was coming so he could show off the fresh gap in his teeth. The man, Keeley mused, made an impression and made it fast.

It wasn't as if she didn't have enough to occupy her mind or her time. She'd found enough tuition students to add another class and was even now snaking her way through the maze of bureaucracy to arrange for three additional subsidized students.

She'd had meetings with the psychologist, the social worker, the parents and the children. The paperwork alone was enough to, well, choke a horse, she admitted. But it would be worth it in the end.

With some amusement, she flipped through the article in *Washingtonian Magazine*. She knew the exposure was responsible for netting her the new full tuition students. The photographs were gorgeous and the text made full use of her background, her Olympic medal and her social standing.

No problem there, she decided, particularly since the academy was mentioned several times.

She glanced at the phone with a little sigh as it rang. It hadn't stopped since the article had been published. The time was coming, Keeley thought, when she was going to have to break down and hire an assistant.

But for now, the school was all hers.

"Good morning, Royal Meadows Riding Academy." Her coolly professional tone warmed when she heard her cousin Maureen's voice.

Fifteen minutes later, she was hanging up and shaking her head. It appeared she was going to dinner and the races that evening. She'd said no—at least Keeley was fairly certain she'd said no five or six times. But nobody held out against Mo for long. She just rolled over you.

Keeley eyed the piles of paperwork on her desk, huffed out a breath when the phone rang again. Just do the first thing, she reminded herself, then do the second, and keep going until it was done.

She'd done the first, the second and the third, when her father came in.

He stopped in the doorway, held up a hand. "Wait, don't tell me. I know you. The face is very familiar." He narrowed his eyes as she rolled hers. "I'm sure I've seen you before, somewhere. Tibet? Mazetlan? At the dinner table a year or two ago."

"It hasn't been more than a week." She reached up as

he bent to kiss her. "But I've missed you, too. I've been swamped here."

"So I've heard." He flipped open the magazine to her article. "Pretty girl. I bet her parents are proud of her."

"I hope so." When the phone rang, she muffled a shriek, waved her hands. "Let the machine get it. It's been ringing off the hook since Sunday. Half the parents who call in to inquire about lessons haven't even asked their kids if they want to ride."

She scooted her chair to the little fridge and took out two bottles of soda. "So thanks."

"For?" Travis prompted as he took the soft drink.

"For always asking."

"Then you're welcome. I hear I'm escorting two lovely women to dinner tonight."

"Mo caught you?"

He chuckled before he tipped back the bottle to drink. "'We haven't had an inter-family gathering in weeks,'" he mimicked. "'Don't you love me anymore?'"

"She always pushes the right button." Keeley studied the toe of her oldest boots. "So...have you heard from Brendon?"

"Late yesterday. They should be home tonight."

"That's good." You'd think the man could have called her once, she thought, scowling at her boots. Sent a telegram, a damn smoke signal.

"I imagine Brian's anxious to get back."

Her head jerked up. "Really?"

"Betty's making progress—as are several of the other yearlings. She's doing particularly well on the practice oval. She's ready for Brian to take her over full-time."

"I caught one of her morning workouts. She looks strong."

"We breed true at Royal Meadows." There was something wistful in his tone that had Keeley lifting her brows.

"What's the matter?"

"Nothing." Travis shrugged it off and rose. "Getting old."

"Don't be ridiculous."

"Yesterday you were riding on my shoulders," he murmured. "The house was full of noise. Clomping up and down the steps, doors slamming. Scattered toys. I don't know how many times I stepped on one of those damned little cars of Brady's."

Turning back, he ran a hand over her hair. "I miss that. I miss all of you."

"Daddy." In one fluid movement she rose and slid her arms around him.

"It's the way it's supposed to work. Three of you off at college, Brendon moving around to get a handle on the business of things. It's what he wants. And you, building your own. But... I miss the crowd of you."

"I promise to slam the door the very first chance I get."

"That might help."

"Sentimental softie. I love that about you."

"Lucky for me." He gave her a quick, hard squeeze, then glanced over as the phone rang again. "Actually I didn't stop in for sentiment, but to give you some business advice." He drew her back. "You need help around here."

"I'm thinking about it. Really," she added when he angled his head. "As soon as I straighten things out I'll look into it."

"I seem to recall you saying the same thing six months ago."

"It just hasn't been the right time. I've got it all under control." Even as she said it, the phone rang again.

"Keeley, getting help doesn't mean you won't be in charge, doesn't mean it won't be your school."

"I know, but…it won't be the same."

"I'm here to tell you nothing stays the same. The farm's more than it was when it passed to me, and less than it will be when it passes to you and your brothers and sisters. But I've put my mark on it. Nothing can change that."

"I guess I just don't want it to get away from me."

"You've already proven you can do it."

"You're right. Of course, you're right. But it isn't easy to find the right person. It would have to be someone good with kids and horses, and who'd be able to pitch in with the administrating to some extent and wouldn't quibble about shoveling manure. Plus I'd have to be able to depend on them, and get along with them. And they'd have to be diplomatic with parents, which is often the trickiest part."

Travis picked up his soft drink again. "I might be able to point you in the right direction there."

"Oh? Listen, Dad, I appreciate it, but you know, a friend of a friend or the son or daughter of an acquaintance. That kind of thing gets very sticky if it doesn't work out."

"Actually, I was thinking of someone a little closer to home. Your mother."

"Ma?" With a half laugh Keeley sat again. "Ma doesn't want this headache, even if she had time for it."

"Shows what you know." Smug now, he drank. "Just mention it to her, casually. I won't say a word about it."

By the time the day's lesson was over, and the last horse groomed and fed, Keeley dragged herself into the house. She wanted nothing more than a long bath and a quiet night. And if she ducked the evening plans, her cousin Mo would dog her like a hound. Better to face an evening out than weeks of nagging.

She moved through the kitchen, into the hall. Her father was right, she realized. How would any of them get used to the quiet? No one was shouting down the stairs or rushing in the door or playing music so loud it vibrated the eardrums.

She paused at the top of the steps, looking right. There was the room Brady and Patrick shared. She still remembered that during one spat Brady had run a line of black tape from the ceiling, down the wall, across the floor, and up again, cutting the room in half.

One had been marked Brady's Territory. The other he'd dubbed No Man's Land.

And how many times had she heard Brendon pound a fist on the wall between his room and theirs ordering them to keep it down before he came in and knocked their heads together?

When she passed Sarah's room, she saw her mother sitting on the bed, stroking a red sweater.

"Ma?"

"Oh." Adelia looked up. Her eyes were damp, but she shook her head and smiled. "You startled me. It's so bloody quiet in this house."

Keeley stepped in. The room had bright blue walls. The curtains and spread picked up that bold hue and matched it with an equally vivid green in wide stripes. It should have been horrible, Keeley mused, as she often did. But it worked.

And it was completely Sarah.

"Do you and Dad share the same brain?" Keeping her voice light, Keeley sat on the bed. "He was feeling sad this morning over the same thing."

"I suppose after all these years together, you pick up the same vibrations or whatever. And Sarah called just a bit ago. She's desperately in need for this particular red sweater, which she can't think how she forgot to take with her. She sounds so happy and busy and grown up."

"They'll all be home next month for Thanksgiving, then again for Christmas."

"I know. Still, if I could think of a way to get away with it, I'd deliver this sweater myself instead of shipping it. Lord, look at the time. I've got to get myself cleaned up and changed for dinner. And so do you."

"Yeah." Keeley pursed her lips in thought while her mother smoothed the sweater one more time and rose. "I'm running behind today," she began. "I seem to be running behind a lot lately."

"That's what happens to successful people."

"I suppose so. And adding on this class is going to crowd my time and energy even more."

"You know I'll give you a hand when you need it, and so will your father." Adelia walked out of the room and into her own to lay Sarah's sweater aside.

"Yes, I appreciate that. I guess I'm going to have to seriously consider something more formal and permanent, though. I really hate to. I mean, taking on an outsider, it's difficult for me. But…"

Keeley let the word hang, surprised when her mother—who usually had something to say—remained silent.

"I don't suppose you'd be interested in working part-time at the school?"

Adelia turned her head, met Keeley's eyes in the mirror over the bureau. "Are you offering me a job?"

"It sounds awfully strange when you put it that way, but

yes. But don't do it because you feel obliged. Only if you think you'd have the time or the inclination."

Adelia spun around, her face brilliant. "What the devil's taken you so long? I'll start tomorrow."

"Really? You really want to?"

"I've been *dying* to. Oh, it's taken every bit of my will-power not to come down there every day until you just got so used to me being around you didn't realize I *was* working there. This is exciting!" She rushed over to give Keeley a hug. "I can't wait to tell your father."

Keeping her arms tight around her daughter, Adelia did a quick dance. "I'm a groom again."

"If I'd known you were available, Dee, and looking for work, I'd've hired you." Burke Logan settled back in his chair and winked at his wife's cousin.

"We like to keep the best on at Royal Meadows." Adelia twinkled at him across the table in the track's dining room. He was as handsome and as dangerous to look at as he'd been nearly twenty years before when she'd first met him.

"Oh, I don't know." Burke trailed a hand over his wife's shoulder. "We have the best bookkeeper around at Three Aces."

"In that case, I want a raise." Erin picked up her wine and sent Burke a challenging look. "A big one. Trevor?" Her voice was smooth, shimmering with Ireland as she addressed her son. "Do you have in mind to eat that pork chop or just use it for decoration?"

"I'm reading the *Racing Form,* Ma."

"His father's son," Erin muttered and snagged the paper from him. "Eat your dinner."

He heaved a sigh as only a twelve-year-old boy could. "I think Topeka in the third, with Lonesome in the fifth and

Hennessy in the sixth for the trifecta. Dad says Topeka's generous and a cinch tip."

At his wife's long stare, Burke cleared his throat. "Stuff that pork chop in your mouth, Trev. Where's Jena?"

"She's fussing with her hair," Mo announced, and snatched a French fry from Travis's plate. "As usual," she added with the worldly air only an older sister could achieve, "the minute she turned fourteen she decided her hair was the bane of her existence. Huh. Like having long, thick, straight-as-a-pin black hair is a problem. This—" she tugged on one of the hundreds of wild red curls that spiraled around her face "—is a problem. If you're going to worry about something as stupid as hair, which I don't. Anyway, you guys have to come over and see this weanling I have my eye on. He's going to be amazing. And if Dad lets me train him…"

She trailed off, slanting a look at her father across the table.

"You'll be in college this time next year," Burke reminded her.

"Not if I can help it," Mo said under her breath.

Recognizing the mutinous look, Erin changed the subject. "Keeley, Burke tells me your new trainer is a natural with the horses, with Travis and with cards as well."

"And I hear he's gorgeous, too," Mo added.

"Where'd you hear that?" Keeley demanded before she could bite her tongue in two.

"Oh, word gets around in our snug little world," Mo said grandly. "And Shelley Mason—one of your kids? Her sister Lorna's in my World History class, a *huge* bore by the way. The class, that is, not Lorna, who's only a small bore. Anyway, she picked Shelley up last week from your place and got a load of the Irish hunk, so I heard all about it. Which is why I'm planning on coming over as soon as I can and getting a load of him myself."

"Trevor, give your sister your pork chop so she can stuff it in her mouth."

"Dad." Giggling, Mo snatched another fry. "I'm just going to look. So, Keeley, is he gorgeous? I respect your opinion more than Lorna Mason's."

"He's too old for you," Keeley said, a bit more sharply than she intended and had Mo rolling her eyes.

"Jeez. I don't want to marry him and have his children."

Travis's laugh prevented Keeley from snapping back with something foolish. "Good thing. Now that I've found someone who comes close to replacing Paddy, I don't intend to lose him to Three Aces."

"Okay." Mo licked salt from her fingertip. "I'll just ogle him."

Annoyed, and feeling ridiculous at the reaction, Keeley pushed back her chair. "I think I'll go down and take a look at the field, and check on Lonesome. He's always a little sulky before a race."

"Cool." Mo sprang up. "I'll go down with you."

Mo rushed out of the dining room, heading out past the betting windows at a fast clip, so that Keeley was forced to step lively to keep pace. "It's going to be so much fun for you, having your mom work at the school. There's nothing like a family operation, you know. Which is all I want. I mean, come on, I don't have to go to college to be a trainer. If I already know what I want to do, and I'm learning how to do it every day right at home, what's college going to do for me?"

"Expand your brain?" Keeley suggested.

Ignoring that, Mo hurried outside where the air had turned crisp. "I know horses, Keeley. You understand what it's like. It's instinct and experience and it's *doing*." She gestured widely. "Well, I've got time to nag my parents into submission."

"No one does it better."

With a laugh, Mo hooked her arm through her cousin's. "I'm so glad to see you. The summer just winged by, you know, with all of us so busy with stuff."

"I know."

They made the turn for the shedrow and the world was suddenly horses.

Some were being prepped for the next race. In the boxes, grooms wrapped long, thin legs that would carry those huge bodies in a blur of speed and power. Trainers with keen eyes and gentle hands moved among the horses to pamper a skittish ride or rev up another.

The hot walkers cooled down horses who'd already run. Legs were examined, iced down. Through the sharp air came the hoofbeats that signaled another field was coming back from the race. Steam rose off the horses' backs, turning into a fine and magical mist.

"Of all the shedrows in all the world." Brendon came out of the stables, grinning.

"You're back."

"Just." He strolled over to rub a hand over Mo's hair. "I talked to Ma a couple of hours ago from the road and she said you were all coming here tonight. So we swung by on the way home."

"We?"

"Yeah, Bri's taking a look at Lonesome, giving him a pep talk. Moodiest damn horse. Figured we might as well catch the race, then I can hook a ride back with you guys and Brian can trailer Zeus back home."

"Sounds like a plan." It pleased her to hear the calm of

her own voice while her heart was galloping. "Actually I came down to take a look at Lonesome myself."

"He's all yours—and Bri's. Hey, I've got time to get some dinner. See you up there."

"Now you can introduce me to the hunk." Mo fell into step beside Keeley.

"I will if you can behave like you have a brain as well as glands."

"It has nothing to do with glands, I'm just curious. Don't worry, I'm taking a page out of your book there when it comes to men."

Keeley stopped at the door to the stables. "Excuse me?"

"You know, guys are fine to look at, or to hang around with occasionally. But there are lots more important things. I'm not going to get involved with one until I'm thirty, soonest."

Keeley wasn't certain whether to be amused or appalled. Then she heard Brian's voice, the lilt of it. And she forgot everything else.

He was in the box with Lonesome, a temperamental roan gelding. The horse moped, as was his habit before a race.

"They ask too much of you, there's no doubt about it," Brian was saying as he checked the wrappings on Lonesome's legs. "It's a terrible cross you have to bear, and you show great courage and fortitude day after day. Perhaps if you win this one I can put a word in for you. You know, extra carrots and that sort of thing, a bit of molasses in the evening. A bigger brass plaque for your box at home."

"That's bribery," Keeley murmured.

Brian turned, his eyes going warm. "That's bargaining," he corrected. "But if I can interest you in a bribe," he began and opened the box door intending to snatch Keeley inside for a much anticipated welcome back kiss.

He nearly stepped over Mo. "Sorry. Didn't see you there."

"I'm short. That's my cross to bear. I'm Mo Logan." She stuck out a friendly hand. "Keeley's cousin from Three Aces."

"Pleased to meet you. You've a horse running tonight, Ms. Logan?"

"Mo. Hennessy. Sixth race. My money says he'll win laughing."

"I'll keep that in mind if I get up to the betting window."

"I want to take a look at Hennessy before his race. Come up to the dining room if you have time, Brian, for food or a drink. The family's all there."

"Thank you for that. Pretty thing," Brian murmured when Mo dashed off.

"She wanted to take a look at you, too. She heard you were a hunk."

"Is that so?" Amused, Brian shifted. "Did you tell her that?"

"I certainly did not. I have more respect for you than to speak of you in such a sexist way."

"Respect's a good thing." He yanked her into the box, crushing his mouth to hers before she could laugh. "But I'm banking on passion just at the moment. Have you passion for me, Keeley?" he murmured against her mouth.

"Apparently." Her ears were ringing. "Oh, Brian, I want—" She strained against him until they bumped into the horse. "You. Now. Somewhere. Can't we...it's been days."

"Four." He wanted to tear off the long slim dress she wore and mount her like a stallion, all blinding heat and primitive need.

He'd thought, convinced himself, that he'd be sensible

about her, kept his wants and wishes under control. And all it had taken was seeing her. Just seeing her. It was exactly as it had been that first time he'd laid his eyes on her. A lightning strike in heart and blood.

"Keeley." He ran kisses over her face, buried his in her hair, then started all over again. "I've such a need for you. It's like burning from the inside out. Come with me, out to the lorry."

"Yes." At that moment, she'd have gone anywhere. It seemed he would swallow her whole. "Hurry. Let's hurry."

She took his hand, fumbled with the door herself. Breathless, she would have stumbled if he hadn't caught her. "Teach me to wear heels in the damn stable," she muttered. "My legs are shaking."

With a nervous laugh she turned back to him. Her legs stopped trembling. At least she couldn't feel them. All she could feel now was the unsteady skipping of her heart.

He was staring at her, his eyes intense. When she'd turned his hands had reached up to frame her face. "You're so beautiful."

She'd never believed words like that mattered. They were so easily, and so often carelessly, said. But they didn't seem easy from him. And there was nothing careless about the tone of his voice. Before she could speak, before she could think of what could be said, there was a shout and the sound of running feet.

"Keeley, hurry, come with me." Oblivious to the intimacy of the scene she'd burst in on, Mo grabbed her hand. "I need backup. The bastard."

"What? What's happened?"

"If he thinks he's going to get away with it, he's got another think coming." Dragging Keeley, Mo barreled through the stables, turned and charged toward a stall.

Keeley could already hear the voices raised in argument. She saw the man first. She recognized him. Peter Tarmack with his oiled hair and cheap pinkie ring made a habit of picking up horses in claiming races, then running them into the ground.

The jockey was a familiar face as well. He was past his prime and, like Tarmack, was known to enjoy a few too many nips from the bottle at the track. Still, he picked up rides now and again when a regular jockey was sick or injured.

"I tell you, Tarmack, I won't ride him. And you won't get anyone else to. He's not fit to run."

"Don't you tell me what's fit. You'll get up and you'll ride, and you'll damn well place. You've been paid."

"Not to ride a sick and injured horse. You'll get your money back."

"What you haven't already put in a bottle."

Because Mo was quivering and had sucked in a breath to speak, Keeley squeezed her hand hard enough to grind bone. "Is there a problem, Larry?"

"Miss Keeley." The jockey yanked off his cap and turned his wrinkled, flustered face to hers. "I'm trying to tell Mr. Tarmack here that his horse isn't fit to race tonight. He's not fit."

"It's not your place to tell me anything. And I don't need one of the almighty Grant's damn whelps interfering in my business."

Before Keeley could respond, Brian had moved in. She blinked and he had hauled Tarmack up to his toes. "That's no way to be speaking to a lady." His voice was quiet, the eye of a storm. And the storm, with all its vengeance, was in his eyes. "You'll want to apologize for that, while you still have teeth to help you form the words."

"Brian, I can handle this."

"You'll handle what you like." He kept his eyes on Tarmack's now bulging ones. "But he'll by God apologize with his very next breath."

"I beg your pardon." Tarmack choked it out, wheezed in air as Brian relaxed his grip a little. "I'm simply trying to deal with a washed-up jockey—and one I've paid in advance."

"You'll get your money back," the jockey replied, then turned to Keeley. "Miss Keeley, I'm not getting up on this ride. He's half lame from a knee spavin, and anybody with eyes can see he's hidebound. He ain't fit to race."

"Excuse me." Her voice viciously cold, she pushed past Tarmack and moved into the box to examine the horse for herself. Within moments, her hands were shaking with rage.

"Mr. Tarmack, if you try to put a jockey on this horse, I'll have you up on charges. In fact, I'm damn well having you up on charges regardless. This gelding's sick, injured and neglected."

"Don't hang that on me. I've only had him a couple weeks."

"And in a couple weeks you haven't noticed his condition? You've been working him despite it?"

"Now you look." He started to take a step forward and found himself looking eye to eye with Brian again. "Listen," he said, his tone shifting to a whine. "Maybe you can be sentimental when you've got money. Me, I make my living moving horses. They don't run, I go in the red."

"How much?" Keeley laid a hand on the gelding's cheek. In her heart, he was already hers. "How much did he cost you?"

"Ah…ten grand."

Brian merely shoved a finger into Tarmack's breastbone. "Pull the other one. It has bells on it."

Tarmack shifted his shoulders. "Maybe it was five thousand. I'd have to check my books."

"You'll have a check for five thousand tomorrow. I'm taking the horse tonight. Brian, would you take a look at him, please?"

"Wait just a minute."

This time it was Keeley who turned and she who shoved Tarmack aside. "Be smart. Take the money. Because whether you do or don't I'm taking this horse with me."

"The knee needs treatment," Brian said after a quick look. It burned his blood to see how the injury had been neglected. "We can deal with that. From the look of him, I'd say he has a good case of bots. He needs tending."

"He'll get tending."

Keeley merely glanced over her shoulder at Tarmack. "You can go." Her voice held the regal ring of dismissal—princess to peasant. "Someone will deliver the check to you in the morning."

The tone burned in Tarmack's gut. She wouldn't be so hoity-toity without her damn bodyguard, he thought. He'd have taught her a little respect if the Irish bastard hadn't been around.

He bunched a fist impotently in his pocket and tried to save face. "I'm not just letting you take the horse and leave me with nothing but your say-so. I don't give a damn who you are."

Brian straightened again, blood in his eye, but Keeley merely held up a hand. "Mo, would you please take Mr. Tarmack to the dining room. If you'd ask my father to write him a check for the five thousand, and I'll straighten it out later."

"Happy to." She grabbed Keeley by the shoulders, kissed her. "I knew you'd do it." Then with a sniff she turned away. "Come with me, Tarmack. You'll get your money."

"I'm sorry, Miss Keeley." Larry ran his cap through his hands. "I didn't know how bad it was till I saw the ride here. I couldn't get up on him seeing how he was."

"You did the right thing. Don't worry."

"He did pay me ahead, like he said."

She nodded, stepped out of the box again, gesturing to him. "How much do you have left?"

"'Bout twenty."

"Come and see me tomorrow. We'll take care of it."

"'Preciate it, Miss Keeley. That horse there, he ain't worth no five, you know."

She studied the gelding. His color was muddy, his face too square for elegance and made homelier still by an off-center blaze of dirty white. And his eyes were unbearably sad.

"Sure he is, Larry. He's worth it to me."

Chapter 9

"You don't have to help with this."

Brian said nothing, simply continued to clip the gelding's legs. Bots were a common enough problem, especially with horses at grass. But this one had been sadly neglected. He had no doubt the eggs the botfly had laid on the gelding's legs had been transferred to the stomach.

"Brian, really." Keeley continued to mix the blister for the knee spavin. "You've had a really long day. I can handle this."

"Sure you can. You can handle this, morons like Tarmack, washed-up jockeys and everything else that comes along before breakfast. Nobody's saying different."

Since the statement wasn't delivered in what could be mistaken for a complimentary tone, Keeley turned to frown at him. "What's wrong with you?"

"There's not a bloody thing wrong with me. But you could use some work. Do you have to do everything yourself, every flaming step and stage of it? Can't you just take help when help's offered and shut the hell up?"

She did shut the hell up, for ten shocked seconds. "I simply assumed that you'd be tired after your trip."

"I'll let you know when I'm tired."

"The gelding here doesn't seem to be the only one with something nasty in his system."

"Well, it's you in my system, princess, and it feels a bit nasty at the moment."

Hurt came first, a quick short-armed jab. Pride sprang in to defend. "I'll be happy to purge you, just like I'll purge this horse tomorrow."

"If I thought it would work," he muttered, "I'd purge myself. You'll want to wait until at least midday," Brian told her. "You can't be sure the last time he was fed."

"I know how to treat stomach-bots, thank you." Gently she began to apply the blister to the injured knee.

"Here, you'll get that all over your clothes."

Keeley jerked away bad-temperedly when Brian reached for the pot of blister. "They're my clothes."

"So you should have more respect for them. You've no business treating a horse in clothes like that. Silk dresses for God's sake."

"I've got a closetful. We princesses tend to."

"Nevertheless." He curled his fingers around the lip of the pot, and under the sick gelding they began a vicious little tug-of-war. He would have laughed, was on the point of it, when he looked at her face and saw that her eyes were wet.

He let go of the pot so abruptly, Keeley fell back on her butt. "What are you doing?" he demanded.

"I'm applying a non-irritating blister to a knee spavin. Now go away and let me get on with it."

"There's no reason to start that up. None at all." Panic

jingled straight to his head, nearly made him dizzy. "This is no place for crying."

"I'm upset. It's my stable. I can cry when and where I choose."

"All right, all right, all right." Desperately he dug into his pocket for a bandanna. "Here, just blow your nose or something."

"Just go to hell or something." Rather grandly, she turned her shoulder on him and continued to apply the blister.

"Keeley, I'm sorry." He wasn't sure for exactly what, but that wasn't here nor there. "Dry your eyes now, *a grha,* and we'll make this lad comfortable for the night."

"Don't take that placating tone with me. I'm not a child or a sick horse."

Brian dragged his hands through his hair, gave it one good yank. "Which tone would you prefer?"

"An honest one." Satisfied the blister was properly applied, she rose. "But I'm afraid the derisive one you've used since we got here fits that category. In your opinion, I'm spoiled, stubborn and too proud to accept help."

Though the tears appeared to have passed, he thought it wise to be cautious. "That's pretty close to the truth," he agreed, getting to his feet. "But it's an interesting mixture, and I've grown fond of it."

"I'm not spoiled."

Brian raised his eyebrows, cocked his head. "Perhaps the word means something different to you Yanks. Seems to me it's not everyone who could casually ask their father to write a check for five thousand dollars for a sick horse."

"I'll pay him back in the morning."

"I've no doubt of it."

Baffled now, she threw up her hands. "Should I have just

left him there, walked away so that idiot Tarmack could find a jockey who would go up on him?"

"No, you did exactly right. But the fact's the same that you could toss around that kind of money without blinking an eye."

Brian walked to the gelding's head to examine his eyes and teeth. It grated on him. He wished it didn't, as it said little for him that her easy dismissal of money scored his pride.

But it had, at that heated moment at the track, slammed the distance between them right in his face.

"You're a generous woman, Keeley."

"But I can afford to be," she finished.

"True enough." He ran his hands down the horse's neck, soothing. "But that doesn't take away from the fact that you are." Slowly he continued to work his way over the horse. "You'll have to forgive me—Irish of my class are generally a bit resentful of the gentry. It's in the blood."

"The class system's in your head, Brian."

That, he thought, wasn't even worth commenting on. What was, was. His fingers found a small knot. "He's a bit of an abscess here. We'll want to bring this to a head."

They'd bring something else to a head, she decided and moved in so they faced each other over the gelding's back. "So tell me, how do men of your class deal with taking women of mine to bed?"

His eyes flashed to hers, held. "I'd keep my hands off you if I could."

"Is that supposed to flatter me?"

"No. It just is, and doesn't flatter either of us." He moved out of the box to get flannel to heat for a hot fermentation.

No, she thought. She'd be damned if she'd leave it at that. "Is that all there is to it, Brian?" she demanded as she followed him out. "Just sex?"

He ran water, hot as his hand could bear, and soaked a large section of flannel in it. "No." He spoke without turning around. "I care about you. That just makes it more difficult."

"It should make it easier."

"It doesn't."

"I don't understand you. Would you be happier if we just jumped each other, without any connection, any understanding or feelings?"

He hauled up the bucket. "Infinitely. But it's too late for that, isn't it?"

Baffled, she walked back into the box behind him. "You're angry with me because you care about me. This water's too hot," she said when she tested it.

"No, it isn't. And I'm not angry with you at t'all." Murmuring to the gelding, he lay the heated flannel over the abscess. "A bit with myself, maybe, but it's more satisfying to take it out on you."

"That, at least, I can understand. Brian, why are we fighting?" She laid a hand over the one he held pressed to the flannel. "We're doing the right thing here tonight. The method of how we got the gelding here isn't as important as what happens to him now."

"You're right, of course." He studied the contrast of their hands. His big, rough from work and hers small and elegant.

"And why we care for each other isn't as important as what we do about it."

About that he wasn't as sure, so he said nothing while she lifted another square of flannel and wrung it out.

Morning dawned misty and cool. As she'd slept poorly, Keeley's mind refused to click into gear. Her usual rush of morning adrenaline deserted her so that she began her daily chores with her body dragging and her brain fogged.

Brian's doing, she thought sulkily. This inconsistency of his, this off-and-on insistence to keep a distance between them was baffling. She'd never run into a problem she couldn't solve, an obstacle she couldn't overcome. But this one, this one man, might just be the exception.

He hurt her, and she hadn't been prepared for it. Could they have spent so much time together, been so intimate, and not understand each other? He cared about her, and that made it a problem. What kind of logic was that? she asked herself. Where was the sense in that kind of thinking?

Caring about someone made all the difference. She'd seen that constant well of compassion in him. It was, she admitted, as attractive, as appealing to her as that long, tough body, that thick, unkempt mane of sun-streaked hair.

The look of him, the face of planes and angles, the bold green eyes, might have stirred her blood—and had, though she'd been more annoyed than pleased initially. But it was the heart, the patience, the nurturing side he refused to acknowledge that had won her interest and respect.

Rather than being a problem, it had been, and was, the solution for her.

How could he look at her now, after all they'd shared, and see only the pampered daughter of a privileged home?

How could he, believing that, have feelings for her?

It was baffling, irritating and very close to infuriating. Or would be, she thought with a yawn, if she wasn't so damned tired.

The lack of energy struck unfairly keen when Mo bounced into the stables. "Just had to come by before I headed off to the eternal hell of school." She popped right into the box where Keeley was examining the injured knee. "How's he doing?"

"He's more comfortable." Testing, Keeley lifted the gelding's foot, bending the knee. He snorted, shied. "But you can see there's still pain."

"Poor guy. Poor big guy." Clucking, Mo patted his flank. "You were such a hero last night, Keel. I mean just stepping in and taking right over. I knew you would."

Keeley's brows drew together. "I didn't take over. I don't take over."

"Sure you did—you always do. The original take-charge gal. Very cool to watch. And this guy's grateful, aren't you, boy? Oh, and the hunk wasn't hard on the eyes, either." Grinning, she gave an obvious and deliberate shudder. "The real physical type. I thought he was going to punch that idiot Tarmack right in the face. Was kinda hoping he would. Anyway, the pair of you made a great team."

"I suppose."

"So, what about those smoldering looks?"

"What smoldering looks?"

"Get out." Mo cheerfully wiggled her eyebrows. "I got singed and I was only an innocent bystander. The guy looks at you like you were the last candy bar on the shelf and he'd die without a chocolate fix."

"That's a ridiculous analogy, and you're imagining things."

"He was going to pound Tarmack into dust for dissing you. Man, I just wanted to melt when he hauled the guy up by the collar. Too romantic."

"There's nothing romantic about a fight. And though I certainly could have handled Tarmack myself, I appreciated Brian's help."

Damn it, she thought. She hadn't even thanked him. Scowling, she stomped out of the box for a pitchfork.

"Yeah, you could have handled him. You handle everything. But not really needing to be rescued sort of makes *being* rescued more exciting, you know."

"No, I don't know," Keeley snapped. "Go to school, Mo. I've got mucking out to do."

"I'm going, I'm going. Sheesh. You must be low on the caffeine intake this morning. I'll come by later to see how the gelding's doing. I've got a kind of vested interest, you know? See you."

"Yeah, fine. Whatever." Keeley muttered to herself as she went to work on the stalls. There was nothing wrong with being able to handle things herself. Nothing wrong with wanting to. And she did appreciate Brian's help.

And she didn't need caffeine.

"I like caffeine," she grumbled. "I enjoy it, and that's entirely different from needing it. Entirely. I could give it up anytime I wanted, and I'd barely miss it."

Annoyed, she snagged the soft drink she'd left on a shelf and guzzled.

All right, so maybe she would miss it. But only because she liked the taste. It wasn't like a craving or an addiction or...

She couldn't say why Brian popped into her head just then. She was certain if he'd seen her staring in a kind of horror at a soft drink bottle, he'd have been amused. It was debatable what his reaction would be if he'd realized she wasn't actually seeing the bottle, but his face.

No, that wasn't a need, either, she thought quickly. She did not *need* Brian Donnelly. It was attraction. Affection— a cautious kind of affection. He was a man who interested her, and whom she admired in many ways. But it wasn't as if she needed...

"Oh God."

It had to be overreaction, she decided, and set the bottle aside as carefully as she would have a container of nitro. What she was going through was something as simple as overromanticizing an affair. That would be natural enough, she told herself, particularly since this was her first.

She didn't want to be in love with him. She began wielding the pitchfork vigorously now, as if to sweat out a fever. She didn't *choose* to be in love with him. That was even more important. When her hands trembled she ignored them and worked harder still.

By the time her mother joined her, Keeley had herself under control enough to casually ask Adelia to work in the office while she exercised Sam.

Keeley Grant had never run from a problem in her life, and she wasn't about to start now. She saddled her mount, then rode off to clear her head before she dealt with the problem at hand.

The portable starting gate was in place on the practice oval. The air was soft and cool. Brian had seen the blush of color coming onto the leaves, the hints of change. Though he imagined it would all be a sight in another week or two, his attention was narrowed onto the horses.

He was working in fields of five, using two yearlings and three experienced racers at a go. This last phase of schooling just prior to public racing would teach him every bit as much as it taught the yearlings.

He needed to watch their style, learn their preferences, their quirks, their strengths. Much of it would be guesses—educated ones to be sure, but guesses nonetheless, at least until they had a few solid races under their belts.

But Brian was very good at guessing.

"I want Tempest on the rail." He chewed on a cigar as it helped him think. "Then The Brooder, then Betty, Caramel and Giant on the outside."

He glanced around at the sound of hoofbeats, then lost

his train of thought as Keeley trotted toward the oval. Irritated, he looked deliberately away and slammed the door on that increasingly wide area of his mind she insisted on occupying.

"I don't want the yearlings rated," he ordered, telling the exercise boys not to hold them back. "Nor punished, either. No more than a tap of the bat to signal. My horses don't need to be whipped to run."

Despite his concentration, he was aware when Keeley dismounted behind him. He took out his stopwatch, turning it over and over in his hand as the field was led to the gate.

"I don't know the yearling at the rail," Keeley said conversationally as she looped her reins around the top rung of the fence.

"Your father named him Tempest in a Teacup, as he's got a small build, but he's full of spirit. You don't often ride this way in the morning."

"No, but I wanted to see the progress. And my new assistant is handling things at the office."

He glanced over. She'd taken the band out of her hair. It flowed wild over her shoulders, but her face was cool and very serious. "Assistant is it? When did this happen?"

"Yesterday. My mother's working with me at the school now. Contrary to some beliefs, I don't insist on handling all the steps and stages by myself, when help is offered."

"Touchy still, are you?"

"Apparently."

"Well, you'll have to snarl at me later. I'm busy. Jim! Hold him steady now," Brian called out as Tempest shied a bit at the gate. "That one still objects a bit to being penned in. There, that's it," he murmured as the horses were loaded and the back gate shut. He held a finger over the timer, plunging when the gates sprang open.

The horses flew out.

He wondered if there was anything that gave his heart more of a knock than that instant, that first rush of speed, that blur of great bodies surging forward on the track.

But through the thrill of it, his eyes missed nothing. The stretch of legs, the clouds of dirt, the figures riding low over the necks.

"She wants the lead, right from the start," he murmured. "Wants the rest tasting her dust."

Caught up, Keeley leaned over the rail as the horses made the first turn. The thunder of hoofbeats drummed in her blood. "She runs well in a crowd. You were right about that. Tempest is a little nervy."

"We might try a shadow roll on him. He wants the outside. He's about endurance. The longer the race, the better he'll like it. There's Betty now. She wants the rail. Aye, she'll hug it like a lover."

Without thinking, he laid his hand over Keeley's on the rail. "Just look at her, will you? That's a champion. She doesn't need any of us. She knows it."

With his hand warm and firm over hers, Keeley watched the horses streak down the backstretch with Betty nearly a length in the lead. Pride and pleasure tangled inside her.

When Brian let out a shout, clicked his watch again, she started to turn, to indulge the giddy thrill by throwing her arms around him. But he was already drawing away.

"That's good time, damn good time. And she'll do better yet." He nodded, his eyes tracking as the riders rose high in their stirrups and slowed their mounts. "I'll find the right race for her, give her a taste of the real thing."

Giving Keeley an absent pat on the shoulder, he vaulted the fence.

She watched him go to the horses, to stroke and compliment Tempest, give the rider a few words before moving on to Betty.

The filly pranced flirtatiously, then lowered her head to nibble delicately on Brian's shoulder.

You're wrong, Keeley thought. Whatever she knows, whatever she is, she needs you.

And so, damn it, do I.

After he'd stroked, nuzzled, praised, and the horses were led away to be cooled down, Brian jumped over the fence again to pick up his clipboard.

"I'd hoped your father would be down to see her first run with a field."

"I'm sure he would have. He must be tied up with something."

With a grunt in response, Brian continued to scribble notes. "Well, I'm running more of the yearlings this morning, so he'll see plenty. How's the gelding?"

"Comfortable. The swelling's down a little. I want to wait until after my class today to drench him. It's a messy business and I don't need a half dozen kids coming around once it starts to work on him."

"Best to wait till late in the day anyway. You want a good twenty-four hours between his last feeding and the drenching. I can do that for you if you're busy."

The automatic refusal was on the tip of her tongue. She nipped it off, took a breath. "Actually, I was hoping you'd find time to take a look at him later."

"I can do that." He glanced up, saw how set and serious her face was. "What is it? Are you that worried?"

"No." She took another breath, ordered herself to relax. "I'm sure everything will be fine." She'd make sure of it, she told herself. One way or the other. "I'll feel better when things are under control, that's all."

She worked it out. She felt better when she had a situation defined and a goal in mind. This one wasn't really so complicated, after all. She wanted Brian. She was fairly certain she was in love with him. Being certain of that would take a little more time, she imagined, a little more consideration.

After all this was new territory and needed to be approached with caution and preparation.

But her feelings for him were strong, and not as one-dimensional as simple attraction.

If it was love, then she needed to make him fall in love with her. She was perfectly willing to work toward what she wanted, as long as she got it in the end.

Pleasantly tired after a long day's work, she gave her horses their evening meal. There was no question about it, she decided. Having her mother help had taken a huge burden of time and effort off her shoulders.

Was it stubbornness, she wondered, that caused her to pull back from a helping hand so often? She didn't think so. But it was something nearly as mulish. She wanted the people she loved and who loved her to be proud of her. And she equated that, foolishly, she admitted, with the need to be perfect.

But she preferred thinking of it as taking responsibility.

Just as she was doing now with Brian, she mused. If she was in love with him, she was responsible for her own feelings. And it was up to her to try to generate those same feelings in him.

If she failed… No, she wouldn't consider that. Once you considered failure you were one step farther away from success.

Moving into the gelding's box, she hung his hay bag and measured out his feed. "It's better tonight, isn't it?" Gently she checked the swelling on his knee. When she heard the footsteps heading down on concrete, she smiled to herself.

"You're feeding him?" Brian stepped into the box. "I couldn't get up here any sooner."

"That's all right. He took the drenching without a quibble. And you can take my word for it, it worked." She straightened up, smiled. "You can see by the way he's eating, he's feeling better."

"Knows he's fallen into roses, he does." Brian examined the injury himself, nodded. "We have a stallion with the strangles, which is what held me up."

"Delicate creatures, aren't they?" She ran her hand over the gelding's withers. "Deceptive. The size of them, the speed and strength. It all shouts power. But under it all, there's the delicacy. You can be fooled by looking at something—at the face, at the form—and judging it without knowing what's inside."

"True enough."

"I'm not delicate, Brian. I have iron bred in me."

He looked at her. "I know you're strong, Keeley. And still, you've skin like a rosebud." Gently he ran his thumb over her cheek. "I have big hands, and they're hard, so I need to take care. It doesn't mean I think you're weak."

"All right."

He turned back to the horse. "Have you named him?"

"As a matter of fact, I have. We had a dog when I was a girl. My mother found him, a very homely stray who started sneaking up to the house. She fed him, gained his confidence. And before my father knew it, he had a big, sloppy mutt on his hands. His name was Finnegan." She laid her cheek on the gelding's, rubbed. "And so now is his."

"You've a sentimental streak along with that iron, Keeley."

"Yes, I do. And a latent romantic one."

"Is that so?" he murmured, a little surprised when she turned and ran her hands up his chest.

"Apparently. I didn't thank you for riding to my rescue last night."

"I don't recall riding anywhere." His lips twitched as she backed him out of the box.

"In a manner of speaking. You cut a bully down to size for me. I was upset and worried about the gelding, so I didn't really think about it at the time. But I did later, and I wanted to thank you."

"Well, you're welcome."

"I haven't finished thanking you." She bit lightly on his bottom lip, heard his quick indrawn breath.

"If that's what you have in mind, you could finish thanking me up in my bedroom."

"Why don't I just show you what I have in mind? Right here."

She had his shirt unbuttoned before he realized they were standing in an empty stall, freshly bedded with hay. "Here?" He laughed, taking both her hands to tug her out again. "I don't think so."

"Here." She countered his move by ramming his back against the side wall. "I know so."

"Don't be ridiculous." His lungs were clogged, and his mind insisted on following suit. "Anyone could come along."

"Live dangerously." She pulled the stall door shut behind them.

"I have been, since I first set eyes on you."

The thrum of the heart in her throat turned her voice husky. "Why stop now? Seduce me, Brian. I dare you."

"I've always found it hard to turn aside a dare." He reached out, tugged the band from her hair. "You cloud my senses, Keeley, like perfume. Before I know it, there's nothing there but you." He slid his hand around to cup the back of her neck, to draw her toward him. "And nothing that needs to be."

His mouth covered hers, soft, smooth in a kiss silky enough to have her gliding down on that alone. She'd asked for seduction knowing seduction wasn't needed.

"I want you, Brian. I wake up wanting you. Kiss me again."

And the way her body simply melted into his, the way her lips warmed and parted, inviting him in had every pulse in his body throbbing like a wound.

"I don't want to be gentle this time." He reversed their position until her back was against the wall, and his eyes, so suddenly dark, burned into hers. "I don't want to be so careful, just this once."

The thrill of it was a bolt through the heart. "Then don't. I'm not fragile like your horses, Brian. Don't be fooled."

"I'll frighten you." He couldn't have said if it was a threat or warning, but her answer was just another dare.

"Try it."

He tore her shirt open, sending buttons flying. He watched her eyes widen in shock even as he crushed his mouth to hers to swallow her gasp. Then his hands were on her, a rough scrape of callus over sensitive skin. Part of him expected her to object, to struggle away, but she only moaned against his savaging mouth, and held on.

When her knees gave like heated butter, he dragged her down to the mound of hay.

He used his mouth on her, his teeth, his tongue. A kind of wild fury. His hands raced over her, rough and possessive in their impatience to have more. To take all.

Her choked cries had the horses moving restlessly in their boxes. As he propelled her over that first breathless edge, she fisted her hands in his hair as if to anchor her-self. Or to drag him with her.

He'd given her tenderness, shown her the beauty of love-making with patience and care. Now he showed her the dark glory of it with reckless demands and bruising hands.

Still she gave. Even with the whirlwind rushing inside him, he felt her give. Flesh dampened until it was slick, hearts pounded until the beat of them seemed to slap the air, but she rolled with him, accepting. Offering.

Even when her eyes were blind, the blue of them blurred as dark as midnight, she stayed with him. The sound of his name rushing through her lips seemed to sing in his blood.

She cried out, arching against his busy mouth when her world shattered into shards bright as glass. There was noth-ing to cling to, no thread to tie her to sanity, and still he drove her harder until the breath tearing from her lungs turned to harsh, primitive pants.

"It's me who has you." Wild to mate, he gripped her hips, jerked them high. "It's me who's in you." And plunged into her as if his life depended on it.

She heard a scream, high, thin, helpless. But it wasn't helplessness she felt. She felt power, outrageous power that pumped through her blood like a drug. Drunk on it, she reared up, her eyes locked on his as she fisted her hands in his hair once more.

She fixed her mouth on his, savaging it as he rode her, hard and fast. And she held on, held on, matching him beat for beat though she thought her body would burst, until she felt him fall.

"It's me," she said on a sob, "who has you." And still holding fast, let herself leap after him.

Chapter 10

As far as Keeley was concerned it was perfect. She'd fallen in love with a man who suited her. They had a strong foundation of common interests, enjoyed each other's company, respected each other's opinions.

He wasn't without flaws, of course. He tended to be moody and his confidence very often crossed the line into arrogance. But those qualities made him who he was.

The problem, as she saw it, was nudging him along from affair to commitment and commitment to marriage. She'd been raised to believe in permanency, in family, in the promise two people made to love for a lifetime.

She really had no choice but to marry Brian and make a life with him. And she was going to see to it he had no choice, either.

It was a bit like training a horse, she supposed. There was a lot of repetition, rewards, patience and affection. And a firm hand under it all.

She thought it would be most sensible for them to become engaged at Christmas, and marry the following summer. Certainly it would be most convenient for them to build their life near Royal Meadows as both of them worked there. Nothing could be simpler.

All she had to do was lead Brian to the same conclusions.

Being the kind of man he was, she imagined he'd want to make the moves. It was a little galling, but she loved him enough to wait until he made his declaration. It wouldn't be with hearts and flowers, she mused as she walked Finnegan around the paddock. Knowing Brian there would be passion, and challenge and just a hint of temper.

She was looking forward to it.

She stopped to check the gelding's leg for any heat or swelling. Gently she picked up his foot to bend the knee. When he showed no signs of discomfort, she gave him a brisk rub on the neck.

"Yeah," she said when he blew affectionately on her shoulder, "feeling pretty good these days, aren't you? I think you're ready for some exercise."

His coat looked healthy again, she noted as she saddled him. Time, care and attention had turned the tide for him. Perhaps he'd never be a beauty, and certainly he was no champion, but he had a sweet nature and a willing spirit.

That was more than enough.

When she swung into the saddle, Finnegan tossed his head, then at her signal started out of the paddock in a dignified walk.

She went cautiously for a time, tuning herself to him, checking for any hitch in his gait that would indicate he was favoring his leg. It pleased her so much to feel him slide into a smooth rhythm that after a few moments she relaxed enough to enjoy the quiet ride.

Fall had used a rich and varied palette this year to paint the trees in bold tones of golds and reds and orange. They swept over the hard blue canvas of sky and flamed under the strong slant of sunlight.

The fields held onto the deep green of high summer. Weanlings danced over the pastures, long legs reaching for speed as they charged their own shadows. Mares, their bellies swollen with the foals they carried, cropped lazily.

On the brown oval, colts and fillies raced in the majestic blur of power that brought thunder to the air.

This painting, Keeley thought, had been hers the whole of her life. The images that came back, repeating season after season. The beauty and strength of it, and the settled knowledge that it would go on year into year.

This she could, and would, pass on to her own children when the time came. The solidity of it, and the responsibilities, the joys and the sweat.

Sitting aside the healing gelding, she felt her throat ache with love. It wasn't just a place, it was a gift. One that had been treasured and tended by her parents. Her part in it, of it, would never be taken for granted.

When she saw Brian leaning on the fence, his attention riveted on the horses pounding down the backstretch, her aching throat seemed to snap shut.

For a moment she could only blink, stunned by the sudden, vicious pressure in her chest. Her skin tingled. There was no other word to describe how nerves swarmed over her in a wash of chills and heat.

As she fought to catch her breath, her heart pounded, a hammer on an anvil. The gelding shied under her, and had danced in a fretful half circle before she thought to control him.

And her hands trembled.

No, this was wrong. This wasn't acceptable at all. Where did this come from—how did she get this ball of terror in her stomach? She'd already accepted that she loved him, hadn't she? And it had been easy, a simple process of steps and study. Her mind was made up, her goals set. Damn it, she'd been pleased by the whole business.

So what was this shaky, dizzy, *painful* sensation, this clutch of panic that made her want to turn her mount sharply around and ride as far away as possible?

She'd been wrong, Keeley realized as she pressed an unsteady hand to her jumpy heart. She'd only been falling in love up to now. How foolish of her to be lulled by the smooth slide of it. This was the moment, she understood that now. This was the moment the bottom dropped away and sent her crashing.

Now the wind was knocked out of her, that same shock of sensation that came from losing your seat over a jump and finding yourself flipping through space until the ground reached up and smacked into you. Jolting bones and head and heart.

Love was an outrageous shock to the system, she thought. It was a wonder anyone survived it.

She was a Grant, Keeley reminded herself and straightened in the saddle. She knew how to take a tumble, just as she knew how to pick herself back up and focus mind and energy on the goal. She wouldn't just survive this knock to the heart. She'd thrive on it. And when she was done with Brian Donnelly, he wouldn't know what had hit him.

She steadied herself much as she had done before competitions. She took slow and deliberate breaths until her pulse rate slowed, focused her mind until it was calm as lake water, then she rode down to face her goal.

Brian turned when he heard her approach. The vague irritation at the interruption vanished when he saw Finnegan. He felt a keen interest there, and passing his clipboard and some instructions to the assistant trainer, moved toward the gelding.

"Well now, you're looking fit and fine, aren't you?" Automatically he bent down to check the injured leg. "No heat. That's good. How long have you had him out?"

"About fifteen minutes, at a walk."

"He could probably take a canter. He's looking good as new, no signs of swelling." Brian straightened, narrowing his eyes against the sun as he looked up at Keeley. "But you? Are you all right? You're a bit pale."

"Am I?" Small wonder, she thought, but smiled as she enjoyed the sensation of holding a secret inside her. "I don't feel pale. But you…" Swimming in the river of discovery, she leaned down. "You look wonderful. Rough and windblown and sexy."

His narrowed eyes flickered, and he stepped back, a little uneasy when she rubbed a hand over his cheek. There were a half a dozen men milling around, he thought. And every one of them had eyes.

"I was called down to the stables early this morning, didn't take time to shave."

She decided to take his evasive move as a challenge rather than an insult. "I like it. Just a little dangerous. If you've got time later, I thought you might help me out."

"With what?"

"Take a ride with me."

"I could do that."

"Good. About five?" She leaned down again and this time took a fistful of his shirt to yank him a step closer. "And, Brian? Don't shave."

* * *

The woman threw him off balance, and he didn't care for it. Giving him those hot looks and intimate little strokes in the middle of the damn morning so he went through the whole of the day itchy.

Worse yet the man who was paying him to work through the day, not to be distracted by his glands, was the woman's father.

It was a situation, Brian thought, and he'd done a great deal to bring it on himself. Still how could he have known in the beginning that he'd become so involved with her on so many levels inside himself? Falling in love had been a hard knock, but he'd taken knocks before. You got bruised and you went on. A bit of attraction was all right, a little flirtation was harmless enough. And the truth was, he'd enjoyed the risk of it. To a point.

But he was well past that point now. Now he was all wrapped up in her and at the same time had become fond of her family. Travis wasn't just a good and fair boss, but was on the way to becoming a kind of friend.

And here he was finding ways to make love to his friend's daughter as often as humanly possible.

Worse than that, he admitted as he strode toward her stables, he was—from time to time—catching himself dreaming. These little fantasies would sneak into his head when he was busy doing something else. He'd find himself wondering how it would all be between Keeley and him if things were different, if they were on the same level, so to speak. And he thought—well, that is if he were the settling down sort—that she might be just the one to settle down with.

If he were interested in rooting in one place with one

person, that is. Which of course, wasn't in his plans at all. Even if it was—which it wasn't—it wouldn't work.

She was clubhouse and he was shedrow, and that was that.

Keeley was just kicking up her heels a bit. He understood about that, couldn't hold it against her. For all the privilege, she'd had a sheltered life and now was taking a few whacks at the boundaries of it. He'd rebelled himself against the borders of his own upbringing by sliding his way out of school and into the stables when he'd still been a boy. Nothing had stopped him, not the arguments, the threats, the punishments.

As soon as he'd been able, he'd left home, moving from stable to stable, track to track. He'd kept loose, he'd kept free and unfettered. And had never looked back. His brothers and sisters married, raised children, planted gardens, worked in steady jobs. They owned things, he thought now, while he owned nothing that couldn't easily fit in his traveling bag or be disposed of when he took to the next road.

When you owned things you had to tend them. Before you knew it, you owned more. Then the weight of them kept your feet planted in one spot.

He flicked a glance up at the pretty stone building that was his quarters, and admired the way it stood out against the evening sky. Flowers in colors of rust and scarlet and gold ran along the foundation, and the truck he'd bought from Paddy was parked like it belonged.

He stopped and, much as Keeley had that morning, turned to survey the land. It was a place, he realized, that could hold a man if he wasn't careful. The openness of it could fool you into believing it wasn't confining, then it would tempt you to plant things—yourself included—until it had you, heart and soul.

It was smart to remember it wasn't his land, any more than the horses were his horses. Or Keeley was his woman.

But when he stepped over toward her paddock, that fantasy snuck up on him again. In the long, soft shadows and quiet light of evening she saddled the big buff-colored gelding he knew she called Honey. Her hair was pinned on top of her head in an absentminded, messy knot that was ridiculously sexy. She wore jeans and a sweater of Kelly green.

She looked...reachable, Brian realized. Like the kind of woman a man wanted with him after a long day's work. There'd be a lot to talk about with this woman, over dinner, in the privacy of bed. Shared loves, shared jokes.

A man could wake up in the morning with a woman like that and not feel trapped, or worry that she did.

Catching himself, Brian shook his head. That was foolish thinking.

"Look at this." Brian walked up to the fence, leaned on it. "You've done all the work already."

"You've caught me on a good day." Keeley checked the cinch, stepped back. She knew his stirrup length now, and his favored bit and bridle. "I had no idea how much time I'd free up by having Ma help out on a regular basis."

"And what do you intend to do with it?"

"Enjoy it." When he opened the gate she led both horses through. "I've been so focused on the work the last couple of years, I haven't stepped back often enough to appreciate the results." She handed him the reins. "I like results."

"Then maybe you'll use some of that free time to come by the track." He vaulted into the saddle once she was mounted. "I'm looking for results there. I have Betty entered in a baby race tomorrow."

"Her maiden race? I wouldn't want to miss that."

"Charles Town. Two o'clock."

"I'll ask my mother to take my afternoon class. I'll be there."

They kept it to a walk, skirting the paddock and heading toward the rise of land swept with trees gone brilliant in the softening slants of sunlight. Overhead a flock of Canada geese arrowed across the evening sky sending out their deep calls.

"Twice daily," Brian said, watching the flight. "Off they go on their travels, honking away, dawn and dusk."

"I've always liked the sound of them. I guess it's something else that says home this time of year." She kept her eyes on the sky until the last call echoed away.

"Uncle Paddy phoned today."

"And how's he doing?"

"More than well. He'd bought himself a pair of young mares. He's decided to try his hand at some breeding."

"Once a horseman," Brian said. "I didn't figure he could keep out of the game."

"You'd miss it, wouldn't you? The smell and the sound of them. Have you ever thought of starting your own place, your own line?"

"No, that's not for me. I'm happy making another man's horses. Once you own, it's a business, isn't it? An enterprise. I've no yearning to be a businessman."

"Some own for the love of it," Keeley pointed out. "And even the business doesn't shadow the feelings."

"In the rare case." Brian looked over, scanning the outbuildings. Yes, this was a place, he thought, built on feelings. "Your father's one, and I knew another once in Cork. But ownership can get in the blood as well, until you lose touch with that feeling. Before you know it, it's all facts and figures and a thirst for profit. That sounds like bars to me."

Interesting, she thought. "Making a living is a prison?"

"The need to make one, and still a better one, first and foremost. That's a trap. My father found his leg caught there."

"Really?" He so rarely mentioned his family. "What does he do?"

"He's a bank clerk. Day after day sitting in a little cage counting other people's money. What a life."

"Well, it's not the life for you."

"Thank God for that. These lads want a bit of a run," he said and kicked Honey into a gallop.

Keeley hissed in frustration but clicked to her mount to match pace. They'd come back to it, she promised herself. She hadn't learned nearly enough about where the man she intended to marry came from.

They rode for an hour before heading back to stable the horses and settle in the rest of her stock for the night. He was half hoping she'd ask him over to the house for dinner again, but she turned to him as they left the stables, lifted a brow.

"Why don't you ask me up for a drink?"

"A drink? There's not much of a variety, but you're welcome."

"It's nice to be asked occasionally." Before he could tuck his hand safely in his pocket, she took it, threaded their fingers together. "You have free time now and again yourself," she said easily. "I wonder if you've heard of the concept of dates. Dinner, movies, drives?"

"I've some experience with them." He glanced at his pickup as they turned toward his quarters. "If you've a yen for a drive, you can climb up into the lorry, but I'd need to shovel it out first."

She huffed out a breath. "That, Donnelly, wasn't the most romantic of invitations."

"Secondhand lorries aren't particularly romantic, and I've forgotten where I parked my glass coach."

"If that's another princess crack—" She broke off, set her teeth. Patience, she reminded herself. She wasn't going to spoil things with an argument. "Never mind. We'll forget the drive." She opened the door herself. "And move straight to dinner."

He caught the scent as soon as he stepped inside. Something aromatic and spicy that reminded him his stomach was about dead empty.

"What is it?"

"What is what?" Then she grinned and sniffed the air. "Oh, what is that? It's chili, one of my specialties. I put it on simmer before my last class."

"You cooked dinner?"

"Mmm." Amused, and very satisfied by his shock, she wandered off into the kitchen. "I didn't think you'd mind, and I knew we'd both be hungry by this time." She lifted the lid on a pot, gave it a quick stir while fragrant steam puffed out. "It's the kind of thing you can just leave and eat when you're ready, which is why it appeals to me. Oh, and I brought over a bottle of Merlot, though beer's never wrong with chili if you'd rather."

"I'm trying to remember the last time someone cooked for me—other than your mother and someone who was related to me."

Even more pleased, she turned to slide her arms around him. "Haven't any of your many women cooked for you?"

"Now and then perhaps, but not in recent memory." Because they were alone, he took her hips, brought her closer. "And I certainly remember none that smelled so appetizing."

"The women? Or the meal?"

"Both." He lowered his mouth to hers, allowed himself the luxury of sinking in. "And it reminds me I'm next to starving."

"What do you want first?" She grazed her teeth over his bottom lip. "Me, or the food?"

"I want you first. And last, it seems."

"That's handy, because I want you first, too." She drew back. "Why don't we clean up? I could use a shower." Laughing, her hands holding his, she pulled him out of the kitchen.

She'd brought over a change of clothes as well. It gave Brian a start to see her casually pulling on fresh jeans. Her hair was still wet from the shower they'd shared, her skin rosy from it. And, he noted, a bit raw in places because he hadn't shaved.

But the wild love they'd made under the hot spray in the steamy room wasn't anywhere near as intimate, anywhere near as *personal* somehow as her having a clean sweater lying neatly folded on the foot of his bed.

She reached for it, then glanced over, catching him staring at her. "What is it?"

He shook his head. There wasn't a way to explain this sense of panic and delight that lived inside him while he watched her dress. "I've rubbed your skin raw." Reaching out, he traced his fingertips over her collarbone. "I should have shaved. You're so soft." He murmured it, trailing those fingers up over her shoulder. "I don't know how I manage to forget that."

When she trembled, he looked up into her face. For a moment she saw the need flash back into his eyes, glinting like the edge of a sword. "Now you're cold. Put your sweater on. I've got some ointment."

The hot edge faded as quickly as it came. It was frustrating, she thought as he rooted into a drawer, that the only time he really broke the tether on his control was when they made love.

He got out a tube and since she'd yet to put the sweater on, squeezed ointment onto his fingers and began to gently rub it on her abraded skin. She recognized the scent.

"That's for horses."

"So?"

She laughed and let him fuss. "Does this make me your mare now?"

"No, you're too young and delicate of bone for that. You're still a filly."

"Are you going to train me, Donnelly?"

"Oh, you're out of my league, Miss Grant." He glanced up, cocked a brow when he saw her grinning at him. "And what amuses you?"

"You can't help it can you? You have to tend."

"I put the marks on you," he muttered as he smoothed on the ointment. "It follows I should see to them."

She lifted a hand to toy with the ends of his damp, gold-tipped hair. "I like being seen to by a man with a tough mind and a soft heart."

That soft heart sighed a little, ached a little. But he spoke lightly. "It's no hardship running my fingers over skin like yours." With his eyes on hers, he used the pad of his thumb to spread ointment over the gentle swell of her breast. "Particularly since you don't seem to have a qualm about standing here half naked and letting me."

"Should I blush and flutter?"

"You're not the fluttering sort. I like that about you." Satisfied, he capped the tube, then tugged the sweater over her head himself. "But I can't have such a fine piece of

God's work catching a chill. There you are." He lifted her hair out of the neck.

"You don't have a hair dryer."

"There's air everywhere in here."

She laughed and dragged her fingers through her damp curls. "It'll have to do. Come on, let's have that wine while I finish up dinner."

He didn't know much about wine, but his first sip told him it was several steps up from what might be the usual accompaniment to so humble a meal as chili.

She seemed more at home in his kitchen than he was himself, finding things in drawers he'd yet to open. When she started to dress the salad, he set his glass aside.

"I'll be back in a minute."

"A minute's all you've got," she called out. "I'm putting the bread in to warm."

Since his answer was the slamming of the door, she shrugged and lit the candles she'd set on the little kitchen table. Cozy, she decided. And just romantic enough to suit two practical-minded people who didn't go in for a lot of fussing.

It was the sort of relaxed, simple meal two people could prepare together at the end of a workday. She intended to see they had more of them, until the man got a clue this was exactly how it was going to be.

Satisfied, she picked up her wine, toasted herself. "To good strong starts," she murmured and drank.

Hearing the door open again, she took the bread out of the oven. "We're set in here, and I'm starving."

She turned to put the basket of bread on the table and saw Brian, and the clutch of mums and zinnias he held in his hand.

"It seemed to call for them," he said.

She stared at the cheerful fall blossoms, then up into his face. "You picked me flowers."

The sheer disbelief in her voice had him moving his shoulders restlessly. "Well, you made me dinner, with wine and candles and the whole of it. Besides, they're your flowers anyway."

"No, they're not." Drowning in love she set the basket down, waited. "Until you give them to me."

"I'll never understand why women are so sentimental over posies." He held them out.

"Thank you." She closed her eyes, buried her face in them. She wanted to remember the exact fragrance, the exact texture. Then lowering them again, she lifted her mouth to his for a kiss. Rubbed her cheek against his.

His arms came around her so suddenly, so tightly, she gasped. "Brian? What is it?"

That gesture, the simple and sweet gesture of cheek against cheek nearly destroyed him. "It's nothing. I just like the way you feel against me when I hold you."

"Hold me any tighter, I'll be through you."

"Sorry." He pressed his lips to her forehead to give himself a moment to compose. "I forget my own strength when I'm starving to death."

"Then sit down and get started. I'll put these in some water."

"I..." He had to say something and cast around for a topic where he wouldn't stutter or say something that would embarrass them both. "I meant to tell you earlier, I looked up Finnegan's records."

There, he thought as he sat and began to dish up salad for both of them. Safe ground. "Of course he's registered as Flight of Fancy."

"Yes, I knew that." She tucked the flowers in a vase, and

set them on the table before joining Brian. "Finnegan suits him better, I think."

"He's yours to call what you like now. His record in his first year of racing was uneven. His blood stock is very decent, but he never came up to potential, and his owners sold him off as a three-year-old."

"I was going to look up his data. You've saved me the trouble." She broke a hunk of bread in half, offered it. "He has good lines, and he responds well. Even after the abuse he hasn't turned common."

"The thing is he did considerably better in his third year. Some of his match-ups were uneven, and in my mind he was a bit overraced. I'd have done things differently if I'd been working with him."

"You do things different, Brian, all around."

"Ah well. In any case, he went into that claiming race and that's how Tarmack got his hands on him."

"Bastard," Keeley said so coolly, Brian cocked his head.

"We won't argue there. I'm thinking you'd be wasting him in your school here. He was born for the track, and that's where he belongs."

Surprised, she frowned over her salad. "You think he should race?"

"I think you should consider it. Seriously. He's a thoroughbred, Keeley, bred to run. The need for it's in his blood. It's only that he's been misused and mismanaged. The athlete's inside him, and though your school's a fine thing, it's not enough for him."

"If he's prone to knee spavins—"

"You don't know that. It's not a hereditary thing. It was an injury a man was responsible for. You could have your father look him over if you don't think I've got the right of it."

She considered a moment, sipped her wine. "I certainly trust your judgment, Brian. It's not that. You and I both know that a horse can lose heart under mistreatment. Heart and spirit. I just wouldn't want to push him."

"Sure, it's up to you."

"Would you work with him?"

"I could." He ladled chili into bowls. "But so could you. You know what to do, what to look for."

She was already shaking her head. "Not for racing. I know my area, and it's not the track. If I consider running him again, I'd want him to have the best."

"That would be me," he said with such easy arrogance she grinned.

"Is that a yes?"

"If your father agrees to having me work your horse on the side, I'm happy to. We'll start him off easy, and see how he goes." He started to leave it at that, then because he thought she'd understand, hoped she would, finished. "It was in his eyes this morning, when you rode him down to the track. It was there. The yearning."

"I didn't see it." She reached over to touch his hand. "I'm glad you did."

"It's my job to see it."

"It's your gift," she corrected. "Your family must be proud of you." She spoke casually, began to eat again, then stared at him, baffled, when he laughed. "Why is that funny?"

"Pride wouldn't exactly be part of their general outlook to my way of thinking."

"Why?"

"People can't find pride in what they don't understand. Not all families, Keeley, are as cozy as yours."

"I'm sorry," she said, and meant it. Not only for whatever lack there was in his family feelings, but for deliberately prying.

"Sure it's not such a matter. We get on all right."

She meant to let it go, to change the subject, but the words burned inside her. "If they're not proud of you, then they're stupid." When he stared, his next bite of chili halfway to his mouth, she shrugged. "I'm sorry, but they are."

Watching her, he started to eat again. Her eyes were snapping, her cheeks flushed, her jaw set. Why the woman was fuming, he realized. "Darling, that's sweet of you to say, but—"

"It's not. It's rude, but I meant it." Snatching up the wine bottle, she topped off both of their glasses. "You have a real talent, and you've earned a strong reputation—or you damn well wouldn't be here at Royal Meadows. What's not to be proud of?" she demanded, with even more heat. "Your father, of all people, should understand."

"Why?"

Her mouth dropped open. "He's the one who introduced you to horses."

"To the track. It wasn't the horses for my father," Brian told her. He was so fascinated by her reaction it didn't occur to him that he was having an in-depth conversation about his family. Something he absolutely never did.

"They were a kind of vehicle. He admired them, certainly. But it was the wagering, the rush of gambling that called to him. Likely still does. That and the chance to take a few pulls from the flask in his pocket without my mother's silent and deadly disapproval. I told you, Keeley, he's a bank clerk."

"What difference does that make?"

All, was what Brian thought, but he struggled to find a more tangible explanation for her. "He stopped looking through the bars of his little cage years back. He and my mother, they married young, not quite the full nine months, you understand, before my oldest sister came along."

"That can be difficult, but still—"

"No, they were content with it. I think they love each other, in their way." He didn't think about those areas much, but since he was in it now, he did his best. "They made their home, raised their children. My father brought in the wage. Though he gambled, we never went hungry—and bills were paid sooner or later. My mother always set a decent table, and our clothes were clean. But it seemed to me that the both of them were just tired out at the end of the day, just from doing."

Keeley remembered an expression of her mother's. *A child could starve with a full plate.* She understood that without love, affection, laughter, the spirit hungered.

"Going your own way shouldn't stop them from being happy for you."

"My brother and my sisters, they're clerks and parents and settled sort of people. I'm a puzzle, and sooner or later when you can't solve a puzzle, you have to think there's something wrong with it. Else there's something wrong with you."

"You ran away," she murmured.

He wasn't sure he liked the phrase, but nodded. "In a sense, I suppose, and as fast as I could. What's the point in looking back?"

But he was looking back, Keeley thought. Looking back over his shoulder, because he was still running away.

Chapter 11

Keeley decided some men simply took longer than others to realize they wanted to go where you were leading them. It was hard to complain since she was having such a wonderful time. She was making it a habit to go to the track once a week, a pleasure she'd cut out of her life while she'd been organizing her academy.

There were still dozens of details that she needed to see to personally—the meetings, the reports and follow-ups on each individual child. She wanted to plan a kind of open house during the holidays, where all the parents, grandparents, foster families could come to the academy. Meet and mingle, and most importantly see the progress their children had made.

But now that her school was on course, and she'd expanded to seven days a week, she was more than happy to turn the classes over to her mother for one day.

She was thrilled to watch Betty's progress, to see for

herself that Brian's instincts had been on target with the filly. Betty was, day after day and week after week, proving herself to be a top competitor and a potential champion.

But even more she was delighted to see Finnegan come to life under Brian's patient, unwavering hand.

Bundled against the chill of a frosty morning, Keeley stood at the fence of the practice oval and waited while Brian gave Larry his instructions on the workout run.

"He gets nervy in the gate, but he breaks clean. You'll need to rate him or he'll lose his wind. He likes a crowd so I want you to keep him in the pack till after the second turn. You let him know then, firm, that you want more. He'll give it to you. He doesn't like running in front, he misses the company."

"I'll keep his eye on the line, Mr. Donnelly. I appreciate you giving me the chance."

"It's Miss Grant's giving you the chance. I smell whiskey on your breath before post time tomorrow, and you won't get a second one."

"Not a drop. We'll run for you, if for nothing but to show that son of a bitch Tarmack how you treat a thoroughbred."

"Fair enough. Let's see how she goes."

Brian walked back to the fence where Keeley stood sipping her soft drink. "I don't know if you made the best choice in jockeys, but he's sober and he's hungry, so it's a good gamble."

"It's not the winning this time, Brian."

He took her bottle, sipped, winced. How the woman could drink such a thing in the morning was beyond him. "It's always the winning."

"You've done a wonderful job with him."

"We won't know that until tomorrow at Pimlico."

"Stop it," she ordered when he slipped through the split

rail fence. "Take credit when it's deserved. That's a horse that's found his pride again," she said as the practice field was led to the gate. "You gave it to him."

"For God's sake, Keeley, he's your horse. I just reminded him he could run."

You're wrong, she thought. You gave him back his pride, just the way you made him your own.

But Brian was already focused on the horse. He took out his stopwatch. "Let's see how well he remembers running this morning."

Mists swam along the ground, a shallow river over the oval. Shards of frost still glittered on the grass while the sun pulsed weakly through the layers of morning clouds. The air was gray and still.

With a ringing clang the gate sprang open. And the horses plunged.

Ground fog tore like thin silver ribbon at the powerful cut of legs. Bodies, glistening from the morning damp, surged past in one sleek blur.

"That's it," Brian murmured. "Keep him centered. That's the way."

"They're beautiful. All of them."

"Got to pace him." Brian watched them round the first turn while the clock in his head ticked off the time. "See, he'll match his rhythm to the leader. It's a game to him now. Out gallivanting with mates, that's all he's thinking."

Keeley laughed, leaned out as her heart began to bump. "How do you know what he's thinking?"

"He told me. Get ready now. Ready now. Aye, that's it. He's strong. He'll never be a beauty, but he's strong. See, he's moving up." Forgetting himself Brian laid a hand on her shoulder, squeezed. "He's got more heart than brains, and it's his heart that runs."

Brian clicked the watch when Finnegan came in, half a length behind the leader. "Well done. Yes, well done. I'd say he'll place for you tomorrow, Miss Grant."

"It doesn't matter."

Sincerely shocked more than offended, he goggled at her. "That's a hell of a thing to say. And what kind of luck is that going to bring us tomorrow, I'd like to know?"

"It's enough to watch him run. And better, to watch you watching him run. Brian." Touched, she laid a hand on his heart. "You've gone and fallen in love with him."

"I love all the horses I train."

"Yes, I've seen that, and understand that because it's the same with me. But you're in love with this one."

Embarrassed because it was true, Brian swung over the fence. "That's a woman for you, making sloppy sentiment out of a job."

She only smiled as Brian walked over to stroke and nuzzle his job.

"That's a fine thing. My daughter and my trainer grooming a competitor."

She glanced over her shoulder, held out a hand for her father as he strode toward her. "Did you see him run?"

"The last few seconds. You've brought him a long way in a short time." Travis pressed a kiss to the top of her head. "I'm proud of you."

She closed her eyes. How easily he said it, how lovely to know he meant it. It made her only more sad, more angry, that Brian had cause to laugh over the idea of his own father having any pride in him.

"You taught me to care, you and Ma. When I saw that horse, I cared because of what you put inside me." She tilted her head up, kissed her father's cheek. "So thanks."

When his arm came around her, she leaned in, warm

and comfortable. "Brian was right. The horse needs to race. It's what he is. I wanted to save him. But Brian knew that wasn't enough. For some it's not enough just to get by."

"You brought this off together."

"You're right." She laughed a little as realization dawned, so clear and bright she wondered how she'd missed it before. "Absolutely right."

She'd canceled classes for the day. It was, Keeley told herself, a kind of holiday. A celebration, she thought, in compassion, understanding and hard work. It wasn't only Finnegan's return to the track, but Betty's first important race. Her parents would be there, and Brendon.

If there was ever a day to close up shop, this was it.

She rode out to the track at dawn, to give herself the pleasure of watching the early workouts, of listening to the track rats, building anticipation.

"You'd think it was the Derby," Brendon said as he walked with her back to the shedrow. "You're hyped."

"I've never owned a racehorse before. And I'm pretty sure he's my first and last. I'm going to enjoy every moment of this, but... It's not my passion. Not like it's yours and Dad's. Even Ma's."

"You channeled your passions into the school. I never thought you'd give up competing, Keel."

"Neither did I. And I never thought I'd find anything that satisfied me as much, challenged me as much."

They stopped as horses were brought back from the early workouts.

Steam rose off their backs, out of the tubs of hot water set outside the stables. It fogged the air, cushioned the sound, blurred the colors.

Hot walkers hustled to cool off the runners, stablehands

and grooms loitered, waiting for their charges. Someone played a mournful little tune on a harmonica, with the ring of the farrier's anvil setting the beat.

"This is your deal here," she said, gesturing as Betty was led by. "Me, I'm happy just to watch."

"Yeah? Then what're you doing here so early?"

"Just carrying on a fine family tradition. I'm going to act as Finnegan's groom."

That was news to Brian, and he wasn't entirely pleased when she announced her intentions. "Owners don't groom. They sit in the grandstands, or up in the restaurant. They stay out of the way."

Keeley continued strapping Finnegan with straw. "How long have you worked at Royal Meadows now?"

His scowl only deepened. "Since midthrough of August."

"Well, that should be long enough for you to have noticed the Grants don't stay out of the way."

"Noticing doesn't mean approving." He studied the way she groomed Finnegan's neck and couldn't find fault. But that was beside the point. "Grooming a horse for showing or schooling or basic riding is a different matter than grooming before a race."

She let out a long-suffering sigh. "Does it look like I know what I'm doing?"

"His legs need to be wrapped."

Saying nothing, she gestured to the wrapping on the line, and the extra clothespins hooked to her jeans.

Not yet convinced, he studied her grooming kit and the other tools of a groomer's trade. The cotton batting, the blankets, the tack.

"The irons haven't been polished."

She glanced at the saddle. "I know how to polish irons."

Brian rocked back on his heels. He needed to see to Betty. She was racing in the second. "He needs to be talked to."

"This is funny, but I know how to talk, too."

Brian swore under his breath. "He prefers singing."

"Excuse me?"

"I said, he prefers singing."

"Oh." Keeley tucked her tongue in her cheek. "Any particular tune? Wait, let me guess. *Finnegan's Wake?*" Brian's steely-eyed stare had her laughing until she had to lean weakly against the gelding. The horse responded by twisting his head and trying to sniff her pockets for apples.

"It's a quick tune," Brian said coolly, "and he likes hearing his name."

"I know the chorus." Gamely Keeley struggled to swallow another giggle. "But I'm not sure I know all the words. There are several verses as I recall."

"Do the best you can," he muttered and strode off. His lips twitched as he heard her launch into the song about the Dubliner who had a tippling way.

When he reached Betty's box, he shook his head. "I should've known. If there's not a Grant one place, there's a Grant in another until you're tripping over them."

Travis gave Betty a last pat on the shoulder. "Is that Keeley I hear singing?"

"She's being sarcastic, but as long as the job's done. She's dug in her heels about grooming Finnegan."

"She comes by it naturally. The hard head as well as the skill."

"Never had so many owners breathing down my neck. We don't need them, do we, darling?" Brian laid his hands on Betty's cheek, and she shook her head, then nibbled his hair.

"Damn horse has a crush on you."

"She may be your lady, sir, but she's my own true love. Aren't you beautiful, my heart?" He stroked, sliding into the Gaelic that had Betty's ears pricked and her body shifting restlessly.

"She likes being excited before a race," Brian murmured. "What do you call it—pumped up like your American football players. Which is a sport that eludes me altogether as they're gathered into circles discussing things most of the time instead of getting on with it."

"I heard you won the pool on last Monday night's game," Travis commented.

"Betting's the only thing about your football I do understand." Brian gathered her reins. "I'll walk her around a bit before we take her down. She likes to parade. You and your missus will want to stay close to the winner's circle."

Travis grinned at him. "We'll be watching from the rail."

"Let's go show off." Brian led Betty out.

Keeley put the final polish on the saddle irons, rolled her now aching shoulders and decided she had enough time to hunt up a soft drink before giving Finnegan a last-minute pep talk.

She stepped outside and blinked in the sudden whitewash of light. The minute her eyes focused she saw Brian sitting near the stable door on an overturned bucket.

Alarm sprinted into her throat. He had his head in his hands and was still as stone.

"What is it? What's wrong?" She leaped forward to drop to the ground beside him. "Betty?" Her breath came short. "I thought Betty was racing."

"She was. She did. She won."

"God, Brian, I thought something was wrong."

He dropped his hands and she could see his eyes were dark, swarming with emotion. "Two and a half lengths," he said. "She won by two and a half lengths, and I swear I don't think she was half trying. Nothing could touch her, do you see? Nothing. Never in my life did I think to have a horse like that under my hands. She's a miracle."

Keeley laid her hands on his knees, sat back on her heels. Passion, she thought. She'd spoken to Brendon of it, but now she was looking at it. "You made her." Before he could speak, she shook her head. "That's what you said to me once. 'I don't break horses. I make them.'"

"I can't get my head round it just now. This field was strong. I put her in thinking now and then you need a lesson in humility. Time for her to grow up, you know what I mean. Face real competition."

Still staggered, he dragged his hands through his hair and laughed. "Well, she'll never learn a damn thing about humility."

"Why aren't you down with her?"

"That's for your parents. She's their horse."

"You've a lot to learn yourself." She got to her feet, brushed off the knees of her jeans. "Well, Finnegan will be going down shortly. Why don't you come in and look him over?"

Brian blew out a breath, sucked in another, then rose. "I think he'll place for you," he told Keeley as he followed her in. "It wouldn't hurt to wager on it."

"I intend to wager on him." While Brian went in to check Finnegan's leg wrappings, she got papers out of the pocket of the jacket she'd laid aside.

"The wrappings look all right." He flicked a finger over the stirrups. "And you polished the irons well enough."

"Glad you approve. Next time you can do it." She held out the papers.

"What's this?"

"Papers giving you half interest in Flight of Fancy, also known as Finnegan."

"What are you talking about?"

"He was half yours anyway, Brian. This just makes it legal."

His palms went cold and damp. "Don't be ridiculous. I can't take that."

She'd expected him to refuse initially, but she hadn't expected him to go pale and snarl. "Why? You helped bring him back. You trained him."

"A couple of weeks work, on my off time. Now put those away and stop being foolish."

When he started to push by her, she simply shifted to block his way. "First, he wouldn't be racing today if it wasn't for you. And second, you're as attached to him as I am. Probably more. If it's the money—"

"It's not the money." Though a part of him knew it was, to some extent. Because it was hers.

"Then what?"

"I don't own horses. I don't want to be an owner."

"That's a pity, because you are an owner. Or a half owner anyway."

"I said I'm not accepting it."

"We'll argue about it later."

"There's nothing to argue about."

She stepped out of the box, smiled sweetly. "You know, Brian, just because you can make a fifteen-hundred-pound horse do what you want, doesn't mean you can budge me one inch. I'm going to go bet on our horse. To win."

"He's not our—" He broke off, swore, as she'd already

flounced out. "And you don't bet to win," he muttered. "It's nothing personal," he said to Finnegan who was watching him with soft, sad eyes. "I just can't be owning things. It's not that I don't have great affection and respect for you, for I do. But what happens if in a year or two down the road I move on? Even if I don't—as it's feeling more and more that I'd wonder why I would—I can't have the woman give me a horse. Even a half a horse. Well, not to worry. We'll straighten it all out later."

He shouldn't have been nervous. It was pitiful. It was just another horse, just another race. It wasn't, as Betty was, a shining gift. This was an apple-loving, sweet-natured gelding who'd already broken down once and had lost far more races than he'd won in his short career.

Brian was fond of him, of course, and wanted him to have his day in the sun. But he had no illusions about this one being a champion.

He was simply guiding the horse toward doing what he'd been born for. And that was run his best.

And still nerves danced in Brian's belly.

"The track's dry and fast," he told Larry as they walked past the backstretch. "That's good for him. The field's crowded, and he likes that, too. Blue Devil's the number six horse, and odds-on favorite. There's reason for that."

"I know Blue Devil." Larry nodded and gnashed a mouthful of gum. "He can slither through a pack like a snake. He gets in the lead, he sets a fast pace."

"I expect that's what he'll do today. I need you to feel what Finnegan's got in him. I don't want you overracing him, but don't hold him back past the first turn. Let him test his legs."

"I'll take care of him, Mr. Donnelly. Here's Miss Grant

come to see us off. He looks fine, Miss Grant. You done good with him."

"Yes." A little breathless from the run back from the betting window, she gave Finnegan a brisk rub. "We did."

When the call sounded for riders up, she stepped back. "Good luck."

"Talk to him." Brian gave Larry a leg up. "Don't forget to talk to him all the way. Don't let him forget what he's there for."

"They look good," Keeley decided. "Here."

"What now?"

"I put fifty down for you."

"You—damn it."

"You can pay me back out of your winnings," she said breezily. "We'd better get to the rail. I don't want to miss the start. Have you seen my family?"

"No. They're around. The lot of you's everywhere." Because she was moving through the crowd, he grabbed her hand. He could imagine her being trampled. "I don't know why you don't go up into the bar where you can watch in civilized surroundings."

"Snob."

"It's not a matter of—" He gave up. "I want you to tear up those papers."

"No. Look they're bringing them to the gate."

"I'm not taking a half interest in your horse."

"Our horse. Who's number three? I lost my *Racing Form*."

"Prime Target, eight to five, likes to come from behind. Keeley, it's a thoughtful gesture, but—"

"It's a sensible one. Okay, here we go." She shot him a brilliant smile. "Our first race."

The bell rang.

They shot out of the gate, ten muscular bodies with men clinging fiercely to their backs. Within seconds they were merged into one speeding form with legs reaching, flying, striking. Silks of red, white, gold, green streamed by in a shock of color. And the sound was huge.

Blindly Keeley groped for Brian's hand and clung.

She lost her breath, and her sense, in the sheer thrill.

Clouds of dust spewed from the dry track, jockeys slanted forward like dolls, and the pack began to break apart at the second turn.

"He's holding onto fourth," Keeley shouted. "He's holding on."

The lead horse edged forward. A head, a half a length. Finnegan bulled up the line, nipping the distance, vying for third. Keeley heard the crowd around her, the solid roar of it, but her heart pounded to the rhythm of hoofbeats.

Those legs stretched, reached, lifted.

"He's gaining." She began to laugh, even as her hand clamped on Brian's, she laughed. From the joy bursting inside her, she might have been riding low on the gelding's back herself. "He's gaining. He's moving up, into second. Would you look at him?"

He was looking, and the grin on his face was wide. "I didn't give him enough credit for guts. Not nearly enough credit. He'll move on the backstretch. If he's still got it in him, he'll move."

And he moved, a big, unhandsome horse at twenty to one odds with a washed-up jockey in the irons. He moved like a bullet, streaking down the dirt, charging the leader, running neck-in-neck with the favorite while the crowd screamed.

Seconds before the finish line, he pulled ahead by a nose.

"He won." Keeley whirled to Brian. She wondered if

the shock on his face mirrored her own. "My God, Brian, he won!"

"Two miracles in one day." He let out a short, baffled laugh, then another, longer. Riding on the thrill, he plucked Keeley off her feet and spun her in circles.

"I never expected it." She threw her arms in the air, then wrapped them around his neck and kissed him. "I never expected him to win."

"You bet on him."

"That was for love, not for reality. I never thought he'd win."

"He did." Brian gave her a last spin before setting her on her feet. "That's what counts."

"We're going to celebrate. Big time."

While Betty's win had left him shaken to the soul by that heady taste of destiny, this was sheer, stupefied delight. He snatched Keeley again and spun her into a quick waltz through the crowd.

"I'll buy you a bottle of champagne."

"Two," she corrected. "One for each of us. We have to get down to the winner's circle."

"You have to. I don't go to winner's circles."

He might behave like a mule, she mused, but he was a man. And she knew which button to push. "You don't have to go for me, or even for yourself. But you have to go for him." She held out a hand.

He wanted to swear but figured it a waste of breath. "I'll go, as his trainer. He's your horse. I don't own any part of him."

"Half," she corrected, trotting to keep up as Brian tugged her along. "But we can discuss which half."

Chapter 12

"Of course I'm seeing to him." Keeley bent to unwrap Finnegan's right foreleg.

"You should be up celebrating."

"This is part of it." She ran her hands carefully up the gelding's leg before pinning the wrapping to the line. "Finnegan and I are going to congratulate each other while I clean him up. But you could do me a favor." She pulled her ticket out of her pocket. "Cash in my winnings."

Brian shook his head. "At the moment I'm too pleased to be annoyed with you for betting my money." With one hand on the horse he leaned over to kiss her. "But I'm not taking half the horse."

Keeley hooked an arm around Finnegan's neck. "You hear that? He doesn't want you."

"Don't say things like that to him."

She laid her cheek against the gelding's. "You're the one hurting his feelings."

As two pairs of eyes studied him, Brian hissed out a breath. "We'll discuss this privately at some other time."

"He needs you. We both do."

The muscles in his belly twisted. "That's unfair."

"That's fact."

He looked so uncomfortable, she sighed. She wanted to throw up her hands, give the man a good thump. But it wasn't the time to rage or demand he take a good look at a woman who loved him.

"We will talk about it." They were going to talk about a great many things, she decided. Very soon. "But for now, we'll just be happy."

He hesitated while she went back to unwrapping Finnegan's legs. "I've been happier in the last few months than I've ever been."

"That doesn't have to change." She finished hanging the wrappings, picked up a dandy brush. "We're a good team, Brian. There's a lot we could do together."

Brian ran a hand down Finnegan's throat. "We've made quite a start here. Would you want to go out after a bit and have some fancy dinner and wine?"

Keeley slanted him a look. "Are you finally asking me for a date?"

"It seems appropriate under the circumstances." Grinning he fingered the betting ticket. "And it seems I've come in to some extra cash."

"Then I'd love to."

"I've got to go check on Betty, make sure she's transported back to the farm."

"If you run into any of my family, tell them where I am, will you?"

"I will. He's had his moment in the sun, hasn't he?" Brian murmured.

Keeley set the brush down, crossing over as Brian opened the stall door. "You've had quite a day, Donnelly."

"I have. I don't know when there's been another like it."

She put her arms around him, resting her head on his shoulder. "There'll be more." For all of us. She tipped back her head. "We'll make more," she promised as she raised her mouth to his.

He could have lost himself in her. It was so easy when he was holding her to slip away from the moment and into the dream.

"You're neglecting your horse." He rested his cheek against hers, closed his eyes. "I'll come back for you."

"I'll be waiting."

But he didn't move, only stood with her gathered close while the love inside him pulsed like light. Then he drew back, taking both of her hands and bringing them to his lips. "Don't forget to give him apples. He's fond of them."

"Yes, I know." It felt as though her heart were shaking. "Brian—"

"I'll be back," he said and strode away before the words rising into his throat could be spoken.

"Something's changed," Keeley whispered. "I felt it." She pressed her hands, still warm from his, to her heart. "Oh, it's been a hell of a day. And it's not over yet." She swung back into the stall where Finnegan stood, watching her patiently. "He loves me. He just can't get his tongue around the words yet, but he loves me. I know it."

She picked up the dandy brush again. "We're going to cross another finish line before the day's over. I've got to make myself beautiful. We'll have candlelight and wine, and…"

She trailed off as she heard the stall door open again. Thinking it was Brian come back, she turned. Her brilliant smile faded into ice when she saw Tarmack.

"You think you pulled a fast one, don't you?"

"You're not welcome here."

"Snatched this horse out from under me. No better than a horse thief. Figure you can get away with it 'cause you're a Grant."

"You were paid your asking price." She spoke coolly. She caught the stink of too much whiskey on his breath. And so, she thought, did Finnegan. The horse was beginning to quiver. Calmly, she hooked her hand in his bridle. "If you have a complaint, take it up with the Racing Commission."

"So your father can pay them off?"

Her head came up. Her eyes went from ice to fire. "Be careful what you say about my father."

"I'll say what I want to say." He moved in, his eyes glazed and mean from drinking. "Cheats, all of you, look-ing down on those of us just trying to make a living. Stole this horse from me." He jabbed a finger into her shoulder. "Said he wasn't fit to run."

"And he wasn't." She wasn't afraid. There were people around, she thought quickly. She had only to call out. But a Grant didn't cry for help at the first tussle. She could deal with a drunk and pitiful bully.

"Fit to run for you, though. To run and win. That purse is mine by rights."

It was only the money, she thought. Just as Brian said, with some, it was all facts and figures, and no feeling. "You've got all the money out of me you'll get." She turned away to brush the gelding. "Now I suggest you leave be-fore I file a complaint."

"Don't you turn your back on me, you little bitch."

It was shock as much as pain that had Keeley gasping when he grabbed her arm and dragged her around. When she tried to jerk free, the sleeve of her shirt tore at the shoulder. Beside her, Finnegan whinnied nervously and shied.

"You look at me when I talk to you. You think you're better than me." He shoved her back against the gelding's side, then yanked her forward again. "You think you're special 'cause your daddy's rolling in money."

"I think," Keeley said with deceptive calm, "that you'd better take your hands off me." She reached in her pocket, closed her fingers, and they were rock steady, around a hoof pick.

It happened fast, a blur of motion and sound. Even as she tugged the makeshift defense free, Finnegan whipped his head and bit Tarmack's shoulder. For the second time Tarmack rapped her hard against the solid wall of the gelding's side, and as he drew back his fist she shouted, leaping to block it from connecting with Finnegan's head.

It skidded over her temple instead, sending a shocking ribbon of pain across her skull, and a haze of pale red over her vision. As she staggered, stumbling around to defend herself and her horse, Brian came through the doors like a vengeful god.

Instinctively Keeley grabbed Finnegan's bridle, to calm him, to balance herself. "It's all right. It's all right now."

But hearing the unmistakable sound of fists against flesh and bone, she ran out.

"Brian, don't!"

His face was blank, a mask without emotion. It seemed all sharp bones and cold eyes. He had Tarmack braced against the wall with a hand over the man's throat, an arm cocked back to deliver another blow. Tarmack's mouth and nose were already bleeding. Keeley grabbed Brian's arm, and hung on like a burr. It felt like gripping hot iron.

"That's enough. It's all right."

Without even a glance, so much as a flicker of acknowl-edgment, Brian shook her off, rammed a ready fist into Tarmack's gut. "He put his hands on you."

"Stop it." Panting, she grabbed his arm again, and wrapped both hers around it. "He didn't hurt me. Let him go, Brian." She could hear Tarmack struggling for air through the hand Brian had banded around his windpipe. "I'm not hurt."

Very slowly, Brian turned his head. When his eyes, flat and cold with violence, met hers, she trembled. "He put his hands on you," he said again, carefully enunciating each word. "Now step back."

"No." She could hear the shouts behind her, see out of the corner of her eye the crowd already forming. And she could smell the blood. "It's enough. Just let him go."

"It's not enough." He started to shake her off again, and Keeley had an image of herself flying free as he flicked her off like a gnat.

She hadn't feared Tarmack, but she was afraid now.

"What's the problem here?"

She could have wept with relief at the sound of her fa-ther's voice. The crowd parted for him. She'd never known one not to. He took one long look at her face, skimmed his gaze over the torn sleeve, and though the hand he laid on her shoulder was gentle, she'd seen the edge come into his eyes.

"Move back, Keeley," he said in a voice of quiet steel.

"Dad." She shook her head, twined around Brian's arm like a vine. "Tell Brian to let him go now. He won't listen to me."

Brian rapped the gasping Tarmack's head against the wall, a kind of absent violence as he once again spoke with rigid patience. "He put his hands on her."

The edge in Travis's eyes went keen, sharp as silver. "Did he touch you?"

"Dad, for God's sake." She lowered her voice. "He'll kill him in a minute."

"Let him go, Brian." Adelia hurried up, took in the situation in one glance. Gently she touched a hand to Brian's shoulder. "You've dealt with him. There's a lad. You're frightening Keeley now."

"Her shirt's torn. Do you see her shirt's torn?" He continued to speak slowly, as if in a foreign tongue. "Take her out of here."

"I will, I will. But let that pathetic man go now. He's not worth it."

Perhaps it was the voice, the lilt of his own country that broke quietly through the rage. Brian loosened his grip and Tarmack wheezed in air.

"He had her trapped in the stall. Trapped, you see, and his hands were on her."

Adelia nodded. Her gaze shifted briefly to her husband's. A lifetime ago he'd dealt with a drunk who'd had her trapped. She understood the barely reined violence in Brian's eyes. "She's all right now. You saw to that."

"I'm not finished." He said it so calmly, Adelia could only blink when his fist flashed out again and had Tarmack sagging to his knees.

"Stop it." Seeing no other way, Keeley stepped between the two men and shoved Brian with both hands. She didn't move him an inch, but the gesture made a point. "That's enough. It's just a torn shirt. He's drunk, and he was stupid. Now that's enough, Brian."

"You're wrong. It won't ever be enough. You've tender skin, Keeley, and he'll have marked it, so it won't ever be enough."

Tarmack was on his hands and knees, retching. In an almost absent move, Travis dragged him to his feet. "I suggest you apologize to my daughter and then be on your way, or I might let this boy loose on you again."

His stomach was jellied with pain, and he could taste his own blood in his mouth. Humiliation struck nearly as hard as he saw the blur of faces watching. "You can go to hell. You and all the rest. I'm bringing charges."

"Go ahead." Travis bared his teeth in a killing smile. "You're drunk and you're stupid, just as my daughter said. And you touched her."

"He was shouting at her, Mr. Grant." Larry elbowed his way through the crowd. "I heard him threatening her when I was coming in to see the horse."

Travis blocked Brian's move forward, felt Brian's muscle quiver under his hand. "Hold on," he said quietly, and turned his attention back to Tarmack. "You stay away from what's mine, Tarmack. If you ever lay hands on my girl again, what Brian can do to you will be nothing against what I will do."

Emboldened as he assumed Brian was now on a leash, Tarmack swiped blood from his face with the back of his fist. "So what if I touched her? Just getting her attention was all. She's not so particular who has his hands on her. She wasn't minding when this two-bit mick was pawing her."

Brian surged forward, but Travis was closer, and nearly as quick. His fist cracked, one short-armed hammer blow, against Tarmack's jaw. The man's eyes rolled back as he collapsed.

"Dee, take Keeley home, will you?" Travis glanced at the crowd, one brow lifted as if he dared for comments. "Would someone call security?"

"We shouldn't have left." Keeley paced the kitchen, stopping at the windows on each pass. Why weren't they back?

"Darling, you're shaking. Come on now, sit and drink your tea."

"I can't. What's wrong with men? They'd have beaten that idiot to a pulp. I'm not that surprised at Brian, I suppose, but I expected more restraint from Dad."

Genuinely surprised, Adelia glanced over. "Why?"

As worry ate through her she raked her hands through her hair. "He's contained. Now you, I could see you taking a few swings…" She winced. "No offense," she said, then saw that her mother was grinning.

"None taken. My temper might be a bit, we'll say, more colorful than your father's. His tends to be cold and deliberate when it's called for. And it was. The man hurt and frightened his little girl."

"His little girl was about to attempt to gut the man with a hoof pick." Keeley blew out a breath. "I've never seen Dad hit anyone, or look like he wanted to keep right on with it."

"He doesn't use his fists overmuch because he doesn't have to. He'll be upset about this, Keeley." Adelia hesitated, then gestured her daughter to a chair. "Sit a minute. Years ago," she began, "shortly after I came to work here, I was down at the stables at night. One of the grooms had been drinking. He had me down in one of the stalls. I couldn't fight him off."

"Oh, Mama."

"He was starting to tear at my clothes when your father came in. I thought he would beat the man to death. He didn't even raise a sweat about it, just laid in with his fists, systematic like, in a cold kind of rage that was more terrifying than the fire. That's what I saw in Brian's face today." Gently she touched the faint bruise on Keeley's temple. "And I can't blame him for it."

"I don't blame him." She gripped her mother's hands.

"This today, this wasn't like that. Tarmack was mad over the horse, and wanted to bully me."

"Threats are threats. If I'd gotten there first, likely I'd have waded in myself. Don't fret so, darling."

"I'm trying not to." She picked up her tea, set it down again. "Ma, what Tarmack said about Brian. About him pawing me. It wasn't like that. It's not like that between us."

"I know that. You're in love with him."

"Yes." It was lovely to say it. "And he loves me. He just hasn't gotten around to saying so yet. Now I'm worried that Dad… Tempers are up, and if he takes what that bastard said the wrong way." She pushed away from the table again. "Why aren't they back?"

She paced another ten minutes, then finally took some aspirin for the headache that snarled in both temples. She drank a cup of tea and told herself she was calm again.

And was up like a shot the minute she heard wheels on gravel. She got to the door in time to see Brian's truck drive by, and her father's pull in behind the house.

"I missed all the excitement." Though his voice was light, Brendon's eyes carried that same glint of temper she'd seen in their father's. "You okay?"

"I'm fine." Though she patted his arm, her gaze was fixed on her father. She could read nothing in his face as he climbed out of the truck. "I'm absolutely fine," she said again, stepping toward him.

"I'd like you to come inside."

Contained, she thought again. It was impressive, and not a little scary, to see all that rage and fury so tightly contained. "I will. I have to see Brian." Her eyes pleaded with his for understanding. "I have to talk to him. I'll be back."

With one quick squeeze of her hand on his arm, she dashed off.

"Let her go, Travis," Adelia said from the doorway. "She needs to deal with this."

Eyes narrowed, he watched his daughter run to another man. "She's got five minutes."

Keeley caught up with Brian before he climbed the steps to his quarters. She called out, increased her pace. "Wait. I was so worried." She would have leaped straight into his arms, but he stepped back. And his face was glacier cold. "What happened?"

"Nothing. Your father dealt with it. The man won't be bothering you again."

"I'm not worried about that," she said shortly. "Are you all right? I started to think you might be in trouble. I should have stayed and given a statement. Everything got so confused."

"There's no trouble, and nothing to be worried about."

"Good. Brian, I wanted to say that I... Oh, God! Your hands." She snatched them, the tears swimming up as she saw his torn knuckles. "Oh, I'm so sorry. Your poor hands. Let's go up. I'll take care of them."

"I can take care of myself."

"They need to be cleaned and—"

"I don't want you hovering."

He yanked his hands free, then cursed when he saw her cheeks go pale with shock, and the first tear slid down. "Damn it, swallow those back. I'm not in the mood to deal with tears on top of everything else."

"Why are you slapping at me this way?"

Guilt and misery rolled through him. "I've things to do." He turned away, started up the stairs. And fury caught up with guilt and misery. "You didn't want me standing up for you." He spun back, his eyes brilliant with temper.

"What are you talking about?"

"I'm good enough for a roll on the sheets or to help with the horses. But not to stand up for you."

"That's absurd." The tears came fast now as reaction from the last few hours set in. "Was I just supposed to stand by and watch while you beat him half to death?"

"Yes." He snapped, gripped her shoulders, shook. "It was for me to see to. You took that from me, and in the end, handed it to your father. It was for me, two-bit mick or not."

"What's going on here?" For the second time that day, Travis walked in on tempers and shouts, Adelia by his side. And this time, he saw his daughter's tear-streaked face. His eyes shot hotly to Brian. "What the hell is going on here?"

"I'm not sure." Keeley blinked at tears as Brian released her. "This idiot here seems to think I share Tarmack's opinion of him because I didn't stand back and let him beat the man to pieces. Apparently by objecting I've tread on his pride." She looked wearily at her mother. "I'm tired."

"Go up to the house," Travis ordered. "I want to speak with Brian."

"I refuse to be sent away like a child again. This is my business. Mine, and—"

"You don't speak in that tone to your father." Brian's sharp order brought varying reactions. Keeley gaped, Travis frowned thoughtfully and Adelia fought back a grin.

"Excuse me, but I'm very tired of being interrupted and ordered around and spoken to like a recalcitrant eight-year-old."

"Then don't behave like one," Brian suggested. "My family might not be fancy, but we were taught respect."

"I don't see what—"

"Be quiet."

The command left her stunned and speechless.

"I apologize for causing yet another scene," he said to Travis. "I'm not altogether settled yet. I didn't thank you for smoothing out whatever trouble there might have been with security."

"There were enough people who saw most of what happened. There'd have been no trouble. Not for you."

"A minute ago you were angry because my father smoothed things out."

Brian spared her a glance. "I'm just angry altogether."

"Oh, that's right." Since violence seemed to be the mood of the day, she gave in to it and stabbed a finger into his shoulder. "You're just angry period. He's got some twisted idea that I don't think he's good enough to defend me against a drunk bully. Well, I have news for you, you hardheaded Irish horse's ass."

Now that her own temper was fired, she curled her hand into a fist and used it to thump his chest. "I was defending myself just fine."

"You half Irish, stiff-necked birdbrain, he's twice your size and then some."

"I was handling it, but I appreciate your help."

"The hell you do. It's just like with everything else. You've got to do it all yourself. No one's as smart as you, or as clever, or as capable. Oh it's fine to give me a whistle if you need a diversion."

"Is that what you think?" She was so livid her voice was barely a croak. "That I make love with you for a diversion? You vile, insulting, disgusting son of a bitch."

She raised her own fists, and might have used them, but Travis stepped in and gripped Brian by the shirt. His voice was quiet, almost matter-of-fact. "I ought to take you apart."

"Oh, Travis." Adelia merely pressed her fingers to her eyes.

"Dad, don't you dare." At wit's end, Keeley threw up her

hands. "I've got an idea. Why don't we all just beat each other senseless today and be done with it?"

"You've a right." Brian kept his eyes on Travis's and kept hands at his sides.

"The hell he does. I'm a grown woman. A grown woman," she repeated rapping a fist lightly on her father's arm. "And I threw myself at him."

She gained some perverse satisfaction when her father turned that frigid stare on her. "That's right. I *threw* myself at him. I wanted him, I went to him, and I seduced him. Now what? Am I grounded?"

"It doesn't matter how it happened. I was experienced, and she wasn't. I'd no right to touch her, and I knew it. In your place I'd be doing some pounding of my own."

"No one's doing any pounding." Adelia moved forward, laid a hand on Travis's arm. "Darling, are you blind? Can't you see what's between them? Now let the boy go. You know damn well he'll stand there and let you pummel him, and you'd get no satisfaction from it."

No, Travis wasn't blind. Looking in Brian's eyes he saw his life shift. His baby, his little girl, had become someone else's woman. The someone else, he noted, looked about as miserable and baffled by the whole business as he felt himself. "What do you intend to do?"

"I can be gone within the hour."

Amusement was bittersweet. "Can you?"

"Yes, sir." For the first time he knew he'd never pack all he needed, all he wanted into his bag. "Reivers is capable enough to hold you until you find another trainer."

Stubborn Irish pride, Travis thought. Well, he'd had a lifetime of experience on how to handle it. "I'll let you know when you're fired, Donnelly. Dee, we still have that shotgun up at the house, don't we?"

"Oh aye," she said without missing a beat. And wondered if she'd ever been more proud of the man she'd married, or had ever loved him more. "I believe I could lay my hands on it."

Yes, amusement was bittersweet, Travis thought as he watched every ounce of color drain from Brian's face. "Good to know. It's always pleased me that my children recognize and appreciate quality." He released Brian, turned to Keeley. "We'll talk later."

Tears were threatening again as she watched her parents walk off, saw her father reach for her mother's hand, forge that link that had always held strong.

"I've competed for a lot of things," she said quietly. "Worked for a lot of things, wanted a lot of things. But underneath it all, what they have has always been the goal." She turned as Brian walked unsteadily to the steps and sat down. "He won't shoot you, Brian, if you decide you still need to run."

It wasn't the shotgun that worried him, but the implication of it. "I think the lot of you are confused. It's been an emotional day."

"Yes, it has."

"I know who I am, Keeley. The second son of not-quite middle-class parents who are one generation out of poverty. My father liked the drink and the horses a bit too much, and my mother was dead-tired most of the time. We got by is all, then got on. I know what I am," he continued. "I'm a damn good trainer of racehorses. I've never stayed in one job, in one spot, more than three years. If you do, it might take hold of you. I never wanted to find myself fenced in."

"And I'm fencing you in."

He looked up then with eyes both weary and wary. "You could. Then where would you be?"

"Talk about birdbrains." She sighed then walked over to him. "I know who I am, Brian. I'm the oldest daughter of beautiful parents. I've been privileged, brought up in a home full of love. I've had advantages."

She lifted a hand when he said nothing, and brushed at the hair that tumbled over his forehead. "I know what I am. I'm a damn good riding teacher, and I'm rooted here. I can make a difference here, have been making one. But I realize I don't want to do it alone. I want to fence you in, Brian," she murmured, framing his face with her hands. "I've been hammering at that damn fence for weeks. Ever since I realized I was in love with you."

His hands came to her wrists, squeezed reflexively, before he got quickly to his feet. "You're mixing things up." Panic arrowed straight into his heart. "I told you sex complicates things."

"Yes, you did. And of course since you're the only man I've been with, how would I know the difference between sex and love? Then again, that doesn't take into account that I'm a smart and self-aware woman, and I know the reason you're the only man I've been with is that you're the only man I've loved. Brian…"

She stepped toward him, humor flashing into her eyes when he stepped back. "I've made up my mind. You know how stubborn I am."

"I train your father's horses."

"So what? My mother groomed them."

"That's a different matter."

"Why? Oh, because she's a woman. How foolish of me not to realize we can't possibly love each other, build a life with each other. Now if you owned Royal Meadows and I worked here, then it would be all right."

"Stop making me sound ridiculous."

"I can't." She spread her hands. "You are ridiculous. I love you anyway. Really, I tried to approach it sensibly. I like doing things in a structured order that makes a beeline for the goal. But…" She shrugged, smiled. "It just doesn't want to work that way with you. I look at you and my heart, well, it just insists on taking over. I love you so much, Brian. Can't you tell me? Can't you look at me and tell me?"

He skimmed his fingertips over the bruise high on her temple. He wanted to tend to it, to her. "If I did there'd be no going back."

"Coward." She watched the heat flash into his eyes, and thought how lovely it was to know him so well.

"You won't push me into a corner."

Now she laughed. "Watch me," she invited and proceeded to back him up against the steps. "I've figured a lot of things out today, Brian. You're scared of me—of what you feel for me. You were the one always pulling back when we were in public, shifting aside when I'd reach for you. It hurt me."

The idea quite simply appalled him. "I never meant to hurt you."

"No, you couldn't. How could I help but fall for you? A hard head and a soft heart. It's irresistible. Still, it did hurt. But I thought it was just the snob in you. I didn't realize it was nerves."

"I'm not a snob, or a coward."

"Put your arms around me. Kiss me. Tell me."

"Damn it." He grabbed her shoulders, then simply held on, unable to push her back or draw her in. "It was the first time I saw you, the first instant. You walked in the room and my heart stopped. Like it had been struck by lightning. I was fine until you walked into the room."

Her knees wanted to buckle. Hard head, soft heart, and

here, suddenly, a staggering sweep of romance. "Why didn't you tell me? Why did you make me wait?"

"I thought I'd get over it."

"Get over it?" Her brow arched up. "Like a head cold?"

"Maybe." He set her aside, paced away to stare out at the hills.

Keeley closed her eyes, let the breeze ruffle her hair, cool her cheeks. When the calm descended, she opened her eyes and smiled. "A good strong head cold's tough to shake off."

"You're telling me. I never wanted to own things," he began with his back still to her. "It was a matter of principle. But when a man decides to settle, things change."

Things change, he thought again. Maybe she had the right of it, and he'd been running for a long time. But in running, hadn't he ended up where he'd been meant to be in the end?

Destiny. He was too Irish not to embrace it when it kept slugging him between the eyes. "I've money put by. Considerable as I've never spent much. There's enough to build a house, or start one anyway. You'd want one close by—for your school, for your family."

She had to close her eyes again. Tears would only fluster him. "Those are the kind of details I usually appreciate, but they just aren't the priority right now. Will you just tell me, Brian. I need you to tell me you love me."

"I'm getting to it." He turned back. "I never thought I wanted family. I want to make children with you, Keeley. I want ours. Please don't cry."

"I'm trying not to. Hurry up."

"I can't be rushed at such a time. Sniffle those back or I'll blunder it. That's the way." He moved to her. "I don't want to own horses, but I can make an exception for the gift you gave me today. As a kind of symbol of things. I didn't have faith in him, not pure faith, that he'd run to win. I didn't have faith in you, either. Give me your hand."

She held it out, clasping his. "Tell me."

"I've never said the words to another woman. You'll be my first, and you'll be my last. I loved you from the first instant, in a kind of blinding flash. Over time the love I have for you has strengthened, and deepened until it's like something alive inside me."

"That's everything I needed to hear." She brought his hand to her cheek. "Marry me, Brian."

"Bloody hell. Will you let me do the asking?"

She had to bite her lip to hold off the watery chuckle. "Sorry."

With a laugh, he plucked her off her feet. "Well, what the hell. Sure I'll marry you."

"Right away."

"Right away." He brushed his lips over her temple. "I love you, Keeley, and since you're birdbrain enough to want to marry a hardheaded Irish horse's ass, I believe it was, I'll go up now and ask your father."

"Ask my—Brian, really."

"I'll do this proper. But maybe I'll take you with me, in case he's found that shotgun."

She laughed, rubbed her cheek against his. "I'll protect you."

He set her on her feet. They began to walk together past the sharply colored fall flowers, the white fences and fields where horses raced their shadows.

When he reached to take her hand, Keeley gripped his firmly. And had everything.

* * * * *

Get 4 FREE REWARDS!

We'll send you 2 FREE Books plus 2 FREE Mystery Gifts.

FREE
Value Over
$20

Both the **Romance** and **Suspense** collections feature compelling novels written by many of today's bestselling authors.

YES! Please send me 2 FREE novels from the Essential Romance or Essential Suspense Collection and my 2 FREE gifts (gifts are worth about $10 retail). After receiving them, if I don't wish to receive any more books, I can return the shipping statement marked "cancel." If I don't cancel, I will receive 4 brand-new novels every month and be billed just $7.24 each in the U.S. or $7.49 each in Canada. That's a savings of up to 28% off the cover price. It's quite a bargain! Shipping and handling is just 50¢ per book in the U.S. and $1.25 per book in Canada.* I understand that accepting the 2 free books and gifts places me under no obligation to buy anything. I can always return a shipment and cancel at any time. The free books and gifts are mine to keep no matter what I decide.

Choose one: ☐ **Essential Romance**
(194/394 MDN GQ6M)

☐ **Essential Suspense**
(191/391 MDN GQ6M)

Name (please print)

Address   Apt. #

City   State/Province   Zip/Postal Code

Email: Please check this box ☐ if you would like to receive newsletters and promotional emails from Harlequin Enterprises ULC and its affiliates. You can unsubscribe anytime.

> Mail to the **Reader Service:**
> **IN U.S.A.:** P.O. Box 1341, Buffalo, NY 14240-8531
> **IN CANADA:** P.O. Box 603, Fort Erie, Ontario L2A 5X3

Want to try 2 free books from another series? Call 1-800-873-8635 or visit www.ReaderService.com.

---

*Terms and prices subject to change without notice. Prices do not include sales taxes, which will be charged (if applicable) based on your state or country of residence. Canadian residents will be charged applicable taxes. Offer not valid in Quebec. This offer is limited to one order per household. Books received may not be as shown. Not valid for current subscribers to the Essential Romance or Essential Suspense Collection. All orders subject to approval. Credit or debit balances in a customer's account(s) may be offset by any other outstanding balance owed by or to the customer. Please allow 4 to 6 weeks for delivery. Offer available while quantities last.

Your Privacy—Your information is being collected by Harlequin Enterprises ULC, operating as Reader Service. For a complete summary of the information we collect, how we use this information and to whom it is disclosed, please visit our privacy notice located at corporate.harlequin.com/privacy-notice. From time to time we may also exchange your personal information with reputable third parties. If you wish to opt out of this sharing of your personal information, please visit readerservice.com/consumerschoice or call 1-800-873-8635. **Notice to California Residents**—Under California law, you have specific rights to control and access your data. For more information on these rights and how to exercise them, visit corporate.harlequin.com/california-privacy.

STRS20MAX